To Love and Cherish

To Love and Cherish

❖ BRIDAL VEIL ISLAND ❖

TRACIE PETERSON
JUDITH MILLER

BETHANY HOUSE PUBLISHERS

a division of Baker Publishing Group
Minneapolis, Minnesota

Published by Bethany House Publishers
11400 Hampshire Avenue South
Bloomington, Minnesota 55438
www.bethanyhouse.com

Bethany House Publishers is a division of
Baker Publishing Group, Grand Rapids, Michigan

Printed in the United States of America

Library of Congress Cataloging-in-Publication Data
Peterson, Tracie.
    To love and cherish / Tracie Peterson and Judith Miller.
        p. cm. — (Bridal veil island)
    ISBN 978-0-7642-1010-5 (hardcover : alk. paper)
    ISBN 978-0-7642-0887-4 (pbk.)
    I. Miller, Judith, 1944– II. Title.
PS3566.E7717T64 2012
813'.54—dc23   2012000970

Scripture quotations are from the King James Version of the Bible.

This is a work of historical reconstruction; the appearances of certain historical figures are therefore inevitable. All other characters, however, are products of the author's imagination, and any resemblance to actual persons, living or dead, is coincidental.

The internet addresses, email addresses, and phone numbers in this book are accurate at the time of publication. They are provided as a resource. Baker Publishing Group does not endorse them or vouch for their content or permanence.

Cover design by John Hamilton Design

12   13   14   15   16   17   7 6 5 4 3 2 1

To
Lori Baney

With thanks for your friendship
and encouragement.

—Judy

CHAPTER 1

Melinda Colson swallowed the lump of frustration lodged in her throat. Her knuckles scratched against the wicker picnic basket as she tucked a cloth napkin around the woven sides. The lid dropped with an unexpected clatter, and she looked up to meet Mrs. Mifflin's surprised gaze.

Her disappointment swelled, and a heavy weight settled in her stomach. "But I understood we weren't departing Bridal Veil Island for another two weeks." Her palms turned damp as she awaited Mrs. Mifflin's response.

"That was our plan, but I've received word that my dear friend, Ida McKinley, will be arriving in Cleveland. We must return home to prepare for her visit." Mrs. Mifflin patted her perspiring upper lip with a lace-edged handkerchief. "There's so much to accomplish before she arrives. I do wish she would have given me a bit more notice."

Melinda's mouth gaped open, and she loosened her grip on the rigid basket handles. "The president's wife is coming to visit you?"

"Indeed she is. Ida has been asked to speak at the commencement exercises at Miss Sanford's school in Cleveland. That's where we first met and became friends. Of course, she was Ida Saxton back then." The older woman pursed her lips and tipped her head slightly. "I'm sure I told you that when you first came to work for me."

Perhaps Mrs. Mifflin had mentioned her connection to Mrs. McKinley, but if so, it hadn't registered at the time. After all, when Melinda first arrived at the Mifflin home, she'd been overwrought with grief. Her thoughts had been focused on her parents' untimely death aboard one of their shipping vessels rather than on Mrs. Mifflin's childhood friends.

"When is she due to arrive in Cleveland? We'll need sufficient time to close the cottage for the season." *Cottage!* A twelve-room two-story Queen Anne home designed by an architectural firm in New York City could hardly be called a cottage, but Mrs. Mifflin enjoyed referring to it as such.

"No need to worry. I've made arrangements with Mr. Zimmerman, the resort superintendent, to have some of the maids from the clubhouse come and take care of closing our lovely Summerset."

"There's no need to go to the expense of hiring maids. I'd be more than happy to remain and close the cottage. Besides, you'll know that everything has been properly attended to if I'm here." Melinda hoped the older woman would heed her suggestion. She didn't want to leave Bridal Veil—not now. And if things went as she hoped, not ever.

Mrs. Mifflin frowned and shook her head. "My dear! How could I possibly get along without you? I need you to fashion my hair and take care of arrangements for the tea. As it is, we'll be hard-pressed to finish all the details on time. You know there's never before been anyone else I could depend upon as my companion."

Melinda disliked being referred to as Mrs. Mifflin's companion, but that was the title the matron had used when she'd interviewed and hired Melinda after her parents' death. At the time, Melinda hadn't argued against the title. Back then she had been in dire need of the income. But perhaps all of that would change today.

"Besides," Mrs. Mifflin continued, "the dues Mr. Mifflin pays to belong to the Bridal Veil Island consortium cover such needs. That was one of the reasons we agreed to join. The island offers a pleasant diversion from the harsh Cleveland winters while also paying strict attention to the necessary services we require. We've even arranged to have the cottage painted later this summer. Of course, I don't expect you to realize all of the benefits we enjoy as members."

Mrs. Mifflin dabbed her face again and startled as the clock chimed the hour. "Goodness, but I do wish there were more time."

Time!

When Melinda glanced at the clock, her pulse quickened. She needed to hurry. If things went as she hoped, Evan Tarlow, the Bridal Veil Island gamekeeper, might surprise her with a proposal at their picnic this afternoon.

But not if I don't get there soon.

The thought was enough to force her to action, and she tightened her hold on the basket handles. This was her afternoon off, and she needed to make good use of these few free hours. "I have a picnic planned for this afternoon, but I'll be certain to have time to pack your trunks this evening."

Mrs. Mifflin's smile faded like a summer bloom in need of rain. "I would think you'd be willing to forgo your afternoon off, Melinda. A picnic with one of the clubhouse maids is of little importance. Especially when you consider *my* current needs."

Melinda forced a smile. "You needn't worry." She tried her best to understand the older woman's anxiety. "I promise I will have your needs cared for." She patted the woman's arm. "I've never failed to have your things ready, no matter the occasion."

Mrs. Mifflin gave a sniff as though she might begin to weep. "It's just that this is more important than anything else. I find it rather selfish of you to put your own desires first."

Early on, Melinda had learned that Mrs. Mifflin believed everything should center on her needs. And although Melinda prayed for the matron each day, she'd not seen much change in her behavior. If Melinda's father had been able to keep his freighting business solvent and insurance on the ships paid, she wouldn't have been forced into these circumstances. With no means of support, any thoughts of marriage to a wealthy husband had disappeared when her parents died at sea. The estate attorney had been brief when he'd set Melinda and her brother, Lawrence, adrift in the uncharted seas of financial misfortune.

But perhaps the insolvency had been a blessing in disguise. During the winter months at Bridal Veil Island, a kinship had developed between Melinda and Evan. His romantic interest had been the high point of each season, and she hoped his attention would lead to a proposal of marriage. By society's standards, Evan didn't have a great deal to offer, but Melinda didn't use the monetary standard of the world to assess a suitor. She'd learned a good heart could be trusted more than money. And Evan possessed a truly good heart. Also, it didn't hurt that he was delightfully handsome.

Melinda hid her smile and lifted the basket from the table. "I'm sorry, Mrs. Mifflin, but I'm unable to change my plans. I know that you would want me to be a woman of my word, just as the pastor encouraged us last Sunday. Remember, you told me to always be sure to keep my promises." She turned and rushed toward the back door, giving a wave over her shoulder. "I won't be long."

"I find your behavior unacceptable, Melinda." When she continued down the steps, Mrs. Mifflin called after her. "Don't be even one minute late or you'll see a decrease in your wages!"

Melinda hurried down the walk. If Evan proposed, she would no longer need to worry about Mrs. Mifflin or the possibility of having her wages decreased.

Her spirits soared as she neared the secluded grassy spot that provided a perfect view of the Argosy River. Two years ago she and Evan had declared this spot their special piece of Bridal Veil. Not that they could actually claim anything on Bridal Veil, for it all belonged to the investors who had purchased the land, but this place afforded them moments of privacy that Melinda found so vital to her own well-being.

A breeze blew the honey-blond curls surrounding her oval face, and she could feel the heat rise in her cheeks as the sun beat down with more intensity than she'd expected. How she disliked her fair complexion that splotched bright pink with only a bit of sunshine. She should have worn her straw-brimmed hat.

"Over here, Melinda!" Evan appeared from behind one of the low-hanging branches of a live oak and waved her forward, his broad smile enhancing his already good looks.

Her throat caught at the sight of him. His broad shoulders and sturdy appearance caused her heart to quicken, yet it was the kind, gentle spirit beneath Evan's ruggedness that had won her heart. He loved this island and he'd taught her to love it, as well. Just like Evan, she'd learned to appreciate the beauty in every inch of this place he called home. Now she prayed it would become her home, too.

"I brought a blanket for us to sit on." He pointed toward the ground beneath the tree.

She smiled as their eyes locked, and Evan's look embraced her with warmth that pulsed through her body. She wanted to blurt out the fact that she was expected to depart in the morning, but she decided to wait for the right moment to tell him. There would be no perfect time to deliver such news, but she didn't want to greet him with Mrs. Mifflin's edict.

"I hope you're hungry." After the two of them sat down on the blanket, she lifted the napkin from atop the basket. "I have your favorite—fried chicken."

He rubbed his palm on his stomach and immediately helped himself to a drumstick. "Umm, this is delicious. I hope you're not too hungry. I think I could eat every piece myself."

Melinda moved the basket closer to him. "You're in luck. My stomach couldn't hold a thing at the moment."

"I hope it's not because you're ill. Harland said we could take a couple of the horses riding this afternoon." His brows furrowed and he hesitated a moment. "If you feel up to it."

Evan's boss, Harland Fields, was charged with supervising the group of men employed as gamekeepers, groundskeepers, and landscapers. In addition, the older man was expected to oversee all of the grounds improvement projects on Bridal Veil.

"I'd love to go riding on the beach." Although they both loved the river view from the clubhouse side of the island, Melinda particularly took pleasure in riding along the ocean on the east side. Frequently she and Evan would walk the two miles to the other side to look for shells and listen to the water lap against the shoreline. Other times, when the horses weren't being used by guests, Harland would let them take the animals out for exercise. At least that's what he called it when nosy guests inquired about the hired help enjoying a ride along the shore.

Evan wrapped up the remaining two pieces of chicken and tucked them back into the basket before grabbing an apple and shining it on the front of his shirt. "I saw a couple of loggerhead turtle nests near the end of the island. Would you like to ride down there and have a look?"

"Yes, that would be wonderful." She tried to sound excited, but her response fell flat.

The apple crunched as Evan bit into it, and a dribble of juice trickled down his chin. Using a corner of her napkin, Melinda wiped the moisture from his face. Her heart fluttered as he covered her hand with his and held it close to his chest. "Something's wrong, Melinda. I can tell. Either you're sick or I've done something to make you unhappy. Which is it?"

No longer able to continue the masquerade, Melinda wilted. "Just before I left the cottage, Mrs. Mifflin announced that we're departing for Cleveland in the morning."

A frown creased Evan's forehead. "But you're not due to leave for two more weeks."

"I know." Melinda detailed what little she'd learned about Mrs. McKinley's approaching visit. "I asked to remain behind and help close the cottage, but Mrs. Mifflin wouldn't hear of it. She says I'm the only one who can properly style her hair and make arrangements for the visit." Melinda sighed. "From the way she talks, you'd think she's expecting me to remain in her employ for the rest of my life." She hoped her last comment would nudge Evan to act. Otherwise, come tomorrow morning, she'd be crossing the Argosy River to the mainland and catching a train back to Cleveland.

"Mr. Mifflin hasn't said anything about canceling the hunt he's planned for tomorrow. Maybe she's confused." While Evan folded the blanket, Melinda arranged the remaining items in the basket. He grabbed the handle and tucked the blanket beneath one arm. She could see he was doing his best to sort fact from possible fiction. "I'm guessing that Mrs. Mifflin has spoken out of turn. I don't think there's any reason for concern."

"Believe me, Evan, there is every reason for concern. I know Dorothea Mifflin, and you can be sure I will be on a train back to Cleveland tomorrow. Unless something or someone stops me."

"Evan!" Harland approached them sitting astride a trotting chestnut mare. With a deft hand, he pulled back on the reins and the horse fell in step alongside them. "Mr. Mifflin canceled the hunt he had scheduled for tomorrow." He tipped his hat to Melinda. "I'm surprised Mrs. Mifflin let you have your afternoon off." The older man smiled down at her before turning his attention back toward Evan. "You need not reschedule Mr. Mifflin's hunt. He tells me they'll be leaving the island tomorrow. 'Course, I'm thinking Melinda already gave you that piece of news." He settled back in the saddle. "You two still planning to go riding?"

"Sure are," Evan said. "I'm going to leave this picnic basket and blanket inside the stable while we're gone."

Harland nodded and leaned around the horse's head. He gave the mare a pat on the neck. "One of you can take Anna Belle. The old girl's ready for a good run." He removed his foot from the stirrup and swung down from the horse. "You two make the most of your time together. It's going to be a long time afore you see each other again."

Melinda's skirt caught between her legs as she whirled around to face Evan. "Maybe not. We haven't had a chance to fully discuss what we might do."

The older man arched his bushy eyebrows. "I'm not seeing there are many choices for the two of you. Once the Mifflins have made a decision, I don't think they'll be changing their minds."

Biting back her thought that there was at least one option available, she permitted Harland to help her astride Anna Belle while Evan went into the stable for his horse. Not until they were alone would she broach the topic of remaining at Bridal Veil. She would need to be delicate in her comments. Although Evan had spoken of his love for her, he'd made no mention of marriage. But marriage followed a declaration of love, didn't it? Surely he had already considered a future with her and would see this as the proper time to propose. After all, she could hardly propose to him.

CHAPTER 2

The wind tugged at Melinda's hair as their horses galloped down the beach toward the south end of the island. Bridal Veil Island was similar to other resorts designed to entice wealthy investors. Life on the island was intended to be relaxing yet luxurious, and the scenery played an important role. Melinda had always loved their time here—more because of Evan than the beauty of the island, but she found that quite appealing, as well. On any other day, she would have been eager to see the loggerhead nests, but today the sea turtles were of little importance to her. Evan pointed toward a spot not far away, and they slowed the horses to a trot.

"Let's ride over to where there's plenty of wild grass, and the horses can graze."

Melinda followed his lead but remained astride Anna Belle until Evan dismounted his own horse and circled around to help her down. She loved the safety and warmth of his broad hands as they held her waist and lowered her to the ground. She tipped her head back to meet his eyes. "Thank you, Evan."

"My pleasure. Our time together is the best part of my day." A golden glint twinkled in his brown eyes, and she wished the moment would go on forever. He grasped her hand. "Over here.

So far there are only two nests, but in a few weeks there will be many more." His voice brimmed with undeniable excitement.

Melinda's desire to remain with him on Bridal Veil washed over her like a tidal wave, and she forced back the threat of tears. How she longed to share in his pleasure today, as she so often had, but unless they developed a plan for their future together, she would experience little joy this day.

He gestured toward the nests and turned to look at her. "What's wrong? Sea turtle nests are nothing to cry about." His words mingled with the high-pitched cawing of the seagulls along the shore, and he stepped closer. He pulled her to his side. "Tell me why you're so sad."

The pain in her heart had become so heavy that it seemed to sink to the depths of her stomach. Didn't he understand that unless something was done, she would leave tomorrow morning? Perhaps she needed to clarify, but she had expected so much more from him. That he would sweep her off her feet in a magnificent embrace and tell her he'd never let her out of his sight again; that he would hold her close and speak of his undying love; that he would propose marriage and her long days as Mrs. Mifflin's companion would be over.

"I'm sad because I don't want to leave Bridal Veil. I don't want to leave you." She waited for his response and silently prayed, *Please, Lord, let him hear my despair and say the words I long to hear.*

"I know. Every year you say you don't want to leave, and every year I wipe away your tears and tell you I will write and that it will be time for you to return before we know it." He smiled and looked at her as though his words should resolve her sadness. "Everything will be fine."

"No it won't!" Several startled terns took wing as she shouted her reply.

He watched the birds take flight. "No need to shout. I can hear you."

"I'm sorry." Her stomach churned as she turned her back toward him. She immediately felt guilty for her harsh response. "This early departure took me by surprise, and I feel as if my world is falling apart. I don't want to leave you, Evan. I lost my parents, and now I feel as though I'm losing you, as well."

He cupped her cheek and wiped away a tear. "My sweet Melinda, I know how hard the loss of your parents has been on you, but the miles separating us aren't permanent. The time will pass quickly, and soon you'll be back on the island, and we can be together again."

"But for how long?"

Melinda noticed the perplexed look in his eyes. It was clear he didn't understand that she loved him and wanted to make her home on Bridal Veil Island, that she longed to work alongside him and be a true helpmeet. Had he not learned that much about her during the four winters she'd lived on the island?

Perhaps the clubhouse maids were correct. They'd often spoken about a man's inability to understand a woman and her feelings. But Melinda had always thought Evan was different. The two of them could talk about everything. At least that's what she had thought.

Each winter they spent all of their free time together, either walking or riding the fifteen-mile length of the island, always eager for new adventure. She'd learned the history of the island, the animals and plants, the birds and sea creatures—and she'd loved each moment.

During her first winter on the island, Evan had described the ebbs and tides of the ocean, never making her feel foolish for her many questions. On other visits, he'd told her stories of the pirates and Civil War soldiers who had rowed into the narrow inlets under cover of night, using the island to hide their booty or deliver supplies to Confederate soldiers. He was a wondrous storyteller, and she'd listened to him for hours, enjoying each exciting tale. Other days, the two of them had walked barefoot in the sand and laughed when the lapping ocean licked at their feet.

"Wait here." Evan ran toward the water's edge, leaned down, and picked up a shell. He returned and reached for her hand. He placed the shell in her palm. "Your favorite, an angel-wing shell." He grinned at her. "I think it's one of the biggest we've found."

Melinda nodded, unable to push out a thank-you, the shell a reminder of their many explorations. She rubbed her finger across one of the sharply beaded ribs. The simple act flooded her mind with unbidden memories that had provided endless fun and, for her, so many new experiences.

Evan had shown Melinda the beauty of the marshlands as the sun shimmered across the wet grasses, and when he learned she'd never caught a fish, he taught her—and how to bait a hook, as well. With dogged determination, he'd taught her to paddle a canoe. A smile tugged at her lips as she recalled nearly tipping the canoe on more than one occasion. There were times when she believed he knew her thoughts before she spoke them and that she knew his.

But that wasn't true today. Today she didn't think he knew her at all.

Evan grasped her shoulders and turned her until they were face-to-face. His dark eyebrows were almost meeting over his eyes as he stared at her. "I understand you don't want to leave—especially since you were to remain another two weeks. But arguing during the little time we have left makes no sense, does it?"

"I don't want to argue, either, but this isn't just about staying another two weeks."

Evan stared at her as though she'd spoken to him in a foreign language. "If it isn't about leaving early, then what is it about?"

"It's about remaining here on the island—forever. About never leaving."

He tipped his head back and shrugged. "Well, no one stays on this island forever. You know that. This is a place where the wealthy come to hide away from the world. Problem is . . . you can't hide forever."

Her frustration mounted to new heights. He was being so practical, and while that was a quality of his she loved, right now she wanted to scream. Maybe she needed to speak in short, concise sentences until it became crystal clear.

"Please listen to me, Evan." She looked deep into his eyes. "I do not want to return to Cleveland—not now, not ever. I want to live the remainder of my life here on Bridal Veil Island."

He tipped his head to the side. "Stay here? What would you do?"

I could be your wife! Oh, how she wanted to say those words to him. Instead, she did her best to remain calm. "I could get a job. Maybe at the clubhouse. Don't they need someone to—"

He shook his head. "It's closed up once all the guests return home. Any jobs here on the island during the summer months are filled—by men."

"But Emma is here year-round." Emma and Garrison O'Sullivan had been living on the island year-round from the time Garrison had been hired to oversee care of the horses and livestock.

"You're right, but there are days when I know she'd rather be anywhere but on this island, especially during the heat of summer when the air is so heavy you can hardly take a breath and everything feels clammy, even the clothes you put on first thing in the morning. Besides, the only reason Emma is here is because she's Garrison's wife."

Melinda let his final words hang between them like a swinging pendulum. Either he didn't understand that marriage was exactly what she wanted, or his declaration of love had meant nothing to him. She didn't want to believe Evan's profession of love had been lightly given, yet could he be so dense on only this one occasion?

Disappointment swept over her as they walked back to the horses. Evan had promised to return the animals by four o'clock so they could be groomed and fed.

She could think of nothing else to say, no other way to make clear what she had hoped would have been a spontaneous reaction from a man in love.

Evan leaned forward to help Melinda as she mounted her horse, his mind whirring with confusion. From the day he'd first met Melinda, he'd thought her near perfect. He'd laughed when the other fellows said they didn't understand women. "You should meet my Melinda," he had replied. He and Melinda had always understood each other, their words as clear as the blue skies over Bridal Veil and their thoughts as interlaced as the strong cotton twine of a fisherman's net.

Until now.

Melinda was searching for a remedy he couldn't give her. Surely she realized he couldn't hire her to fill some nonexistent position. He didn't have the authority to hire anyone. And had there been a job available, where would she live? The only acceptable place would be with Garrison and Emma O'Sullivan, and they didn't have a lot of extra room for anyone else in their little cottage. Of course there was Emma's sewing room, but that wasn't the point. Having another person move into your home would change things. Emma might be agreeable to such an arrangement. She might even like having another woman around to keep her company during the summer months. But Garrison O'Sullivan was another story—he was a man who didn't like change. Moving into the O'Sullivans' home would be impossible, and it was the last place where he wanted to see Melinda.

By morning he was sure Melinda would accept the fact that there was no choice but to return. Still, his heart ached at the tears in her eyes. He loved her and didn't want to see her so unhappy. He'd have to write many letters so that their time apart would pass quickly.

The following morning Evan arrived at Summerset Cottage. Though not the largest cottage on Bridal Veil, no expense had been spared in furnishing the home or landscaping the grounds. Bridal Veil gardeners had been employed to plant and care for the azaleas, hyacinths, ferns, and palms that surrounded the wrap-around porch and glassed sunroom, and Evan thought the men had done an excellent job.

The practice of naming homes had begun with Bridal Fair, the original mansion constructed on the island. That home had belonged to the Cunninghams, who had lived there long before the island had been purchased for a resort. As Evan had heard it said, Victor Morley, the developer, had been a good friend of the Cunningham family. When they fell upon hard times, he had proposed the island a perfect location for a resort. After the grand lodge had been built, others had purchased lots to build their own island getaways, and naming those houses had continued with each new cottage. Referring to the expansive structures that dotted Bridal Veil Island as cottages seemed a bit of a misnomer, especially to the workers who had constructed the lavish houses and the servants employed to work in them. They were certainly the grandest of any Evan had ever known, and he was happy that he could be a part of this stately island.

Wiping the tops of his boots on the back of his pants, Evan rechecked his appearance as best he could before bounding up the steps. His heart picked up a beat in his eagerness to see Melinda before she departed with the Mifflins. When she approached the door, she looked no happier than when they'd parted company yesterday. "Good morning," he said in his cheeriest voice.

"Come in, Evan." Melinda pushed open the door. "There's no denying it's morning, but I wouldn't say it's good."

"Anything I can do to help?"

She opened her mouth but quickly mashed her lips together and poured him a cup of coffee. "Bottom of the pot," she said.

He nodded. "Thanks. Sure I can't do anything?" He glanced around the room. The kitchen in Summerset wasn't large, but a large kitchen wasn't needed. Most of the guests joined together in the clubhouse to enjoy their meals, and little cooking was performed in the private residences.

"Indeed you can, Evan." Mrs. Mifflin entered the kitchen, her jaw set at a determined angle. "The wagon was supposed to be here a half hour ago to take our belongings down to the boat. At this rate we're going to miss the train."

Evan set his coffee cup on the table. "I'll see if I can locate the wagon." He hiked one shoulder and gave Melinda an apologetic smile before rushing out the door. At the end of the walkway, he spotted the vehicle and waved to the driver—Alfred Toomie. No wonder it was late.

Still waving at Alfred, Evan trotted toward the rumbling wagon and shouted, "Come on, Alfred. The Mifflins are going to miss their train if they don't get over to Biscayne!"

Alfred gave the reins a halfhearted slap across the horses' rumps. In spite of the listless direction, the horses picked up their pace.

When the horses finally came to a halt in front of the Mifflins' cottage, Evan scolded Alfred for his tardiness. "Now get in there and help carry the trunks out here before Mrs. Mifflin reports you to Mr. O'Sullivan and you lose your job."

Evan doubted the young man cared if he got fired, for his father took the boy's pay each week. Still, Alfred had a responsibility to perform his work as expected. The boy pushed a hank of dirty blond hair off his forehead. He looked as though he hadn't had a bath for some time, and he smelled that way, too.

"If you do a good job, you might even get a tip that you can hide from your father." Evan winked and hoped that bit of news would encourage the young fellow. And if Mrs. Mifflin didn't give him an extra coin, Evan would.

In all the scurrying about to load the wagon and transport the Mifflins and Melinda in the carriage, there wasn't time for the two of them to talk until they were at the dock. Evan stood beside Melinda while the trunks were being loaded onto the *Bessie II*, the launch that would deliver them across the river to the Georgia mainland, where they would board a train headed north.

Evan reached for Melinda's hand. "I know you're unhappy to be leaving, but I'm just as unhappy to see you go. I love you, Melinda. Promise me you'll write as soon as possible."

One side of her mouth twisted up into a little smile. "You love me? Really, Evan?"

"Of course, you silly goose. Why don't you believe me? Last week I pledged my love to you and you said you loved me, as well. Why do you question me now?"

"I suppose because it seems you are happily sending me away."

He shook his head and touched her cheek. "I never said I was happy about your leaving, but we both know we have little to say in the matter. We are both dependent upon the direction of others." As if to stress this point, Mrs. Mifflin approached.

"Come along, Melinda. There isn't time to dillydally." She grasped Melinda's arm in a possessive manner.

Melinda leaned close to Evan, straining to whisper in his ear. "We'd have had plenty of say if you had asked me to stay." That said, she turned and hurried to the boat.

CHAPTER 3

Evan wanted to run after her and jump aboard the launch. He wanted to have a little more time to grasp what she'd been thinking and try to understand her abrupt comment. He wanted to assure her that at no time had he thought she'd expected, or even wanted, him to ask her to remain on Bridal Veil. During the past months, there had been no mention of Melinda remaining—not by either of them. How could she stay? There were no lodgings, no jobs for women. The very idea made no sense. Perhaps she thought he had some special sway with the management.

He watched the boat gain speed as it steamed across the water toward the mainland. In a final effort to show his commitment, Evan yanked his hat from his head and waved it high in the air. If Melinda saw him, she didn't acknowledge the gesture. He lowered his arm and continued to stare after the boat, his hat loosely dangling between his fingers.

"That lady didn't give me no money." Alfred Toomie stood beside him with his dirty hand turned palm side up. "I hauled all them trunks like you told me, but that woman just turned the other way like she never saw me afore."

Evan reached into his pocket and withdrew a coin. He hadn't truly expected Mrs. Mifflin to tip the boy. Service was expected on the island—good service—without any gratuity. "You need to do good work all of the time, Alfred. You were hired to do a job, and it's your responsibility to do it as well as you can." He placed the coin in Alfred's hand. "The Bible tells us that we should do our work as if it's an offering to the Lord. Do you know what that means?"

Alfred bobbed his head, and a strand of his unwashed hair dropped across his forehead. "Means that when I do somethin', I should do it as good as I can so's to make God happy." He flashed a wide grin. "Is that right, Evan?"

"Yes, that's right. Will you promise me that you'll start doing that?"

"I promise, but is it okay if I keep a tip if it's offered?"

Evan chuckled. "Yes, Alfred. Now get on back to the stables with that wagon before Mr. O'Sullivan thinks you've gotten lost along the way."

While Alfred returned to the wagon, Evan glanced over his shoulder for one final look at the *Bessie II*. In the distance, he could still make out the launch, but he could no longer distinguish the passengers. With a sense of urgency nipping at his heels, he mounted his horse and headed for the hunting lodge.

The lodge wasn't huge, not when compared to the guests' cottages or the accommodations offered in the clubhouse, but it did provide adequate living quarters for Harland Fields and Evan, and it had a large parlor that was used by guests as a place to gather prior to leaving on their hunts. With only an hour before he would lead the next hunt, Evan hoped there would be time to write a letter to Melinda.

If he could send a letter that would go to the mainland in the morning, perhaps it would arrive in Cleveland and be waiting when she arrived home. There seemed to be no other way he could assure her of his love.

❧❧

"Evan!"

The pen dropped from Evan's hand the moment he heard Harland call for him. Quickly sealing the envelope, he shoved it into his pocket. He'd been so intent on his letter writing that he hadn't heard the voices of the guests now gathered in the parlor down below.

He grabbed his hat and rushed down the narrow steps. "Sorry, Harland, I got distracted."

The older man's brow creased and he shook his head. "No time for excuses. You've got a big group waiting to get out there and try to shoot at something. Make sure it ain't one another—or you."

The two men had begun to share that admonition a number of years ago—after one of the guests had accidentally discharged a rifle and missed Harland by only inches.

"I'll do my best to keep us all safe and show them a good time." Although it was late in the morning to begin a hunt, the men sometimes preferred a leisurely breakfast rather than an early start. Most claimed it was their wives who caused the morning delays, but Evan knew better. Many of these men enjoyed a slow start to the day here on Bridal Veil.

Today he gathered the group of "come-latelys," as he and Harland referred to the late arrivals, and led them toward the barn. With any luck, Garrison would have the horses saddled and Evan could provide the group with a good time—even if they didn't bag any animals.

It mattered little to Evan what time of day they rode out so long as they enjoyed the adventure. Only when guests complained about their lack of success on a hunt did Evan become annoyed. And some of them did complain. Only last week he'd heard one of the men say, "Maybe we need a gamekeeper who can do his job and stock the island with animals to hunt. Isn't that why we keep him here year-round?"

He'd mentioned the incident to Harland, but the older man assured Evan there was no reason for worry. "They need an excuse when they return home empty-handed. You know they won't take the blame themselves. Don't worry yourself, Evan. Your job is secure, and the men who make the decisions on Bridal Veil all like you. They know you're good at what you do."

Evan liked to think he was good at his position, for he'd always taken pride in a job well done. Whether helping muck the barn when they were short of help or hunting wild boar to eradicate them from the island, he always tried to do his very best. Today, however, his thoughts weren't on the hunt. Instead of keeping a sharp eye out for any birds or animals that a guest might want to bring down, his thoughts wandered to Melinda.

He'd been praying his letter would help soothe the anger that had flashed in her eyes when she'd wheeled away from him on the dock.

Melinda followed Mrs. Mifflin to the glass-enclosed cabin of the launch and settled beside the older woman. Mrs. Mifflin had insisted upon leaving the boat railing once they left the dock, saying the breeze would ruin her hair. But the matron's curls were tightly pinned and a large hat was perched atop her head, leaving little chance any curl could go astray. From the glass windows that lined the seating area in the cabin, Melinda had seen Evan standing on the dock waving his hat, but she hadn't acknowledged him. Mrs. Mifflin would have considered such forward conduct a breach of proper behavior. She hoped her actions hadn't hurt him. She was still chiding herself for her final comment to him. Evan loved her, and she had acted like a spoiled child.

But I wanted so much for him to propose, she thought. In fact, she had been convinced he would ride up at the last minute—just like a knight in stories of old. He would appear upon his fine horse, sweep her into his arms, and ride away with her. She smiled sadly. "But that is not what happened."

"What did you say?" Mrs. Mifflin questioned.

Melinda shook her head. "Nothing of consequence."

The older woman's worrisome nature took hold before they stepped off the boat in Biscayne, and she didn't give Melinda a minute's peace when they boarded the train. "We have so much to accomplish before Ida's visit. I simply don't know how we'll complete everything before she arrives." Mrs. Mifflin leaned close and lowered her voice. "Until I give you permission, make certain you don't say anything to the other servants. I don't want word of Ida's visit leaked through idle gossip." On and on, her nervous mantra continued. Mr. Mifflin did his best to calm his wife, but when all his efforts failed, he retreated to the gentlemen's car and left Melinda to deal with the woman.

The journey wasn't giving Melinda much time to think about Evan. Instead of writing him the letter he'd requested, her time was devoted to making lists and copious notes of the many tasks to be completed the moment they arrived home.

"I purchased stationery in Biscayne, and I think you should write out invitations to the tea I'm going to host during Ida's visit." Mrs. Mifflin withdrew a sheaf of writing paper from a brown bag and shoved it in Melinda's direction. "First, let's decide upon the exact wording for the invitation, and then you may begin to write them out while I finalize the list."

At each stop along the way, Mrs. Mifflin talked at length about all that must be done—until she fell ill at their stop in Baltimore.

Melinda hated herself for feeling relief that they would be delayed. She truly didn't want the older woman to suffer sickness, but the farther they traveled, the more hopeless Melinda felt. She needed time to think things through.

Mr. Mifflin fetched a doctor, who came to the hotel room and decided Mrs. Mifflin likely was suffering from a mild case of food poisoning—the doctor blamed the oysters she'd eaten the night before. He chided her for not having more sense than to partake of such a dish in a month without an *r*, prescribed a very watered down dose of laudanum, and suggested rest. Mr. Mifflin privately explained away the illness as a case of nerves. Either way, the delay did nothing to ease Melinda's worries. And Mrs. Mifflin, in her sickbed, was more demanding than ever.

By the time they finally arrived in Cleveland, Melinda's nerves were frayed, but the invitations had been written, and there were more lists than she cared to think about. Thankfully, Mr. Mifflin had wired ahead to inform Sally and Matthew, two of the servants, of their return.

Mrs. Mifflin waved Sally aside as she strode toward the stairway. "I do hope you've been tending to the necessary cleaning, Sally. We have an important guest arriving, and if I find any dust or dirt in this house, you can expect to see a decrease in your wages." Without waiting for a response, she ordered Matthew to fetch her trunks. "And see that those invitations are delivered, Melinda."

Sally looked at Melinda and clucked her tongue. A sprite of a woman, the maid had been with the Mifflins for more than ten years. "Doesn't appear that her time of rest on the island has helped Mrs. Mifflin's disposition any, has it?"

Melinda shook her head. "Nor mine."

The maid chuckled. "No wonder those sons of theirs never come home to visit. I wouldn't be here, either, if I didn't need the money."

Melinda ignored the remark. Sally loved to gossip, especially about her employers. There was no denying the Mifflins' sons, Cyrus, and his brother, Malcolm, seldom visited their parents, but both had attended boarding schools from an early age. Currently, both were enrolled at Oxford University, and visits home were expected to be rare. Still, it gave Sally something to chatter about when there was little other gossip.

On several occasions Melinda had taken Sally aside and gently spoken of the damage gossip could inflict upon others. When her early attempts failed, Melinda had pointed out Scriptures against the practice. Sally had patiently listened, but Melinda knew her words had fallen on deaf ears. It seemed nothing would bridle the maid's tongue.

"So who's this important guest the missus mentioned, and what kind of invitations were she speaking of?" Sally stepped closer and lowered her voice. "Ever since that telegram arrived from the mister, I've been wondering myself silly what could be so important that the missus would hurry home two weeks ahead of schedule. I know she likes to mix with those other rich folks on that island."

Sally's questions could lead Melinda down a path she didn't care to tread. If word of Mrs. McKinley's arrival became common knowledge among the servants of Cleveland society before their mistresses knew, Mrs. Mifflin would claim complete and utter embarrassment. And Melinda would be the one held responsible for the social gaffe.

"A dear friend of Mrs. Mifflin—one with whom she attended school many years ago—is going to be in the city. They haven't seen each other for a number of years."

The excitement in Sally's eyes faded and her lips drooped. "Oh, is that all? And here I was expecting to learn a good piece of . . ." She stopped before actually saying she had hoped for a bit of gossip to pass along to her friends. Not that Sally needed to make such an admission. Long ago, Melinda had learned Sally couldn't be trusted to keep a secret. The woman might be an excellent housekeeper, but she failed miserably at maintaining a confidence.

"So the invitations are for what? A tea? A dinner party?"

"A tea in honor of her friend."

Sally started up the stairs and then stopped. "So when is this friend arriving? I suppose I'll need to air out the guest room."

Melinda sighed. "No need to air out the room just yet. Mrs. Mifflin will give you orders when she wants you to do so. Her friend won't arrive for several weeks."

"Several weeks?" Sally stopped on the stairway and leaned across the banister. "I wouldn't think she'd rush home to prepare for a friend who isn't arriving for several weeks. Heaven knows she's expected me to prepare for a huge dinner party in less time than that. And why the worry over dust and the rush to get the invitations sent out?"

"If you have other questions, you should direct them to Mrs. Mifflin, Sally. Like you, I do as I'm told."

Sally bent so low that Melinda thought she might topple over the banister. "I think you know more than you're telling me, but I'm not one to be pushy." She waved her index finger back and forth. "One thing for sure—it won't take long for me to find out what all this hubble-bubble is about."

Melinda didn't doubt that remark—not in the least. Sally would be hunting down information like a bloodhound sniffing out a scent. Until she'd satisfied her curiosity, there would be no stopping the woman. "By the way, there's a letter waiting for you on the table in the kitchen. Maybe that will raise your spirits a bit."

"A letter?"

The maid winked. "From that Evan fellow at Bridal Veil Island.

He didn't waste a speck of time getting a letter off to you, now did he?" She chortled and continued up the stairs. "If you've got nothing else to share with me, I best get upstairs and help the missus unpack, or she'll be ringing that bell of hers. Go on now and see what your fellow has to say."

Knowing Sally, she'd probably already read the contents of the letter. The woman did, after all, consider herself quite proficient at steaming open the mail.

CHAPTER 4

Melinda strode into the kitchen and retrieved her letter. Sally had placed the envelope in the center of the table for all who entered to see. The sight caused Melinda a moment of irritation, but she supposed it truly didn't matter. Had Sally placed the letter somewhere out of sight, she still would have told anyone within earshot that Melinda had received mail. Anyone except their mistress, of course. Sally didn't want Mrs. Mifflin to get the idea her servants gossiped. But Melinda knew nothing was off limits with Sally. In spite of Melinda's admonitions, the maid shared every jot and tittle with anyone who would fill her ears with a few interesting tidbits of their own.

A quick examination of the seal didn't reveal any evidence of tampering, but that didn't mean Sally hadn't read the letter. It simply meant she'd done an excellent job of hiding her reprehensible handiwork.

"What's done is done," she muttered as she ran her finger beneath the seal and removed the letter.

"You speaking to me, Miss Melinda?" Matthew stood in the doorway, his large hands shoved inside the pockets of his work pants.

Melinda slipped the pages into the envelope. "No, I was talking to myself," she said with a sheepish grin. "I didn't hear you come down the hallway, Matthew. Are you finished carrying all those trunks upstairs so soon?"

He bobbed his head, his gaze fixed on the envelope in her hand. "Got your letter, I see. That Evan sounds like he's a nice young man. Seems he's mighty sorry you—" Eyes wide with realization of what he'd said, Matthew clapped his palm across his lips.

"Sally read my letter to you, didn't she?" When he didn't immediately respond, Melinda stepped closer. "I know you don't want to get her in trouble, but Sally oversteps far too many boundaries. Reading my mail is very disrespectful."

"Yes, ma'am, it is. You're right about that, and I told her so, but she said you wouldn't find out." He hung his head. "But me and my big mouth went and let it slip. She's gonna be mighty unhappy with me, and that's a fact."

Though Matthew had apparently been a willing listener, it was Sally who'd carried out the offense. "I won't say anything to reveal you, Matthew, but I hope that you won't take part in Sally's misdeeds in the future."

When he lifted his head, sorrow shone in his brown eyes. "Thank you. I'll do my best to keep away when Sally's spreading her tales." He pointed his thumb toward the ceiling. "The missus said I should deliver the invitations to the post office for you."

Melinda nodded and motioned for Matthew to follow her to the hallway, where she removed the stack of invitations from the leather traveling bag that had once been one of Mrs. Mifflin's possessions. In addition to her wages, Melinda received dresses, gowns, and other belongings Mrs. Mifflin declared unusable or out of fashion—a benefit bestowed upon most ladies' maids. Though the two women didn't share the same size or style, Melinda had a talent for sewing, and she'd soon learned to fashion the castoffs into attire that better suited her own taste.

Leaning down, she unclasped the satchel and removed the invitations. "Here you are. Be sure you don't drop any of them. I don't think Mrs. Mifflin would forgive either of us if an invitation went astray."

Matthew reached for the envelopes. "I'll be careful. You can count on me." Tucking the invitations into the crook of his arm, he shot her a smile before he departed.

Melinda returned his smile and leaned forward to clasp the travel case. Before the death of her parents, Melinda enjoyed the many luxuries granted children born into families of wealth. In the past, she'd even worn gowns that surpassed the quality of those belonging to her current mistress. However, life had changed. And so had Melinda. After her parents' death, Melinda learned that the worldly possessions she'd once thought so important no longer held the same allure. Possessions were a cold replacement for love, and she wanted to build her life on things that truly mattered—love and family.

Less than two weeks ago, she had thought that her love for Evan was going to mean marriage and a home at Bridal Veil. Now, she wasn't so sure. After making certain Sally was nowhere in sight, she returned to the kitchen, sat down at the table, and withdrew Evan's letter from the envelope.

Dear Melinda,

I am sorry we didn't have enough time to discuss our future before you returned to Cleveland. I know you were unhappy with me, and I think maybe you doubt my love. I hope that isn't true, because I meant what I said to you. I love you very much, and even though I only got up my courage to tell you this year, I have loved you since the very first winter you came to Bridal Veil. I know I will always love you.

I didn't know what to think when you said I should have asked you to stay. I still can't figure out how you thought that would work out. There aren't any jobs for women during the summer months, and there's no place where you could have lived except maybe with Garrison and Emma. Garrison is a good man, but he wouldn't welcome the idea of having another woman in his house. He already complains that Emma talks too much. Imagine what he'd think if there were two women chattering all the time.

Melinda rested the letter on the table and glanced heavenward. Men! Why was it they assumed that if two women were together they would be constantly talking? Besides, she hadn't meant that she wanted to stay and live with Garrison and Emma. She sighed, picked up the letter, and continued to read.

The women servants' quarters close down during the summer, and you couldn't have lived here at the hunting lodge with two men. So maybe you think I shouldn't have been perplexed, but I was—and I still am. You hadn't even mentioned staying here and if you had, I would have explained all the reasons why it was impossible. If you think about this a little more, maybe you can understand my confusion. I love you very much and hope that you will write and tell me that you feel the same. Please don't keep me waiting to hear from you, as I am truly worried you may be angry enough to seek the affection of another. I don't ever want that to happen. I look forward to next winter when we can discuss this in person.

With love and hope,
Evan

The letter was certainly contrite. She wanted to deny her feelings of disappointment but found it impossible at the moment. Perhaps she shouldn't have expected Evan to sweep her into his arms and carry her off to the church for a spontaneous wedding ceremony. Still, he could have done more than stand on the dock and wave his cap when they were halfway across the river.

"Reading your letter, are ya?" Sally pranced into the kitchen and gave her a wink. "What's your fellow got to say? I'll bet he's itching to marry you, isn't he?"

The thought of Sally reading Evan's letter caused Melinda to wince. Not only did she loathe the idea of her personal information becoming fodder for the gossip mill, but what if Mrs. Mifflin got wind of her desire to marry Evan? The woman would do her best to squelch any such plan. Over and over, she'd said she would never let Melinda leave her employ; she constantly declared Melinda to be the only lady's maid who possessed the deportment and ability to serve her well. Though the older woman chuckled when she said she'd never let her leave, both Melinda and Mrs. Mifflin knew there was much truth in what she said. Once Mrs. Mifflin set her mind to do something, she usually found a way. And if she couldn't, her husband could.

"How can you possibly be finished unpacking all the trunks so soon?" Melinda asked, fending off Sally's question with one of her own, a ploy she'd learned from her mother years ago.

"Oh, I'm nowhere near done, but the missus wants a cup of tea. And with any luck she'll decide upon a nap after her tea. That way I can finish without her ordering me about at every turn. From the way she sits there on her chair telling me where to put this and where to put that, you'd think I didn't know where anything belonged."

"I doubt she thinks any such thing. We're all aware that you're well acquainted with every item in this house and every bit of business, as well." Melinda pushed her chair away from the table and stood.

"Now, what's that supposed to mean? You think I have my nose in places where it don't belong, is that what you're saying?"

"I think you already know the answer to that question, Sally." Melinda turned and walked out of the kitchen.

She needed to write to Evan, but first she needed to give some thought and prayer to the content of her missive. Better to take her time so she wouldn't later regret her words.

◆◆

Evan's footsteps pounded along the hard dirt path as he approached the hunting lodge. He greeted Harland as he lifted his hat and swiped the perspiration from his forehead. "Hot for May, don't you think?"

Harland sat in a rocking chair, ready to walk to the dining hall for the noonday meal. "Come morning, it'll be June first. The heat shouldn't surprise you too much." Delilah, the cat they'd inherited from the Morley family when they'd begun their renovations of Bridal Fair, rested on Harland's lap. "Looks like you worked up a sweat." A soft chuckle escaped his lips as he gave the rocking chair a backward push with the tip of his boot.

Delilah jumped down and sauntered toward Evan. He reached down and scratched the cat's ears. He'd been told the cat possessed different abilities than her sire, Samson. While Samson had detected bad-tempered guests, Delilah's talents were founded in her ability to sense bad weather. Harland said Delilah could sense a storm moving in before the weatherman over in Biscayne could. Evan had seen the cat become restless, arch, and scream high-pitched meows before a storm would hit, so he didn't dispute her aptitude.

Evan stopped at the bottom of the wooden steps and looked up at the older man. "Sometimes it's a waste of good time taking those fancy folks out to hunt. They're more interested in talking about their finances than listening to what I tell them."

He clomped up the steps. "And then they complain 'cause they don't have anything to show off when they get done."

Harland gave him a sideways glance. "Sounds like you got something more than a bunch of halfhearted hunters stuck in your craw. What's eating at you, boy?"

"Nothing. I'm just tired of guests who can't be satisfied." He stepped toward the door. "I better get washed up or we'll be late for dinner. Give me a couple minutes." He didn't wait for a reply. Even if the dinner bell rang, he knew Harland would wait for him. The cooks at the large cabin that had been converted into a dining hall might give Evan a hard time if he was late—might even refuse to feed him. But they'd never say a word to Harland. He'd been there longer than any of them, and they respected him both for his knowledge and for his kind nature.

A person always knew where he stood with Harland. He spoke the truth, but always with kindness. When Evan had asked him how he managed to remain so even tempered when things went wrong, he'd laughed and said, "I'm a man of reason. There's a reason why things happen. If I stay calm, it's easier to figure out that reason."

Evan yanked off his sweaty shirt and stared in the mirror as he washed his face and neck. Was he ever going to hear from Melinda? A launch from Biscayne delivered the mail and newspapers each day, and each day he held his breath as he riffled through the workers' mail that was dumped on a long table at the back of the dining room.

Years ago the mail had been delivered less often, but when the guests complained, the change was made to daily deliveries. Of course, the bag of mail first went to the clubhouse, where it was sorted. Any mail for workers was bagged and then sent to the dining room, where it could be picked up.

Evan buttoned his clean work shirt, slicked back his wet hair, and hurried down the narrow stairway before the bell clanged in the distance. "I'm ready. Sorry to keep you waiting."

"No need to be sorry. Been using the time to converse with the Lord." Harland pushed up from his chair. "How 'bout you, Evan? You been talking to the Lord lately?"

"Not much." Evan kept his gaze fixed on the path.

It had been Harland who had led Evan to the Lord years ago. Evan hadn't been working on Bridal Veil for long when he realized Harland was different from most of the men in his life. Harland possessed a silent kind of strength that kept him going no matter the circumstances—and not just dragging along, but moving forward with a positive attitude and a smile on his face. When Evan attempted to praise him for being a good example, Harland shook off the compliment like a dog drying wet fur. "Don't set your sights on me for an example," he'd said, pointing toward heaven. "You need to strive to be like Jesus, not like me."

From that time forward, Harland had willingly pointed Evan to Scriptures that had helped him understand he needed Jesus in his life. For too many years, he'd dwelled on the pain of a father who had withheld his love and the loss of his mother when he was twelve. Instead of fond memories of his family, Evan's were of late-night arguments over money and broken promises, his father's anger when his mother became ill, and shouted blame placed on everyone except Evan's brother, James.

While his mother had been affectionate toward Evan, his father had reserved praise and affection for James. Once his mother died, Evan grew up surrounded by coldness. It wasn't until he met Harland that he'd truly learned the warmth God's love provided. There was no denying he still had a long way to go before he developed the kind of loving attitude the Bible talked about, but he'd been trying. Some days he was more successful than others. Today wasn't one of those successful days.

Harland reached up and patted him on the shoulder. "Might help if you spend some time with the Lord." There wasn't condemnation in his voice, only concern. "I know it always helps me when things aren't going so good." A red-throated wild turkey strutted across the trail. "And if you want to talk to me, I've got a listening ear."

Evan nodded and ducked his head beneath a low-hanging branch of a live oak that shaded their path. "I know you do. It's Melinda. I haven't had a letter from her. When she left, I asked her to write to me as soon as possible." He kicked a small rock with his toe. "She was unhappy when she left, and now I'm afraid that she's decided I'm not the man for her."

Harland tipped his head to the side. "And have you written to her?"

"The very day she left here. I put it in the mail the following day."

"Before you go jumping to conclusions, why don't you give it a little more time? Knowing Mrs. Mifflin, I'm sure she keeps Melinda mighty busy. And with them returning home early, I'm guessing it caused more work than usual for her." Harland waved to a couple of the workers as they approached the dining hall. "Besides, all this fretting isn't gonna make a letter get here any sooner. And if Melinda is the woman God intends for you, He's already got it planned out."

Evan forced a smile. He knew Harland was right, but knowing something and accepting it were two different things.

CHAPTER 5

June 1898

Melinda sat down at the small desk in the corner of her room and picked up her pen. Every day since her return to Cleveland, she had attempted to write to Evan. But with each attempt she had failed. The words simply wouldn't come. She prayed and prayed that the Lord would give her the perfect words to fill the pages. Finally, those words had become clear, and now she could only hope that Evan hadn't lost patience while waiting to hear from her.

She knew her concerns were well founded. When she had first returned to Cleveland, a letter arrived almost every day, but over the past week she'd received only one, and it had been brief. Evan ended the letter with two questions. *Is all hope lost? Should I quit writing to you?*

She began her letter with an apology for her delayed reply. As she continued to write, the words spilled from her pen as though they'd been bottled up in her head for an eternity. She couldn't seem to write quickly enough to keep up with her thoughts. Thoughts that were far different from the ones she'd had when she'd left Bridal Veil Island.

First let me give you an absolute NO to your latest questions. All hope is not lost, and I very much want you to continue writing to me. I have now had time to consider my actions and have been seeking God's guidance as to my response. During this time of thought and prayer, I realized that my actions were foolhardy and selfish. I love you and didn't want to leave the island. I know from your letters that you shared those same feelings. However, when you didn't ask me to stay, I felt rejected and unloved.

After reading your first letter, it became clear that your reaction was based upon logical and reasoned thinking, while my desire to remain was based upon my emotions and more impracticable nature. The Lord has shown me that your practicality is an excellent virtue and one needed in any good and strong relationship between a . . .

She hesitated, her pen hovering over the page. She didn't want to say husband and wife—it seemed too presumptuous in this first letter. After all, Evan had declared his love, but he had never uttered the word *marriage.* "Man and woman," she whispered. Yes, that would be a much better choice. Once again she began to write.

. . . man and woman. As I have continued to consider your actions, I am most thankful that you had my welfare and concern at heart. The fact that you deeply cared about my comfort and where I could live speaks volumes to me. I do pray that my delayed response has not caused you too much worry. Please know that though we are separated by distance, my heart remains yours.

Once she'd completed her apology and assured Evan of her love, Melinda continued with the happenings at the Mifflin residence since her return. She didn't know if he would want to read of her worry over Sally's loose tongue or Mrs. Mifflin's tiresome behavior, but in the past he had urged her to tell him the small details of her life. Besides, it gave her a safe place to release some of her frustration, frustration that stemmed from her difficulties with both women.

I must close for now. I hope all my ramblings have not put you to sleep. I will have less to write next time, for I promise I will not wait long before posting another letter. Remember that I love you and eagerly await the time when we can once again be together.

With love and devotion,
Melinda

❦

Mrs. Mifflin was in her glory. There was no other way to explain the woman's euphoria. Because most members of Cleveland society had been vacationing elsewhere during the winter, word of Mrs. McKinley's arrival and the tea being hosted at the Mifflin residence didn't circulate until one week prior to the big event.

Melinda wasn't certain what pleased her mistress the most. The fact that she was hosting the president's wife in her home or the fact that she'd been able to keep the secret from leaking out ahead of time. There was no denying that her friends were more than a little impressed—and more than a little envious.

When Mrs. McKinley's letter arrived saying that she and her two servants would be delighted to stay at the home of the Mifflins rather than take lonely rooms in a hotel, Mrs. Mifflin had shown the letter to all of her acquaintances. "Ida and I have always been very close—like sisters," she would say while tucking the letter back into its official envelope. When further questions arose, she would respond as if she weekly corresponded with the president's wife, though Melinda had never seen any such letters. And with Sally checking the mail, Melinda knew she would have heard about regular correspondence from the executive mansion.

Mrs. Mifflin was basking in the attention, accepting every invitation to call on her society friends prior to Mrs. McKinley's arrival. Today she was to pay a call on Lucy Hollister. As with all of her other visits, she insisted Melinda accompany her.

Although Melinda had requested permission to remain at home, her mistress didn't relent. "You know I don't like to pay calls by myself."

That had been the end of the discussion. Now Melinda dutifully sat beside her mistress as the carriage delivered them to the mansion of Hubert and Lucy Hollister. She supposed she should be grateful for the privilege of attending such affairs. To act as personal maid or companion to a woman of society was a great honor. Scullery maids and mere household servants would never see such moments, except from the serving side. Even so, these events were a painful reminder of the life she'd once had.

"Now, do not forget, if asked, that Ida and I have been the dearest of friends since our youth." Mrs. Mifflin's proud bearing mirrored her tone. "You may even let it drop in conversation, should you be addressed, that I've been invited to the White House on many occasions."

"Yes, ma'am." Melinda knew better than to comment further.

Once inside the house, Melinda was directed to a chair in the far corner of the parlor while the two matrons shared tea near the fireplace and Mrs. Mifflin spun stories of her close friendship with the president's wife.

"My Hubert says the president's wife suffers from poor health, and he doubts she'll actually be well enough for a visit to Cleveland next week."

Surprised when Mrs. Hollister raised her voice enough to be heard in the far corners of the room, Melinda looked up from her stitching. Mrs. Mifflin's smile disappeared, and her shoulders lifted to a squared angle that would have made a military officer proud. "Her health has been failing for some years now, so I've alerted Dr. Braden to be at the ready." She spoke with such authority that even Melinda had believed her reply—until they returned to the carriage.

"Drive us to Dr. Braden's office, Matthew," she said.

Melinda lightly grasped the woman's arm before they stepped up into the carriage. "Wouldn't it be easier to telephone the doctor from home? His office is quite some distance from here, and I know there is much you wish to accomplish before Mr. Mifflin returns home for the evening."

Mrs. Mifflin stiffened at the suggestion. Melinda sighed. Like most of the wealthy women of Cleveland, Mrs. Mifflin had insisted upon having a telephone in their home. However, she and the other women seldom used the device. Word had quickly passed among them that the operators listened in on all of the calls and were quick to repeat everything they heard.

"Calling on that telephone would be no different than telling Sally I was going to Dr. Braden's office. Everyone in Cleveland would know before I even arrived at his office." She pressed her hand to her chest as she settled on the carriage seat. "I didn't realize Ida had succumbed to poor health—she said nothing in her letter. However, I don't want anything to go awry while she's staying at our house." She glanced at Melinda from beneath hooded eyes. "And since I'm going directly to the doctor's office, my comment to Lucy wasn't really a falsehood."

Melinda didn't respond. If Mrs. Mifflin believed it so, nothing Melinda said would change her mind. Instead, Melinda thought of her own mother, who had been so much more giving and gracious than Mrs. Mifflin or her friends. Yet Melinda's mother had held just as respectable a position in society. But unlike most of them, her mother had cared about people. Melinda could remember her mother once sitting up all night with their housekeeper when the poor woman had caught influenza. Other times, she remembered her mother's generosity with the servants—giving them extra food to take home to family members and giving them generous bonuses every holiday.

The memory made Melinda more melancholy than she already was. How she missed her mother and father. The years since their deaths had flown by in many ways; in others it seemed that just yesterday she had been sitting beside her mother in a carriage just like this.

"Remember, Melinda, mercy is always better than pride. People will say and do things with which you will take umbrage, but it is always better to err on the side of mercy. Mercy gives, where pride takes."

Melinda nodded as if hearing her mother speak the words once again. Life with Mrs. Mifflin had snuffed out a great deal of Melinda's merciful thoughts. She didn't like to admit it, but Mrs. Mifflin's influence had not exactly been good. Melinda knew herself to be judgmental and critical. She thought of Evan. She'd even been critical with him—questioning his love for her—placing expectations on their relationship that she had no right to infer.

She sighed. *Lord, help me to be more merciful. Help me to be more like Mother and less like Mrs. Mifflin.*

❖❖

Evan entered the hunting lodge and removed his hunting boots. Delilah rubbed against his pant leg and greeted him with a purr. "It's good to see you, too, Delilah." He reached down and scratched the cat behind her ears.

There had been four men on the hunt today, each an avid sportsman. In truth, the four of them could have done quite well without Evan, but rules were rules, and one of his primary jobs during the season was to lead all of the hunts. For some groups he needed to be an instructor as well as a guide. Today's group required neither. He'd been pleased, albeit somewhat surprised, that they had embraced him as a fellow hunter rather than an employee.

Of course, he'd worked at Bridal Veil long enough to know that much depended upon the mix of guests on each hunt. Although these men had treated him as an equal today, if one or two of them hunted with different guests in the future, their behavior would likely be less friendly. It was the way of things among the wealthy visitors, and Evan had learned to accept it.

When he'd first arrived, Harland had said, *"Always remember that we may all be equal in God's eyes, but our employers don't see things that way."* Evan had never forgotten Harland's words of caution.

He looked up at the sound of footsteps on the front porch and greeted Harland as the older man walked inside.

"Heard you had a good hunt. Mr. Mossman told me the group got their limit of duck and quail. He also said you were an excellent guide and he plans to tell Mr. Morley you are one employee they shouldn't ever lose." A wide grin spread across Harland's face. "That should make up for any comments you've had from the come-latelys."

Evan nodded. "I suppose it does. Thanks for telling me, Harland." He picked up his hunting boots. "I'm going to take these upstairs and get my work boots. Think I'll stop at the dining room on my way to the barn and see if the mail's been dropped off."

"No need. I've already been there."

Evan's hopes plummeted. The happiness he'd felt only moments earlier vanished like a morning mist. "In that case, I'll go get my work boots and go to the barn."

"You might want to read this first." Harland reached into his back pants pocket and removed an envelope. "I saw this on the table and took the liberty of picking it up. Didn't reckon you'd mind."

Evan stared at the envelope, unable to believe his eyes.

Harland flapped the envelope. "Well, you gonna take it or you want me to open it?"

His heart pounded a new beat as he reached for the cream-colored envelope. "Thanks, but I think I'd rather do it myself." Happiness that Melinda had finally written flooded him with unbridled joy. He felt like a six-year-old on Christmas morning until he stuck his finger beneath the seal. What if she'd written to tell him she no longer wanted him to write, no longer wanted him? He glanced at Harland.

"Well, go on. Open it. Not looking inside doesn't change what she's already written." The older man knew what Evan had been thinking. "Don't let worry and fear get the best of you now that you got a letter from her."

Evan unsealed the envelope before he could give it further thought. He forced his gaze back and forth across the lines before looking up at Harland. "She says she's sorry she didn't write sooner, but she was waiting for guidance from the Lord."

Harland nodded. "That was wise. I think she's a smart gal. What else?"

"She says she acted foolish and she loves me." He grinned at Harland. "She also said—"

Harland put his hands up. "That's enough. You keep the rest private between the two of you. I just wanted to make sure you got good news. Didn't want you taking off for Cleveland and leaving me here to take care of things on my own this summer."

"You don't need to worry about that any longer, Harland. I'm here to stay."

❧❧

The day of the tea, as everyone in the Mifflin household had come to refer to June twenty-third, dawned sunny and mild. Quite perfect! At least that's what Mrs. Mifflin had declared when she descended the stairs for breakfast. Mrs. McKinley had given her speech at Miss Sanford's commencement exercises two days before, but since then she'd been resting in her rooms and taking her meals there, as well. Her two maids scurried in and out to request anything their mistress required. They were careful to make their needs known only to Melinda or to Mrs. Mifflin. Melinda wasn't certain if they'd been advised against speaking to any of the other servants, but Sally had taken offense that they were ignoring her.

Melinda was passing through the upstairs hall when Sally approached. "If Mrs. McKinley and her maids think me untrustworthy, maybe I shouldn't be helping prepare for the tea. Neither of them will so much as acknowledge me." Sally crossed her arms tight across her chest and tipped her nose toward the ceiling.

"Do cease such talk, Sally. No one except Mrs. Mifflin has spoken to Mrs. McKinley. Besides, communication with Mrs. McKinley and her staff has nothing to do with your duties downstairs." Worried the conversation might be overheard by the Mifflins' prestigious houseguest, Melinda guided the maid toward the stairs. "Let's continue this conversation elsewhere."

Once they entered the kitchen, Melinda directed Sally to a far corner where they wouldn't be heard by the other staff—all of them busy preparing the delicate tea sandwiches and various pastries that would be served later in the day. "Right now you are needed here in the kitchen to keep the staff working in a timely manner. Later you'll be needed to see that the service goes as planned. Your ability to make this a wonderful event is of utmost importance to Mrs. Mifflin."

Sally's shoulders relaxed. "I suppose you're right. And if I do my best work with the tea, I'm sure the president's wife will thank me."

Melinda wasn't certain Mrs. McKinley would go so far as to thank the staff for performing their duties, but she didn't express that thought to Sally.

After one final assessment of the parlor, dining room, and kitchen, Melinda ascended the stairs. With only two hours until the guests would begin to arrive, Mrs. Mifflin would expect a detailed report when Melinda entered to help her dress for the tea. Thankfully, she could honestly state that everything was in order.

With her thoughts centered upon how she would fashion Mrs. Mifflin's hair, Melinda hurried down the hallway. She would like to try a different style that would flatter the older woman's sharp features and narrow face, but that likely wouldn't happen today.

Holding the rail as she took the final step into the upper hallway, Melinda turned when the door to Mrs. McKinley's rooms clicked and her lady's maid appeared. "My mistress wishes to speak to you."

"Me?"

The only answer was a slight nod. "Please, don't keep her waiting." The words rang with an air of urgency that caused Melinda to hasten forward without further question. "In here," the maid said, leading Melinda through the sitting room and across the threshold into the bedroom.

Melinda stared across the room and attempted to hide her alarm. She'd captured only a fleeting glance of the tiny woman when she'd arrived, and there had been no introductions. Jean, her lady's maid, had been clear that her mistress needed to rest.

"How may I be of service to you, Mrs. McKinley?" Melinda thought she should curtsy or somehow acknowledge the status of the president's wife, but she didn't know the protocol for this particular circumstance, so she remained as stiff as a board just inside the doorway.

"Do step closer," Mrs. McKinley said.

When the president's wife struggled to gain a more upright position in the bed, Jean rushed forward and tucked another pillow behind her. Her dark brown hair splayed across the pillow like unruly feathers.

Melinda attempted to hide her concern as she did the woman's bidding. To see Mrs. McKinley abed when there remained only two hours to dress and prepare for the tea caused a knot to settle in the pit of her stomach. The woman's pale complexion only served to deepen Melinda's concern. "Do you continue to feel weary, Mrs. McKinley?"

"I have not fully recovered from the rigors of my travel. I fear it will be impossible for me to be in attendance at the tea this afternoon. I know Dorothea will be terribly disappointed. I also know that in her younger years she was prone to fainting or painful headaches when she received distressing news." Mrs. McKinley reached for Melinda's hand and gave a gentle squeeze. "I'm relying upon you to deliver this news in the most delicate manner possible. Will you do that for me?"

Melinda swallowed the knot that had risen from her stomach to her throat. "I'll do my best." She could manage no more than a whisper. "Mrs. Mifflin is going to be very disappointed."

"I know she is. That's why I'm depending upon you. I thought it best you speak with her rather than have one of my maids deliver the news." Mrs. McKinley released her hold on Melinda's hand. "Poor Dorothea has gone to so much trouble that it truly pains me to let her down."

"But you must, madam." Jean's words were heavy with worry, and she lifted her head to look directly into Melinda's eyes. "My mistress attempted to get up and dress for the tea, but she hasn't the strength. Please report that any further activity will only prolong Mrs. McKinley's poor condition."

Condition? Since their arrival, neither Mrs. McKinley nor her maids had mentioned any sort of condition. A condition suggested long-term illness, yet they had spoken only of weariness from their travels. Perhaps Mrs. McKinley needed a doctor. What if Mrs. Hollister was correct about the president's wife suffering from ill health? What if she died? Though ridiculous, the thought sent a shiver scurrying down Melinda's spine. "I would be pleased to send for Mrs. Mifflin's family physician. She has already alerted him that you would be visiting. He agreed to make himself available should you become ill during your visit."

"Thank you, but there's no need for a physician. Rest is the answer. By tomorrow I should be much better." She glanced at the porcelain clock on the mahogany dressing table. "You'd better go to Dorothea. I'm sure she is waiting for you to assist her."

Melinda wanted to remain and further encourage a visit from the doctor, but time wouldn't permit. "I'll do my best to deliver your news with care, but Mrs. Mifflin may want to come and speak to you privately."

"I would be pleased to receive her, but if she could wait for several hours. I need to sleep."

Jean hurried to the side of the bed and gently removed the extra pillow from the bed. "Of course you do, mistress. I'll pull the drapes and see that you're not disturbed." The maid sent a warning look in Melinda's direction.

"I'll advise Mrs. Mifflin that you'll be resting." Melinda turned and hurried from the room.

She raced down the hallway as though her skirts were on

fire. Mrs. Mifflin would be prepared to scold her soundly. The moment she opened the door, Mrs. Mifflin strode toward her with anger flashing in her eyes. "There you are! Of all days to keep me waiting, how could you be late today? Ida will think me a horrid hostess."

"She won't think any such thing; she is your dear friend. Why don't you sit down at your dressing table and I'll fashion your hair. We have more than enough time." Melinda waited until the woman was seated. She picked up the brush and slowly drew it through the older woman's hair. "I am late because Mrs. McKinley requested a short visit with me."

"Whatever for? Did you see her gown? What color is she wearing?" Mrs. Mifflin met Melinda's eyes in the mirror.

"She asked that I tell you she isn't feeling well enough to attend the tea." Melinda waited a moment, choosing her words carefully. "Her complexion is very pale, and her attempt to dress for the afternoon festivities proved impossible." Melinda continued to brush, hoping the motion would calm her mistress. "I inquired if she needed the care of a physician, but she refused." Mrs. Mifflin remained surprisingly calm while Melinda parted her hair in the center and brushed her dark locks. "Do you prefer loose curls around your temples?"

Her mistress gave only a curt nod. Mrs. Mifflin was trying to mask her feelings, but she wasn't doing a very good job.

Melinda felt sorry for the woman and decided to do her best to offer encouragement and perhaps a little mercy. "Mrs. McKinley knew that you would be terribly disappointed. She cares very much for your well-being and hopes sincerely that her bad news won't cause you too much despair. She said you might visit her later . . . in a few hours . . . after she's had a rest."

Using a deft hand, Melinda finished styling Mrs. Mifflin's hair in quick time. She was amazed that the older woman had remained calm. In fact, she didn't utter a word as Melinda assisted her into her corset and layer of petticoats. When she'd finished adjusting the gown, Mrs. Mifflin turned to gaze in the mirror.

"I'll need my jewels." She sat down in front of the dressing table and waited while Melinda removed them from the case.

Perhaps this was going to go better than anticipated. She had expected Mrs. Mifflin to show some kind of emotion. In fact, she'd expected Mrs. Mifflin to take to her own bed rather than face the women who would soon be arriving.

Melinda arranged the gold necklace encrusted with small emeralds around Mrs. Mifflin's neck. "Perfect. You look absolutely lovely."

Mrs. Mifflin gave a slight nod, pushed up from the dressing table, and immediately fainted.

CHAPTER 6

Summer had slowly melded into fall, and with each passing day Melinda's desire to return to Bridal Veil grew stronger. Her longings weren't at all helped by Mrs. Mifflin's disposition. The first few days after the fiasco, the older woman had barely managed to run the household. After Ida McKinley's departure, however, Melinda's mistress had taken to bed and was given to long hours of sobbing.

Mrs. Mifflin's frustrated sorrows over the tea for Mrs. McKinley had finally subsided, though she continued to refer to the incident as "the greatest disappointment of my life." The president's wife had extended her regrets with handwritten notes to each of the invited guests, delighting the matrons of Cleveland society and elevating Mrs. Mifflin's status among her friends. Once assured her position among the social elite remained intact, her outlook greatly improved. She had risen from her bed much like a mythical phoenix from the ashes to start life anew.

Evan's weekly letters helped ease the distance between them, but they couldn't compete with having him near her side. Reading his letters over and over had become a nightly ritual. In the past he hadn't shared much about his off-season work, and now becoming familiar with his daily routine during the summer months caused her to feel a new closeness to him.

The details of how Evan and Harland had spent weeks setting controlled fires in the hunting areas to encourage new growth had surprised her. She couldn't imagine that burning the underbrush and grass would have a positive effect on the land, but that's what Evan and Harland did each summer. Combined with the summer heat, it was one of Evan's least favorite tasks, but he said the process helped to provide the best conditions to increase wildlife for the next hunting season. With such attention and care, it was no wonder guests had little difficulty bagging deer, marsh hens, bluebill, quail, grouse, and pheasant.

As assistant gamekeeper, Evan was expected to ensure the animal population remained well developed. His tasks had expanded to include the upkeep of the hunting lodge in addition to lending a hand at the stables and wherever else he might be needed. Melinda couldn't help but wonder what duties she might take on as the wife of such a man. Perhaps she would be called upon to assist with the wives of the guests who hunted, but she wasn't exactly certain what that assistance might entail.

It seemed there was no end to the many chores that needed attention—and there were few workers left to complete them. Evan spoke of working night and day and having little time for simple necessities such as washing clothes and cooking. Melinda smiled to herself. She would point out in her letters that these were the jobs a wife could perform in order to ease the burden of a workingman. Even the hotel and club superintendent of Bridal Veil Island had a helper, although it wasn't in the capacity of wife.

Mr. Zimmerman worked at a resort in the Adirondacks during the summer months, so he delegated his supervisory duties on Bridal Veil to his temporary assistant, Mr. Nordegren. The investors always turned over a long list of tasks that they expected to see completed before their return in early winter.

While Evan's letters made it clear there was little time for anything but hard work during the humid summers, Melinda did smile when she read that he and Harland took occasional dips in the ocean. "Harland isn't very fond of being in the water, so he rolls up his pant legs and stands there watching while I get myself soaked from head to toe. He says that's enough to cool him off, but not for me." She grinned each time she pictured Harland with his pants rolled up to his knees.

Melinda's letters to Evan didn't include much lighthearted news. Instead, when she put pen to paper, her letters detailed the boring activities of Cleveland society. While she'd once been in the midst of such activity, she now sat on the fringes when she accompanied Mrs. Mifflin to her teas and soirees. No longer did she harbor a desire to return to a life among the wealthy residents of Cleveland. Now she wished only to leave Mrs. Mifflin's employ and marry Evan. Each of his letters expressed a strong love for her, but he hadn't yet written the four words she longed to hear: *Will you marry me?*

"Melinda!" Mrs. Mifflin's shout brought her back to the present and sent her rushing down the hallway. She'd been lost in reading Evan's letter and completely forgotten the time. Flinging open the door, she was met by Mrs. Mifflin's angry frown. "Where have you been? You know Lucy Hollister can't abide people arriving late to her home."

Melinda inhaled a deep breath and approached in a calm fashion. If she appeared flustered, it would only heighten Mrs. Mifflin's ill-tempered manner. "There's no need for concern. You'll be ready in plenty of time. Matthew knows to have the carriage around front, and your dress is ready." She pointed to the chair in front of the dressing table. "It won't take long to fashion your hair."

Mrs. Mifflin looked into the oversized mirror attached to her dressing table and focused on Melinda's attire. Her eyebrows dipped a notch. "I see you made some alterations to that dress. The color becomes you."

"Thank you. Your gowns are always of the finest quality, and this shade of green is one of my favorites." Melinda hoped the small talk would continue to calm her mistress.

"The lace at the neckline is a nice touch. You added that, as well, didn't you?"

Melinda nodded. "I removed it from one of my old worn dresses."

"It's good that you've learned to make do. I count myself fortunate that I've been able to help you in your time of need." She straightened her shoulders. "I'm sure you feel much the same, since your parents did nothing to provide for your well-being in their passing. That is why it is such a public disgrace to incur debt. It only serves to humiliate those left behind."

The woman's comments stabbed like a hot poker. She continued to allude to the failure of Melinda's parents to leave an inheritance. She appeared to enjoy the opportunity to reopen Melinda's slowly healing wounds. In truth, Melinda cared little about the inheritance; it was the fact that her parents had been living a lie that pained her. Never once had they mentioned their financial difficulties to her or to her brother, Lawrence.

"I'm pleased that you continue to find my assistance to your liking." There was so much more she wanted to say, but Melinda knew her place. Unless she intended to speak words of praise, a lady's maid should remain silent. *And that is all I am. A companion and maid to a woman of means. Nothing more.*

"Sally tells me you continue to receive letters from that hunter at Bridal Veil. I do trust you're not encouraging him."

Melinda cringed at the comment. Would Sally never quit prying? The clock chimed as she placed a final pin in a curl. At least she'd been saved from the need for a direct response. "We'd best hurry or you'll be late."

On more than one occasion Melinda had requested permission to remain at home rather than accompany the older woman to her social functions, but Mrs. Mifflin had made it clear she would not grant approval. Like the other ladies' maids, Melinda was a symbol of Mrs. Mifflin's social status. Much like the jewels and accessories worn by their mistresses, the maids had to be shown off, as well.

That afternoon's gathering was no different than the hundreds that had gone before. The genteel ladies of Cleveland gathered in Lucy Hollister's parlor, and after a few cursory bits of conversation, the maids were dismissed to sit in the expansive hallway or on the veranda that surrounded the Hollister home. Of course, they weren't supposed to be out of earshot, in case their mistresses would send the butler to fetch them. Melinda chose to sit outdoors. She'd tucked her stitching and a copy of *Emma* into her bag. Mrs. Mifflin had loaned her the book as well as some of Jane Austen's other books. Although Melinda read all of Austen's novels while a student, she'd been taking pleasure in them once again.

Spotting several chairs under a large buckeye tree, she wandered away from the porch. No doubt Mrs. Mifflin would be unhappy if she saw her so far away from the house, but the tree would provide her a quiet, shady place to read. Better to apologize than seek permission—that was the servants' oft-quoted mantra at the Mifflin household, and one Melinda had adopted of late.

Melinda was soon lost in her book. From her earlier reading, she recalled the arrival of Frank Churchill's friend Jane Fairfax and Emma's reaction to the young woman, but it didn't diminish her pleasure as she continued to read.

She didn't hear the sound of approaching footsteps and let out a gasp when two large hands covered her eyes. Someone leaned close to her ear—a man—and whispered, "Guess who?"

"I have no idea, but you best unhand me before I scream for help!"

The shield dropped away from her eyes, and Melinda twisted around in the lawn chair. Recognition was immediate. "Lawrence! Where did you come from?" Her book clattered to the grass when she reached to embrace her brother. With his arms still encircling her, she leaned back and looked into his eyes. "I can't believe this."

He chuckled and squeezed her a bit tighter. "You can believe it. I'm quite real. Surely you didn't think you'd never set eyes on your brother again."

"No, of course not, but you haven't kept in touch, and I've been worried. The last I heard from you was before you accepted a position on a ship and said you planned to sail the seas and make your fortune."

His hazel eyes twinkled as he released her from his arms. "I've accomplished part of what I set out to do." He leaned down, retrieved her book, and then motioned for her to sit down before he took the chair beside her. "I've sailed the seas, but I haven't yet made my fortune." He grinned. "But I'm still working on it."

"Doing what?"

"At the moment I'm working as a groomsman and jockey for Harris Dangerfield." He leaned back in the chair and stretched his legs in front of him. "Rather surprising for the son of Kathleen and Lincoln Colson, wouldn't you agree? I'm a tad taller than most jockeys, but my thinness is to my advantage."

Melinda heard the pain in his voice. "It's honest work, Lawrence. And hard work never hurt anyone. Isn't that what everyone says?"

Their parents' deaths had been difficult for both of them, but she had worried about Lawrence and his love of gambling. Her father had done his best to keep Lawrence on a tight rein, but mostly it had been unsuccessful. Like a moth to a flame, Lawrence was drawn to wagering on cards, horses, and everything else.

"Maybe, but I don't plan to work hard for the rest of my life. I'll find a way to make my fortune. But I'll not follow in Father's footsteps and lose it all."

Bitterness replaced the pain she'd detected in his voice only a few moments earlier, but she was pleased to hear that he didn't plan on losing his fortune once he'd made it. Perhaps he'd truly given up his penchant for gambling.

He leaned forward and grasped her hand. "And you shouldn't be working as a lady's maid. To see you kowtow to the likes of Dorothea Mifflin would have destroyed our mother."

"Well, it is far better than living on the streets. I'm thankful I received the education and training that allowed me to secure honorable work." She glanced around to make certain no one else was nearby. "But I don't think I'll be working for Mrs. Mifflin much longer."

He released her hand and once again relaxed in the chair. "And how are you going to manage that feat?"

"I'm in love with the assistant gamekeeper at Bridal Veil Island." She hesitated a moment. "The Mifflins spend most of the winter months there. I met Evan at Bridal Veil, Evan Tarlow. We were introduced the first year I went to work for the Mifflins." Her words gushed forth like water streaming from a well-primed pump. "I think you'd like him."

"I realize your opportunity to marry someone from the upper class has disappeared, Melinda. But surely you could find someone better suited than a gamekeeper living on a remote island down in Georgia. Is that really what you want?" His eyebrows arched into twin peaks.

"He hasn't yet asked me to marry him, but when he does, I won't hesitate for a minute. He's a wonderful man, and I want to spend the rest of my life with him. Where we live doesn't matter to me as long as I'm with Evan." She jutted her chin for emphasis.

"Then, if that's what you want, I'll wish you all the happiness in the world when—or should I say *if*—you marry him." He grinned and shrugged his shoulders. "Living on that island would probably be better than dealing with Dorothea Mifflin. She seldom has a kind word to say about anyone." He shook his head. "And her husband bullies any of his business associates who show the slightest sign of weakness. Father always said that Cyrus and Dorothea were a match deserving each other."

"That isn't kind, Lawrence." During the years since her parents' deaths, Melinda had missed her brother and his jocular attitude. Throughout his life, Lawrence had been able to make his way without exerting much effort. He let his good looks and humor—and the family money—carry him. But his carefree days had ended when their parents died.

"I came back to Cleveland to spend time with my sister, and now I discover you'll soon be leaving for Georgia. Maybe I should have remained aboard those steamers."

"No, you should not! I won't be leaving Cleveland all that soon. I don't think Mr. and Mrs. Mifflin will want to leave until after Christmas, but I'm hoping I'm wrong." Melinda had been doing her best to encourage a departure prior to Thanksgiving but had met with little success. "What was it like, living like that these past years? I can't imagine sailing from one place to the next, never sure where I'd be." She glanced toward the front porch. Several of the maids were returning into the hallway. "I want to hear all about the places you visited."

"And you will. I have a number of souvenirs for you." He combed his fingers through his thick blond hair. "I know I should have written, but I've never been good at that sort of thing."

She smiled and patted his arm. "You're forgiven. I'm just pleased that we've reunited. Tell me, after all those years at sea, how did you ever happen to be hired to work as a jockey and groomsman for Mr. Dangerfield?"

"I'm a man of many talents, dear sister. I never lost my love for horses and continued to ride whenever we were on land. When I got back here, a fellow asked me to ride his horse in a local race. Of course, I won." He puffed out his chest and laughed. "Mr. Dangerfield happened to be there and approached me afterward. I've been with him the past few weeks."

She hoped his mention of racing didn't mean he was still gambling. "I have a wonderful idea, Lawrence. Why don't you come to Bridal Veil when I go down with the Mifflins? There are stables on the island, and the wealthy guests all bring their horses. I'm sure Evan would put in a good word so that you could get work. I'll write a letter and ask him. There are lots of servants and employees who come for the season, so we have our own social gatherings. It's really quite nice."

"Any young ladies who might interest me?"

"There are a great many there. Servants as well as the daughters of the wealthy investors, but I don't think you'd better attempt to woo any of the debutantes. Their fathers want suitors from their own social class." She reached for his hand and gave it a squeeze. "Please consider it, Lawrence. It would be so grand to have you there." Before Lawrence could weigh her request, Mrs. Mifflin stepped on the veranda and glanced about. Melinda jumped to her feet. "I have to go, but come see me and consider what I've said."

Lawrence retrieved her stitching bag and studied the title of her book as he handed it to her. "*Emma.* Still the romantic, I see." He leaned forward and brushed a kiss on her cheek. "I'll think about Bridal Veil."

"I have to hurry," she said. With the bag in one hand and book in the other, she scurried toward the front porch. Mrs. Mifflin wouldn't be happy. She didn't like to be kept waiting.

The older woman sighed as Melinda neared her side. "I thought you maids were told to wait in the hallway or on the veranda." She squinted out at the lawn. "And who is that man you were with? Did I see him kiss your cheek?"

Melinda tucked her book back into her bag. "My brother, Lawrence. You remember him, don't you?" Mrs. Mifflin said nothing but hurried to the carriage as if the presence of Lawrence were something she must escape.

Matthew assisted them into the carriage, and once they were on their way, Mrs. Mifflin took up the conversation. "I thought Lawrence had gone to sea. Cyrus said he was always a disappointment to your father." With a flick of her wrist, she opened her fan.

"That's not true. My father loved Lawrence." Her father might not have approved of some of Lawrence's choices, but he had never spoken of disappointment in his son. "Lawrence was at sea. He's traveled to many countries, but now he's come back to Cleveland and is working for a Mr. Dangerfield."

"Doing what? I don't think Harris Dangerfield owns a ship."

"Lawrence tells me he's been hired as a groomsman and jockey for the Dangerfield family."

"My, my. Whatever would your poor mother and father think of that? While Lawrence was off at sea, there weren't any questions about him. For all anyone knew he could have been captain to his own ship. But now that he's back in Cleveland and working as a groomsman . . . dear me." She clasped a hand to her bodice and shook her head. "He's truly going to be an embarrassment to your family name, isn't he?"

Even Mrs. Mifflin's unkind comments couldn't crush Melinda's pleasure at having her brother return to the city. Besides, when the wealthy residents of Cleveland realized her parents had died penniless, they'd crossed the Colson name off their social lists faster than it took to ring their servants for a pen. There was no longer a family name for Lawrence, or her, to embarrass.

CHAPTER 7

OCTOBER 1898

Sharing supper with the O'Sullivans had become a time Evan cherished. Being with the older couple always made Evan feel cared for. It calmed his spirit in a way he couldn't explain. Tonight, however, there was a storm brewing, and no one felt even the slightest sense of calm. Only moments before, Garrison O'Sullivan had made his way outside to check the skies.

He returned with a look of worry and addressed Harland, who was eating with them, as well. "Wind's picking up a little more, Harland. I'm thinkin' ya may be right about gettin' the animals to safety. I'll get on down to the barn and saddle a couple of horses. If y'er a mind to, you can come and help me move the rest of the horses and the cattle to the pasture. We can only hope they won't go wanderin' too far when the storm moves in." He grabbed his cap from a peg near the door. "If we lose the livestock, there's gonna be more than a wee bit of complainin' from the owners."

Emma waved a dish towel in the air. "Be sure and take care of the milk cows, Garrison. There's plenty of folks dependin' on milk from the dairy during the winter months." Her lips tipped up in a grin. "And I depend on 'em all year round."

"I do na need ya telling me how to do me job, Emma, darlin'. I'll be taking care of all the animals. I know full well they're important to everyone—you and me included." Garrison slapped his hat on his head. There was an edge to his voice that Evan knew had nothing to do with his irritation at Emma and everything to do with the storm.

"I'll be with you as soon as I give Evan some instructions." Harland turned toward Evan. "I want you to go over to the workers' quarters and roust the fellows over there. Between all of them, maybe they can get around and make sure everything is secure. Have several of them check the clubhouse to see that shutters are closed good and tight and the doors secured. Send the others to check as many of the cottages as you can. Close and tighten shutters on any that need it."

Most of the cottages had been shuttered when the owners went north for the summer. Still, there were a few, like the Mifflins, who had departed in a rush and might not have checked to see that their cottages had been properly secured by their servants.

"You go to the boathouse. Take Alfred with you. He'll listen to you, and you'll need help in there."

Evan nodded. Only a dozen men lived on the island this time of year. The seasonal workers returned home when the guests departed at the end of winter, and the rest of the workers who helped with painting and maintenance during the off-season months lived in Biscayne and arrived by boat each morning. Those men had already departed for the night.

Alfred had the same opportunity to go home to Biscayne each night. But with a drinking, mean-spirited father, he preferred living in the workers' quarters year-round. Each payday Alfred would take the launch across the river and give his wages to his father, and then he'd return to the island. He was far from their best employee, but Evan had a soft spot for him. Probably because the young man wanted to please his father but never could. Evan had felt the same way until he'd come to Bridal Veil and met Harland. Not that coming here had changed the relationship with his father, but Harland had shown him that a relationship with God could ease that pain and provide him the loving father he'd always desired. Evan had tried to show that to Alfred, as well, but he didn't know if Alfred had fully accepted the idea of a loving heavenly Father.

Harland sopped the last of his stew with a crust of bread and shoved it into his mouth before pushing up from the table. "Hurry and finish, Evan. We've got little light left to help guide us."

Evan swallowed his final bite and nodded. "I'm right behind you. Thank you again for the food, Mrs. O'Sullivan. It was the best I've had in many a day."

She turned from the dishes she'd set to soak in the sink. "I'm thinkin' it's the best you've had since the last time you set your feet under my table." She chuckled and lifted a soapy hand from the water. "Best be gettin' down the road, or I'll be accused of holdin' ya back with me chatter."

Evan waved and opened the front door. A gust of wind yanked it from his hand and slammed it against the house. "I'm sorry!" he shouted while gaining a good hold on the door and pushing it closed.

There was no denying the wind had picked up in the short time since they'd entered the O'Sullivan cottage. If it kept up at this rate, he might be forced to agree with Harland that there was a good chance of a hurricane headed in their direction. The thought, more than the biting wind, caused a shiver to course through his body.

Leaning forward, he angled his head down and pushed against the blustery weather. With each step forward, he felt the escalating winds attempt to push him back. Swirling coils of air filled with dirt, sand, and debris pummeled his face and hands like flying shards of glass.

Thankful when he finally arrived at the workers' quarters, Evan beat on the door several times before he opened it. Had the weather been otherwise, he would have waited for one of the men to invite him inside; these quarters, were, after all, their home. But today he pushed aside any thought of good manners. A huge gust of wind and debris followed him inside.

Other than Alfred, who was sitting on his bed looking at a magazine, the men were huddled together in a far corner of the room playing cards. The group turned in unison, startled to see their cards, papers, and other belongings swirl about the room. Johnny Boyd jumped to his feet. "Close that door!"

"It's closed," Evan called out. "I need all of you men to come with me. Put on your slickers, and if there's an extra, I'd like to borrow it. There's work that needs to be done with this storm moving in."

"I'm not going out in this," one of the men responded. "There's lightning off in the distance, and it's been thundering for the last few minutes. The lights have been flickering here all evening."

"These are Harland's instructions, not mine. You'll be answering to him if you go against his orders."

Another fellow remained in his chair. "I didn't sign up to go out in a hurricane. I'd rather look for another job than take my chances being killed in that storm." He waved to a row of pegs along the wall. "You're welcome to use my raincoat, though."

Alfred got up from his bed. "I'll go with you, Evan." He crossed the room and grabbed his raincoat.

Of the twelve men in the room, only five donned their slickers.

Except for Alfred, worry lines etched the men's faces. Evan understood. Their worried looks were a near match for his own mounting concern. With the storm growing, there was no way they'd be able to reach even a third of the cottages. He sent Johnny to the clubhouse and the other three men in opposite directions with orders to check as many cottages as possible and then return to their quarters. "You come with me to the boathouse, Alfred. And you'd best fasten your slicker."

One of the men shouted a profanity as they opened the door and another huge gust blasted into the room, but Evan paid the fellow no heed. He was disappointed by their attitude but not totally surprised. Nobody wanted to go out in this weather. Well, almost nobody—Alfred was delighted.

The men divided to head out in different directions. As they separated, Evan shouted, "Keep yourselves safe!"

The wind moaned through tree limbs bowed low against the strain of the onslaught. A bolt of lightning crisscrossed the sky, quickly followed by a deafening clap of thunder that shook Evan to his core. Alfred cupped his hands to his mouth and shouted, "It's beautiful, ain't it?"

A tree limb cracked then crashed to the ground not more than five feet away. The heavens opened and pummeled the earth with torrents of rain. Alfred tripped on a fallen branch and sprawled across the muddy path in front of him. Once again a flash of lightning bolted through the sky. Evan's feet slipped in the mud as he grabbed hold of Alfred's arm and fought to pull him up. The young man's slicker flapped around him. Why hadn't he fastened the coat?

Alfred grinned at him. "Thanks, Evan."

Evan looped arms with Alfred and the two of them slogged forward. Only a short distance to go and they'd be at the boathouse. How he wished Captain Holloway was still in charge.

When he'd been the overseer of the boathouse and captain of the *Bessie II*, he had lived in quarters above the boathouse. When a storm threatened, Captain Holloway always took charge of the boats. But after he'd suffered heart problems two years ago, the good captain had been forced to quit his job.

The new captain, Richard Fleming, had accepted the position under a different set of circumstances. Married with two children, Captain Fleming had notified the investors that a cottage better suited a man with a wife and family. Although the living quarters above the boathouse were large enough for his family, Captain Fleming's wife had objected to living in the structure. She cited worries over their children—a fact that was easily enough understood, since a large portion of the boathouse floated in the river to provide easy access for the vessels when they entered the building for storage and repair. Captain Fleming and his family departed Bridal Veil as soon as the season ended. Just like the investors, the captain and his family enjoyed a cooler climate during the summer months. When November returned, so would Captain Fleming and his family.

During the captain's absence, security of the boathouse was another of the many tasks assigned to Harland. And with Mr. Nordegren gone on his week of vacation, Harland was in charge. In truth, the workmen all depended upon Harland for guidance, whether Mr. Nordegren was present or not. The assistant manager cared a great deal about the clubhouse maintenance and repairs, but his scope of concern didn't move far beyond the exterior of the large hotel complex.

Evan held tight to Alfred as a crashing swell buffeted the boathouse and drenched the two of them. If this continued through the night, the damage would be even greater than Harland had estimated. Black water continued to rise and fall against the building in giant punishing waves. Once inside, he and Alfred managed to light several of the lanterns that hung low from the rafters. Though many of the buildings and cottages on Bridal Veil now had electricity, wiring the boathouse still remained on the investors' list of pending improvements. Besides, if the electricity was still working anywhere on the island, Evan doubted it would remain operable much longer.

He directed Alfred to the far side of the boathouse. "The ropes will stretch with the tidal surges, which will toss the boats about, so do your best to tie them down good and tight."

There weren't as many boats on the far side, and Evan knew the young man moved at a slow pace. He didn't doubt that Alfred would do his best, but no matter the circumstance, Alfred only moved at one speed—slow. There was nothing they could do to make the boathouse any more secure. If the force of the storm caused the boathouse to capsize, all of the boats would be damaged, but he continued to pray the storm would soon subside.

Alfred held a lantern in one hand and did his best to remain upright as he closed the distance between them. "I'm going to go out and see the sky, Evan."

"No, Alfred! Stay in here!"

If Alfred heard Evan, he didn't heed him. He opened the rear door and disappeared into the darkness. The boathouse rocked with a vengeance, and water surged from beneath the boats. A clap of thunder followed a wild streak of lightning and an onslaught of riotous winds. Evan lost his footing and clung to one of the thick beams that supported the roof.

When the waters briefly calmed enough that he could gain his balance, Evan picked his way to the doorway, clutching at ropes and beams to steady himself until he pulled open the door. "Alfred! Alfred!" He lifted his lantern high in the air and swung it in every direction, continuing to shout the boy's name. But Alfred was nowhere to be seen.

The despair that ripped at Evan's heart was soon joined by threatening fear and uncertainty. He didn't know what to do. To remain at the boathouse would likely be a death sentence for any man, yet he didn't want to chance deserting Alfred. Evan's head told him that the giant surge that had knocked him to the boathouse deck a short time ago had surely washed Alfred away, but his heart told him there could be a chance the young man had survived.

Over and over he shouted Alfred's name into the howling wind that continued to batter everything in its path. His thoughts raced in an attempt to reach some acceptable decision. "If Harland were here, what would he tell me to do?" He shouted the question into the high-pitched storm. When no answer came, he looked toward heaven and cried out to God, "What am I to do? Do I leave him and try to save myself? I don't know if he's alive. Show me what to do, God!"

A bolt of lightning flashed overhead and lit up the sky. Beneath the shining light, the decking that surrounded the exterior of the boathouse appeared as black and shiny as patent leather. Debris deposited by the ebb and flow of the waves lay scattered atop the deck awaiting the next surge that would wash it out to sea. Evan turned toward the far end of the deck, and his eyes fell upon what looked like Alfred's slicker. He edged his way down the short distance and retrieved the raincoat. His throat caught and his tears mingled with the rain that pelted him as he clutched the coat to his chest.

CHAPTER 8

Still clutching Alfred's raincoat, Evan slowly fought his way back to the hunting lodge. The rain had subsided, but rumbles of thunder and flashes of lightning warned there was more to come. Battered and worn, he had no idea how long his struggle against the elements had taken before he finally dragged himself up the steps to the hunting lodge. With his remaining strength, he pushed open the door and fell inside the room.

"Evan!" Harland crossed the distance between them in several long strides. "I've been praying for your safety, boy." Using his shoulder, Harland pushed the door closed and then fell against it as the wind once again raised a screeching howl. "You didn't get back here any too soon. I think we're in for another round."

Evan dropped Alfred's slicker onto the floor. His stomach lurched at the sight of the rumpled raincoat. Surges of pounding guilt and sorrow now replaced the battering he'd withstood from the storm. He couldn't tell Harland what had happened—not yet. The words wouldn't come, even if he tried. "What time is it?"

"Near three o'clock. We've got at least four more hours until we see any sign of daylight. And if this doesn't let up, it will be even longer." He grabbed a towel and blanket and handed them to Evan. "Best get out of those wet clothes." He raked his fingers through his hair. "You were gone so long I was beginning to think the Lord hadn't heard my prayers."

Delilah padded to Evan's side and wound between his legs before quickly moving away. Evan gestured to the cat. "Best stay clear of me if you don't want to get wet, Delilah." He glanced at Harland. "Delilah got anything to say about this weather?"

Harland shook his head. "Nothing good."

Evan looked around the room. Harland had done his best to fortify the downstairs against the wind and rain. A heavy gun cabinet had been moved in front of one window while other large pieces of furniture blocked the other windows and rear door.

"Now that you're back here safe and sound, I'm gonna push this bookcase in front of the door."

"It's too heavy. Let me help you." Evan jumped to his feet, and between the two of them, they moved the heavy piece of furniture close enough to block the front door.

Once they'd completed the task, Harland motioned toward the stairs. "Now you best go up and change out of those wet clothes."

Evan didn't argue. His bones felt as though they'd been chilled to the marrow and would never again feel warmth. When he returned downstairs, Harland was sitting in one of the large leather chairs, his forehead wrinkled with concern. "The men get back to their quarters? I hope they had the sense to block the windows. You tell 'em to block the windows?"

"I think they know to block the windows, Harland." Most of those men knew more about storms and hurricanes than Evan did. They'd lived on the coast for all of their lives. "Only a few of them were willing to go out in the storm and help secure the cottages and clubhouse. I don't know if they're safe. I couldn't make it over there once I left the boathouse."

"Don't like hearing the men wouldn't follow orders. Some of 'em may find themselves without a job if they try that again."

Harland's words cut Evan like a sharp knife, and he dropped to one of the chairs. If Alfred had refused to go, he'd still be alive. His throat closed as he pointed to the rain slicker on the floor. How could he tell Harland about Alfred if he couldn't even say the boy's name? Harland cast a glance at the raincoat before his gaze settled on Evan.

"That belong to one of our men? Is someone missing out in the storm?" The alarm in his voice matched the panic that flashed in his eyes. "Who is it? What happened, Evan? Tell me!" He jumped up from his chair and crossed the distance between them in three long strides. "Who did we lose out there?"

"Alfred." He covered his face with his palms as he choked out the boy's name. "I didn't keep him safe, Harland."

"Tell me what happened." The older man sat down in the chair beside him.

Once Evan was able to speak, he told how Alfred went out to watch the storm. "I shouted at him to stay inside." Grief choked him as he told how he'd searched for the young man but found nothing except for the raincoat. "I told him to fasten it, but he didn't listen."

Harland patted his shoulder. "Fastened or not, the raincoat wouldn't have saved him if a surge hit the boathouse deck. You can't blame yourself, Evan. He didn't listen to your warning." Harland leaned back and stroked his chin. "Doesn't look like you believe me, but if there's blame that needs placing for the boy's death, you can put it square on my shoulders. I'm the one who told you to take him to the boathouse, so the fault is mine, not yours."

Evan shook his head. "This isn't your fault, Harland."

"And it isn't yours, either. It was an accident—a sad and tragic accident that will haunt both of us for a long time to come. I think it might help both of us if we did some Bible reading and praying." He smiled, but the sadness in his eyes didn't disappear. "You want to join me?"

The lights flickered and Evan glanced at a lamp between the chairs. "We may need to read by lantern light if the electricity gives out, but I know it would help me to do some Bible reading. Maybe I'll find something that will help take away some of this guilt."

"The boy had choices, Evan. He could listen to your counsel and remain safe, or go about his own way and deal with the consequences. I don't mean to sound harsh, but we've each and every one of us got those same choices to make. Some of us make mistakes and live to try again. Sometimes those mistakes are deadly. Either way, it ain't up to us to make another fella's choices. If Alfred would have done as he was told, he'd be right here with us."

"It hurts just the same," Evan admitted. "No matter who's to blame."

"Indeed it does." Harland handed him one of the Bibles from the bookcase. "But this is the best salve I know. You might want to start with Romans, chapter eight."

Evan hadn't finished reading the chapter when Delilah arched her back and screeched an ear-splitting yowl. The electricity went off at the same moment, and Evan was thankful they'd taken care to light a lantern. With a ferocity that caused the hunting lodge to shudder around them, the storm returned with renewed force. From behind their furniture barricades, glass shattered, and the wind did battle with the heavy wooden objects. Rain seeped through the windows and beneath the doors.

The heavy chest they'd moved in front of a side window teetered. "Help me hold it in place!" Both men pushed to hold their weight against the chest while Harland prayed aloud for strength. "I think the worst of the storm is upon us, Evan. Pray the winds will shift and move away from the islands and mainland."

Evan prayed.

The hours passed like days. The wind, thunder, lightning, and rain continued, but by midmorning the storm had lost much of its intensity. The two men sloshed through the water that had entered the lodge during the tidal surge that hit in the early morning hours. Delilah remained safe and dry on the stairway leading to the second floor, watching Evan and Harland as they pushed the bookcase away from the front door.

Evan gestured toward the cat. "Looks like Delilah may have to live on the stairs and second floor until we get all this water out of here."

Harland chuckled. "You can be sure she won't get her paws wet, and that's a fact." He grunted as he moved the bookcase far enough to open the door. "Might as well get out here and see what's left of the place."

The skies remained dark and foreboding, but Harland appeared calm. Uprooted trees had been tossed about like sticks. A giant cypress blocked the main path from the lodge, the limbs stretched in awkward angles like broken appendages, but Harland motioned him forward. "Getting this tree out of the path will be one of our first tasks. Let's make our way over to the O'Sullivans' place, and then we'll move on to the workers' quarters, the boathouse, the clubhouse, and the cottages. Best to check out the damage and then decide what needs our attention right away. Don't even need to go see the windmill—it was probably the first thing to fall."

Evan stared in disbelief as they picked their way through the piles of debris that blocked their path at every turn. A gnawing emptiness settled in the pit of his stomach, the void deepening with each remembrance of Alfred's death. The thought of finding other dead or wounded workers pressed on him like a heavy weight. At least Melinda was safe.

CHAPTER 9

Melinda sat at a distance keeping a close watch for Mrs. Mifflin's gesture. This afternoon's gathering was the first tea the matron had hosted since her failed social for Mrs. McKinley. All of the servants had received explicit instructions that blunders would not be tolerated. And, as usual, they'd heard Mrs. Mifflin's habitual warning that their wages would be decreased if anyone made a mistake.

Sally grinned and gently elbowed Melinda when Mrs. Mifflin had issued the customary edict. Yet they knew the words were more than an idle threat. She would execute her promise if she deemed it necessary. None of the servants could afford a decrease in their wages, but they worried more about the matron's temperamental repercussions than any reduction in pay. So on this particular day all of the servants were striving to please.

Once tea had been served and on Mrs. Mifflin's signal, Melinda would make her way to the piano and entertain the guests while they enjoyed the afternoon repast. "Don't play too loud," Mrs. Mifflin had sternly instructed. "I want the music to fill any silences but be soft enough to permit unhindered conversation."

On other occasions Melinda had been granted permission to read while she waited to serve Mrs. Mifflin's needs. Today, however, her gaze would remain fixed upon her mistress. The guests, smaller in number than those who had been invited to Mrs. McKinley's tea, were seated in the parlor, while Melinda remained on the perimeter, close to the piano, within sight of Mrs. Mifflin and also within earshot of any conversations. The matrons' perfumes soon overpowered the room. Scents of spring flowers mingled with heavier musky aromas in a blend that soon caused Melinda's eyes to water. She touched the corner of her handkerchief to her eyes, thankful the ladies would be in the other room while she played the piano. Sneezing during her presentation would be unacceptable.

Martha Genesee, one of Mrs. Mifflin's close friends, snapped open her fan. "It's warm for October, don't you think, Dorothea?" She whisked the fan back and forth in front of her nose.

"A little, but we often have these final spurts of summer during early fall." Although Mrs. Mifflin appeared to have placed her full attention on her guest, Melinda could see her employer's eyes darting about the dining room to ensure all was going smoothly. Soon Sally would have everything properly set in the dining room, and Mrs. Mifflin could relax.

"Edward and I were horrified by the news coming from Georgia. With that terrible hurricane and some of the islands underwater . . ." Her voice trailed off and she flapped the fan back and forth as though she might faint. "What did Cyrus have to say? Has he heard anything from Mr. Zimmerman or Victor Morley? Edward is eager for news and said I should inquire. He knows Cyrus keeps abreast of such matters. We'd considered going down before Christmas this year, but if Bridal Veil has flooded, we won't be going at all."

Melinda scooted to the edge of her chair, certain she'd heard Mrs. Genesee mention Georgia and some of the islands being underwater. Shock turned to panic as the words registered in her consciousness. She longed to grab Mrs. Genesee by the arm and force the woman to repeat every word she'd said. It took everything in Melinda's power to sit at attention and remain quiet, to smile with folded hands resting on her lap, as though all remained perfect with the world. She silently berated herself for daydreaming instead of keeping an ear on the conversation.

Mrs. Mifflin frowned and clucked her tongue. "Such an unpleasant topic to discuss during tea, Martha."

"It wasn't my idea to discuss the disaster. Edward reminded me several times that I should inquire. He'll be unhappy if I have nothing to relate. The newspapers have reported a variety of articles, and all of them differ. He doesn't know what to believe."

Disaster? Melinda heard the word as clearly as the chimes of the parlor clock. Myriad questions lodged in her throat, but she dared not say a word. She pressed her damp palms down the front of her silk moiré skirt and strained forward, afraid to miss a word yet frightened of what would be said.

"Now, Martha, you know how newspapermen like to exaggerate. They all want fascinating headlines so they'll sell more papers than their competitors." Mrs. Mifflin tipped her head toward Mrs. Genesee, but she cast a quick glance at Melinda.

Sally stepped into the kitchen doorway, and the moment Mrs. Mifflin looked in her direction, the maid gave an affirmative nod. Mrs. Mifflin stood and invited the ladies into the dining room. As they made their way into the other room, Mrs. Mifflin approached Melinda.

"I've decided you should begin to play now. Please take your place at the piano." Mrs. Mifflin looked at the piano and then back at Melinda.

She stood, but her feet wouldn't move. "Has Bridal Veil been struck by a hurricane?" Her throat caught as she awaited an answer.

Mrs. Mifflin's eyes turned dark. "Were you eavesdropping on my conversation with Mrs. Genesee, Melinda?"

"I wasn't—"

"Go to the piano. We will discuss this after my guests depart. And play well. I don't want my guests to hear any sour notes."

Hands trembling, Melinda took her seat at the piano. Worried or not, she must play well. Otherwise, she'd gain little information from Mrs. Mifflin. She inhaled a deep breath and caught her lower lip between her teeth. She must concentrate. "Please, Lord, help me play well," she whispered.

For the remainder of the afternoon, her fingers moved effortlessly across the keys, playing the concertos of Mozart, Beethoven, and Chopin that she'd memorized during her endless hours of practice. Now she was thankful for the years of piano lessons that made it possible for her to perform under such pressure and worry. Several of the ladies clapped when she completed Mozart's Concerto no. 21.

Mrs. Genesee strolled toward the piano. "I do love that piece, and you play beautifully."

Melinda glanced at Mrs. Mifflin. Had she been playing too loudly? The matron's expression appeared detached, which generally was not a good sign. The ladies had finished their tea, and more of them now strolled into the parlor and gathered around the piano.

Mrs. Williston took a seat near the piano. "I'm so pleased you supplied us with entertainment, Dorothea. I do appreciate an opportunity to enjoy artistic talent along with our tea. I had planned to have poetry readings at my next gathering. I think we could all benefit from more than idle chatter, don't you agree, ladies?"

"Indeed! Leave it to Dorothea to be the one who encourages us to expand our cultural horizons." With a smile large enough to swallow her face, Mrs. Genesee gestured toward their hostess.

A polite round of applause followed. While Melinda worried over the news she'd heard and the safety of Evan and the other employees on Bridal Veil, the ladies discussed a variety of offerings they might introduce at future gatherings. She longed for them to leave so that she could make further inquiry. None of the servants had mentioned anything about a storm, but how would they know? Most of them cared little about the world outside of Cleveland.

When the last of the guests had departed, Mrs. Mifflin gestured for Melinda to follow her upstairs. She hoped the guests' approval of her music would temper Mrs. Mifflin's earlier displeasure. She remained at a short distance behind Mrs. Mifflin while she climbed the steps. The older woman glanced over her shoulder when she arrived at the top of the staircase. "I cannot abide this dress any longer. The lace has scratched my neckline the entire afternoon." She strode to the mirror in the upstairs hallway and leaned forward for a better view. "Look at these red splotches. Everywhere the lace touches, I have a red mark. You need to do something to fix the neckline, or this dress is unwearable."

"I'll see to it this evening." Melinda followed Mrs. Mifflin into her sitting room and then into her bedroom, where she set to work unfastening the dress and corset. Mrs. Mifflin frowned as she touched her fingers to her neckline. "Your guests appeared to enjoy themselves this afternoon." Perhaps a bit of conversation would distract Mrs. Mifflin from her concern over the neckline of her gown.

"They did, indeed. Your musical training proved a benefit to all of us. At least your mother did not fail you in that area. I am pleased the ladies have decided to use our gatherings for more than idle chatter, which ultimately leads to unfounded gossip." She removed the dress from her shoulders and let it fall to the floor. "In the future, you need to refrain from eavesdropping, Melinda." She stepped out of the dress that lay in folds around her feet. "I don't intend to decrease your wages for the improper behavior, but only because you redeemed yourself at the keyboard."

"Thank you, Mrs. Mifflin. I truly was not eavesdropping. It was only when I heard mention of Bridal Veil that my attention was drawn to Mrs. Genesee's comments. Surely you can understand my extreme worry over the employees residing on the island, especially if a hurricane has left them flooded." Melinda lifted the gown from the floor and then removed a day dress from the wardrobe—one that didn't have any lace embellishment.

Mrs. Mifflin's eyebrows dipped low above her eyes. "You're worried about all of the employees or one employee in particular?"

"My concern is for all of them, as well as for those who may be stranded on the other islands. Of course I'm extremely distressed that something may have happened to Evan."

"So I would assume. Sally tells me that he continues to write you every week. Sometimes even more often." Her frown deepened. "You truly should cease this letter writing nonsense, Melinda. Though I find it inappropriate, I haven't forbade you from keeping company with a gamekeeper while we're on the island. I realize he's a pleasant diversion during your time off, but there's no need to continue corresponding throughout the year." She fussed with the bodice of her dress. "I find it completely inappropriate that the two of you would exchange words of affection with each other."

Melinda was stunned to hear Mrs. Mifflin mention the possibility of forbidding her to keep company with Evan on her time off work. But it was her final remark that truly gained her attention. "Words of affection?" Anger welled in her chest, but she forced an even tone. Sally had obviously been up to her old ways again. "Why would you think such a thing?"

"As I've often mentioned, with a bit of persuasion, Sally can be most informative. She does enjoy an extra coin in her pocket now and again."

"Since it would seem she has been steaming open my mail and sharing the contents when it is to her advantage, you already know of my deep feelings for Evan, so it should come as no surprise that I would be very distressed to think he'd been stranded on Bridal Veil during a hurricane." Melinda looked away, but not before Mrs. Mifflin noticed her tears.

"There's no need to become overwrought. I'm sure Martha Genesee was exaggerating what she'd heard. She loves to make a story out of nothing. When Cyrus returns for supper, I promise to inquire. Surely you realize that if there was any need for concern, he would have already mentioned the storm."

Melinda didn't know any such thing. Mr. Mifflin never discussed anything of consequence with his wife—at least not when she was attending to the woman. Instead, their hours together consisted of small talk and long silences. Melinda thanked the woman, but waiting for Mr. Mifflin's return would surely seem an eternity. In the meantime, she would go downstairs and ask the other servants if they'd heard anything about the storm. She also planned to have a word with Sally about her snoopy behavior.

Melinda started toward the door, but Mrs. Mifflin stopped her. "This would be an excellent opportunity for you to begin removing that lace on my gown."

Melinda sighed. Instead of carrying through with her plans, she'd be stuck in Mrs. Mifflin's sitting room removing tiny stitches from lace while Mrs. Mifflin wrote a letter to her cousin in New York.

Careful not to rip either gown or embellishment, Melinda had detached the lace by the time Mr. Mifflin returned home. When the downstairs door opened, she turned toward the sitting-room door. If Mrs. Mifflin wasn't in the downstairs parlor, Mr. Mifflin usually greeted his wife in her sitting room. Melinda fervently hoped he would do so today. She strained to hear the sound of footfalls on the carpeted stairs and silently cheered when she finally heard Mr. Mifflin approach.

He tapped before entering the room. "I see you ladies are hard at work. How did your tea go this afternoon, my dear?" He crossed the room and placed a fleeting kiss on his wife's cheek. "I thought you might be resting after an afternoon of activity."

Mrs. Mifflin set aside the pen and paper. "I would have enjoyed a short nap, but I have correspondence that must be answered. What with all the plans for today's social, I'm behind in my replies. There's so much that requires my attention, it seems unending at times."

"You do a marvelous job, my dear. No one could ever complain about your adherence to proper social etiquette." He glanced toward Melinda. "Isn't that correct, Melinda?"

"You're absolutely right, sir. Your wife's accomplishments are exemplary. Even today, her guests were praising her abilities."

Mrs. Mifflin preened while she explained. "They lauded me with a host of compliments." She gave a little shrug. "And all because I had Melinda play the piano." Uttering Melinda's name seemed to jar the older woman's memory. "Tell me, Cyrus, has there been any word of a hurricane hitting Bridal Veil? Martha Genesee said she and Edward had heard reports of damage to some of the islands off the coast of Georgia. Edward instructed her to inquire, but I knew nothing to report."

"Nothing definite yet, although I do know there was damage in Biscayne. A storm, but I don't know if it was a genuine hurricane. The reports have been varied, and I can't say we know anything of a precise nature just yet."

Mrs. Mifflin looked up at her husband. "Melinda is concerned about some of her friends who remain on the island throughout the year. Perhaps you could telegraph and make certain there haven't been any injuries."

He nodded. "But a visit to the telegraph office can wait until morning. I'm ready for supper." He patted his stomach. "Besides, any damage is already done, and whether I inquire now or tomorrow won't make much difference."

Melinda bit her lip. How could the man be so indifferent to those who might be injured or in need of aid, people charged with keeping his property maintained and safe during the summer months? She tried to recall if she'd ever observed her parents act with such coldness toward those of a lower class. If they had, she couldn't remember, and for that she was thankful.

"Come along, Dorothea. Let's see what the cook has prepared for us. I'm famished."

Outside the door, Melinda turned in the opposite direction and went down the back stairway into the kitchen. Though she was permitted to use the front stairs, the staff ate in the kitchen, and she wanted to speak to Sally.

Once the meal had been served to Mr. and Mrs. Mifflin, the servants gathered around their own table. After Matthew said a quick prayer, Sally passed a bowl of creamed potatoes. "You got your share of notice today, didn't ya, Melinda?"

Melinda bristled. Sally was never pleased when one of the other servants received attention, and right now Melinda had little patience for the woman's jealousy. "It wasn't my desire to be noticed. I was ordered to play the piano, just like you're ordered to prepare meals."

"Maybe so, but you did your best to play tunes that would gain ya the most attention. All them trills and such. You didn't fool me. You were hoping those ladies would take notice."

Melinda wanted to explain that what she'd been playing weren't "tunes" but concertos, but then she'd sound as pompous as Mrs. Mifflin. "I didn't choose the pieces. They were selected by Mrs. Mifflin. If you'd like to ask her, she'll confirm what I've told you."

"Bah!" Sally waved the serving spoon. "Ain't worth my time to ask."

Melinda waited until the roast beef and potatoes had been passed around the table. "I'd like to speak to you privately after we finish supper, Sally." She kept her voice low so that the others wouldn't hear her request.

Sally looked up from her plate. "If you got something to say, you can say it in front of all of us. I got nothing to hide from anyone sittin' round this table."

Melinda hesitated. She didn't want to embarrass the woman.

Sally leaned in her direction. "Go ahead! Say what you got to say and be done with it."

"Mrs. Mifflin tells me you've repeated information you gathered from reading my personal mail. I knew you'd told her I was receiving letters from Evan, but I didn't realize you'd continued reading them and passing along the contents." She frowned at the maid. "In our previous conversation, I was quite clear when I said you should never again open and read my mail."

A chorus of gasps followed the disclosure, and Sally waved the other servants to silence. "Ain't what you think. I didn't want to do it but the missus made me. She said she wanted to know what was going on between you and Evan. Said she didn't want to lose you as her lady's maid."

"She also mentioned that you gave her the information in exchange for extra money."

Sally's fork clattered onto the china plate. "Is that what she told you? That I've been reading your letters so she'd give me extra money?"

Melinda tipped her head and arched her brows. "That's what she said. And what do you say?"

"I took money from her. But even if she hadn't offered money, I would have done what she told me. I need my job, and if she says to steam open and read your letters, then that's what I had to do." Sally glared at the other servants. "Don't act like you'd do any different. If you was threatened with losing your job, you'd do the same thing—you just don't want to admit it to Melinda."

"I'd like to think I would do the right thing, Sally, but sometimes we don't know until we're confronted with a situation." The other servants resumed eating their meal. Given a choice of reporting on another servant or earning a living, they would choose to continue working, too. There was no denying that in this instance Mrs. Mifflin was far more to blame than Sally.

"Well, I'm hoping you'll forgive me. And I hope Evan and those other folks weren't injured in the storm." She shoved a forkful of potatoes into her mouth.

"You know about the hurricane?"

Sally swallowed the mouthful of potatoes. "I know the mister is going to send a telegraph in the morning." She grinned and waved her fork to include the other servants seated at the table.

Melinda forced a feeble smile. There were no secrets in this household—not even one.

CHAPTER 10

The next morning concentration proved near impossible for Melinda. As the lunch hour approached, she watched for any sign of Mr. Mifflin. Occasionally he returned home for the noonday meal. Melinda hoped today would be one of those occasions.

"Do sit down, Melinda. Your pacing makes me nervous." Mrs. Mifflin waved toward the brocade-covered chair. "Why don't you read to me?"

Melinda was well aware that Mrs. Mifflin's question was actually a command. Instead of sitting, Melinda walked toward the library. She glanced over her shoulder as she neared the door. "Did you have a particular book in mind?"

"You choose. I trust your judgment."

Melinda considered her volume of *Emma*. She'd had little time to read and would enjoy completing the book, but she couldn't very well begin reading in the middle of the story. Then again, perhaps she could, since Mrs. Mifflin usually fell asleep while she read to her. She grinned at the thought but pushed it aside as she studied the bookshelves. Certainly Mrs. Mifflin wouldn't enjoy listening to any of the history volumes that lined her husband's bookshelves. Melinda traced her finger along the spines, hoping to find something that might capture the woman's interest as well as her own. She rested her hand on a volume of poetry as the front door opened. Her heart jumped in her chest when she heard the sound of Mr. Mifflin's voice.

Though she wanted to run the short distance to the parlor, she willed herself to proceed down the hallway at a normal pace. Still clutching the book, she stopped at the parlor doorway. Mr. and Mrs. Mifflin sat on the divan, their heads close together and their voices low.

When neither acknowledged her presence, she extended the book of poetry. "I located a book I think you'll enjoy, Mrs. Mifflin." She hesitated for a moment. "I apologize. I didn't mean to interrupt your private conversation." They startled and turned toward her in unison. Neither said a word; they simply stared at her. She tapped the book with the index finger of her left hand. "You told me to retrieve a book from the library."

It seemed foolish telling Mrs. Mifflin what she already knew, yet it appeared she needed to be nudged from her silence. The woman stared a moment longer. "Oh yes. I did, didn't I? Well, there isn't time for reading at the moment. Cyrus has returned for the noonday meal."

"So I see."

Mr. Mifflin stood and tugged on the hem of the too-small vest that didn't quite cover his protruding belly. "Melinda!" He stood and said her name as though she had just appeared. "I told Dorothea that I wanted to speak to you, and here you are." He made it sound as though she'd dropped from the ceiling.

"You have word about the storm?" Her fingers tightened around the volume of poetry.

"I sent a telegraph early this morning, and already I've had one in return." He smiled. "The damage on the mainland was somewhat greater than on the islands, though none of the damage is of a magnitude to cause concern. Mr. Nordegren would be on his annual vacation at this time, so I sent an additional telegraph to Harland Fields, since he takes charge during Mr. Nordegren's absence. I told him that if there was anything they needed, he should contact me. He sent word they're accustomed to these storms, and they'll have the water damage cleaned up in no time." He swung his hands wide. "So you see, there's no reason for continued worry."

"I'm surprised you received word so soon, but you've set my mind at ease. I thank you for your kindness—both of you." Melinda pressed the book to her chest and backed up a few steps. "If you'll excuse me, I'll tend to some matters while the two of you enjoy your lunch."

Mr. Mifflin's normally pale complexion darkened to a ruddy shade. He fumbled in his vest pocket rather than look at Melinda. "Yes, yes. We'll do that. Come along, Dorothea."

Mrs. Mifflin grasped her husband's arm. She patted Melinda's arm as they passed by. "You see? I told you Cyrus would take care of this. No need for worry."

Melinda waited in the hall until the couple made their way toward the dining room. Once they were out of sight, she rushed to the kitchen, where the aroma of fish chowder filled the room. Still clutching the book to her chest, she leaned against one of the worktables and exhaled a huge sigh.

Napkin tucked in his collar, Matthew sat at the table awaiting the noonday meal. "Good news, Melinda?"

She grinned and nodded. "Very good news."

Sally lifted a tureen of the soup and headed toward the dining room. "Well, wait until we're all in here to tell it."

Once they'd gathered around the table, she repeated Mr. Mifflin's report. All of them celebrated with her, but it was Sally who grasped her arm before she left the room once they'd finished their meal. "I truly am sorry about what I've done, Melinda. I hope you'll forgive me. If a life on that island with Evan is what you want, then I hope your dream will come true."

Melinda swallowed the lump in her throat, touched by Sally's apology. The woman seldom apologized for anything, especially her bad behavior. "Thank you, Sally. And you are forgiven, but I do hope you won't read any more of my mail."

The maid winked. "Since the missus was so willing to let the cat out of the bag, I can tell her you've taken to hiding your mail from me."

"And you'll be able to honestly speak those words, because that's exactly what I'll do." Melinda winked in return.

❖

The following morning, Melinda tucked the letter she'd written the previous evening into her pocket. She would wait until Matthew prepared to take Mr. Mifflin to work and ask him to post it on his way home. She could trust Matthew—he didn't count steaming letters open as one of his skills.

At the sound of a tap on her door, she glanced toward the clock, fearing she'd misjudged the time. There was a half hour remaining until time for breakfast. She was unaccustomed to anyone knocking on her door, especially so early in the morning. Opening the door a crack, she peeked out. "Sally! What are you doing up here? You should be cooking breakfast."

"The other two maids are able to stir a pot of oatmeal and scramble eggs." Not waiting for an invitation, she pushed her way into the room. "I don't want to be seen by the missus. I got something to tell you." She closed the door behind her and motioned Melinda to the other side of the room.

Her heart hammered and her chest tightened as she followed Sally across the room. This wasn't going to be good news. She could see it in Sally's eyes. "What is it?"

"I heard the mister and missus talking last night. About the storm down in Georgia. The mister lied to you."

The room swirled and Melinda grabbed hold of Sally's arm. "No! He wouldn't." Even as she spoke, she knew Mr. Mifflin would—both of them would. She moved to the side of the bed and sat down. "Tell me exactly what they said."

Sally dropped down beside her and scooted close. "That storm was a hurricane. He said there was lots of damage in Biscayne, but he didn't know for sure about Bridal Veil because all the telegraph wires are down."

"What?" Melinda twisted around to look Sally in the eyes. "But he said . . ."

Sally bobbed her head. "We both know what he said to you. But the truth is that he couldn't send or receive any telegrams because the wires are all down." She glanced toward the door. "He told the missus to be sure and keep any newspapers out of the house because there's been a few articles in the newspaper, and there's sure to be more once the telegraphs are back to working." Sally grasped Melinda's hand and gave a gentle squeeze. "I'm truly sorry, Melinda, but I figure it's better to know the truth than to be thinking everything is fine and dandy when your Evan might be—"

"Did Mr. Mifflin say if there had been any deaths reported?" She squeezed the maid's hand until she grimaced. "I'm sorry. I didn't mean to hurt you, but please tell me the truth."

"He said one newspaper reported there had been some deaths in Biscayne, but they didn't have reports from all of the coastal islands." Sally got to her feet. "I'm sure he's all right, Melinda. You need to keep yourself busy while you wait for word. I'm sure Evan will mail you a letter as soon as he's able. He'll know you're worried about him."

Melinda knew the maid was correct. Evan would write—if he

was able. But what if he'd been injured and needed her? They had pledged their love to each other, and it was only right that she go to him. He'd do the same for her . . . . she was certain he would. She jumped up from the bed and paced back and forth. "I need to do more than sit here and keep busy, Sally."

The maid frowned. "Now look what I've done. You're going to fret and stew. I shouldn't have told you." She glanced toward the clock. "I got to get back downstairs, but promise me you won't tell the missus I was listening at their door."

Melinda looked up, her mind in a daze. "What?" She shook her head. "No, I won't tell them it was you, Sally. Thank you for telling me."

Sally tightened her lips into a tight seam. She turned around when she neared the door. "Don't do anything you'll later regret, Melinda. Think things through before you make any plans."

"Would you tell Mrs. Mifflin I sent word that I'm not feeling well and won't be down until later this morning?"

Sally nodded. "That will be the truth—you're white as a bed-sheet." She peeked out the door before she slipped into the hallway.

Once the door clicked behind her, Melinda tried to gather her thoughts. Though it was difficult to believe Mr. Mifflin would tell her outright lies, she believed Sally had spoken the truth. After all, Mrs. Mifflin had been clear that she thought letter writing and any possible relationship with Evan should cease.

Surely they realized she would eventually hear of the hurricane and know the truth. How did they plan to explain? More fabrications? She imagined Mr. Mifflin explaining away his deception by saying he'd been telegraphed incorrect information or some other such story. Perhaps they thought she would hear from Evan by the time she learned of the hurricane and her worries would have already vanished—and Mrs. Mifflin wouldn't need to fear losing her lady's maid.

Melinda longed to understand why anyone would do such a thing to another. Would Mrs. Mifflin withhold such information from a friend, or was this form of treatment reserved only for servants? Then again, perhaps they withheld the truth whenever it worked to their advantage. Dwelling on what they had done wouldn't help her. Right now she needed a plan.

She would not remain in a house where people lied in order to control her actions. The very thought sickened her.

"I don't know exactly what to do, Lord, but I know I need to learn the truth."

❦

Several hours had passed when Sally once again tapped on Melinda's door. "The missus wasn't happy. She had an appointment this morning, and Mary had to help her dress and fix her hair. Poor Mary. She couldn't do anything to suit the missus. The girl came back downstairs in tears. I'm supposed to tell you that you need to be up and about by late this afternoon. There's a party of some sort, and you'll be needed."

The woman's gaze settled on the clothing Melinda had removed from the wardrobe. "Would you ask Matthew to bring up my old trunk from the storage shed out back? I believe that's where he put it when I moved here."

Sally's mouth gaped open. "You're leavin'?"

"I must. But I need to accomplish a great deal before Mrs. Mifflin returns. I'm going downstairs to make a telephone call. I need to contact my brother."

"But you can't give up a good job without the prospects of something else. It's not sensible. Evan hasn't even asked you to marry him."

Melinda said nothing but fixed Sally with a stare. The woman finally seemed to realize that Melinda's mind was made up.

"Matthew's gone. He's taken the missus to her appointment, but I can ask Timothy, the young fella that helps with the gardening, if you'd like." Sally shook her head. "I don't think you should use that telephone. The missus says the operators repeat every word they hear. Word travels fast, so if you want to keep your conversation private, you best send a note." She pointed to the desk. "Write a note. Timothy can take it to your brother after he brings your trunk from the shed."

"I don't think I need to worry about the operators telling Mrs. Mifflin what I have to say, Sally. Once she returns home, I plan to tell her myself."

They walked down the front stairs, and while Melinda rang the operator, Sally went off in search of Timothy. After asking the operator to connect her with the Dangerfield residence, she listened to four short rings followed by one long. Finally a servant answered. Melinda did her best to speak with as much authority as possible. "This is Melinda, Mrs. Mifflin's lady's maid, calling from the Mifflin residence. I need to speak with Lawrence Colson. It's an emergency."

She was surprised when the servant didn't question her further. "I'll have to send someone to fetch him out in the barns. Shall I have him return the call, or do you wish to remain on the line?" Though it would make more sense to hang up, she didn't want to take a chance that Lawrence wouldn't call back. If he was gone for some reason, she'd prefer to have the Dangerfields' servant tell her. "I'll remain on the line, thank you."

While she waited, Sally returned to report Timothy had taken her trunk up the back stairway and placed it in her room. "I had him bring along the two suitcases you brought with you, as well."

"Thank you, Sally. I'm sure that I'll put them to good use." Melinda still held the receiver to her ear. "I'm waiting on my brother to come to the phone. He's out in the barns."

Sally gave a nod. "If you'd like, I can go up and begin to fold and pack some of your belongings."

The offer surprised Melinda. The woman wasn't usually generous with her time. "You don't need to do that, Sally. I'm sure you have other work that needs your attention."

"Nothing that won't wait. I'd like to help. It's the least I can do after telling all of your business to Mrs. Mifflin." She waited for a moment, but when Melinda didn't immediately respond, she touched her arm. "Please. I truly want to do something to help you."

Melinda wasn't sure what to do. She could certainly use the help, but she didn't want to get Sally in trouble should Mrs. Mifflin return home earlier than expected. "Go ahead and begin. I'll be up as soon as I speak with Lawrence." The smile that spread across Sally's face was as bright as sunshine on a summer day. "You'd think I'd given her a raise in pay," Melinda murmured.

"Hello. This is Lawrence Colson. Who's calling, please?"

"Lawrence. It's Melinda. Listen carefully." She related all that had occurred over the past few days before she inhaled a deep breath. "I'm leaving for Georgia later today, Lawrence. I have enough money saved to pay for my train ticket, and I have enough to purchase one for you, if you'll come with me." The silence was deafening. "Please say you'll come with me, Lawrence. I don't want to travel to Georgia on my own."

"Melinda, this is madness. Think about it for a moment. Unless your friend has proposed, you are imposing yourself . . . Well, I don't mean it exactly that way. But . . . well . . . has he asked you to marry him?"

Melinda ignored the question. She knew the foolishness of leaving a good job to go off in search of a man who might or might not love her enough to make her his wife, but she couldn't help herself. She loved Evan. She needed to know if he was safe. She needed to see that he was alive—even if he didn't want her.

"Please come with me, Lawrence. Please. I promise I'll never ask anything else of you."

For a moment he said nothing and Melinda feared he would refuse. "How much time do I have before we depart?"

Unable to withhold her excitement, she shrieked with joy. "You'll come with me? Do you mean it?"

He laughed. "You've ruined my hearing with that screaming, but yes, I'll meet you at the station. What time?"

"You have to be there by four o'clock. And Lawrence, don't be late."

"I'll meet you there—four o'clock."

Making this journey would be so much easier with Lawrence along. She whispered a prayer of thanks as she hiked her skirt and ran up the steps. "And please keep Evan safe. Please."

―――――――

Lawrence considered his sister's actions rash, but they played right into his own needs—the most urgent of which was to put some distance between himself and Cleveland. His sister's emotional decision to go in search of a man who hadn't even declared himself would normally have caused Lawrence some worry. She was, after all, the last of his family, and he did desire for her to remain safe.

When he'd seen her installed as a lady's maid to Mrs. Mifflin, Lawrence had felt it acceptable to make his own way in the world. It wasn't that he no longer cared about Melinda, but rather he felt inadequate to help her. In truth, he didn't feel capable of helping much of anyone.

He forgot about his duties and made his way quickly to the small room he'd been given off the stable. There was precious little to pack, but what few things he had, Lawrence intended to keep. Within a few minutes he was all but ready to go.

"Where have you been?" a gruff male voice called as Lawrence made his way to the far stall in the stable.

"I've been packing. I'm needed elsewhere."

The older man gave him a look that suggested Lawrence had lost his mind. "And what of your job here? You've not given notice."

Lawrence shrugged and gave a smile. "I suppose you can consider this my resignation. A family member is in need of my help, and I can't refuse."

Melinda completed her packing, and Timothy placed her trunk and cases in the front hallway, ready for her departure. She sat waiting in the parlor for Mrs. Mifflin's return. When she heard the horses clopping along the front driveway, she stepped to the foyer.

Mrs. Mifflin swept past her. "I'm pleased to see you're feeling better. I hope you've pressed my gown."

"No, I haven't pressed your gown, but I'm sure Mary will see to it."

The woman stopped and turned toward her. "And why would Mary see to it?" She noticed the trunk and cases. "And what are these? Do we have unexpected guests?"

"No, they are mine. I'm leaving, Mrs. Mifflin. I'm going to Bridal Veil to see if Evan has been injured in the hurricane."

The older woman's complexion turned ashen, and she motioned to the parlor. "I must sit down. Come in here." Melinda followed her into the room. Mrs. Mifflin opened her fan and flapped it with enough ferocity to cool both of them. "You're not thinking clearly, Melinda. My husband explained that there was no need for worry. There was only a storm, but you've let your emotions get the best of you, and you're acting in an irrational manner." She looked up at Melinda. "Do sit down so that we can talk."

"I don't have time for a lengthy discussion, Mrs. Mifflin. I plan to leave for the train station very soon." She had more than sufficient time before the train would arrive, but she knew that if she delayed her departure, the older woman would attempt to prevent her from leaving.

"You can't do this. You haven't given me proper notice. I have engagements and need your assistance. This is totally uncalled for and improper behavior for a lady's maid. Now sit down and be reasonable."

Melinda remained standing. "Mrs. Mifflin, I know there was a hurricane and that the destruction in Biscayne was significant. I also know that there has been no word from Bridal Veil and the damage to the island is unknown at this time. Although you knew of my concern for Evan, you and Mr. Mifflin gave me false information. I fail to understand how you could be so cruel. I love Evan, and I must go to him."

"Go to him?" Mrs. Mifflin croaked the words from between her dry lips. "And what will you do once you find him? Get married? He hasn't even proposed marriage. What if he was simply dallying with your affections? You'll be giving up your position here in Cleveland, and you'll have no way to support yourself."

"Evan hasn't been dallying with my affections. He is a sincere and wonderful man, and I know he will marry me." Anger welled in her chest. How dare this woman toss about such accusations? She only knew Evan as a servant to order about—not as a man of honor and love.

Mrs. Mifflin toyed with her fan for a moment. "Perhaps he will. But what if he died in the storm? Then what will you do?" Her eyes sparkled as though she almost wished him dead. "If you leave me, I won't give you a letter of reference, and if you come back to Cleveland, I'll see that you won't find employment. You need to consider your decision carefully, Melinda. Even if one of the wealthy Georgia matrons decided to hire a Northern girl, she'd require exemplary references."

Melinda's stomach roiled as the woman slung her angry threats. She hadn't considered the possibility that Evan might not want to marry her. And she hadn't let herself think that he might be dead. Injured perhaps, but not dead. The thought that she might encounter any of those circumstances caused a ripple of fear to march up and down her spine. " 'For God hath not given us the spirit of fear; but of power, and of love, and of a sound mind.' " She murmured the words from Second Timothy.

"What was that?" Mrs. Mifflin cupped her hand behind one ear. "Did you say you're of sound mind? If that be the case, then I know you've decided to remain in Cleveland."

Melinda shook her head. "I said that God has not given me a spirit of fear; but of power, and of love, and of a sound mind. It's a verse from the Bible. And it means that I am leaving on the next train. Should I need a reference in the future, I hope that you will reconsider your ill feelings and give an honest report. If not, I will put my trust in God."

Mrs. Mifflin pushed to her feet and stepped forward until the two of them were nose to nose. "I will do exactly as I've promised. You may depend upon it! And don't think that you may use my carriage to take you to the train station. The staff is here to serve me, not an ungrateful servant."

Melinda took a backward step. "I hadn't considered imposing upon you or your staff, Mrs. Mifflin. I've sent for a hansom cab." Mrs. Mifflin gave a disgruntled huff and made her way to the stairs.

"You'll regret not treating me fairly."

Melinda didn't remind the woman that it was her lies and those of Mr. Mifflin that were most unfair. The woman's threats

111

frightened Melinda but weren't enough to outweigh her fears for Evan and his well-being. Melinda opened her mouth to call after Mrs. Mifflin and remind her of the pay she owed for the previous week. It was money Melinda very much needed. She hesitated a moment longer watching the woman retreat.

She'll never pay me.

Mrs. Mifflin disappeared upstairs. There was no possibility the angry woman would hand over money now—especially since Melinda had failed to give any notice. It was no doubt the first of many sacrifices she would have to make in order to reach Evan. Drawing a deep breath, Melinda knew that the time had come to leave. Her hands trembled as she reached for her cases.

"I'll take those out to the front for you, Melinda." Matthew smiled at her. "She's gone upstairs and will never know. Besides, I don't care if she does. It's only right that I help you."

Sally, Mary, and several other servants tiptoed down the hall to bid her good-bye and wish her well while Matthew carried her baggage to the front sidewalk. Tears threatened, but she swallowed hard and forced them to remain at bay. Matthew waited by her side until the cab arrived and then helped her inside. "You take care, Melinda, and be sure to write. We'll all want to be hearing from you. I can't read, but you know Sally can read real good." His lips curved in a lopsided grin.

He lifted his hat and waved as the carriage pulled away. She swiped away a tear that rolled down her cheek. Though she felt no sorrow in leaving Mr. and Mrs. Mifflin, she would miss all of the servants—even Sally and her snooping ways. The impact of what she'd just done settled over her as she leaned back against the leather carriage seat. Had she made a terrible mistake? Would Evan be angry that she'd come? One question after another popped into her head, each one more frightening than the last. Her lightweight gloves were damp with perspiration, and her heart pounded in her ears like a gonging bell. "Please, Lord, take away my spirit of fear and replace it with your power."

She lurched forward as the carriage jolted to a stop in front of the train station. The cab driver jumped down, opened the door, and helped her down. "You want me to take that trunk and your bags inside the station?" Before she could answer, he continued. "Cost ya extra if I do."

She nodded and motioned for him to assist her. She directed him to place the baggage near the ticket counter, handed him several coins from her reticule, and stepped to the window.

The ticket agent offered a beleaguered smile. "Where to, ma'am?"

"Biscayne, Georgia. Two tickets."

He looked up and stared at her for a moment. "Can't get you into Biscayne. There's been a hurricane. No trains in or out. I can get you as far as Savannah, but there's no trains beyond that point."

Her heart plummeted. She didn't know how they'd get from Savannah to Biscayne, but perhaps Lawrence would have some ideas. They'd have enough time that perhaps he could come up with a plan.

"That's fine. I'll take two tickets to Savannah." Of course, she knew it had to be fine. She had no other choice. She paid for the tickets, located a porter to take care of her baggage, and began her search for Lawrence.

The clock struck the half hour and still there was no sign of Lawrence. She paced the station, looking in every direction, praying he would appear. As the clock ticked on, she walked to the front doors and out of the station. She'd turned to return inside when she saw a huge black horse racing toward the station at breakneck speed. The rider waved his hat overhead.

She stared at the sight, unable to believe her eyes. Was it?

Could it be? She narrowed her eyes as horse and rider drew closer. It was! Lawrence was riding the horse like a jockey intent on winning a race. Moments later he was in front of the station, pulling back on the reins until the horse came to an abrupt halt.

Her brother grinned down at her. "I bet you thought I wasn't going to make it, but here I am." He leaned forward and patted the horse's neck. "And this big fellow is coming along with us."

Words failed her.

CHAPTER 11

Three days had passed before Old Sam appeared at the hunting lodge. "Thought I better get across the river and see how you fared through the storm. I woulda come sooner, but things is a mess, and I've been waitin' to make sure the tides had settled for good." He scratched his head and glanced about. "I took a look in the boathouse 'fore I came inland. Some of the boats took quite a beatin', but I was glad to see the dock wasn't damaged too bad. At least boats can tie up and folks can get on and off board."

Harland nodded. "We've been down there to look things over, Sam. We'll get to the repairs as soon as we can, but right now, those boats aren't on the top of the list."

In spite of Alfred's and Evan's best efforts, some of the launches belonging to the investors had been severely battered, and all had taken on water when several beams and three-quarters of one wall of the boathouse had given way.

"Come on in and sit down. We got a pot of coffee, and I'd like to hear what you can tell us about Biscayne."

The fisherman followed Harland inside and settled in the sitting room. "The storm hit pretty bad, but it was worse further south. Least that's the news I'm hearin' from off the fishing boats coming in the past two days. There's no electricity and lots of damage along the wharves. The winds shifted away from Bridal Veil and slammed into us with more force." He shook his head. "Lots of folks suffered big losses, but only two dead at last report."

According to Sam, there were supplies available that hadn't been ruined in the storm, but after hearing the older man describe the loss and damage, Evan had his doubts. "We're going to need to hire workers. You think there will be any men wanting to work here on the island?" Evan arched his brows and waited. He worried most of the men would be hiring out in Biscayne.

"Don't think you'll have much problem. Be jest like all the other storms. Word spreads north, and men make their way down here 'cause they need money." He took a drink of his coffee. "I'm jest glad to see things is all right here—or as good as they can be after a hurricane. If you fellas is wantin' to come over to Biscayne, I can come back and get ya in a day or two. Bring a list of the supplies you need. Should be plenty of workers coming in by then."

Their list of needs would be long, and it certainly couldn't be filled in one order, but the man spoke with enough authority that Evan said he'd be thankful to have Sam return for them.

While they continued to visit, neither Evan nor Harland mentioned Alfred's death. The two of them had agreed they would deliver the news to his family themselves. But if Old Sam carried word there'd been no injuries or deaths on the island, Alfred's parents might receive that false report. If so, it would be a double cruelty for Evan and Harland to show up and deliver news of their son's death.

Evan finally decided he must say something before Sam departed. Relating the story took more out of him than he'd imagined. When he finished, his body ached as though he'd been beaten. "Please say nothing until we have a chance to speak with Alfred's parents ourselves."

"You got my word. I won't say a thing. It's best they hear it from you, but I'm guessing his father will miss the boy's pay more than he'll miss the boy." Sam had ferried Alfred back and forth from time to time. He knew Alfred had no desire to live at home—and he knew why, as well.

Before Sam departed, Evan handed him a letter to Melinda. If she knew of the storm, he didn't want her to worry. "Don't expect her to get it for a while," Sam cautioned. "The rails are out from below Savannah to Jacksonville, so there's no trains running and no mail coming in or going out." There was no way of knowing when the rails would be repaired or how soon the trains would be back on schedule, but Evan hoped word of the hurricane wouldn't cause Melinda to worry unnecessarily or to do anything rash.

The following day, Harland dropped to the couch and rested his head on the cushioned frame. "I've decided it's time for me to give up my job here at Bridal Veil. I'm just too old to carry this heavy load, Evan. There comes a time when a man knows it's time to look for work that suits his age, and my time has come. This place needs someone younger, not an old man like me."

"That's just weariness talking. All this damage from the hurricane has you worn down. I wish we could see more progress, too, but it's been only a few days. We'll get the job done. Besides, you're not old, Harland." Evan hoped to see some sign of agreement from his friend and mentor, but the older man's weary expression didn't change.

Delilah brushed past Evan, jumped onto the couch, and settled in Harland's lap. The older man combed his fingers through the cat's thick fur. "It's more than the storm. My bones ache most every day, and I feel a strain I never experienced in the past. The investors keep expanding this place, and my responsibilities grow right along with all those extras they keep adding. I don't feel up to the job anymore. Once Mr. Nordegren gets back, I'm going to tell him he should put you in charge. You're the one who should take over this job."

"Me?" Fear and panic knotted together and settled on Evan's chest like a rock. With the recent storm, the pressure to get everything back to normal had magnified beyond imagination. "Are you joking? With all this damage and work that needs to be completed before the season, this place can't get along without you. I could never oversee all this work, Harland. You're the one with the experience to get us through this mess."

"Additional people will be hired to help with the damage and preparations. Besides, there's no better way to learn than to jump in and do things, and this is the perfect time. I won't leave you until you feel equipped, but if I didn't think you were capable, I'd never suggest the idea to Mr. Nordegren or to Mr. Zimmerman." He lifted his head a few inches and looked Evan in the eye. "You're the right man for the job, Evan, so no use arguing with me." That said, he returned to his previous position and closed his eyes.

Evan waited, hoping Harland would sit up so they could discuss the matter a little more. When Harland didn't move, Evan yanked off his work boots and took them out to the porch. After they'd sat in the sun for a while, he would beat them against the railing to knock off the dried mud. Since the hurricane, it was the most cleaning his boots had received, and if it hadn't been for Garrison's wife, he'd be wearing filthy clothes. The routine had changed for all of them. Life had turned upside down, and now Harland was planning to further toss things about. His stomach churned as though he'd swallowed a glass of sour milk. Harland believed in him, but could he really step in and prove himself adequate to the job? Memories of his father's condemning insults plagued him.

"You'll never amount to anything, Evan. You're worthless."

Evan grimaced. It was as if his father were standing in the same room with him now. *"Your brother James has always been the only one I could rely on."*

"Leave the boy be," Evan's mother often declared in his defense. Unfortunately it usually resulted in horrible arguments between husband and wife. James thought it almost entertaining. There was something sadistic in the pleasure he took from watching their father bully their mother.

Evan pressed his hands to his head as if to force the images from his mind. His parents had been dreadfully unhappy together. His mother had died a broken and lonely woman. No doubt death had been a sweet release. But it hadn't been so for Evan. He'd been rejected and criticized throughout his childhood and cast off as a young adult.

But Harland believed in him in a way that his own father never had.

Squaring his shoulders, Evan vowed to be worthy of that trust. One way or another, he would prove to Harland and everyone else that he was of value. But the thought of Harland leaving was troubling. Evan went back into the lodge prepared to discuss the matter, but Harland appeared to be asleep.

Evan looked at the old man and shook his head. They'd made little progress on the cleanup, and now Harland was talking of pulling out before the real work had even begun. Only the necessities had received immediate attention. All of the men had helped round up the animals, check owners' cottages, and inspect the many outbuildings for damage. They'd been grateful when they discovered they'd lost only one cow and an old workhorse. Garrison held out hope that when they completed the survey of the island, they'd locate both. Harland wasn't so sure. And now he planned to leave them. Evan could scarcely imagine the island without the old man.

His footsteps muffled by thick work socks, Evan took the steps two at a time and grabbed his other pair of boots. Carrying the shoes in one hand, he plopped down in a straight-backed chair near Harland and tugged the back of a boot until his foot slid into position. The noise caused Harland to stir.

"You feeling up to going over to the cottages, or you need to rest?"

Harland yawned. "Give me an hour or so, and then I'll join you over there. Which cottage you going to first?" Harland had assigned the men living in the workers' quarters to begin repairs to the clubhouse. The cottages of the investors were important, but many more had permanent rooms in the clubhouse. At the moment, they needed to please the majority—and that meant seeing to the clubhouse.

Evan didn't hesitate. "I think I'll go to Bridal Fair first. After the clubhouse, it probably deserves our attention next, don't you think?"

Harland grinned and nodded. "I knew you were the right choice for this job, my boy. You're using your head to make good decisions." He tapped his index finger to the side of his forehead and then resumed stroking Delilah. "I'll meet you over there in an hour or so. You best stop and see if Emma will feed you before you set out."

"I'll see if she can pack me a sandwich to take along. It will save me some time." After a final glance over his shoulder, Evan leaned down and wrapped his hand around the wooden handle of the toolbox. He'd need more than a handheld toolbox to complete all the needed repairs, but with these he could at least begin.

His boots squished in the muddy path, yet birds chirped

overhead as though all was right with the world. They remained undisturbed by the storm that had wreaked havoc along the Eastern Coast only days before. A yellow warbler sat high on an exposed branch and sang a bright clear song as Evan passed by. That bird might be calm, but he wasn't. He didn't know whether he should be honored by Harland's decision to recommend him as a replacement or run for the hills. Being a gamekeeper was one thing, but managing and supervising grounds and improvements, overseeing the landscape work, and managing the wildlife was an immense responsibility—not to mention supervising all the men. Much more responsibility than he'd ever imagined. For a fleeting moment, his chest swelled with pride, but soon that feeling was replaced with fear and echoed insults from his father. Forcing them aside, Evan did his best to maintain a positive attitude, but the questions poured in faster than he could answer.

How could they accomplish all the necessary work before the first guests returned for the season in less than three months? Harland had spoken of new employees, and no doubt it would be the only way to accomplish the cleanup, but where would they come from? As grounds and game manager, he would be held accountable. And if he didn't succeed, he might be out of a job in short order.

What would Melinda think? He wondered if she'd be pleased and believe him equal to the job. What would she think if he was without work and forced to leave Bridal Veil because the investors chose someone else? He pictured her smiling and full of assurance—cheering him on with words of encouragement— telling him he could accomplish anything he set his mind to. If the investors selected him for the position, he hoped that would prove true. He shifted the toolbox to his other hand and grinned at the idea. Only a short time ago, he didn't think it possible to accept the position, but now he was envisioning himself in charge.

"Where is it yar headin', Evan?" Emma O'Sullivan's question yanked him back to the present. She was standing in mud to her ankles, pinning wet trousers onto a sagging clothesline.

"I'm going over to Bridal Fair to begin some repairs on Mr. Morley's place. Thought I'd stop by here first and see if I could ride one of the horses over." He pushed his hat back on his head and grinned. "I was hoping maybe I could talk you out of a sandwich to take with me, too."

She'd wedged a clothes basket between branches of a fallen tree to keep it off the muddy ground. "I'll need me a few more minutes to finish hanging these clothes, and then I'll fetch you somethin' to take with ya. Go on over to the barn and get ya one of the horses saddled up. Garrison's out mending fences."

The far end of the barn roof had collapsed, but the rest of the structure remained sound. And the O'Sullivan cottage hadn't suffered a great deal of damage. Garrison had set to work and immediately repaired some roof shingles, and Emma had mopped and swept out the murky water that had remained after the rains subsided. Fortunately, their cottage, like many of the others, sat high enough that it hadn't flooded, but rain had come through broken windows and a damaged roof. The remaining outbuildings had suffered their share of damage, but once the men set to work, it wouldn't take long to have them repaired. The problem would be how soon they could complete all the other repairs before getting to the barn and outbuildings.

By the time Evan finished saddling the horse and led her out of the barn, Emma had returned indoors. He walked the horse to the house, tied her to a thick branch of the uprooted tree, and proceeded up the front steps.

"Bring yarself on in here," Emma called. "I'm just about done."

Evan stepped to the door and hesitated until he saw that Emma was still wearing her muddy boots. A tarp had been laid like a rug from the door to the kitchen. Obviously this made it easier for Emma to work and not have to discard her boots or worry about the floor. Evan crossed the threshold and watched as Emma placed two thick sandwiches in a pail.

"Haven't had time to do me any baking since all this mess with the storm, but I put ya a couple of apples in there and a jug of milk." She swiped her hands down her apron. "Garrison thought the milk cows would be slow giving milk, but they been doing jest fine. Those old cows are like me—takes more than a storm to get 'em out of sorts." She tipped her head back and laughed.

Evan had to admire the woman. Most would be ready to pack their bags and leave, but not Emma O'Sullivan. There wasn't much she didn't seem to take in her stride—except maybe her husband's occasional bad humor. "Thank you, Emma. Harland and I sure do appreciate the fact that you've taken to feeding us since all of this happened."

"There's enough men's work that needs to be done without the two of you having to cook your own meals. I'm happy to do it." She lifted the pail and handed it to him. "Speakin' of Harland, where's he at this fine day? Working so hard he can't stop for a bite to eat?"

Evan didn't want to say he was resting. Emma would tease and tell him he was getting old, and Harland didn't need to hear that kind of talk right now. "He's over at the hunting lodge, but he plans to join me later."

"Well, I'll be here, and that's a fact." She followed Evan outside and watched as he mounted his horse.

As if to prove mightier than the storm, the sun's rays beat down with an unrelenting intensity. The sweltering heat mingled with the damp vegetation and produced a stench of musty decay that filled his nostrils and permeated his clothes.

When he got to Bridal Fair, Evan moved tree branches that had been ripped from the live oaks. They would provide good fuel once they'd dried. He chopped at the pieces only when necessary to cut them down to a size he could handle; otherwise it was the kind of work that could wait.

Debris had blown across the porch, gouging holes here and there, but nothing that couldn't be repaired. Evan inspected the windows and found all but one had survived without damage. He measured the dimensions and wrote down what was needed to replace the glass. Next he would inspect the attic to see if the storm had put any holes in the roof.

Evan thought the odor would disappear once he began his work inside Bridal Fair, but it had remained. A nagging reminder of the storm and its devastation. Upstairs the roof appeared solid, much to his relief. There was already plenty of work to be done, and he was glad to see that little of it would be required for Bridal Fair.

For the rest of the day, Evan worked at Bridal Fair seeing to the minor issues. No doubt Mr. Morley would be pleased to see the old house had survived. Evan was confident that once transportation was available, Mr. Morley himself would come to check on the situation. He had always been a man of detail and would not leave the island's condition to a mere letter. Most of the other investors' cottages had suffered the loss of gutters, shingles, and windows, as well as some rain damage. In a few places the problems were much greater—especially at the clubhouse. Morley would see to it that order was restored at any cost.

Evan made a mental checklist of all that needed to be replaced or repaired on the island. In addition to the clubhouse and the cottages, the wharf would need a great deal of repair; the windmill would need to be resurrected; new bathhouses as well as fishermen's houses would need to be constructed to replace the ones that had washed away. The orchards planted by the landscaping crew were now gone, and the exterior grounds at all of the cottages were in dire need of cleanup and replanting. All day he expected Harland to appear, but when the older man hadn't shown up by late afternoon, Evan gave up on the idea of receiving any help and departed for the O'Sullivans'.

The oppressive humidity seeped through his clothing, and his shirt stuck to his body like a second skin. He'd be glad for a bath and a change of clothes. He spotted Harland and Garrison coming from the barn as he approached. His mount, sensing she'd arrived home and eager for something to eat, headed straight for the barn without prompting. As the horse drew closer to the men, Evan called out to Harland, "Thought you were going to come over to Bridal Fair and lend a hand."

Harland chuckled and shook his head.

"Sure and he planned to, but I needed him more than you, boyo. I found that lost cow, but she was bogged in mud. Needed help gettin' her out." Garrison pointed his thumb toward the barn. "She's safe and sound inside. Once ya take care of Molly, come on in and sit down for yer supper."

Seeing to the needs of the horse came first, but Evan's stomach protested while he cared for the animal. Once he'd finished, he gave the horse a pat on the rump and headed for the cottage. He tried his best to avoid stepping in deep mud as he picked his way toward the house, but it proved impossible. When he reached the porch, he noticed the tarp that had previously protected Emma's floor was now hanging over the rail. Evan dropped to the front step, removed his boots, and placed them alongside the other pairs of shoes outside the door. He entered the house and, after one look at everyone's sock-clad feet, laughed out loud. To his way of thinking, this was one sight to behold. He glanced heavenward. "Thank you, Lord. I needed a good laugh."

❖

Old Sam arrived on schedule a couple of days later. With a detailed list in his pocket, Evan boarded the fishing boat with Harland close on his heels. The previous night Harland had added several items to Evan's list after they'd returned home from the O'Sullivans', but he'd praised Evan's efforts.

As they grew closer to Biscayne, Evan's chest tightened. The strong winds had pushed several large vessels ashore in the Biscayne harbor as well as a pilot boat that had come to rest in a perpendicular fashion that defied gravity. Sam pointed to the docks, which had all suffered lifting to some degree. "The water pounded them from underneath while the wind beat them about from overhead. Only a few that won't need repairs."

A fog of pungent air hung over the harbor like an inhospitable guardian of the ruins. In spite of the heat, Evan shivered at the sight. *So much, so much.* The words repeated over and over in his head. He hadn't expected to see such extensive destruction. Even if he had, there was no way his mind could have pictured the sight.

They pulled alongside one of the wharfs that had received minimal damage. Sam pointed toward the town. "Be careful as ya go—it's treacherous walking through these streets with all the flooding. Never know what's underneath that water. Especially down here near the docks, where there's cargo that's been tossed about."

Evan stepped onto the dock and stood mesmerized for several moments. He needed to take stock of his surroundings before he could move any further. His mind couldn't grasp the horrific spectacle. The shocking details overpowered his brain.

Harland grasped his arm. "Come on, Evan. I know it's a terrible sight, but we won't accomplish anything standing here."

"When you want to return, Harland?" Old Sam was hunched over, tying off his fishing boat.

"We'll be back by late afternoon—five o'clock. That suit you?" The fisherman waved and nodded. "I'll be here."

With bandannas covering their noses and mouths to avoid the stench, men were working feverishly along the wharves. A short distance from where they stood were hundreds of thousands of feet of lumber that had been awaiting shipment. Now, it would likely be washed away. As Harland guided him down the street, Evan stared at the once-brick-fronted buildings that now gaped open like yawning caverns. The bricks that had once provided shelter, the furnishings and merchandise that had provided livelihood—all had been swept away. And along with it, the waters had washed away the work and dreams of so many men.

The two men sloshed through the water until they ascended a hill that led them into another part of the town. "I'm glad Sam loaned us these wading boots, or we'd be looking to purchase shoes before we left." Harland glanced at Evan. "Down there on the right is where Alfred's family lives. I thought we should stop there first."

Evan tightened his hands into two fists and felt his stomach clench. How do you tell parents their son has died? Especially someone as young as Alfred. "This is going to be hard." He wanted to turn and run. Instead, he stopped in the middle of the street. "I don't know if I can do this, Harland."

The older man pulled him to the side of a ramshackle building. "Let's pray before we go meet with them." Harland didn't give him a chance to reply. He bowed his head and asked the Lord to give them the proper words of comfort for Alfred's family and to ease the pain of their loss. He prayed for some other things, but Evan didn't hear the words—he was worrying about the reaction they would receive. Harland raised his head and tugged on Evan's arm. "Putting it off will only make it harder."

Harland raised his hand to knock, but before he struck the wood with his knuckles, the door opened and a bulbous-nosed, broad-shouldered man filled the doorway. He leaned forward, his eyes menacing. "Who are ya, and whadd'ya want?" His foul breath hung in the air, and Evan took a backward step.

"I'm Evan Tarlow and this is Harland Fields." He hesitated a moment. "From over at Bridal Veil. We've come about Alfred."

"What's he done now?" The man's complexion flared to a reddish-purple hue. "He better not of gotten himself fired, or I'll whip the tar outta him. We need that money to pay the rent." His dark stringy hair fell across his forehead. "Where is he anyway?" He looked out at the street.

When it was evident the man wasn't going to invite them inside or inquire about his son's welfare, Harland took the lead. "Is your wife at home, Mr. Toomie?"

"She's busy feedin' the young'uns—what little we got to give 'em. You tell Alfred he better get over here with his pay and not to be holdin' none of it back neither."

Evan could stand no more of the man's comments. "Mr. Toomie, Alfred won't be bringing any more money to you. We've come to tell you that he died in the hurricane. We're very sorry to bring you this news, but we wanted to personally deliver it to you in case you had any questions."

At first the man stared at Evan as though he'd spoken in a foreign language, but as the realization sunk in, he raked his fingers through the strands of greasy hair. "What are we supposed to do for help with our rent? I need Alfred's wages to pay the bills."

Anger welled in Evan's chest. He wasn't a violent man, but he wanted to punch Mr. Toomie in the nose. How could he be so callous about his son's death? He hadn't even asked for any particulars—he didn't care about anything except Alfred's wages. No wonder the boy had chosen to live on Bridal Veil rather than return home at night.

Harland reached into his pocket. "I brought the wages still due Alfred." Mr. Toomie ripped the money from Harland's hand and shoved it into his pocket. "If you're concerned about the rent and money for food, Mr. Toomie, we're in need of workers to help with the cleanup over on Bridal Veil. I'd be willing to give you a try and see if you're up to the work."

The man sputtered and glared at Harland as though he'd spoken an obscenity. "You think I should come over there and clean up muck and mire from the storm?" He snorted. "That ain't nothing a man like me is willing to do, but I got me another boy. He's younger than Alfred, but I'd be willing to hire him out to ya." He glanced over his shoulder. "Bobby!"

"No, Mr. Toomie, don't bother to call the boy. We need men to help with this work. It would be far too dangerous for a young lad, but if you change your mind, we'll be in town until five o'clock hiring workers."

A scrawny young boy no more than eight years old poked his head around the doorframe. "Who're they, Pa?"

"Get back inside, Bobby." Mr. Toomie gestured toward the lad. "He'd be some help to ya—could wiggle into places where men won't fit, if need be."

Harland shook his head. "I wouldn't want to take the risk. Please tell your wife that we're sorry for her loss." He hesitated. "And yours, as well."

"Alfred was a kind young man." Evan choked out the words.

"Bah! He was a worthless boy. Never could seem to figure out his head from his toes, and now he's done. Well, I say it was bound to happen what with such a waste of a human bein'."

Tears welled in Evan's eyes at the insults. The man might as well have been his own father hurling abusive comments about Evan's failings. He quickly turned away as Harland made some comment. It was only moments, however, before Harland joined him on the street.

Evan swiped his eyes with his shirtsleeve. "He's a poor excuse of a man."

"That he is. But we need to pray for Mr. Toomie. I told him we would, and I figure that's the only hope that man has to straighten out his life. So we'll pray for him. Right?"

"Yes, and for his boy, Bobby, as well."

CHAPTER 12

Lawrence looked at the cards in his hand—two queens, an ace, a three, and a five. The hand was lousy, but his face didn't so much as twitch. He'd learned quite well how to mask his emotions. Losing his parents had been his first lesson, and the lessons just kept coming after that. Now, after all this time, rather than feeling the pain, he had gained.

"So what's it going to be?" the man opposite asked.

"I think I'm happy with this hand, and I call."

A groan could be heard from the others around the table. Everyone but the dealer folded and reached for their drinks. Lawrence looked at the man and shrugged. "Guess that just leaves you and me."

The man looked at the money on the table and then at his hand. Finally, he threw his cards down. "I'm out."

Lawrence smiled and put his cards on the table before reaching for the pot. The men moaned at the sight of the single pair. To keep from making enemies of his financial contributors, Lawrence threw several bills back on the table. "Drinks are on me. I'm afraid I need to go attend to family business."

He made his way from the game and headed to the livery where he'd stabled his horse. He owed the owner for another week of care and didn't want to do anything to make the man suspicious.

Making his way through the dimly lit stable, Lawrence found the black and smiled. He pulled a lump of sugar from his pocket and gave it to the horse. "We did good today. A few more games like that, and we'll have more than enough money to make our way to California."

"So you're California bound, eh?" the liveryman asked, joining Lawrence.

"It's been a thought," Lawrence replied. More of a dream he'd never been able to quite commit to. Commitment wasn't his best asset. Lawrence reached into his pocket and drew out his money. Peeling off several bills, he handed them to the man.

"Give him the best."

The man took the money and nodded. "You gonna ride him today?"

Lawrence shook his head. He knew the energetic horse needed a good long run, but he didn't have the time. "Maybe have someone take him for a run later this evening." He threw the man a coin. "Give him this."

"Yes, sir." The man tucked the money into his pocket. "I could have one of the boys take him out now."

"No. I'd rather not have him out in the heat of the day." *Or the light of the day*, he thought.

❖

Melinda stood at the window of her hotel room and stared down at the street below. If Lawrence returned at this very moment, she would throttle him! While her every waking hour was consumed with worries over Evan and Bridal Veil, Lawrence was busy filling his days and nights at any gaming establishment that would permit him entry. When she'd confronted him about gambling while on the train, he'd denied her accusation—at least in the beginning. After she'd actually seen him when she passed through the club car on her way to dinner, he'd given up all pretenses. After all, he'd been holding a fistful of cards and she'd seen the money in the center of the table. To deny he'd been participating would have been absurd. That's what he'd said when she'd confronted him, and she had agreed. Later, he'd acknowledged that the horse for which she'd paid passage had also been won in a game of cards in Cleveland. Though she'd given him a tongue-lashing, he had simply chuckled and promised to repay her once they arrived at their destination.

The journey to Savannah had taken far longer than either of them had anticipated. Though they'd made good time in the beginning, storm damage along the East Coast had caused them to take alternate routes as they progressed farther south. They'd finally arrived, but rail travel out of Savannah remained unavailable except to those heading north or west. The news had created anxiety for her, but Lawrence hadn't minded. He'd been using the time to fatten his wallet. When she complained, he pointed out it was his winnings that were paying for their hotel rooms and had permitted him to repay her for his train ticket and passage for his horse. That fact aside, she didn't approve of his habit.

Today Melinda had decided a breath of fresh air was in order. She stood in front of the mirror, pinned her hat in place, and picked up one of Mrs. Mifflin's hand-me-down parasols. Lawrence might not approve, but she couldn't remain cooped up in a hotel room waiting for him to locate transportation out of Savannah. Besides, she thought he'd become more devoted to spending time at the gaming tables than to seeking adequate travel arrangements. Walking about the city alone might prove daunting to some women, but she'd never been a wilting violet when it came to a challenge. And with no one to question the suitability of her unaccompanied excursion, she exited the hotel room and descended the carpeted staircase to the main floor of the hotel.

Without any idea how to locate travel information, she decided a visit to a local milliner might be a good place to start. A small shop where she could visit with someone who knew the city should provide the necessary particulars. She straightened her shoulders and, with purpose in her stride, headed toward the front doors of the hotel.

She came to an abrupt halt when a bellboy stepped in front of her. "Are you departing the hotel, miss?"

She tipped her head to one side and smiled. "That is my intention—once you step out of my path."

"Alone? Mr. Colson won't be accompanying you?"

She thought his behavior somewhat obtuse since Lawrence was nowhere to be seen. "Yes. Very much alone."

He nodded toward a door at the other side of the foyer. "The ladies' door is over there. Unaccompanied ladies use the door leading to Abercorn Street rather than this one."

"I didn't realize." Melinda glanced at the door. "But then, I've never departed a hotel unaccompanied." Memories of the many hotels she'd visited with her parents during her younger years flooded her mind as the bellboy walked alongside her. She felt quite alone, but with each passing day she'd gained greater inner strength. "You wouldn't happen to know where I might find available transportation to Biscayne, would you?"

He leaned closer and a hank of thick dark brown hair fell across his forehead. "You know there was a hurricane down in Biscayne, don't you?"

"I'm fully aware of the hurricane. That is what has detained us here in Savannah. And though I find your city lovely and the hospitality of the hotel staff wonderful, I have . . . friends in the Biscayne area, and I'm concerned about their welfare."

He pushed the hair off his forehead. "In that case, I'd say your best chance would be one of the barges heading down that way, but I don't think the accommodations would be suitable." The young man frowned at the idea. "Besides, ladies shouldn't go down to the dock by themselves. You might have your brother see if there are any other vessels sailing in that direction."

"I'll do that. Thank you for your kindness."

He hesitated before opening the door for her. "You're not going down to the docks, are you, Miss Colson?"

She didn't want to lie to the boy. He'd been so kind and she could see the concern in his eyes. He was likely worried he'd get in trouble if anything happened to her. She flashed a bright smile. "Are you able to tell me where I might find a milliner's shop?"

A sigh of relief escaped his lips, and his look of concern vanished. "Oh yes. Not far from here you'll find the finest milliner in all of Savannah." He provided exacting details before he opened the door. "You have a wonderful afternoon, Miss Colson. And I hope you find a hat to your liking."

She waved and headed off in the direction of the milliner's shop. The weather was beautiful and she'd seen little of Savannah. The Mifflins had stopped on a few occasions during their travels to Bridal Veil Island, but Melinda's time had been spent in a hotel room looking after Mrs. Mifflin's needs. She knew it wouldn't be cold when she stepped outdoors, yet the balmy temperature still surprised her. The profusion of greenery that remained on the trees provided shade as well as a feeling of spring rather than fall.

Melinda stopped in front of a dress shop and let her gaze wander over several gowns that decorated the window before proceeding on to the milliner's shop. A gold and black sign hung from ornate framework that extended over the sidewalk and could be viewed at a distance. The proprietor of Leota's Millinery wasn't taking a chance that shoppers would overlook her store. The window, tastefully decorated, contained a variety of beautiful hats. Not that Melinda could afford one of them, but she might secure a bit more information before going to the docks. Besides, she could honestly report to the bellboy that she'd visited the store.

She didn't notice the man who had approached until he tapped his finger on the display window. "That one would look quite attractive on you."

"Excuse me, but I was preparing to go inside." As she turned, she gained a better view of the man and was startled by his striking good looks. Tall and broad-shouldered, his dark hair had been combed to perfection and his brown eyes danced with amusement. A quick appraisal of his clothing revealed he was a man of affluence. Or, like her, he'd received his expensive clothing from a former employer.

"Then let me open the door for you. I'm going inside myself." He stepped around her, grasped the door handle, and gave her a charming smile.

Without thinking, she returned the smile. "Looking to replace your derby?" She didn't know what had come over her, bantering with a complete stranger. His carefree and genial manner had caused her to act before thinking.

He chuckled and pointed to a hat as they entered the store. "Do you think this one might look good on me?"

Two bright blue feathers of at least twelve inches in height waved from atop the crown and were offset on either side by ruffled gauze that had been fastened on the brim with beaded rings. A satin bow of huge proportions adorned the back brim. Melinda tipped her head to the side and surveyed the chapeau. "I don't know if the color is quite right for the suit you're wearing."

His laughter filled the front end of the shop. "You have a very quick wit, Miss . . ."

Melinda hesitated, suddenly aware that she'd likely given a very poor impression. This man had likely mistaken her for a flirt who gave out her name to men on a regular basis.

Before Melinda had decided upon a proper response, a well-dressed lady stepped around one of the narrow counters and directed a broad smile at the gentleman. "Mr. Powers! Welcome. Is your aunt with you?" The woman glanced toward the door.

He chuckled and shook his head. "I'm afraid she's a bit under the weather and asked if I would pick up the hat she ordered from you. She believes she must have it before she attends some function or other early next week. Since I was coming to the area, I offered to stop." He lowered his head as if confiding a deep secret. "She says I am to be sure that you've added all of the feathers that she requested."

A slight look of irritation crossed the woman's face before she offered him another bright smile. "I have never adorned a hat for your aunt that wasn't exactly to her specifications."

The man she'd referred to as Mr. Powers nodded. "I'm sure your work has been pure perfection, Mrs. Frederick. Unfortunately, my aunt is one of those affluent people who believes her wealth causes others to sometimes take advantage." He tightened his lips as though embarrassed he'd been required to mention his aunt's eccentricity. He reached into his pocket and withdrew a piece of paper.

Mrs. Frederick clapped a hand to the embroidered velvet bands that adorned the yoke of her gown. "She sent a list with you?" She directed a fleeting look at Melinda.

He hiked one shoulder and grinned. "You see? My aunt doesn't trust me, either."

Mr. Powers' attempt to make light of the matter hadn't set

Mrs. Frederick at ease. Indeed, her level of discomfort seemed to increase, and Melinda's presence appeared to be adding to the cause. She should leave the shop. After all, she had no intention of purchasing a hat, and she didn't want the shop owner to think further conversation with Mr. Powers would influence her.

"I believe I'll leave you two to your business. I'm merely passing through Savannah and stopped for help with directions. You're busy at the moment." Melinda took a backward step toward the door, but the woman reached for her arm.

"There's no need to hurry off. We have several hats that would look stunning on you." She pointed at a lovely hat in the far corner of the shop. "That hat would be lovely with the dress you're wearing—not that your current hat isn't quite fashionable."

No doubt the humble shop owner constantly worried about offending her customers. Melinda smiled. "It is a bit old, but I spruced it up with new ribbon." She hoped her comment would let the woman know she wasn't someone who could afford to purchase anything from her fashionable shop.

"I'm very familiar with Savannah, and I'd be pleased to direct you to your destination, Miss . . . ?" There it was—another attempt to gain her identity. He grinned. "Mrs. Frederick will vouch for the fact that even though we haven't been properly introduced, it is safe to speak to me."

Eager to please, the woman bobbed her head. "Mr. Powers is quite reputable—a true gentleman. He is the nephew of Levi and Margaret Powers, who are very well known here in Savannah. The family goes back many, many years."

Melinda understood what the shop owner was telling her: The Powers name could be associated with influence and old money—at least in Savannah. She nodded at Mr. Powers. "Miss Melinda Colson of Cleveland, Ohio."

"I'm pleased to make your acquaintance, Miss Colson. I am

Preston Powers, recently returned to Savannah from Baltimore."
Once Mrs. Frederick excused herself to fetch the hat for his aunt,
Mr. Powers positioned himself between Melinda and the door.
"As I said, I would be pleased to assist you with your directions."

"That's most kind of you, Mr. Powers, but I must be on my
way. I'm sure my brother will worry if I don't soon return to
the hotel." That was a bit of an exaggeration, for she doubted
Lawrence would return to the hotel until time for a late supper,
but she didn't want this man to think she'd come to the city
unaccompanied.

Mrs. Frederick bustled forward carrying a large hatbox and bal-
anced it atop the counter. "Let's go over your list, Mr. Powers."

Before she could remove the lid, he grasped the cord and lifted
the box from the counter. "I don't truly believe there's any need
for such an examination, Mrs. Frederick. We both know the hat
is perfection. Besides, I'm sure I can rely upon you to keep our
little secret."

She preened, obviously pleased with his decision. "Your aunt
will never know that we didn't go over the list." She clasped her
fingers together in a knot, lifted them to her lips, and turned her
hand. "My lips are sealed."

He leaned forward and gave a slight bow. "As are mine, dear
lady." He turned to Melinda. "And now, Miss Colson, my time
and directions are at your disposal. Where are we off to?" He
opened the front door. "Perhaps one of our lovely parks?"

"Actually, I'm interested in going to the docks."

"The docks? Whatever for?" He stopped short. "The docks
aren't safe for a woman alone. Were you truly planning to go
there unaccompanied?"

"I'm braver than most women, Mr. Powers, and I'm in need
of information. I need to arrange passage to Bridal Veil Island.
I'm told the trains won't be running to Biscayne for at least

another week, and I'm simply unwilling to remain in Savannah any longer."

"You understand there's been severe damage in Biscayne and Bridal Veil, as well." He took her arm and guided her across the street.

"I know about the hurricane, though I haven't been able to gain an accurate report of the damage on Bridal Veil. The telegraph wires are restored to Biscayne, but not on any of the islands." She glanced about. "Are we headed toward the docks?"

"Yes, though I'm not certain you'll meet with success finding passage. It's mostly freighters carrying supplies going south—no passenger vessels. I can tell you that Bridal Veil wasn't hit as hard as Jekyl Island to the south. That resort suffered a good bit of damage." He grew thoughtful. "But there was one report that a fellow died on Bridal Veil. A name wasn't given, only that he was a permanent worker there—one of the younger men."

Her stomach knotted and bile rose in the back of her throat. "How do you know this, Mr. Powers?" She clenched her hands into fists to stop the shaking.

"There was a report from a freighter, and then I saw it in the newspaper. Of course, you can't trust what they say in the newspapers. Those fellows are always eager for a big headline. However, I think this report was true. We have relatives in Chicago who own a cottage on Bridal Veil, and they wrote to my aunt and uncle here in Savannah. Seems they heard about this fellow's death from Victor Morley. Not sure who he is, but my aunt and uncle said the information would be accurate if it came from him."

The more Mr. Powers talked, the more Melinda's fears escalated. What if Evan had been the one who died? Her collar suddenly felt far too tight. She tucked her fingers inside the neckline and gave a tug. The unyielding collar and pungent odors of fish and dirty bodies emanating from the wharf assailed her. She opened her fan and hoped the movement of air would do some good. Her knees wobbled as she considered the possibility of a future without Evan. If her future didn't include a home with Evan on Bridal Veil, where would she go? There would be no work for her in Cleveland—Mrs. Mifflin would see to that. Without any letter of reference, it would be impossible to secure a position as a lady's maid. And she certainly couldn't depend upon Lawrence. She loved her brother, but he was as unpredictable as the weather.

Mr. Powers stopped and looked at her. "You're quite pale, Miss Colson. Is it something I've said? Why don't you sit down?" He withdrew his handkerchief and brushed off a rickety bench.

"Thank you for your concern, but I'll be fine." As if to prove her point, she inhaled a deep breath and squared her shoulders. There wasn't time to sit. She needed to secure passage to Bridal Veil as soon as possible.

"If you're sure." He gestured to a storefront along the wharf. "This is a freighting business office. We may have some luck here." He hesitated outside the door. "Tell me, Miss Colson, why are you so intent upon going to an island that has so recently been devastated by a hurricane?"

"I have a dear friend who remains on the island year-round. I've heard nothing and am very concerned."

She didn't explain that she hoped to make her home on Bridal Veil or that his news of a death on Bridal Veil could alter her life. Mr. Powers had been kind to escort her, but she wouldn't share her personal business with him.

❖❖

She'd done her best to send Mr. Powers on his way once they were away from the dock. She'd even told him his aunt was likely waiting to examine her new hat, but nothing she tried met with success. Instead of making small talk with a stranger, she wanted to be alone with her thoughts. She wanted to believe Evan was alive, but she now realized her impulsive behavior might prove disastrous.

"Here we are," she said when they arrived at the entrance to the hotel. "Thank you again for your assistance."

"Oh, I should escort you inside. Otherwise, you'll be expected to use the other entrance, Miss Colson." He didn't wait for a reply before tipping his hat to the bellboy and leading her forward.

They'd barely cleared the door when she spotted Lawrence descending the staircase. He rushed toward her, but his gaze was fastened upon the man at her side. "I have been worried, sister. I inquired at the front desk. One of the bellboys said you'd gone shopping for a hat, but I doubted his report."

He stopped only long enough to inhale a quick breath. His attention settled on the hatbox in Mr. Powers' hand. "Where have you been, and who is this?" His brows arched as he turned toward Melinda.

"This is Mr. Preston Powers. He was kind enough to escort me to the docks so that I could inquire about arrangements for our passage to Bridal Veil." She narrowed her eyes. "At the docks I learned that passage has been available for five days. Five days, Lawrence."

"Truly? Well, I haven't gotten back down there. I've been keeping myself otherwise occupied." He extended his hand to Mr. Powers. "It's a pleasure to meet you, sir, and I thank you for looking after my sister." His lips curved in a roguish grin. "I'm sure you understand that I've discovered a great many ways to occupy my time in your fair city."

Mr. Powers gripped Lawrence's hand. "I'm pleased to hear you are fond of our city. Perhaps you'll permit me to show you and your sister some of the places I most enjoy."

"My sister and I don't enjoy many of the same pastimes, Mr. Powers. While I enjoy a good game of cards, the horse races, and a glass of bourbon, she prefers more genteel outings." Lawrence chuckled. "What about you, Mr. Powers? Do you enjoy a good game of cards?"

He nodded. "On occasion, Mr. Colson."

Melinda glared at her brother. "It matters little what either of you enjoy, Lawrence. We are departing in the morning at eight o'clock. I've booked passage on a freighter to Biscayne. The accommodations aren't the best, but the distance isn't great, so we shouldn't be on board for long. And if you want to bring that horse along, you'll need to pay for his passage."

She turned to Mr. Powers. "Thank you again for your kindness. I do hope that your aunt will be pleased with her hat." That said, she turned and hurried toward the carpeted staircase.

When she reached the upper floor, she stopped and looked over the rail and into the lobby. Her brother and Mr. Powers were departing the hotel together—likely in search of a card game.

CHAPTER 13

Melinda stepped off the freighter in Biscayne. A foul odor assaulted her senses, and for a moment she remained speechless, unable to grasp the extent of the damage that surrounded them. Debris lined the coastal shores and the town resembled the aftermath of a great battle. She marveled that there weren't more deaths from the storm, given the extensive damage.

"How could anyone survive such destruction?" she asked to no one in particular.

"If you look close, you can see the waterline on the buildings." Her brother pointed to the faint mark that stood nearly as high as Melinda's height. "I hope I'll be able to find a suitable place for my horse."

Melinda looked at him in disgust. "Your horse is the least of things to worry about, Lawrence."

"Careful as ya go there, miss," one of the sailors called. "Some of them planks is loose. Don't want ya fallin' in the water." The sailor was leading the horse off the freighter and handed the reins to Lawrence once they were on the pier. "Ya might want to walk on up ahead of the horse."

Instead of worrying over Melinda's safety, Lawrence glanced

at the tilted boards, then back toward the sailor. "Are you telling me this dock could give way under the weight of my horse?"

The sailor lifted a corner of the dirty kerchief tied around his neck and wiped his upper lip. "Can't say for sure. Ain't much of nothin' safe after a hurricane, 'specially the pilings that hold up these docks." He grinned, his stubby yellow teeth protruding like ripe kernels on an ear of corn.

Melinda didn't wait for further explanation before making her way to the end of the pier. She wasn't certain the area along the wharf was much better. The captain of the freighter had told them a great deal of progress had been made toward cleanup in Biscayne, but she now questioned his appraisal. A confusion of boxes, barrels, cotton bales, mattresses, broken furniture, doors, timbers, dry goods, and every other conceivable item lay strewn about in utter chaos. The rising temperature and humidity served to create a gut-wrenching stench that caused her to reach for her handkerchief and press it to her nose. What must it have looked like before their arrival? How had anyone survived this?

She glanced about, hoping she might see Old Sam's trawler. If anyone could tell her about Evan, it would be Old Sam. But neither Old Sam nor his boat was anywhere in sight. Still, she was one step nearer to Evan. At least she prayed she was closer to him. She had prayed she would find Evan vibrant and fit and that he would be pleased to see her. Since leaving Cleveland, she'd been plagued by Mrs. Mifflin's warnings. And when she'd heard one of the Bridal Veil workers had died, her worries had compounded. Her emotions wavered back and forth—from deep foreboding and sadness to crushing panic and fear.

Over the past weeks, Melinda had lain awake at night thinking of all the possibilities—most causing her fear to deepen. She'd finally succumbed to the knowledge that she needed to place her trust in God. But knowing what she should do and actually doing it proved difficult. Over and over, she'd asked God to erase her fears, give her peace, and replace her worries with trust in Him. For short periods of time, she would meet with success, but soon she'd snatch back her fears and hold them close, as if they were dear friends rather than her enemies.

The captain had their luggage taken to the large wharf, where several of the steamship and freighting companies had their warehouses and storefronts. She stopped in front of the Shining Star Steamship Company office and turned toward her brother, who was following at a short distance. She pointed at the doorway. "I'm going inside to see if there are any boats going to the islands."

Lawrence frowned. "I think we'd do better talking to some of the fishermen. A steamship isn't going to be crossing the river to the islands."

"I'm quite aware of that, Lawrence, but I didn't think you'd want to lead your horse out on those rickety planks where the launches and fishing boats are tied."

He tipped his head and smirked. "Guess you could hold onto the reins and I could go down there and ask around."

She shook her head. "Better for me to go." It wasn't that she minded the horse. In fact, she thought the animal was beautiful. And though she didn't consider herself well trained, she was certain her riding ability would surprise Lawrence. Evan had taught her to ride the first winter she'd been on Bridal Veil. Since then, the two of them had taken many rides along the hard-packed beaches on the eastern side of the island.

He patted the horse's sleek coat. "And why is it better for you to go?"

She pointed to the horse. "If you want passage for your animal, I think we'll need a barge, not a fishing boat. Why don't you tie him over there and come in with me."

She was willing to pay for her own passage to Bridal Veil, but she wasn't paying for the horse. She'd overheard some of the sailors talking and knew her brother had used his time on the freighter to advantage. A number of them had commented on the fact that he'd emptied their pockets with his card games. When they'd been alone, she had criticized his behavior, but she now realized it was going to take more than a few words to change her brother's gaming habits. In truth, it seemed his penchant for gaming had grown stronger since their parents' deaths.

He hesitated and glanced about, his gaze settling on some of the ne'er-do-wells lingering on the docks. He turned and gestured to a boy of about ten. "I've a shiny coin for you if you'll look after my horse." He pulled the boy close and gave him instructions to shout at the top of his lungs should anyone come near the horse.

"Don't you worry, sir. Folks as far as St. Simons will hear me shout if anyone tries to touch this beautiful horse." The boy grasped the reins and wrapped them around his hand before making a fist. "No one will get him away from me. You can be sure of it."

Once inside the shipping office, Lawrence took charge and within a short time had completed arrangements. While Melinda would go to Bridal Veil, he would wait and accompany his horse on a barge. The local manager of the shipping line didn't encourage them to remain in the area. "Lots of damage here in Biscayne, and Bridal Veil got its share, too. You might want to wait and come back during the regular season. Even without the hurricane, this isn't the best time to vacation in these parts."

Melinda stepped close to the counter. "We're not here on vacation. I have friends who work on Bridal Veil Island. I've come to make certain they're not injured. And we're hoping to help with the repairs to the island."

"Speak for yourself," Lawrence muttered.

When the agent looked away to give a sailor instructions,

Melinda nudged her brother. "We do plan to help, Lawrence. Otherwise, why are you here?"

Once the sailor departed, the manager turned back to them and pointed out the launch for Melinda. Since entering the office, she'd been fearful of asking, but finally she inhaled a deep breath. "Do you know anything about a death on Bridal Veil?"

The agent's smile vanished and he glanced out the door. "Sad thing to lose anyone in a hurricane, but when it's a young man, full of life . . ." He fisted his hand and touched his chest. "It hurts your heart."

"Did you know him?" Melinda's voice cracked.

"That I did. Not well, since he lived over on the island, but his family lives here in Biscayne, so the boy was back and forth each week to bring his pay to his pa."

Melinda didn't realize she'd been holding her breath until the tightness in her chest made it feel as though it might explode. She exhaled a whoosh of air. "Then it wasn't Evan Tarlow?"

"No, not Evan, though I know him also. It was Alfred Toomie. Young fella that helped loading baggage and the like—least that's what his pa told me. His family lives up on the hill a ways."

Melinda didn't want to rejoice at the news, but relief washed over her like a spring rain. "And Evan Tarlow wasn't injured?"

"Evan's fine. He's been over here to the mainland a few times for supplies and to hire men to help with the cleanup. From what I've heard, no one else was hurt over there. Just the Toomie boy."

Melinda attempted to recollect if she'd ever seen Alfred, but she didn't recall the name. There had been any number of young boys who came and went, most of them nameless faces. She regretted the fact that she'd never bothered to ask any of them their names. She shuddered at the thought that she'd adopted more of Mrs. Mifflin's ways than she wanted to admit.

Momentarily engulfed by her own guilt, Melinda reached into

her reticule. "I don't have a lot of money, but perhaps a dollar or two would help the family."

The agent nodded. "I'm sure it would, but Frank Toomie would spend it on liquor instead of food for his family. It would be better to take your money to the grocer and ask him to place a credit on Mrs. Toomie's account." He gestured toward the dock. "You won't have time, miss." He turned his attention to Lawrence. "Perhaps your friend could see to it while he awaits the arrival of the barge."

After requesting the location of the store, Melinda and Lawrence left the office. She handed him the money, and though he briefly objected to the task, he finally agreed. He stood on the dock and waved as the launch pulled away from the dilapidated dock.

"Soon all will be back to the way it was before the storm," the owner of the launch told her. "Much progress has been made."

Melinda had heard that remark earlier in the day, but after viewing only a small portion of Biscayne, she remained unconvinced. "What of Bridal Veil? Have you been on the island?"

"No," he said, shaking his head, "but Old Sam says the damage there isn't as great." He chuckled. "'Course there wasn't as much for those winds to tear down on the island as there was on the mainland."

She supposed that was true, but after seeing homes and buildings completely leveled in Biscayne, Melinda wondered about the extravagant cottages that dotted Bridal Veil, especially Summerset Cottage. Surely the owners would be eager for a report. Perhaps Mr. Morley or one of the other investors had already been there and assessed the damage.

As the launch churned the dark river waters, she imagined Evan waiting at the dock to meet her, his arms open wide and his welcome exuberant. But when the dock came into view, there was no one waiting to greet her. What remained of the dock appeared sound, yet much smaller than the original. The captain edged the boat alongside the pier and directed one of the men to offload her baggage.

"Guess you know how to get to the lodge from here," the captain said.

Melinda thanked him. As the launch pulled away, she forced a deep breath. Was it the weight of her decisions or the damp air that made it difficult to breathe? A warbler chirped overhead, as if to urge her on. Grasping the handles of a smaller bag, she gathered her courage and then headed in the direction of the hunting lodge.

The uprooted cypress trees, twisted palmettos, and debris-laden paths proved the island hadn't escaped the storm. Although the roots of the huge live oaks had held the giant trees in the ground, most of the branches had been stripped. Gone were the frothy veils of moss. Gone, too, were the rich green, everlasting leaves that had caused the giant trees to bear the name live oak. They now stood like naked sentinels silently observing the ravages of the storm. She continued along the muddy path, trying to absorb the transformation of the landscape.

The hem of her skirt caught on a protruding branch, and she leaned down to untangle the fabric. Her damp clothing clung to her body like a second skin, yet in spite of the heat, Melinda shivered. Finally comprehending the power of the hurricane gave rise to another fear. Would making her home on this island mean she might face such a storm in the future? And if it did, was this where she truly wanted to live the remainder of her life? As she rounded the final turn to the hunting lodge, the question assailed her like a battering wind.

Brushing damp strands of hair from her forehead, she climbed the steps and knocked on the door. She dropped her bag on the porch and turned the doorknob. "Evan! Harland! Is anyone here?"

When no answer came, she stepped into the sitting room and glanced toward the stairs. Surely they wouldn't still be in bed—it was far too late in the day. She jumped and turned at the sound of metal crashing onto the wood floor. "Delilah! You scared me to death. And look what you've done." Apparently the cat had jumped down from a higher perch and landed on the metal pan. "You tipped over your food." Unruffled by Melinda's scolding, the cat padded to her side, purred, and brushed against the fullness of Melinda's skirt. As she strutted back toward her food, the cat's white-tipped tail waved like a flag in the morning breeze.

Other than Delilah's scattered food, the lodge appeared in perfect order. After she had viewed so much chaos, the neat surroundings jarred her sensibilities. She stooped down and gathered the food back into the metal pan, but a part of her thought the small mess appropriate—as if it fit much better than the tidiness. Delilah remained close by her side and intently watched. "You need not worry. I won't eat any of your food." Melinda chuckled and scratched the cat's ear.

Once she'd finished, Melinda stood and looked down at Delilah. "So where are Evan and Harland, Delilah? Too bad you can't talk." She strode to the porch, picked up her bag, and placed it inside the door. The cat sat nearby staring at her. "I think I'll go see if Emma is about. Maybe she can tell me where I'll find Evan. You be sure and pass along my whereabouts to Evan if he returns, Delilah."

She laughed aloud at her silliness. Her brother would think she'd lost her mind if he heard her talking to a cat. Then again, he talked to horses, so maybe not. She grinned and turned toward Delilah. "You be good. I'll be back in a little while."

The short hike to the O'Sullivan cabin further muddied the lower quarter of Melinda's skirt. Her knuckles would turn raw trying to scrub the muck from this dress. As for her shoes, who could say how long it would take for them to dry. And once the leather dried, it would likely become brittle and pinch her feet. Her legs ached from the constant pull of the thick mud as it tried to take her shoes captive with each forward step. *Not much farther. Not much farther.* She chanted the words to herself until she finally spotted Emma scrubbing the front porch. A smile tugged at her lips.

"Emma!" Had the mud permitted, she would have raced to the porch and embraced the woman in a tight hug. Instead, she continued to trudge on at a snail's pace.

Cupping one hand to shade her eyes, Emma stepped to the porch rail and bent forward. "Am I seeing things or is that you, Melinda?" Emma edged to one side and strained against the railing. "It is you! I can hardly believe my eyes. Where did you come from, lass?" She walked down the stairs and met Melinda at the bottom step.

Melinda extended her arms and accepted the older woman's embrace. "I'm alone. I came over on a launch from Savannah. My trunks and suitcases are on the dock." She leaned back a few inches and met the woman's clear, blue-eyed gaze. "I'm planning to stay."

"Stay? Here? Now?" She stepped back and nearly toppled on the stairs as her ankle struck against the wooden edge. Concern replaced the sparkle in her eyes. "Ya must be jokin' with me. Have ya not looked around on yer way here?"

"I did, but it's concern over Evan that brought me back, Emma. When I heard about the damage, I couldn't remain in Cleveland. Can you tell me how he is?"

"We're all fine—especially Evan. 'Course, he's younger than us. We've been workin' hard to get things back in shape. Harland finally was able to hire a few men that 'ave come over to help get things back in order before the season. 'Course we'll be needin' more."

Learning Evan wasn't the man who had died had eased Melinda's concerns while in Biscayne, but it hadn't totally erased them. Hearing Emma's assurance lifted a weight from her shoulders that she'd carried ever since hearing of the hurricane. She felt pounds lighter, if such a thing were possible. Unable to contain her joy, she pecked Emma on the cheek. "I would have been here sooner, but—"

The older woman held up her hand. "Come in and sit down. I'll make us some tea, and you can tell me your story while I put my feet up." She pointed to her swollen ankles. "This weather does me no good at all. My ankles could pass for watermelons."

Melinda didn't want Emma to think her rude, but it was Evan she wanted to see. "Do you know where I can find Evan?"

She shook her head. "Best to wait here. Harland has him supervising projects all over the island. No tellin' where he's at. And even if I knew, he'd probably be off someplace else before ya got there." Emma shot her a grin. "Won't hurt ya to wait a little longer. Sure, and it'll make seeing him all the sweeter when you finally set eyes on him."

CHAPTER 14

Though Emma had questioned Melinda's decision to return, the woman had certainly made use of her during the three hours since her arrival. While Emma washed windows, she set Melinda to work ironing the curtains she'd washed the day before. "Ya might as well keep going once ya iron the curtains. There's plenty of ironing in my laundry basket, and that's a fact." She shook her head. "Up till now, it's Garrison's been keepin' me busy. He's more worried about the animals than this cottage."

Melinda hadn't minded ironing the curtains. And she'd rather enjoyed pressing Garrison's shirts and Emma's skirts and shirt-waists. Together with Emma's never-ending questions, the chore had helped pass the time. She lifted Emma's plaid skirt from the wooden ironing board and examined her work.

"No need to be so careful with the ironin', lass. With all this mud, I'm havin' to wash clothes most every day. That skirt will be wet and wrinkled ten minutes after I settle it on me hips."

Melinda giggled. "Well, at least you and I will know that it looked good for a short time. It was a smart idea to lay a tarp like a rug." Melinda pointed to the floor. "I'm sure that saves a lot of cleaning."

Emma nodded. "I can't be takin' the time to shed my shoes every time I need to go in and out. It's funny, but I never realized just how many trips I make until after the hurricane."

"I suppose it would never have occurred to me, either." A horse whinnied in the distance and Melinda hurried to the front door. "Do you think that's Evan?"

Emma dipped her cloth into the bucket of water and shrugged. "Could be Evan or Harland or Garrison—or maybe all three. A little early for 'em to be returning for supper, but ya never know these days." She clucked her tongue. "I've not even set the potatoes to boil, so they may be waitin' a while if it's supper they're wanting." She wrung out the wet cloth and waved it in Melinda's direction. "Get on out there and see before you bust a button."

Melinda didn't wait for any further encouragement. Her shoes thudded across the tarped wooden floor like a muffled drum beating out a marching quickstep. She pushed open the door and immediately covered her mouth with one hand. She best not screech and alarm Emma! She wasn't certain if Evan spotted her before she saw him, but by the time she made it to the porch railing, he was off the horse and up the steps.

His clothes and boots were covered with mud—some dry and some wet, but when he rushed toward her, she didn't hesitate to accept his embrace. "I can't believe my eyes! What are you doing here?" He nestled his face in her hair. Lifting his head, he gazed into her eyes. "Did you receive my letter?"

Melinda studied the creases that lined his face. "No. I didn't receive your letter. You look tired, Evan." She traced her fingers along the side of his face. "It's wonderful to see you. I've been so worried."

He leaned forward and covered her lips with a kiss that left her breathless. Melinda struggled to regain her composure and rested her hands against his chest. Beneath her fingers, his heartbeat pounded as rapidly as her own. He captured her fingers in one of his hands and held them tight against his chest. "I can't believe you're truly here. I keep expecting to wake up and discover this is a dream." A slow smile spread across his face. "I promise you that if this is a dream, I don't ever want to wake up."

She lifted her fingers to his lips, and he kissed them. "This isn't a dream, Evan. I was afraid you'd be unhappy that I'd come."

"How could I possibly be unhappy to see the woman I love?" Their eyes locked in a silent caress that confirmed their love for each other. "I'm only sorry that my letter didn't arrive and that you've been worried about me." He continued to hold her close. "Still, I must admit that it makes me feel good to know that you were so concerned that you traveled all this distance in such difficult circumstances." He glanced over his shoulder as if he expected someone else to appear. "How long will you be staying?"

Her breath caught. Perhaps the best way to handle his question was with one of her own. "How long would you like me to stay?"

He continued to hold her hand, but he took a small backward step. "I don't think that's my decision to make. What did Mr. and Mrs. Mifflin say? I doubt they'd be willing to let you stay down here until the season begins, would they?" He didn't give her a chance to answer before he continued. "I'm surprised they even agreed to let you come down here at all, especially unaccompanied." Once again, he glanced around.

She now understood his confusion. He realized she wouldn't have traveled from Cleveland to Bridal Veil by herself. He was expecting to see her traveling companion somewhere nearby. She had so much to tell him, she didn't know where to start, but Lawrence was probably the best place to begin. After that, she'd ease into telling him that she was no longer employed and planned to remain on Bridal Veil—if he'd have her.

While they sat on the railing, her words spilled out like water from a toppled jug. She told him of the journey by train and freighter, about Lawrence and his willingness to come with her, the horse he'd brought along, and the fact that he'd soon be arriving from Biscayne. "Just as soon as he can arrange for a barge to bring the horse over. He insisted on waiting in Biscayne. I think he worries more about the horse than he does about himself—if that's possible."

Emma poked her head out the front door. "Harland and Garrison with you, Evan?"

His eyes grew wide and he shook his head. "No. I came back for some equipment out of the barn." He pushed away from the porch rail. "Garrison and Harland are gonna be wondering what's happened to me." He leaned forward and pecked Melinda on the cheek. "I'll be back in a couple hours, and we'll talk more. I'll have to see about someplace for you to stay during your visit."

Visit? Before she could correct the misunderstanding, Evan was down the front steps and loping toward the barn. The suction of the mud caused his feet to rise to the top of his boots with each step. When she had mentioned Lawrence's horse, Evan had appeared confused, but there would be plenty of time to explain later tonight. Once he understood she was here to stay, everything would become clear. And once it became clear, she prayed he would be pleased with her decision. She stared toward the barn. But what if he wasn't pleased? What if he thought she should have remained in Cleveland? What if he thought she'd been foolish to risk everything? Suddenly her heart pounded a new beat—one that propelled fear through her body with the speed of lightning.

❖ ❖

With his thoughts as jumbled as the tools he'd gathered from the barn, Evan headed to the clubhouse. Work had progressed at a steady rate, and they would soon be ready to hire staff to clean the interior and make certain the rooms would meet guests' expectations once the season began.

Until a week ago, Mr. Nordegren had remained on vacation because of his inability to make adequate travel arrangements. At least that's what he'd told Harland. Since then Mr. Nordegren had assumed many of the duties, especially those regarding the clubhouse—if only in regard to making decisions. For the physical labor, he looked to Harland and Evan to see that the workers completed the assigned tasks.

Evan had done his best to sort out the reactions he'd been having ever since he'd seen Melinda standing on the porch. He'd run the full gamut of emotions—everything from disbelief, delight, alarm, and worry, to joy, fear, apprehension, astonishment, and elation. At the moment he was totally perplexed. He'd always considered Melinda a woman who gave a great deal of thought and consideration to her decisions—more predictable than impulsive. Yet she'd surprised him at her departure earlier in the year, and her sudden return today surprised him even more. Now he didn't know what to think of this woman he loved. Was she contemplative or compulsive? He was no longer sure. And the fact that her brother had brought a horse with him made no sense at all.

Harland's shout pulled him from his thoughts. "Over here! We already finished on the other side." He waved his hat. "Thought maybe we was gonna have to send a search party out to find you." Harland finger-combed his thinning white hair and plopped his hat on the back of his head with a grin.

Evan pulled back on the reins, dismounted the mare, and dropped the tools onto the ground. "No search party needed. I knew where I was going and how to get back just fine." He looked down at the older man. "You're not gonna believe who's back at the O'Sullivan cabin." He tied the reins to a thick fallen branch while he waited for Harland's response.

The older man reached into his pocket and withdrew a piece of paper. "I got no idea, but I'm hoping it's Old Sam and he brought us his catch of the day." He patted his stomach. "My belly is already growling, but we got work to get done." He pointed to the shrubs and new plantings that Mr. Nordegren had purchased and shipped to the island. "I need you to get these fellows organized and have them follow this layout Mr. Nordegren drew for the plantings." He extended the drawing toward Evan and chuckled, his eyes alight with laughter. "Oh, I bet you're still wanting to tell me who's over at the cabin, aren't ya?"

A broad smile returned to Evan's lips as he bobbed his head. "I sure am. It's Melinda! She was standing on the O'Sullivans' porch when I got there. I could hardly believe my eyes. I still can't believe it." He stopped and stared at Harland for a moment. "Maybe she'll be gone when I get back—maybe this is just a dream and I'm going to wake up."

"I don't know about a dream, but it's gonna be a nightmare if you don't get these men moving. If we don't get these plants in the ground before supper, Mr. Nordegren is going to be mighty unhappy." Harland patted him on the shoulder. "I'm surprised to hear your gal is back here. Maybe you better think about where she's going to stay. You might check with Mr. Nordegren and see what he thinks is best. How long's she staying?"

Evan hiked a shoulder. "I'm not sure. We didn't get to talk long enough for me to find out."

"That a fact?" Harland winked. "As long as you were gone, I'd think you'd have every last detail. Then again, I'll bet you were too moon-eyed to ask any questions."

"I was not moon-eyed, but she did look good to me." Evan chuckled as he walked off with the drawing, but he didn't fail to notice Harland rubbing his lower back.

There was no denying all this heavy work was getting to the

older man. Each night he suffered with aches and pains, although he tried to hide his increasing discomfort. The day Mr. Nordegren returned, Harland had told him of his desire to quit, but the assistant supervisor was unwilling to accept his resignation. He insisted they wait until Mr. Zimmerman, the general manager, returned. Mr. Nordegren had gone on to explain that even after Mr. Zimmerman gave his blessing, it would take the agreement of the primary investors to approve Evan for Harland's position—and that could possibly take until the middle or the end of the season. The assistant supervisor's decision hadn't set well with Harland.

Evan swiped perspiration from his face, his thoughts jumping from Melinda to the work at hand. Perhaps he should speak to Mr. Nordegren and see if she could stay in the maids' quarters on the lower level of the clubhouse. He wasn't certain that would be a good solution, but she couldn't stay in any of the private homes. The O'Sullivans didn't have enough space for her, and she couldn't stay in the hunting lodge. It seemed the only choice would be the clubhouse—or perhaps she'd gained permission from the Mifflins to stay at Summerset Cottage.

"Not there!" He strode toward one of the workers and pointed to the drawing. "That palm goes on the other side." He silently chastised himself for letting his thoughts wander. If he was going to please Mr. Nordegren, there could be no mistakes. And convincing the assistant supervisor of his abilities was the first step toward securing the position Harland would soon vacate. And that job would be the only way he could support a wife and family.

His position as Harland's assistant paid enough for him to save a little each month. In addition, his living quarters and food had been provided. But the pay hadn't been a consideration when Evan accepted the job. He'd wanted the experience and the chance for advancement the position might afford him. Thus far, his decision had proved a good one, as he'd learned a great deal.

Now he must see if the investors agreed. Would they offer him Harland's job and compensate him accordingly? Or would they seek someone else—someone older with more experience? If so, it would be the end of Evan's dream to remain on Bridal Veil. It would mean he must find work and make his home elsewhere. Without the hope of advancement, he simply could not remain.

A short time later, Mr. Nordegren appeared on the front porch of the clubhouse, and Evan smiled. Always impeccably dressed, Mr. Nordegren's overall appearance was difficult to process, for the man's expensive clothing didn't match the rest of his look. Due to a short neck, Mr. Nordegren's full and unkempt beard rested on his cravat like a grizzled fringe that was at odds with the otherwise perfect picture of a hotel manager. Each season Evan was convinced the man would return without the hairy thicket on his chin, but each year he was wrong.

With long, purposeful strides, he approached Mr. Nordegren. "If you have a minute, I have something I want to discuss with you." Evan turned his gaze back to the workers. "I hope you find the plantings to your liking. We plan to have them completed by suppertime."

Mr. Nordegren nodded his head. "They look very good, but you must make sure they are watered, or they will be dead before the end of the month."

These men understood the necessity of watering freshly planted flowers and trees without a reminder from Evan or from Mr. Nordegren, but Evan voiced his agreement. "I have a friend—a young lady who has worked here on Bridal Veil for the Mifflin family—and she is in need of a place to stay during her visit. I was wondering if she might take a room in the maids' quarters here at the clubhouse."

Mr. Nordegren stroked his whiskers. "I'm not sure if that's suitable." He continued to stare into the distance with unblinking dark eyes. "Is she looking for work? We're going to be hiring women to begin cleaning rooms within the next week. Emma O'Sullivan is going to assume her former position as head house-keeper. She might be willing to hire her. In that event, she could be housed in the maids' quarters with the other women Emma hires." He scratched his chin. "Until then, you'll likely need to make other arrangements. Perhaps over in Biscayne?"

Evan didn't know what surprised him more. The fact that Emma had agreed to return to her duties as head housekeeper or that Mr. Nordegren thought Melinda should be housed in Biscayne until she hired on as a housekeeper. And what would Melinda think of the news? After traveling such a distance in such difficult circumstances, she would be more than a little displeased. He must come up with some other plan.

CHAPTER 15

The minute they had finished their work at the clubhouse, Evan hurried back to the hunting lodge, cleaned up, and returned to the O'Sullivan cottage, where he discovered the question of Melinda's accommodations had been settled by Emma. The older woman had been clear: Melinda would stay with them. Evan was surprised by the news—especially since their space was limited and Garrison wasn't known to be fond of company. But Garrison had nodded his silent agreement, and Evan didn't argue. He felt as though the couple had lifted part of the weight from his shoulders. Not that he believed Melinda a burden, but he'd been totally unprepared to have her suddenly appear.

"If there's a bit of time before supper, I'd like to visit with Melinda." Evan glanced at the stove, where Emma was busy frying potatoes. "But I don't want to hold things up. If it's better for us to wait until—"

Emma interrupted before he could finish the sentence. "Go on, the both of ya." She winked at Evan. "I'm thinkin' ya got a lot to say to this lass."

Evan could feel the heat rise in his cheeks. Emma could embarrass the hide off a horse if she set her mind to it. He held the door open for Melinda and followed her onto the porch. "Why don't we sit over here." He guided her to two chairs that were a short distance away.

His stomach clenched and he wasn't sure if it was from hunger or nerves, but he suspected it was the latter. He didn't even know how to begin this conversation. Should he just blurt out his questions? He was delighted to see Melinda, and he didn't want to appear ungrateful that she'd journeyed all this distance, yet her unexpected arrival perplexed him. Why hadn't she waited to receive word from him before embarking on such a dangerous trip?

While he attempted to come up with a way to begin their conversation, she sat down in one of the chairs and turned toward him. "I know you're surprised to see me, but when I heard about all the devastation down here, I had to come and make certain you weren't injured." She lifted a stray curl from the side of her face and tucked it behind her ear. "And you cannot imagine how frightened I was when I learned that someone on Bridal Veil had died in the hurricane." She clasped a hand to her chest. "My heart nearly burst with fear that it was you—especially when I heard it was a young man who lived on Bridal Veil year-round." She reached for his hand. "I was so afraid that I would arrive and find you . . ." Touching her fingers to her mouth, she shook her head. "I cannot even say the word."

The sight of Alfred's raincoat lying on the dock flashed through Evan's mind, a fresh reminder of the boy and his death. Evan's mood turned somber as he met Melinda's gaze. "I wrote to you as soon as I could, but mail service wasn't going through for a number of days. If you had waited a few more days, my letter probably would have arrived."

Her head snapped back as if he'd slapped her. "Are you saying you wish I hadn't come?"

He hadn't meant to hurt her, but there was no denying his

words had caused pain. "I am very pleased to see you, Melinda. You know I love you, but—"

"But what? Do you wish I would have remained in Cleveland?"

Confusion and anger replaced the pain he'd observed only moments earlier. This wasn't turning out at all as he'd hoped. "No, that's not what I said. I'm worried about you being here in these horrible conditions. There's so much work that must be completed before the season opens, and I'll have little time for visiting with you."

"*Visiting?*" Her mouth gaped open and she stared at him as though he'd grown another head.

What had he done? The offense in her tone was enough to alert him he hadn't said what she'd wanted to hear, but truth was truth. He didn't have time for company right now.

"I'm not here to visit, Evan. I'm here to spend the rest of my life. I quit my job with the Mifflins. I'm here, my possessions are here, and I have nowhere else to go." Her eyes filled with tears, and she covered her face with her hands.

He pulled his chair closer. "Please, Melinda. Don't cry. We can work this out." He forced a smile. "There's no problem so big that we can't find a solution. If you don't want to return north, I'm certain there are positions for ladies' maids in Savannah and maybe even Biscayne—that would be even better. If you located a position in Biscayne, we could see each other more often."

She lifted her tear-streaked face. "Evan Tarlow, what is wrong with you? Haven't you heard a word I've said?"

He bobbed his head to affirm that he had, in fact, heard every word she'd said. Why was she getting upset again? Hadn't he said they'd find a solution? Hadn't he offered some viable options for her? He leaned back in the chair and raked his fingers through his thick brown hair.

"It seems everything I say is wrong. Maybe you'd better begin at the beginning, and I'll remain silent until you finish."

Melinda leaned forward. "Perhaps that is the best idea. But you need to listen carefully so you'll understand that those solutions you've suggested aren't helpful."

He wished she hadn't said that—now he was going to be thinking about why his ideas wouldn't work once she began her explanation. His thoughts were already drifting in that direction when she tapped him on the hand and brought him back to the present. He folded his hands together and focused on the somewhat involved tale of Melinda's departure, her lack of a reference letter, the trials of the long train ride, the wait in Savannah, the voyage on the freighter, and the difficulties with her brother and his horse.

His words must be chosen with care. Melinda needed his reassurance that everything would be fine. His fingers tingled as he unclasped his hands. He'd clenched them with such intensity that the blood supply to his fingers had been diminished. "I spoke with Mr. Nordegren over at the clubhouse earlier today and asked if you could use one of the rooms in the maids' quarters. I didn't realize Emma had agreed you could stay here," he quickly added.

She nodded her head. Feeling somewhat encouraged, he continued. "I didn't know you were planning to remain on the island indefinitely, but Mr. Nordegren said there would soon be positions open for help preparing the rooms for the season."

"Go on." Her shoulders stiffened, a sure sign something he said hadn't settled well with her.

"I know the work is far beneath your abilities, but he said Emma will be in charge, and I know you enjoy her company. The job would at least provide a small income, lodging, and meals." He leaned forward. "Does that sound like something you'd be willing to do until we have time to come up with a more suitable position?" Her brow furrowed, and he knew he'd not said what she wanted to hear.

"I'm going to come right out with this, Evan. The position I was hoping you'd offer is that of your wife." She inhaled a deep breath. "I know that's very forward of me and not at all proper etiquette, but you professed your love this summer, and I was clear when I departed that I had hoped you would ask me to stay. Now that I'm here, it seems you still don't think marriage is a suitable solution to this dilemma."

Had he been in an upright position and tapped with a feather, Evan would have fallen to the ground. "Marriage?" He'd felt this same woozy feeling when he'd been sick several years ago. He rubbed his hand across his forehead and forced himself to remain calm. He loved Melinda, but he wasn't prepared for marriage—not now.

He grasped her hands, once again surprised by the silky feel of them between his callused fingers. "I want you to listen to me very carefully—with the same clarity you asked of me while you explained your journey."

"I will." He heard the expectation in her voice.

"Marriage is something I desire with all of my heart, but not now." He flinched when she withdrew her hands and folded them in her lap. "Before you become angry or hurt, let me tell you why."

Her shoulders remained stiff and unyielding while he told her of the commitment he'd made years ago: He would never marry until he could support a wife and children in a suitable manner. Though he didn't like discussing his past, he knew Melinda deserved a deeper explanation. "I watched my own parents on our farm, Melinda. My mother worked herself to an early grave, and still there wasn't enough money to go around. My father was determined to keep the farm so that my brother, James, would receive a proper inheritance. He didn't seem to care that he was killing his wife in the process. But even at a young age, I could see what was happening, how my mother was losing trust and hope, how the hard work and lack of rest stole her life. I vowed that would never happen to a wife of mine." He looked into her eyes. "And I meant it."

He glanced toward the window. The smell of frying potatoes and roasted meat drifted from inside the cottage, and his stomach rumbled. "My job as Harland's assistant couldn't possibly support us."

The look of utter disbelief returned to her eyes as she continued to press the fabric of her tan-and-brown-checked skirt with one palm. "I understand about your mother and father, but that isn't us. And if I worked at the clubhouse, wouldn't that be enough?"

"No, but even if it were, that isn't what I want for us. I know you may not understand, Melinda, but I'm not willing to have your wages help support us." He fastened his gaze on the horizon. "I made a commitment that I can't break. If I do, I'll consider myself a failure, and that isn't what you want for a husband."

"But what about your commitment to me? You said you love me. Does that not include marriage?" Another tear trickled down her cheek and plopped onto her skirt.

"Of course it includes marriage." He went on to explain Harland's decision to resign from his position. "Harland has recommended me to succeed him, but he doesn't have the final say."

"Who does and when will they decide?" Her face brightened and she scooted to the edge of her chair.

"First Mr. Nordegren has to speak to Mr. Zimmerman. Then Mr. Zimmerman has to speak to Mr. Morley, and if he approves of the suggestion, he'll go to the primary investors for a vote."

Her smile faded. "That could take a long time."

He nodded. "Mr. Nordegren said it might be the middle or the end of the season before they reach a decision. My best guess is the end of the season."

"But why? Why couldn't they simply take care of it before the season begins?"

Evan couldn't speak with authority about why things happened the way they did, but she expected some sort of answer—he could tell from the impatient tone of her voice. "Since there's been a hurricane, and we have all this damage to take care of, they'll want the most experienced people on hand to make certain the season opens on time, and the guests' expectations are met without interruption. Harland is far more experienced than I am, and they'll look to him for answers should any unforeseen problems arise." Evan shrugged his shoulders. "That's the only answer I can give you, Melinda. I really don't know how the investors make their decisions any more than you do."

Her lip quivered and she pulled a handkerchief from her pocket. "I'm sorry to be such a crybaby, but this isn't how I pictured our reunion. I had such dreams—such high hopes."

Using his index finger, he tipped her chin upward and looked into her eyes. "You needn't forget either one. I love you, Melinda, and one day we will be married. I promise. I'm only asking that you wait until I can be the husband I need to be and the husband you deserve." He squeezed her hand. "One day I want a houseful of children, and I don't ever want you to worry about how you'll feed them or if there will be enough money to buy a new dress." He hoped his words would encourage her.

"Those things aren't what make a good marriage, Evan. It's love that makes a strong union between a husband and wife."

"I agree. Both love and trust are very important, but worries over money can cause lots of bickering and destroy both love and trust. I saw that with my parents, and I don't want that to happen to us. It's better to be prepared before we say our vows. You need to trust me in this."

Emma clanged a metal spoon against one of her iron skillets and called from inside. "You two best be getting yarselves in here, or Harland and Garrison are gonna eat yar share of the food."

Evan pushed up from the chair. "We can talk more later. Better not keep Emma waiting." He hesitated a minute, hoping for a response, but Melinda simply nodded.

Melinda wasn't sure what she should think. Evan had declared his love several times during their conversation, but the outcome hadn't been what she'd hoped for—what she'd planned for. And what about Lawrence? Though she'd mentioned he'd come with her, she hadn't actually inquired about a job for him. Would Garrison or Harland be willing to hire him? Given her brother's dislike of physical labor, she wondered if she should even suggest such a thing.

Yet Lawrence and his horse would likely be here tomorrow or the next day. She poked the prongs of her fork into the potatoes and pushed them around the plate. "I was wondering if there might be some work for my brother when he arrives. He's excellent with horses—in fact, he's bringing his own horse with him." She forced a bright smile as she glanced back and forth between Harland and Garrison. She hoped her concern wasn't evident. "He'd truly be a big help with the horses, especially once the guests arrive and bring some of their animals."

Mr. O'Sullivan shoved a bite of stewed tomatoes into his mouth as he looked at her. "Well, the guests won't be here until January, but with all this damage, I'm thinkin' we could put him to work. All the sheds and barns need repair, and I'm thinkin'

Emma wouldn't mind if he'd take over some of the milkin'. He any good with a saw and hammer?"

Melinda swallowed hard. She didn't have any idea if her brother had ever pounded a nail or sawed a board in his life, but he must have performed some of those tasks while he'd been sailing around the world these past four years. Didn't sailors have to make repairs that required the use of tools? Surely Lawrence had done some of that kind of work.

She met Mr. O'Sullivan's steady gaze. "I think he could prove a good help to you." She hoped her comment was strong enough to gain Lawrence a job, yet not so boastful that Mr. O'Sullivan would be angry with her if he proved inept. Perhaps she should add a little more. "He had been sailing for the past few years and then worked as a jockey and horse trainer for a gentleman in Cleveland before deciding to accompany me."

Mr. O'Sullivan's bushy eyebrows lifted on his forehead. "A jockey, ya say? I s'pose we can give him a try, but if he can't earn his keep, then it's back to the racetrack with 'im."

"That's only fair." Melinda forced a smile. She'd need to have a long talk with Lawrence once he arrived.

She looked across the table and was met by Evan's worried expression. Since leaving Cleveland, nothing had gone as she'd expected. She prayed nothing else would go wrong!

CHAPTER 16

Melinda and Emma had barely settled at the table, both of them eager to join the men for the noonday meal, when a barge horn blasted a signal for help. The five of them jumped up from their chairs in unison. Garrison frowned as he yanked his hat from a peg by the door, Harland only a few steps behind him.

"Come along, Evan. No tellin' what trouble there may be down at the dock. Must be someone in trouble, for sure."

"We'll come along with ya," Emma said, gathering a basket from the other room. "I'll take along my medicine and bandages in case someone needs some mendin'."

Melinda gasped. "You think there's been some sort of accident?"

"Can't never tell," Emma said. "Grab your bonnet and come along." The men were already out of sight by the time Emma and Melinda hurried down the front porch steps. They hadn't gone far when the older woman's chest began to heave as she puffed for air. "We're gonna have to slow a bit or it's me that will be needin' the medical care." She panted out the words and gestured to Melinda to slow down.

Melinda glanced in the direction of the dock. What if someone was in need of immediate help? "I could take the basket and go ahead, if you'd like."

Emma shook her head. "Garrison will send Evan on the run if they need something before we get there. I'm thinking Dr. Faraday should have heard the signal, but there's no way to be sure."

They weren't far from the dock when the barge sounded another blast. Moments later Garrison, Evan, and Harland appeared in the distance with Lawrence, his horse following behind.

Emma came to an abrupt halt, and Melinda nearly toppled into her. "So was all that horn blowin' just to announce a visitor?"

Melinda skirted around Emma and hurried forward. "Lawrence! Those blasts from the barge horn nearly frightened us to death." She hoped her brother's actions hadn't gotten things off to a bad start. Her brother had said he'd follow her to the island, but she had expected him yesterday. Either he'd decided he was enjoying Biscayne, or he hadn't been able to secure passage on a barge before now. Emma certainly appeared disgruntled by the interruption, but she wasn't sure about the men.

"Don't blame me, Melinda. It wasn't my idea. When I told the captain I didn't know which direction I should go to locate you, he blasted the horn." He shot her a mischievous grin and gestured toward the men. "And look—it worked. In fact, it appears that half the island's inhabitants have come to greet me."

Emma frowned at him. "We're far from half of what lives here, but we're the ones you managed to yank away from the dinner table." All the hurrying had caused her cheeks to turn the shade of fresh-picked cherries. She pulled a handkerchief from her skirt pocket and swiped it across her face. "I'm guessin' you'd be Melinda's brother."

He grinned at Emma. "Only on the days when I don't embarrass her." He nudged Melinda's arm. "And those are few and far between, aren't they?"

"You can behave properly when you've a mind to, and I suggest that this is as good a time as any to begin."

Garrison had stepped near the horse and was stroking the animal's body. "You say you won this animal in a game of cards, do ya?"

Lawrence turned toward the older man. "That's right. A beauty, isn't he?"

"Aye, that he is—and not a beauty that I'd think a man would be willin' to gamble away." His bushy eyebrows settled low on his heavy brow.

"I'm sure you're not accusing me of stealing the animal, sir."

Melinda flinched at her brother's remark, but Lawrence didn't appear to notice. He turned and met the older man's hard stare. Her brother hadn't been on the island more than ten minutes and already she sensed trouble brewing.

Emma shifted the basket to her left arm. "Come along, Garrison. It's not like the lad or his horse are stepping off into the river. You can talk to him and look at the animal back at the house. Dinner is getting cold."

The men fell into line without a word. In some matters, Garrison might be in charge, but there was no denying that when it came to preparing and serving the meals, Emma was in command. Once they'd returned, the men sat around the table and properly introduced themselves while Emma and Melinda reheated the food.

Garrison pointed his thumb toward the front of the house, where Lawrence had tied his horse. "So tell me again 'bout how you won that horse, 'cause I'm thinkin' I may need to take up playin' cards if a man can become the owner of a beauty like that one."

Evan chuckled. "Well, I think you'd have to spend a lot of time honing your gaming skills before you'd want to make such a large wager." He settled in his chair while Lawrence explained.

"The game started early in the day and went well into the night," Lawrence began. "There were a full half dozen men who started, but one by one the game grew too rich for their blood. By the time the clock struck midnight, it was down to just two of us. Unfortunately for the owner, he'd had too much to drink and possessed too little skill at cards." Lawrence crossed his arms over his chest. "I gave him an opportunity to change his mind, but he was determined."

"Aye, liquor can mess with a man's thinkin', and that's a fact." Garrison narrowed his eyes a bit. "So you gave him a chance to back out, ya say?"

Lawrence nodded. "I told him he'd be sorry come morning, but he believed he had a winning hand. Didn't think he could lose."

"I'm surprised he signed the bill of sale once he'd lost, especially if he'd been drinkin'. Many's the time a drinkin' man will fight rather than pay up, especially when there are no witnesses."

"And how would you be knowin' that, Garrison O'Sullivan?" Lips pressed together, Emma perched a fist on one hip and stared at her husband.

"Now, Emma, you know I found meself in such places before the Lord grabbed me by the scruff of the neck."

Harland chuckled. "And the good Lord had plenty of help from Emma, too."

"Aye, that He did," Garrison replied while dipping his fork into the fried potatoes Emma had scooped onto his plate. He swallowed the mouthful of food and then pointed his fork at Lawrence. "So you have a legal bill of sale for that horse?"

Lawrence frowned, obviously annoyed by the continued line of questioning. "Yes, I do. Would it make you feel better to see it?"

Garrison shook his head. "If yar sayin' it's true, then I believe ya. Just don't want no stolen horses on this island. What's the animal's name?"

Lawrence hesitated. "Priceless Journey."

The older man nodded. "Well, he's a priceless animal, and that's a fact."

Melinda watched the exchange between Mr. O'Sullivan and her brother. She'd been living away from her brother for the past four years, and much about Lawrence had changed. The look in his eyes was sincere enough to make her believe, yet there was something in his tone that didn't sound quite right. He'd mentioned that horse's name during their travels, and she was sure it wasn't Priceless Journey. What was he hiding?

After supper she called Lawrence aside. "You appeared to be concealing something when you spoke to Mr. O'Sullivan about that horse. And I thought you gave me a different name for the horse—something about black and running or some such thing, but I'm sure it wasn't Priceless Journey."

Her brother chuckled. "You worry far too much, Melinda. No matter what the name, that horse belongs to me, and I have a bill of sale as proof. There's no need for concern. In fact, I've heard tell that worry causes women's faces to wrinkle at an early age, and I wouldn't want that happening to my sister." He nodded toward the front door. "I think I'll go and take Priceless Journey to the barn."

She stared after Lawrence as he walked out of the house. In spite of her brother's assurances, he'd been unable to still her fears.

As December arrived, Melinda continued to marvel at her brother's ability to settle into this new life. Although Lawrence avoided as much heavy work as possible, he managed to remain in good stead with Mr. O'Sullivan. Lawrence said it was because the older man appreciated his ability with horses and wanted him around when the season opened. Evan thought it had more to do with her brother's ability to pull the wool over Mr. O'Sullivan's eyes.

Melinda decided it was probably a combination of both. Lawrence had proved his capability to work with horses, both as a rider and a trainer, though he wasn't much help when it came to mucking the barn or performing any other distasteful or tedious work. Most of the time, he offered the promise of riding a horse to charm one of the newly hired younger fellows into completing his mundane chores for him.

In considering the events since her brother's arrival, Melinda judged that Lawrence had adapted more quickly than she had. For her, much of this new life had required a great deal of adjustment. Though she'd been living in the maids' quarters at the clubhouse for more than a month now, she still hadn't gotten used to the distance her new living arrangement had created between Evan and her. Lawrence was living in the hunting lodge with Evan and Harland, which suited him just fine.

Melinda hadn't wanted to move from the O'Sullivan home, although she realized the time had come. When other cleaning women had been hired to help at the clubhouse, Mr. O'Sullivan made it clear he missed his privacy. He'd assured his wife that Melinda would now be safe at the clubhouse. Emma knew her husband had already extended his hospitality beyond normal limits, and she explained she couldn't press for more. She assured Melinda that Garrison was right. Melinda would be safe now that the other women were moving in to work at the lodge. Melinda couldn't possibly explain that her misgivings had nothing to do with safety but rather with having to leave Evan's nearness. When the day for her move arrived, Melinda had hoped the older woman would change her mind, but that hadn't occurred.

The clubhouse living quarters had created a new loneliness for Melinda. Instead of spending her evenings with Evan, Harland, Lawrence, and the O'Sullivans, she now spent her free time surrounded by strangers. And try as she might to befriend the other maids, the women seemed determined to keep her at arm's length after one of them shared that she remembered Melinda was Mrs. Mifflin's lady's maid.

Even during the days, her time with Emma was limited. As her supervisor, Emma didn't want to be accused of special treatment or exhibiting a preference for Melinda. "I told you t'would not be easy," Emma told her one day. "Our friendship will only make things more difficult for you."

"I don't care. I'm so happy to be here—to have a purpose and be allowed to stay."

"Well, just remember, once the cleanup and preparations are accomplished, you may well find your purpose removed."

"Oh, but surely they will see I'm a hard worker and keep me on. Not only that, but I have your friendship, and surely you will put in a good word for me."

Emma smiled. "Always, but for now I cannot show any favoritism."

Melinda knew the older woman was correct, but it didn't stop her from seeking out Emma. Each morning she'd wait by the front door of the clubhouse. Before Emma could catch her breath, Melinda would shoot questions at her in rapid succession. The questions didn't change much from day to day: Did Evan send a message for her? What time did Evan return home for supper? What progress were they making? Did Evan mention her name? Did he say if he'd come over to visit on Sunday? On and on it would go until she'd eventually quiz Emma about Lawrence.

But today as Melinda waited, she promised herself not to badger Emma when she arrived. She spotted Emma approaching and bit her lip.

"Good morning, lass. Aren't you going to start your inquisition?"

"Not today."

"Too bad."

"Why? Did Evan send a message for me? Is he all right?"

"See? That didn't take long." Emma laughed and pulled a folded sheet of paper from her pocket. "I suppose you'll be wanting this."

Melinda's heart pounded a new beat at the sight of Evan's handwriting. She quickly read the brief message and pressed the folded page to her bodice. "Thank you, Emma!"

Emma chuckled. "No need to be thankin' me. I didn't write it. But I hope that bit of news from Evan is going to make this day a better one for ya." She winked and continued into the clubhouse. "Now that the roof is fixed, we need to get to those rooms on the upper floor. The rugs need to be taken up and carried outdoors to clean." Emma glanced around. "Where is everyone?"

"They're finishing breakfast. The cook overslept this morning."

Emma's kind features wrinkled into a frown. "That cook may find herself on a launch back to Biscayne if she keeps up her sloppy habits. That's two times in the past week." She lifted a basket from her arm. "Would ya go and fetch her for me, lass? I need to be havin' a talk with her. And tell the others to get up to the fourth floor and start taking out the rugs."

Melinda scurried off toward the clubhouse kitchen to do Emma's bidding. The other women were finishing their breakfast when she reached the doorway, and she waved toward the cook. "Miss Emma wants to see you in the front parlor." She turned to the others. "And we're supposed to begin taking out the rugs on the fourth floor."

Groans circulated around the table, but it was the cook who directed a look of contempt at Melinda. "Been in there reporting on us, I see," she hissed and gave Melinda a push with her hip as she passed by.

"No." She looked at the other women. "Th-that's not what happened. Miss Emma—"

They pushed away from the table and headed off toward the rear stairs. She hurried after the women, and though she attempted to explain, they ignored her. Frustration replaced her earlier delight over Evan's note. She'd be given no opportunity to explain. Instead, the women would believe the cook and think she'd been reporting on them.

Melinda sighed. There was no changing what had already happened. It seemed she had little control over anything in her life. She'd thought coming to Bridal Veil would enable her to begin a new life with Evan, and together they would share opportunities as husband and wife. Instead, Mr. Morley and his investors controlled their future.

Kneeling down, Melinda began to roll up one of the many carpets. Her thoughts turned to the last time she'd spoken with Evan. It had been shortly after her move to the maids' quarters, when Mr. Morley had come to survey the damage. At that same time, Mr. Morley had also presented plans for expansion of activities on the island. The investors had decided that due to the other renovations taking place on the island, this would be a perfect time to construct both a racetrack and a golf course for the pleasure of the guests. They'd decided the new activities would attract additional visitors and investors who would, in turn, help pay for the renovations. Melinda had hoped these new projects might mean an immediate advancement for Evan.

Unfortunately, Mr. Morley had been unyielding in his position with Harland. The investors wanted him to remain as supervisor until the projects were completed. If Harland agreed, they would appoint Evan to work hand-in-hand with him, and when the two projects were completed, Evan would be selected to replace Harland. The older man hadn't been fond of the investors' high-handed strategy, but he'd agreed—for Evan's sake.

She had tried to match Evan's excitement over the news, but

hearing about his added duties had hit like a punch to the midsection. She had no one to blame but herself—she'd made the decision to come to the island without first talking to him, and she needed to accept his decision. Each night she repeated these things, but during the long days when the other girls wouldn't visit with her or the many evenings when Evan didn't come by, loneliness wrapped itself around her and created doubt.

As another hard day of work progressed, the women's complaints increased. Dragging the carpets down several flights of stairs and beating them was arduous enough, but the thought of hoisting them back up the stairs was more than the women cared to imagine. In addition, Emma had ordered that the floors be scrubbed and a fresh coat of wax applied before the rugs could be returned upstairs. When one of the girls tripped while attempting to carry a rug upstairs, Melinda intervened and spoke to Emma.

"Unless you want the women to suffer injury, you'll need some men to carry the rugs back upstairs."

"I'm thinkin' you're probably right. Should've thought of that myself. Tell 'em to leave the rugs once they're clean."

Pleased by the older woman's response, Melinda hurried to tell the others, but they curled their lips and muttered unkind remarks about her friendship with Emma. In spite of her attempts to help, there was no pleasing the women—at least not where she was concerned.

By late afternoon, attitudes hadn't changed much. Throughout supper, the other maids murmured about Emma's playing favorites and the fact that Melinda had more privileges than the rest of them. Melinda didn't argue with them or tell them she followed the same rules as they did. But they resented the fact that Evan could call on her during weekday evenings, while most of the other men were restricted to weekend visits. She had considered pointing out that the privilege was Evan's and not hers, but it wouldn't have changed their thinking. Besides, Evan had never visited during the week.

Their comments stung, but Melinda refused to let them ruin her evening. Any minute now, Evan would arrive and their time together was already far too short to be destroyed by gossipy girls.

Hoping to avoid further remarks, Melinda gathered a quilt from her room and walked outside to wait for Evan. A few moments later, two of the women followed her out the door, but they soon headed off in another direction. When more than twenty minutes had passed, she withdrew the note from her pocket. Perhaps she'd misread the time. "It says five-thirty." She glanced toward the setting sun. What was keeping him? If he didn't hurry, they'd have little time to themselves.

The two maids rounded the path from the opposite direction. "Get stood up, did you?"

Before Melinda could respond, the other girl chimed in. "Serves you right. The rest of us have to wait until the weekend to see our fellows."

Melinda could hear the others join their laughter a short time after they walked inside the living quarters. A tear trickled down her cheek. Why did they find such pleasure in her unhappiness? She swiped away the tear, determined to remain until darkness fell.

A sigh escaped her lips when Evan appeared a short time later. The setting sun cast a shimmer of gold across his dark brown hair and accentuated his chiseled features as he approached.

He pulled back on the reins and dismounted a bay gelding, one of the horses that remained on the island year-round. Evan turned and grinned. "It's nice to see you out here waiting for me. I hope that means you're as eager to see me as I am to be here."

"I'm always delighted to see you. I only wish you would visit more often and arrive on time." She'd tried to appear cheery, but it proved impossible.

Evan tied the horse to a low-hanging branch of a live oak and strode toward her. "You sound unhappy." He tipped his head to one side and met her gaze. "I'm sorry that I'm late, but we worked longer than expected, and I didn't want to come visit you without cleaning up." He chuckled. "I doubt you'd be pleased to be around me if I smelled like the muck from a barn."

He leaned forward and kissed her cheek. "I wish I could be here more often, but you know how busy I am. By the time I finally get home at night, I'm so tired I drop into bed and am usually asleep before I've finished praying." He lifted his nose and sniffed. "You smell wonderful. Is that lilac?"

She nodded. "You could smell my perfume every night if we were married."

His smile faded. "Once everything is in order, the horse track and golf course have been completed, and I've been appointed to take Harland's position, we'll be married." He grasped her hand and brushed a kiss across her fingers. "You'll become so tired of seeing me, you'll long for the days when you lived in the clubhouse."

She inhaled a breath and forced a smile. "I don't think that will ever happen, but I would like to hear what's been completed so far. Maybe that will make me feel a little better." Though it would soon be dark, she spread the multicolored quilt beneath a large cypress tree, where they were out of sight of the door to the maids' quarters.

Evan dropped down beside her. "We're making great progress on the racetrack. It's going to be a mile and a quarter oval. Lawrence spoke with the architect, and the men agreed that would be best. Lawrence says the shorter tracks are more popular now."

"Lawrence? Since when is Lawrence in charge?"

He shook his head. "Oh, Lawrence isn't in charge, but he does know a great deal about racetracks—much more than any of us could have imagined. And he's been willing to share all of his insights with the architect."

Melinda didn't doubt that piece of news. Her brother would be more than pleased to give advice about a new racetrack, especially if it meant he didn't have to perform any manual labor. And it seemed Lawrence had figured out how to charm Evan, as well as the other men.

"The location is completely staked out, and the workers have cleared the land." His eyes were alight with excitement. "By the middle of next week, we hope to have the ground leveled. Harland and I managed to hire additional workers from up north." He leaned forward and rested his arm across one knee. "It's going to be magnificent, Melinda. The architect has drawn up the landscaping plans, and there will be grandstands that will compete with those at Churchill Downs. If Mr. Morley and the investors agree, we'll have *triple* spires on our grandstands."

"I take it there is something particularly special about triple spires."

Evan nodded. "Indeed. The grandstands at Churchill Downs have only double spires. Mr. Morley asked us to have the track ready by the time the first visitors arrive for the season. If possible, he wants the track here to outshine Churchill Downs."

"With all that needs to be completed, it sounds as though I'll see little of you." A slight breeze fluttered through the tree's branches, and Melinda brushed a strand of hair from her forehead. "What about the golf course? Surely the investors don't expect both to be completed before the season."

"As long as they'll let us hire enough men, I think we can accomplish a great deal. Of course, it keeps Harland and me busy just running back and forth to make sure everyone is doing what they're supposed to. Some of the men are fair workers, but others need constant watching. We need to get some good supervisors in place, and that's a fact. However, as long as we have decent putting greens prepared, I think they'll be satisfied for the short term."

Melinda picked at a thread in the quilt. "Maybe once there are a few more supervisors, you'll find more time to come and visit. I've been so lonely since moving out of the O'Sullivans' cottage."

He scooted back on the quilt as though he wanted to escape her discouraging words. "I know, but there's nothing I can do to lessen the time I'm at work. Harland depends on me."

Tears pricked her eyes. "I depend on you, too. Doesn't that count?"

He cupped the side of her face in his palm. "Of course it counts—more than anything. You're the reason I'm determined to do the best job possible during these next few months. I'm going to make certain I'm offered Harland's job so that I can take care of my beautiful wife." He leaned forward and kissed her lips. "You know I love you, Melinda, and you need to trust me. All this hard work is going to provide us with what we need to begin our family." He murmured the words as he pulled her closer and kissed the top of her head.

She placed her hands against his chest and looked into his eyes. "All I want is you, Evan. I'm not afraid of building a life together. You don't have to prove anything to me. Working together will create unity and let us grow as a couple."

He shook his head. "You know I can't marry you yet."

She withdrew her hands from his chest and turned away in frustration. "I know you won't. You're the one who has no trust. You don't trust me. I'm strong and capable, but you won't let me prove it."

"That's not true, and your words aren't fair." Evan's tone was edged with anger. "I've tried to explain my position. I've assured you of my love. However, if we're going to have these kinds of conversations each time we're together . . . well . . . I think we'd be better apart."

Melinda knew deep inside that he made a good point, but still she couldn't force her heart to cooperate. Why wouldn't he even consider changing his plans? She'd given up so much to come here and be with him. She'd been willing to forgo her future security with the Mifflins without any assurance Evan would marry her, yet she wondered if he would have considered doing the same. He spoke of his love for her, but his actions didn't seem to match the words. If she was willing to take a chance on their future, why wasn't he?

She glanced toward the sky as the wind picked up. "There's a storm moving in. You probably need to return the horse before it starts to rain."

The darkening shadows didn't hide his look of surprise. "If you want me to leave, I will."

"No, Evan, I don't want you to leave. I want you always to be by my side, but it seems that isn't the way things are working out." She paused and gave him a smile. "I'm sorry I'm so impatient. I've never been good at waiting."

CHAPTER 17

Melinda glanced up from sweeping the front porch and was surprised to see Pastor Webley crossing the expansive clubhouse lawn.

His bald pate shone in the morning sun, and he waved in greeting. "Good morning to you, Melinda!"

Holding the broom with one hand, she waved in return. "Good morning, Pastor Webley." She stepped toward the edge of the porch. "I'm surprised to see you've arrived so soon. Few of the guests will arrive until after the New Year, and with the hurricane damage this year, some are postponing their arrival until even later."

That was the latest word the workers had received from Mr. Morley. Of course, that was subject to change, for the guests who owned their own cottages weren't required to reserve their rooms in advance like those who rented apartments in the clubhouse.

The preacher stopped at the foot of the steps and glanced back over his shoulder. "I'm amazed at how good everything looks. I didn't expect so much progress."

"Lots of workers and long hours can accomplish a great deal, Preacher. Just ask Evan."

The pastor arched his brows at her remark, but he didn't ask her to elaborate. He mounted the steps and met her gaze. "You say you're surprised to see me here, but I may add that I'm every bit as surprised to see you, Melinda. Have the Mifflins already arrived?"

Melinda was sure the preacher hadn't been on the island long, or he would have already heard she no longer worked for the Mifflins. While he sat on one of the wicker chairs, Melinda continued to sweep and tell him about the recent happenings. His facial expressions altered several times during her story, changing from bewilderment to amazement and then to concern.

When she finished, he tugged at his white collar. "Well, now. That's quite an exciting couple of months you've had, isn't it?"

She gave him a halfhearted smile. "I suppose you could call it that, but for me it hasn't seemed near as exciting as disappointing."

"Disappointing because the plans you made didn't happen as you expected?"

She nodded. "I thought Evan would be happy to see me, and I was sure he'd want to marry right away, but he's determined to secure Harland's position before we get married. He has his ideas of how things must be before we can wed."

"Ahh." The preacher bobbed his head. "So Evan had plans and you had plans, but you hadn't shared your plans with each other. In turn, that caused this big tangled mess. Is that the way of it?"

Melinda frowned. "Well, not exactly. Had it not been for the hurricane, I wouldn't have come down here. But because I was worried about Evan, I gave up my position and came."

"And you thought that since you were here, the two of you should just go ahead and get married now, rather than wait until he's sure he can provide for a wife and family. Is that right?"

Her frown deepened. "I suppose, if you put it that way, but we had pledged our love to each other before I left in May."

"Um-hum." He bobbed his head and rubbed his chin. "Did you do some praying about this decision before you left Cleveland?"

She didn't like admitting to the preacher that the thought

hadn't crossed her mind. Her worry about Evan had been her only concern. "No, I can't say that I did."

"I'm not surprised to hear you say that. When trouble hits, most of us think we know exactly what we need to do." He pointed toward the sky. "Instead of looking to God for help, we decide we know what's best. That kind of thinking can cause us to rush ahead of His plans for us."

"So you think God is blocking the way for Evan and me to marry? Why would He do such a thing? The Bible encourages marriage—it says that it's not good for man to be alone. It says that charity—love—is the most important thing of all."

"You're right. And the Lord may want you and Evan to marry. I'm just wondering if maybe you're trying to move forward while the wagon brake is still engaged." He motioned for her to sit down. "You ever see a team of horses trying to move a wagon before the brake has been released?" He didn't wait for her answer. "I can tell you it ends up with lots of pulling and very little progress. But once the driver releases the brake, the wagon takes off lickety-split." He slapped his hands together with a loud crack. "Now they can get moving forward because they're all thinking and working together, and the obstacles have been removed."

"So you think I was wrong to come down here?" Her palms turned damp against the broom handle. She didn't want the pastor to say she'd been wrong. Those thoughts had already taken hold of her far too many times since she'd set foot on the island. Besides, what was she to do? She had no place to go. Her lips trembled as she awaited his response.

He smiled and rested his arms across his legs. "I don't know for certain what you should have done, Melinda. But I think maybe you're trying to push your time schedule on everyone else, and it doesn't appear to be working very well. It's making you unhappy, and it's making Evan unhappy. I'd say you need to spend some time in prayer and see what happens—without forcing your wishes on anyone else." He leaned back in his chair. "Not an easy thing to do."

She agreed. Not only would it be hard to do, she wasn't at all sure she wanted to try. "I'll give your suggestion some thought."

"And some prayer, I hope." He chuckled and slapped his hands atop his legs. "Since you're here, I'm wondering if I could impose upon you a bit. As you can see, I arrived early this year. I wanted to be certain the church would be in good repair when the guests arrive."

"Emma told me the church roof was the first one to be repaired, although she said the inside didn't suffer much damage. The floors have been scrubbed and waxed, so there isn't much more that needs to be done before the guests return." Melinda glanced in the direction of the church. "Of course, I assume you've already been inside."

"I have. And it looks perfect. I couldn't be more pleased. I was thankful to see the damage hadn't occurred near the front of the church. The piano wasn't damaged at all—at least not that I could tell."

"No, it's perfect. Emma had me try it, and it sounds just fine. And none of the stained-glass windows were broken, either."

"Almost as if God had wrapped it in His hands to shield it from the storm." The preacher slid his palm over his bald head. "About the piano—I know that you play. Mrs. Mifflin mentioned your fine abilities to me only last season. I wondered if I could convince you to play the music for a Christmas program at the church."

Melinda stared at him. Except for private staff that came to the island with the investors and other guests, workers didn't attend church services at the lovely stained-glass-windowed church where Pastor Webley preached his Sunday sermons. "You're going to have the program at the church?" She leaned a little closer. "Who is going to attend?"

"Why, the workers, of course. There's no reason they can't have a program in the church, is there?"

Melinda shrugged. "I'm not the one to answer that question, but before you make any more plans, maybe you should check with Mr. Nordegren or Mr. Zimmerman. Gatherings for the workers aren't usually held in the church."

"I'll speak to Mr. Zimmerman, and I'm certain he'll agree I can hold a Christmas program there for everyone."

Melinda stood and picked up the broom. "You let me know what you decide, and if you want me to play the piano, I'll do my best."

The day before Christmas, the weather turned colder than usual, and by evening everyone attending the Christmas program had donned warm shawls or jackets. Mr. Zimmerman had agreed the program could be presented in the church. Afterward, they would dismiss to the dining hall in the workers' quarters, where a supper would be served and Mr. Zimmerman would offer Christmas greetings from the owners and investors.

The decision had surprised everyone but Pastor Webley. He'd been confident from the outset. Even before he'd gained Mr. Zimmerman's permission, he'd enlisted Emma and Melinda to decorate the church. They'd done their best, using a few of Emma's decorations from home along with some candles and ribbons that had been packed away in the church. After ironing the ribbons, Melinda had fashioned them into crisp bows to surround the candles, which added a festive touch.

Evan grasped Melinda's elbow as they entered the small church. "You and Emma did a fine job decorating."

"Thank you, Evan." His words warmed her heart as he escorted her to the front of the church, where she settled on the piano bench and began to play.

The candlelight provided a warm glow throughout the small church. Christmas without snow would be strange for Melinda, but lacking freezing weather or a sleigh ride, she nevertheless planned to savor every moment of this first Christmas with Evan. While she played the piano, the workers joined together to sing "Glory Be to God on High" followed by "Joy to the World." After they finished singing, a number of costumed employees participated in vignettes depicting the Christmas story. Pastor Webley then presented a short message on the joy of giving year-round—not only during the Christmas season.

"I'd be glad to give all year long if I had as much money as the folks who own this island," one of the workers mumbled as they departed the church. A couple of the other men agreed and laughed.

Emma stopped and turned around to face the men. "Ya missed the point of what the preacher was tellin' ya."

Garrison took hold of his wife's arm. "Come along, Emma. They're not wantin' to hear another sermon from you."

Emma continued alongside her husband. "Maybe not, but it sounds as though they're needin' one."

Evan and Melinda followed the older couple, with Lawrence and Harland a short distance behind them. Once they arrived at the dining hall, the men visited together while the women completed arrangements and served the meal that had been prepared and kept warm on the banked fires of the cookstoves during the church service. The contents of roasting pans, pots, and kettles were emptied into serving bowls for all to enjoy a festive meal that began with oyster stew. Between mouthfuls, the men offered compliments for the roasted turkey, oyster stuffing, carrots in creamy white sauce, baked sweet potatoes, boiled onions, and fluffy rolls they slathered with peach marmalade. They groaned with delight when presented with a choice of pecan, pumpkin, or molasses pie.

"I'll take a slice of each!" one of the men hollered.

"And you'll explode if you try!" another called out.

Laughter filled the room but quieted when Mr. Zimmerman stepped forward. "The owners and investors of Bridal Veil asked that I extend their best wishes for a merry Christmas to everyone, and they are hopeful the New Year will be a prosperous one for all. They are anticipating their return to Bridal Veil and realize that you workers have been required to perform yeomen's service this winter in order to accomplish all that has been expected for the upcoming season." He cleared his throat. "And they are exceedingly thankful."

Shoving one hand into his pocket, he glanced about the crowd. "Of course, you've been paid for those long hours you've worked, but as added thanks, I'll be placing envelopes on the far table." He tugged on his mustache and chuckled. "I'll be watching to make certain you take only the one that bears your name."

An air of anticipation reached new heights as benches scraped on the wood floors and the workers lined up to pick up their envelopes. "I hope it's enough to buy fabric for a new dress," one of the maids whispered to her friend.

"I hope it's enough to pay for the gifts I put on my account at the general store over in Biscayne," another replied.

Evan squeezed Melinda's hand and leaned close to her ear. "I hope it's enough to pay for a lovely wedding next year."

"A simple wedding would be fine with me."

He grinned down at her. "Once you begin to plan, I think you'll change your mind."

"And when do you think I should begin to plan? We haven't set a date."

He shifted to his other foot and allowed a bit of space between them. "It would probably be best to wait until after the season."

Her heart plummeted. She'd thought that as soon as he completed the racetrack and golf course, they would marry. Now it seemed he wanted to wait until after the season—that would mean next May or early June. Her lips trembled, but she tightened them into a thin seam. She wouldn't cry, not in front of all these people.

When she didn't offer any response, Evan appeared not to notice. Instead, he greeted Mr. Zimmerman with a hearty handshake and asked him to join them at their table when he'd finished his duties. Once the envelopes had been picked up, most of the workers disappeared to their quarters. Many would rise early Christmas morning to ride the launch over to join their families in Biscayne. For the remainder, it would be a day of rest and relaxation.

Mr. Zimmerman approached their table. "The owners specifically asked that I offer their gratitude to you men who have worked so hard on the racetrack and putting green. There's a great deal of excitement, and with each passing day I receive letters requesting reservations in the clubhouse."

"For sure, it's the attraction of the racetrack," Garrison said. "Far more men are interested in the races than in hitting a ball in the grass."

Mr. Zimmerman chuckled and patted Garrison's shoulder. "Golf is growing in popularity, too, especially among the wealthy, though I agree there is nothing as exciting as a good horse race."

Mr. Nordegren approached and joined them. "I wonder if it's the racing or the wagering that entices men to the track."

"I'm guessin' it would be the gamblin', for ya don't see many who go to gamin' halls or racetracks and do na place a wager." Garrison withdrew his pipe from an inside pocket and filled the bowl with tobacco. "Men lose all good sense when it comes to wagerin'." He pointed his pipe at Lawrence. "That beauty of an animal that Lawrence now owns is a prime example."

Mr. Zimmerman arched a brow. "And what animal is that?"

Before Lawrence could answer, Mr. O'Sullivan told how Lawrence had won the horse while playing cards with a gentleman who had more money than good sense.

The supervisor frowned. "You will need permission if you plan to race him. I don't know if the investors will permit a worker to—"

"No need for concern, Mr. Zimmerman," Lawrence said. "I don't plan to race the horse. In fact, if we can find another location on the island, I'd prefer to keep him stabled away from the other horses. I don't want the guests asking to ride him." He glanced at the supervisor. "If I keep him in another place, it should avoid any questions or problems."

Mr. Zimmerman tweaked the tip of his mustache. "I'm sure Garrison can offer you another place. There's an old stone structure over near the chicken coops that might suffice." He turned toward Garrison. "That would work, don't you think?"

Garrison nodded. "As long as he doesn't mind hauling feed and hay over there, it will do."

Emma chuckled. "I think it is a good plan. He can feed the chickens and gather the eggs while he's there."

Mr. Zimmerman smiled and stood. "I think Mr. Nordegren and I will head back to the clubhouse. I need to finish going over some of my paper work."

Once the dishes had been cleared and washed, the crowd had dwindled, and by the time the supervisors departed, there were only a few workers remaining.

"I hope you don't have to go just yet, Melinda. I thought we could spend a little more time together." Evan tapped his pocket. "I have a gift for you."

"I thought we would exchange gifts after church tomorrow." She'd sensed his excitement, but she wanted to wait and exchange their gifts on Christmas Day. Today had already been filled with activity. Tomorrow they'd be well rested and have time to enjoy their time together without interruption.

He pulled her aside while the others circled around them and then left. "I'll attend church with you, but after dinner I'll need to work."

"But tomorrow is Christmas, and it's also Sunday. Why do you need to work?" She swallowed hard to hold back her tears, but the thought that he planned to leave her alone on Christmas Day proved too much, and a tear escaped her eye.

His earlier excitement disappeared. He wiped away her tear and smiled. "There's no need for unhappiness, Melinda. We're going to be together every Christmas for the rest of our lives—this is just the first. And I promise I won't be gone all afternoon." He lifted her chin with the tip of his finger. "Does that help?"

She nodded her head, knowing that her attitude was childish. She had tried so hard to do as the pastor had suggested and pray about the situation, but she knew her prayers were lacking . . . as was her faith. "A little time is better than none at all. Do you still want to exchange gifts this evening?"

He grinned. "I don't think I can wait until tomorrow."

Hand in hand, they walked back to the maids' quarters. Though she had hoped he would agree to wait until tomorrow, excitement took hold of her as they neared the clubhouse. What gift had he selected for her? Melinda hurried to her room and retrieved the small wrapped package from the top drawer of her chest. They'd agreed they wouldn't spend any money on their presents. Instead, they would save for their future. She hoped he would be pleased with her gift and that he'd kept to their promise.

With the wrapped package in hand and heart pounding an erratic beat, Melinda rushed back outdoors. Evan led her around to the front porch, and they sat down on the steps. "I don't think Mr. Zimmerman will mind if we use the steps for a little while."

Melinda giggled, ducked her head, and glanced up the wide stairway. "If we tried to sit on the porch, I think he would issue a warning, but I doubt he can see us clear down here." She extended the gaily wrapped package. "I do hope you'll like it."

He carefully untied the red cord and lifted away the paper. He looked into her eyes before he opened the box. "I will be pleased with any gift you give me."

Unable to contain her excitement, she bounced on the step. "Go ahead. Open it."

Evan lifted the lid and withdrew the brass pocket compass from inside the velvet-lined case. "It's beautiful."

"It was my father's, and I want you to have it."

"But what about Lawrence? Shouldn't this be his?"

She shook her head. "My father offered it to him when he turned eighteen, but he didn't want it. He said the only compass he would ever need was the stars."

Evan leaned forward and kissed her cheek. "Thank you. I will cherish it—because it belonged to you and to your father before that."

"And this is for you," he said. "It belonged to my grandmother, and then my mother. I don't remember ever seeing Mother wear it, but she'd take it out from time to time and look at it. She'd tell me how she remembered her mother wearing it, and that she wanted me to have it, since she didn't have a daughter. It's the only possession I kept with me when I left home."

She opened the small box. Nestled inside was a silver and turquoise pin. Melinda lifted it from the box. "It's beautiful, Evan." She ran her finger around the outer silver edges. "Knowing it belonged to your grandmother and your mother makes it even more special to me."

Evan gazed down at Melinda, unable to believe his good fortune. Any man would be pleased to have such a beautiful woman on his arm, but it was more than beauty that had drawn Evan to Melinda. From their first meeting, he'd been smitten by her ability to speak freely with him. She had told him of the loving home she'd enjoyed as a child and her desire to provide the same kind of home for her own children one day. Evan's heart had swelled as she'd revealed her hopes for the future, for Melinda's desires perfectly matched his own. He, too, wanted a home filled with love and laughter rather than anger.

Of course, he'd later learned that Melinda could be impetuous, but he'd soon found the quality endearing. Unlike his own childhood, where he would be throttled for failure to follow his father's strict instructions, Melinda's parents had encouraged her spontaneity and considered such behavior creative. Evan concurred—most of the time. And at this moment, he could find no fault in this lovely woman who had professed her love for him.

He drew her close, not caring if anyone might see. "I love you, Melinda, and I look forward to the day you'll become my wife."

She tipped her head to accept the warmth of his lingering kiss and melted into his arms. Evan sighed. If only Melinda would be patient . . .

CHAPTER 18

JANUARY 1899

With her hands folded to keep them from shaking, Melinda sat in the upholstered gilt-wood armchair outside Mr. Zimmerman's office door. She hoped her outward appearance didn't reflect the inner turmoil she'd experienced since being summoned to the supervisor's office. At the moment, her stomach jiggled like a bowl of egg whites awaiting the whirl of a Dover eggbeater.

At the creaking of the door, she jumped and glanced over her shoulder. "Do come in, Miss Colson." Mr. Zimmerman stepped to the side to permit her entrance. He left the door ajar, obviously wanting to avoid any appearance of impropriety. He motioned for her to be seated before he circled the desk and took his place in a swiveling mahogany chair. He sighed as he shuffled through a stack of paper work. Finally he extracted two pieces of paper and placed them on top of the pile.

As usual, he was impeccably groomed. Each end of his mustache tipped at a flawless angle, and the part down the middle of his hair was perfectly straight. Not a wrinkle could be found in his pinstriped suit and matching vest. His white collar and cuffs had been starched to perfection, and his bow tie perched at his neck with aligned precision. One look at the man caused Melinda to rub the scuffed toe of her shoe against the back of her stocking.

His eyeglasses rested on the tip of his beaklike nose. Though she'd never before noticed, everything about Mr. Zimmerman was long and angular, even his fingers. He tapped one of the bony appendages on the piece of paper. "I have a matter of importance to discuss with you, Miss Colson. One that I hope will benefit you as well as the entire membership of the Bridal Veil consortium."

She waited, uncertain if he expected a reply. The movement in her stomach changed from jiggling to whirring. An image of the biscuits and sausage gravy she'd eaten for breakfast flashed through her mind. She touched her fingers to her mouth and swallowed hard. If she lost her breakfast and stained the Aubusson carpet in Mr. Zimmerman's office, she would surely faint of embarrassment.

"We are expecting a record number of new guests this season." He lifted his head and beamed at her. "And there has been no decline in the number of returning guests. It should prove a banner year for us."

She bobbed her head. "I was pleased to hear your report at the Christmas dinner. I'm sure Mr. Morley and the other investors will be very pleased." She smiled in return, still not knowing what he wanted.

He folded his hands and rotated his chair back and forth. "As you may know, I work at another resort during the summer months. The Sagamore, located in the Adirondacks in New York. You may be familiar?" His dark eyebrows arched high above his eyes.

"I've heard some of the ladies speak of visiting the Adirondacks during the summer months, but I'm not personally familiar with the area."

Like a preening bird, he inched his neck to new heights. If he'd had plumage instead of his shiny black hair, he likely would have fluttered and spread his feathers into a giant colorful fan. Melinda tightened her lips to keep from smiling at the thought.

"Suffice it to say that the Sagamore is beyond lovely—not that Bridal Veil isn't one day going to be comparable or surpass some of the other resorts. However, in order to do so, we must make certain our guests are provided every possible amenity." He picked up a pencil and tapped it on the piece of paper.

"Yes, of course. And I believe everyone has been working very hard toward that end." Did he think the maids were slacking with their work? Why didn't he simply tell her why he'd called her into his office? "Has there been some complaint about our efforts?"

"No, quite the contrary. But as I was saying, we need to find additional ways to keep our guests occupied. We need to provide them with new and innovative experiences during their visits."

Her thoughts raced as she attempted to understand what he was leading to. "I believe the racetrack and the new putting greens will help in that regard, don't you?"

"Yes, but it's the women I am considering at this particular moment. While there are some who might enjoy the horse races, I think there are many who will find themselves with additional time—time that will need to be occupied so they don't become unhappy." He leaned across the desk and pointed the pencil in Melinda's direction. "That is where you come in, Miss Colson."

"Me? How so?" Her heart skipped a beat.

"While I was at the Sagamore, they implemented the position of a 'leisure activities manager' to coordinate activities for the women and children during times when their husbands were off hunting or fishing, as well as arrange dances and small parties during the evenings. You, Miss Colson, are the perfect person for that position."

"A leisure activities manager?" Melinda's hand went to her mouth to suppress a squeal of pure pleasure. Such a position would mean she'd have a permanent home on the island. She wouldn't have to be away from Evan.

"What would such a job entail, and why do you think I would be perfect for the position, Mr. Zimmerman?" Her stomach churned as she thought of Mrs. Mifflin's warning. What if her former employers arrived and created a terrible scene. The humiliation would be horrid.

"You possess the education, poise, and natural beauty to interact with the guests in a way that will put them at ease. I'm aware of your background, Miss Colson. The first year you accompanied Mrs. Mifflin, she told me of the tragic death of your parents and how she'd offered you a position after learning of their financial woes. Of course, that isn't what's important at the moment. Right now, it is of great value that you are better educated than many of the ladies, and that you know how to conduct yourself in society."

Melinda held up her hand. She needed to stop this discussion before it went any further. "You need to know that I didn't leave my employment with the Mifflins under the best of circumstances. I was worried about . . . I needed to know that . . . Well, what I'm trying to say is that if I accept this position, I think Mr. and Mrs. Mifflin will be extremely unhappy."

He chuckled and shook his head. "You don't need to worry about Dorothea and Cyrus Mifflin. Mr. Morley has resolved that situation in its entirety, and they will not object."

"But how did you—"

"There is very little we don't know about our employees, Miss Colson. Especially those we consider valuable to the operation of Bridal Veil. When I saw how well you worked at the menial labor tasks, I knew you would be perfect. Suffice it to say, the matter is resolved, and the Mifflins wish you well in this new endeavor."

"Oh, I don't know what to say." She couldn't keep from smiling. "That's good news indeed, but I'm still uncertain about the position and if I am qualified."

"You are more than qualified. You'll have an office here in the clubhouse, and you will arrange and coordinate plans and appointments for guests to rent paddleboats, go horseback riding, play tennis, or participate in polo matches. For activities that require horses, you will coordinate with Garrison O'Sullivan or his staff. In addition, we want you to work with the chefs to plan special teas, birthday parties, bridal parties—the list goes on. Part of the position will be for you to come up with some unique ideas of entertainment for our guests."

Now that she knew the Mifflins wouldn't object and she'd heard some of the requirements, Melinda's excitement mounted. "Perhaps some of the guests would enjoy special river cruises or scavenger hunts. Or even a masquerade or costume ball."

Mr. Zimmerman jotted down her comments. "I knew you would be the perfect choice. I like all of those ideas, Miss Colson. We're going to be expanding the putting greens so that guests can enjoy a full golf course. Evan and Harland are going to be quite busy during the season."

She wanted to say they'd already been quite busy during the off-season but decided she'd best remain silent. Not only would Evan be expected to oversee construction of the new golf course, but once the guests arrived, he'd be required to take the men out on hunts and conduct all of his previous tasks, all for the same pay. Somehow, it didn't seem right. As far as Melinda was concerned, this meant only one thing: Evan would have less time for her during the coming months. She tried to cheer herself with the thought that if she accepted this new position, she would be busy, as well.

"I'm planning to have your office in the alcove off the main entry by the grand staircase."

She gasped in surprise. "My own office?"

"Indeed. This will make you readily accessible to the guests. I've already arranged for a small desk and a chair that will fit nicely. You'll need appointment books, ledgers, and a variety of other supplies. You'll receive a budget and an account so that items may be purchased for teas and so forth." He leaned forward. "Of course, those costs will then be charged to the guests, but we can go over those matters as you begin to book events."

She listened carefully to his talk of budgets, ledgers, and supplies, but there had been no mention of her wages. Surely he would increase her pay. She had no idea how the supervisor might react if she mentioned money, but if she planned to accept the position, she should know the pay. And she should exhibit the ability to speak up about such things, shouldn't she? "You haven't mentioned the wages for this new position, Mr. Zimmerman. I assume that I'll receive more than my current wages."

He chuckled and rubbed his hands together. "I knew I'd selected the right person for this position. Before I brought you in here, I argued with myself about whether you'd have the courage to speak up and ask about your pay."

"And what did you decide?"

"I decided you would ask about the pay before you accepted the position." He grinned and his thin face wrinkled like a dried apple. "And though you've expressed interest in the job, I didn't fail to note that you've not yet accepted my offer." He inhaled a deep breath. "We will triple your current wages for the first month. If your performance is as good as we all expect, your pay will be further increased and you will be moved to a small apartment of your own. The board of investors will decide the amount of your wages, which will be based on the job you do."

"In that case, I accept the position, Mr. Zimmerman." Triple her current wages was more than Melinda had anticipated. She'd be making as much as when she'd been employed by the Mifflins. Of course, she wouldn't have the extra benefits such as hand-me-down clothing—and clothing would be an important part of her position. Then again, if she wore a uniform of some sort, she wouldn't be required to concern herself with clothing. "What about my attire? Will I wear a uniform of sorts, or am I expected to wear dresses that will integrate well with the guests?"

Mr. Zimmerman tugged one end of his mustache. "I hadn't given that any particular thought. I believe we could have a seamstress over in Biscayne create skirts and shirtwaists that would be appropriate for days in the office. When you are directing more formal functions for the ladies, it might be preferable to wear something more formal." He peered over his wire-rimmed glasses. "Would that be a possibility?"

"I do have some dresses I've refashioned, ones that previously belonged to Mrs. Mifflin. If you think it would be appropriate, I could wear those gowns when necessary." Melinda hoped she wouldn't be required to wear one of the gowns in Mrs. Mifflin's presence, for the older woman would likely make embarrassing comments in front of the other guests.

"To be honest, I'm not certain I'm qualified to make this decision. I'll speak to Mr. Morley and he'll seek advice from his wife. For the present, I believe you should plan on the skirts and shirtwaists. When you go to Biscayne, you can make arrangements with a seamstress, and have her bill sent here to my attention." The clock in the hallway chimed, and Mr. Zimmerman pushed up from his desk. "Why don't we take a look at the space for your office. That way you'll have a better idea of anything you might need to purchase."

Melinda and Mr. Zimmerman strode toward the front of the hotel. Melinda hadn't previously taken much note of the small alcove, but the supervisor was correct. It provided the perfect spot for an office. She would be immediately accessible to guests when they entered or prepared to depart the hotel. The location would prove beneficial to her as well as to the guests.

Her back was turned when Emma approached and stepped to her side. "Is there something amiss? Did the first-floor maid forget to clean the alcove?"

Mr. Zimmerman shook his head. "Everything is fine, Emma. Miss Colson is inspecting her new office. She's accepted a position as our leisure activities manager, so that means you'll need to hire another maid."

Melinda met Emma's surprised expression. "I have a permanent job, right here."

Emma rested her fist on one hip and grinned. "Well, glad I am to hear ya've hired this lass for something better than cleaning rooms. Ya've made a good choice, for sure." Emma tapped the side of her head with a finger. "Melinda's got lots of brains, she does, and she'll do a good job for ya."

The supervisor patted Emma's shoulder and chuckled. "I'm sure the investors will be pleased to hear you approve, Emma."

"Oh, go on with ya, Mr. Zimmerman. We both know they don't care what I think, but sometimes even the likes of me knows when things is being done right." She waved toward Mr. Zimmerman's office. "I was coming by to tell ya that I'm going over to Biscayne this afternoon and to see if there was anything you'd be needin'."

"Nothing I can think of at the moment. But Miss Colson has

quite a list of things to purchase, so she might want to accompany you." He turned toward Melinda. "What do you say, Miss Colson? Are you ready to begin purchasing the items you'll need for your new position?"

Melinda grabbed hold of Emma's arm and shifted from foot to foot. "Oh yes. That would be wonderful. And thank you, Mr. Zimmerman. I appreciate your confidence, and I promise I won't disappoint you." She continued to hold on to Emma, her fingers squeezing into the flesh of the older woman's arm.

Emma let out a yelp and tugged her arm. "Turn me loose before you leave bruises on me arm, lass."

"Oh, I'm sorry—I'm so excited." Melinda clasped a palm to her bodice. "I'll be frugal with my choices while shopping, and I'll continue to think of new ideas."

Mr. Zimmerman rocked on his heels, obviously pleased with her enthusiasm. "No need to be overly concerned about your budget. Purchase whatever is needed—and ask the seamstress to rush on your clothing."

Melinda hurried after Emma but stopped and turned before she'd crossed the foyer. "When am I to begin, Mr. Zimmerman?"

"Why, tomorrow morning, Miss Colson. Our first guests registered yesterday, and our numbers will increase each day. Until the seamstress completes your clothing, you may wear your own attire. Whatever you deem suitable. I trust your judgment. Oh, and perhaps you should purchase some new shoes."

Melinda looked down at the scuffed leather that peeked out from beneath her hem. "I promise you, I will."

Melinda could barely contain her delight. For a brief moment, she considered skipping across the shiny Minton tile. Though she found it impossible to hide her bright smile, she squared her shoulders like a lady and held her head high. If she began skipping, Mr. Zimmerman might reconsider his choice.

Emma and Melinda had descended the outer stairs to the clubhouse when Melinda spotted Evan with a man she'd never before seen. Excited, she waved to him, but he turned away. Surprised, she quickened her pace and headed toward the men, but Emma grabbed her arm. "I wouldn't be interrupting Evan right now. That's Mr. Hubbard, our first guest of the season. I heard Evan and Harland chattin' this mornin', and these are some kind of important talks. Mr. Hubbard is here as a guest, but it's business he's handlin', as well."

Melinda understood she must heed Emma's advice. To interrupt Evan during business wouldn't be proper. She longed to tell him her news, but it would need to wait until later. "What kind of business? Do you know?"

Emma locked arms and leaned closer. "One of the maids overheard them talkin' in the main parlor afore they went outside. She says they were talkin' about the golf course needin' to be completed before the middle of March and that they hired some special fella that's to meet with Evan up in Savannah."

Melinda gasped. "In Savannah? When?"

"Daisy says he's leavin' tomorrow."

"For how long?" Melinda knew Daisy quite well. Much like the Mifflins' maid, Sally, Daisy enjoyed listening in on any conversation and repeating every word she heard. It mattered little whether it was the hired help, fishermen, or guests. She thought any snippet of conversation worth a listen—and worth repeating, too. No doubt she'd stationed herself outside the main parlor and listened to the entire conversation. Though she didn't approve of Daisy's behavior, Melinda wanted to know all the maid had discovered.

Emma shrugged. "She didn't say, but she did tell me there was talk that the golf course had to be bigger and better than the one on Jekyl Island because of some very special event in March."

"I don't see how that's going to be possible," Melinda said. "And what event could be so important that they'd have to complete the golf course? There are enough activities that I'd think the men could get by with just the putting greens for another season."

"You know how these rich folks can be. What they want, they want—and they want it right now."

Melinda did know. In fact, the words stung her a bit. Once again, she could see how her disgruntled attitude mirrored that of her former employers. She drew a deep breath and tried to dismiss any thoughts of unfairness this new demand would create.

Still, it didn't seem possible that after all Evan had done to prepare for the season, he'd now be expected to have a golf course ready by mid-March. If he was going to be at the beck and call of guests and board members every minute of every day, maybe securing Harland's job wasn't going to be so wonderful. Maybe they needed to discuss an adjustment to their plans.

CHAPTER 19

Although he hadn't missed a word Mr. Hubbard had uttered, Evan saw Melinda's excited wave when she and Emma crossed the lawn in front of the clubhouse earlier in the morning. He'd also observed her look of surprise when he hadn't acknowledged her, but he knew Mr. Hubbard wouldn't be pleased by an interruption, especially one of a personal nature. However, the moment he and Mr. Hubbard parted company, Evan went in search of her. He wanted to explain and apologize, but he couldn't find Melinda; he found only Daisy.

The maid was on her way to the Harrison cottage, located not far from the clubhouse, and she had been more than pleased to share news of Melinda. "She and Miss Emma have gone over to Biscayne to purchase supplies. Of course, I get to stay here and work. The Harrison family arrives tomorrow, and they want their cottage aired and readied for their arrival." She shifted her basket of cleaning supplies from one hand to the other. "You'd think Miss Emma would let us take turns going over to Biscayne for supplies, but it's always Melinda that gets to go along. 'Course we all know they're friends, so we've gotten used to Miss Emma playing favorites."

Daisy's comments surprised him, for she knew he and Melinda planned to wed. Had she simply forgotten his relationship to Melinda, or was she hoping he'd repeat her comments to Emma and perhaps help her cause? He had to admit that he frequently misunderstood the ways of women. Melinda was one of the few women he'd ever understood, and even then it wasn't always easy. Like most men, Melinda usually conversed in a frank and straightforward manner, while other women he'd known beat around the bush. Still, there were days when he felt at odds to comprehend his beloved's thinking.

He decided it best to ignore the maid's critical remarks. "Did you happen to hear them say when they would return?"

"Not until close to suppertime, from the sounds of it. They both had long lists to fill—at least that's what they said." She came to a halt in front of the Harrison cottage. "'Course, Miss Emma has plenty of friends over in Biscayne, so they may be stopping to have a cup of tea and some biscuits while they're *shopping*." She leaned down and pulled some weeds from the side of the stone path leading to the door. "Looks like one of the gardeners needs to get over here and pull some weeds before morning. Can't expect me to clean both inside and out."

Although there were few weeds and little trimming was needed, Evan agreed. "I'll send someone over straightaway. Don't you worry about the shrubs or the yard."

She hiked a shoulder and tipped her nose toward the sky. "I didn't intend to." Before Evan turned to leave, she grasped the sleeve of his jacket. "I'm guessing you're wanting to talk to Melinda about all the time she spent in Mr. Zimmerman's office early this morning." She gave him an exaggerated wink. "Or maybe you already know?"

He shook his head. "I didn't know she met with Mr. Zimmerman this morning."

Daisy nudged him in the side. "If you wasn't so good looking, I'd tell you to watch out for him." She cackled as she withdrew a key from her pocket and ambled toward the cottage door.

Evan watched her walk away and then headed off. "Always looking to start something. If she can't find any gossip, she'll spin some of her own," he muttered. Still, her words remained with him—not that he was worried about Mr. Zimmerman stealing Melinda's affections, but why had she been in his office this morning? Was she in some kind of trouble? He knew she performed her duties well, yet there was always the chance something could have gone wrong. Or perhaps the Mifflins had contacted Mr. Zimmerman and raised a fuss.

Though Evan knew it would do no good to worry, he clenched his jaw as he cut across the grassy area and hurried toward the lodge. When he spotted one of the gardeners working at the Brown cottage, he stopped and tucked his fingers in his mouth and let loose a shrill whistle. The older man looked up from the shrubs he'd been pruning and waved.

Evan cupped his hands to his mouth. "Need you to go over to the Harrison cottage and get the lawn and shrubs looking perfect. They arrive tomorrow."

The gardener lifted his hat and waved it overhead. "Should be finished here in about fifteen minutes. I'll head over there next."

Evan continued on his way to the barn, where he would stop and borrow one of the horses. Before departing for Savannah tomorrow, he wanted to take another look at the area that had been staked out for the golf course. From what Mr. Hubbard had told him, the specialist in Savannah wanted to do away with the plan they'd previously laid out and begin anew. Such an idea sounded foolish to Evan, especially since this specialist hadn't even seen the area they'd plotted.

Evan tromped up the steps of the hunting lodge and hoped

Harland would be there. He knew the older man could offer some insight on how to best prepare for a meeting with the golf course specialist. He pushed open the door and stopped just inside. Delilah raced down the steps and greeted him with a yowling meow.

With a frown, he walked toward the cat. "What's the matter, girl? No one around to give you any attention?" He leaned down to pet her, but she ran up the steps, stopped at the top, and made another yowling noise. "What's wrong with you, Delilah? I offered to pet you and you ran off. I don't have time to chase after you." He strode to the large desk and withdrew a tablet of paper. If he made some drawings of the plotted course as well as the surrounding land, perhaps it would help.

When Evan glanced upstairs, Delilah poked her head between the wood railing that ran the length of the upstairs hallway, yowled, and ran toward Harland's bedroom. He dropped the paper and pencil on the table and hurried up the steps. He couldn't tell if the cat was trying to tell him something or if she simply wanted his attention, but her behavior was unusual and baffled him.

"I'm coming, Delilah, and you'd better not have a dead mouse or bird up here, or I'm not going to be happy with you." Evan took the stairs two at a time and stopped at the top of the steps. Delilah peeked around the corner of Harland's door—this time her meow sounded close to normal. Evan strode down the hall to the doorway. His breath caught when he spotted Harland lying on the bedroom floor.

"Harland!" Evan dropped to his knees and felt the older man's forehead. Uncertain what to do, he placed his hand on Harland's chest to see if he could feel him breathing. When he felt a slight movement of Harland's chest, he leaned close to his ear. "Can you hear me, Harland? Are you injured?"

The man groaned and his eyelids fluttered. Delilah rushed

close to the other side of Harland's body, curled up beside him, and purred. "I don't think so. Don't know what happened." He rolled to his side. "Help me onto the bed."

"I don't know if I should move you. Something might be broken. Maybe I should get the doctor first."

Harland pushed to his side, unwilling to wait any longer. "Nothing's broken, just help me up."

Evan braced one leg along the bed's sideboard and carefully lifted Harland to the bed. There were small cuts along one side of his face where he'd hit the floor, and his cheek had already begun to bruise. "Do you know what happened? Did you trip on something? Do you think you fainted, or what?"

"I was feeling tired all morning and decided to come up here and rest for a while. When I got to the top of the steps, I was having some trouble getting my breath, and the next thing I knew, I was waking up on the floor."

"I think I should go fetch the doctor. I know Emma isn't over at the house, but if Garrison's around the barn, I'll have him come and sit with you until we get back."

"There's no need to go after Doc Faraday. I'm feeling fine now. You go on about whatever you were doing, and I'll rest for a while. I'll be good as new once I rest some. And I don't need anyone to come and sit with me. What's Garrison going to do? Pull up a chair and stare at me while I sleep?" A few wisps of hair fluttered around Harland's forehead as he shook his head. The white strands accentuated the stark pallor of the older man's complexion. "Garrison has work to do, and I'll not have him sit here doing nothing while you run off for a doctor I don't need."

"This is one time I won't follow your orders, Harland. You may think you'll be fine, but I want to hear that from a doctor. Like it or not, I'm going to get Dr. Faraday."

After fetching a glass of water and placing it near the bedside,

Evan hurried to the barn. Garrison was nowhere in sight, but one of the young boys who helped in the barns poked his head from inside one of the stalls. "Are you wanting a horse, Mr. Evan?"

"Yes, but I'll see to saddling him. I need you to do something else for me." It would take the boy far longer to saddle the horse than to do it himself. Besides, Harland couldn't complain quite so much if he sent the young fellow rather than Garrison to stay with him. As soon as Evan had explained what had happened, the boy took off on a run, his arms pumping as though he couldn't get to the lodge fast enough. Evan grinned as he saddled the horse. Sitting in a sickroom for a while would likely be a welcome relief for someone who spent the day mucking stalls.

Evan was well on his way to the infirmary when he realized that instead of riding for the doctor, he should have remained behind and sent the boy to fetch Dr. Faraday. He gritted his teeth and clenched the reins tight in his fist. After all, what could a young boy do if Harland suddenly had another attack of some sort?

He tightened his legs and nudged the horse to a gallop, thankful he didn't have much farther to go. The sound of the approaching horse must have alerted the doctor, for he came running outside as Evan arrived. Pulling back on the reins, he quickly explained.

"Sounds like it may be his heart acting up again. I'll get my bag and follow you in my buggy."

"He has a heart problem?"

The doctor stopped on the porch. "He does. That's why I told him he needed to give up his work here on the island. I thought he was going to take my advice last year, but it seems he's determined to stay a while longer."

Thoughts racing, Evan gave the left rein a tug and turned the horse back toward the path. His friend had remained at the island to help him, and now his health was suffering because of it. Why hadn't Harland told him? Evan silently chided himself.

He knew why: Harland was a man who would lend a helping hand no matter the consequences to himself.

A quick reflection over the past months was enough to cause him shame. He'd noticed Harland slowing down, and on a couple of occasions he'd seen the older man clutch at his chest. Why had he willingly accepted Harland's feeble excuses? Why hadn't he pursued each occurrence and insisted upon more detailed answers from his friend? Evan knew exactly why. Losing Harland meant the investors might not offer him the position he wanted. Evan bowed his head. After all Harland had done for him, he'd been willing to pretend he hadn't noticed.

"Forgive me, Lord. How selfish I've been." Evan muttered the prayer as he arrived back at the lodge. He ran upstairs, where Harland remained abed and the young boy sat near the window looking outdoors. Evan motioned to the boy, thanked him, and sent him back to the barn. Harland's eyes remained closed, and Evan lifted the chair, positioned it beside the bed, and sat down.

Harland raised an eyelid and peeked out at him. "You gonna sit there and watch me sleep?"

"Since you're awake, I don't guess I'll be watching you sleep. Besides, the doctor's on the way to check you. He tells me you've got heart problems and he told you a year ago to quit your job." He leaned closer. "Why didn't you tell me, Harland? I'm finding it hard to forgive myself that you're suffering on my account."

Harland flitted his hand. "I'm not suffering, and I didn't stay here only on your account. When the investors said they wanted me to stay until you were trained, I was flattered. Imagine, an old man like me being swayed by a few words of praise." He shook his head. "I have only myself to blame for any harm I've done to myself, but I can tell you I have no regrets, Evan. I'm certain you'll be appointed to take my place so long as you keep your nose to the grindstone."

"What's this I hear about my favorite patient taking a fall?" Dr. Faraday strode into the room and placed his black leather bag at the end of Harland's bed. "Not very good about following your doctor's orders, are you, Harland?"

He shrugged a shoulder. "I may listen a little closer in the future, Doc." He moved his head so he could see around the doctor. "Evan, you need to go check on that golf course. The doctor doesn't need your help and neither do I. Go take care of your job. That's an order."

The doctor chuckled. "You're going to make him sorry he came to fetch me if you keep talking to him like that, Harland."

Harland chuckled. "Sometimes that's the only way I can get him to listen."

Evan gave a mock salute. "I'm on my way, but I'm counting on the doctor to provide me with a list of orders, and I'll expect you to follow every one of them."

———

Evan tucked the paper and pen into his pocket before he departed the hunting lodge. He'd lost a great deal of time, but there was still plenty of daylight to accomplish his task. He hadn't gone far when he heard the sound of a horse's hooves following him. Glancing over his shoulder, he caught sight of Lawrence approaching on Priceless Journey.

Evan reined his horse to one side and permitted Lawrence to come alongside. "I thought you were keeping your horse on the other side of the island."

"I am, but he likes to run, and I thought I'd give him a bit of exercise today. If there's no one out at the racetrack, I thought I'd take him out and see how he does."

Evan squinted against the reflection of the sun on Lawrence's silver-trimmed saddle. "Did that fancy saddle come with the horse?"

Lawrence grinned. "It did and I must say that winning a horse like Mid—I mean, like Priceless Journey makes it difficult to give up gambling."

"Maybe so, but I'd guess losing that animal made it easier for the owner of the horse to quit wagering."

"Never can tell," Lawrence said. "Some men think the next win is only one roll of the dice away. No matter what they lose, they never quit thinking they'll win the next time."

"There's no doubt the racetrack is going to create a lot of gambling. I hope the investors don't regret it." Evan glanced over at Lawrence. "You haven't changed your mind about running your horse, have you?" He bent forward to miss a low-hanging branch in the path. "If an employee owned a finer racehorse than the guests will be bringing in, it could become an issue and cause some unnecessary problems."

"Don't worry. I don't plan to race him this season. If I'm around next year, we'll see what happens. I may even find someone to purchase him. Besides, I enjoy a good game of cards more than betting on horses."

Evan wondered if Melinda had informed her brother about the rules against fraternizing with guests. He hoped Lawrence wasn't forming plans that would gain him access to gambling with the guests.

He'd best mention his concern to her. He'd add that to his list of things to discuss with Melinda—just as soon as she returned from Biscayne.

CHAPTER 20

Melinda was pleased to find Pastor Webley accompanying them home to Bridal Veil Island later that day. She and Emma had arranged for a variety of supplies to be shipped, and even now, Emma was busy with instructions for securing the load.

"How are you this day, Melinda?"

She smiled and took a seat beside the older man. "I'm quite well."

The pastor removed his gold-rimmed glasses and gently wiped the lenses. "I hope that you are in better spirits than you were prior to Christmas."

"I am. I just accepted a new job today. Mr. Zimmerman is going to have me taking care of the guests' leisure activities. It will mean a raise in pay."

"That is good news."

She nodded. "I've been thinking about it all day. The additional money will surely mean that Evan and I can marry soon."

"Are those your plans again?" His lips curved in a good-natured grin.

Melinda didn't want him robbing her of the joy she'd felt all day. "I suppose they are. I haven't had a chance to tell Evan yet, but I hardly see how he could deny it to be a very good idea."

The pastor's expression sobered. "May I be frank with you, Melinda?"

She didn't like the tone of his voice, but she agreed nevertheless. "Of course. I would never want anything but honesty and frank discussion between us."

"I thought as much." He replaced the glasses on his face and settled his hands over his rounded belly. "Men and women think very differently from one another. Evan has spoken to me on several occasions, and I feel very confident from those talks that he will not wish to be dependent upon his wife's work to support their well-being."

Melinda frowned. Evan had said as much. "I realize he worries that I will work too hard. His mother did, and he feels it put her in an early grave. But the Bible says I am to be his helper—does it not?"

"True enough, but it also says that you must submit yourself to Evan's authority. Are you prepared to heed that, as well? After all, we cannot pick and choose which verses we will honor."

Her cheerful spirit wilted. "So you think my new position will do nothing to hurry my marriage."

"I cannot say with certainty, but it is my opinion that Evan will be happy for you, but he will continue to delay the marriage until he feels he can provide amply. And, Melinda, that is an excellent quality in a husband. You mustn't try to dissuade him."

A prick of guilt stabbed at her conscience. As much as she wanted to agree with his comment, Melinda felt at odds. She had been so happy throughout the day. She'd even spoken to the seamstress about the cost and design of a wedding dress. Not that she'd made any commitment.

"I hope I haven't discouraged you too much."

She looked at the pastor and sighed. "I feel there is so much I have to learn. One minute I'm convinced that my thoughts and plans must surely come from God himself, and the next I hear the voice of reason through someone I respect."

He nodded and reached over to pat the top of her gloved hand. "Never stop listening for the voice of God. He will answer . . . if you ask Him to. He will listen to all of your concerns and guide your heart."

❧❦

As early evening arrived, Evan was waiting near the dock when the *Bessie II* finally returned from Biscayne. He hurried toward the boat as the captain carefully steered it alongside the dock. The moment he spotted Melinda and Emma, he waved, but the ladies didn't see him. Melinda was saying something to Pastor Webley, and Emma was busy commanding the crew. Before disembarking, the older woman gave orders to several of the boys from the island who were charged with unloading goods from the boat.

"Can I be of assistance?" Evan asked.

Melinda smiled as their gazes met, and Emma handed him a heavy basket of goods.

"I'm guessin' you missed my cookin', and that's why you're waiting on the dock." She chuckled and glanced over her shoulder at Melinda. "Or is it the pretty lass followin' behind me that you're waitin' to see?"

"I'm always pleased to see you, Emma, but you're right that I was waiting for Melinda." The older woman gave him a look of mock disappointment and Evan laughed. "We did appreciate the food you left for us to warm for our supper. Garrison said he would be a poor substitute for you."

"I'm sure you and Harland would fare just as well. Harland can make a powerful good stew."

"Speaking of Harland, you need to know he's fallen ill. Doc says it's his heart."

"Oh no," Melinda said, looking to the pastor.

Pastor Webley had overheard the conversation. "Is he at the hunting lodge?"

Evan nodded with a smile. "We've all but tied him in bed."

"With your permission, I will go and see him." The pastor looked to the ladies and gave a slight nod. "If you'll excuse me, ladies."

"Of course." Emma pressed her hand to her bodice. "Harland has been lookin' poorly the past year, but he's always claimin' to be fine. Sounds like he wasn't telling the truth! What's the doctor sayin' about his recovery?"

"He had told Harland to quit his position a year ago, but with this last episode, Doc Faraday says he's going to tell Mr. Zimmerman that Harland's medical condition will prevent him from doing his job."

"Harland won't like that one little bit," Emma said. "He's not a man who's gonna take kindly to being ordered off his job."

"Maybe not, but I think he understands now. Although he hadn't told any of us, the problem with his heart isn't new. I think he may move to his brother's home somewhere outside Savannah, though I'm not sure his plans are definite."

"We go off for a few hours, and things turn upside down around here." Emma stopped to make certain the boys were following with the supplies. She grumbled and motioned to Melinda. "You go on ahead with Evan. Those boys are gonna break that glassware for the dining room if I don't get after them." She turned and headed toward the boys while calling out directives.

Pleased they would have some time alone to talk, Evan slowed his pace until Melinda was beside him. "I'm sorry I couldn't acknowledge you this morning."

"Emma explained."

"I knew Mr. Hubbard wouldn't be pleased by an interruption. He's a board member who has invested extra funds to promote the golf course." He touched her arm. "You know I wouldn't intentionally do anything to hurt you. Please forgive me."

She offered him an endearing smile. "There's nothing to forgive. And now may I tell you my news?"

"You have my full attention."

She grinned and stepped around a branch in the path. Her enthusiasm spilled forth like a bubbling brook as she described her new position. When she'd finished, she grasped his arm. "Isn't it wonderful? I can save a great deal of money toward setting up our home, and it will give me an opportunity to use some of my training and education."

Emma shouted at the boys to take the crates and boxes to the servants' entrance at the rear of the clubhouse while Melinda and Evan continued across the lawn toward the maids' quarters.

Evan nodded his head, yet the news caused an unexpected sense of foreboding. He should be delighted that Melinda would no longer be required to work as a maid cleaning rooms. She was an educated young woman with many talents, and Mr. Zimmerman planned to put her abilities to good use. From what Melinda told him, Mr. Zimmerman had been careful to obtain the approval of Mr. and Mrs. Mifflin before offering the position. The supervisor had left nothing to chance.

"Isn't it wonderful, Evan?" Melinda continued to bubble with excitement. He wouldn't have been surprised to see her jump up and down. "Let's sit down for a few minutes." She grasped his arm and moved toward the live oak. "I've already thought of several ideas that I think will be welcome changes to the guests' usual routine."

He felt a stab of protectiveness. "Usual routine? What does that mean? Riding and hunting? I don't think you're going to find the men willing to give up their activities in order to play croquet with their wives."

Her mouth dropped open, and she backed away as she released her grip on his arm. "This isn't a competition, Evan. It's a way to increase the number of activities for the guests. I understand that some of the ladies enjoy riding and hunting, but most do not. If there are more options, the wives will be willing to remain here at Bridal Veil for longer visits. At least that is Mr. Zimmerman's way of thinking. He's seen it prove useful in his employment at another resort."

Evan bowed his head. He'd spoken without thinking. His remark had come from feelings of fear and pride. Since learning of Harland's medical condition earlier in the day, he'd been worried, both about Harland and about losing the promotion at Bridal Veil. "I'm sorry, Melinda. I owe you another apology. I'm having trouble figuring out everything that's going on right now, but I can tell you that I'm very worried about my job. I have no way of knowing if the investors are going to hire me for Harland's position. With his illness, it means they'll have to make a decision sooner than expected, and who can say if they'll consider me qualified."

Her eyes softened and she stepped closer. "I accept your apology. I do understand some of your concern. There have been so many changes since the hurricane. But Harland will vouch for you, and they know that he's placed you in charge of almost all of the work. He'll tell them that you were the one who took responsibility and provided oversight for building the racetrack and grandstands, and that you're going to oversee work on the new golf course." She tipped her head to look into his eyes. "And you need to trust God—isn't that what Harland has told you in the past?"

"It's what the Bible says we're to do, but it isn't as easy for me as it is for Harland. I still struggle with the idea that God has time to take care of the simple things that affect my life."

Melinda motioned for him to sit beside her on the thick low-hanging branch of the live oak. "You're not alone, Evan. I often have to pray that God will strengthen my belief. Have you read in chapter nine of Mark where a father brings his demon-possessed son to Jesus and asks Him to have compassion on them and help them?"

Evan nodded. "Yes. And Jesus tells him that everything is possible for one who believes."

Melinda smiled and squeezed his hand. "And then the man says, 'Lord, I believe; help thou mine unbelief.' I think we need to add that to our prayers."

He leaned forward and rested his arms on his knees. "You're right. The only way I can become more trusting is to ask God to increase my faith."

Several of the maids walked outside. Their chatter and laughter carried on the breeze, and Melinda glanced over her shoulder. "I probably should go soon, or there will be more jealous remarks from the maids."

Her comment spurred Evan back to the present. "Is Mr. Zimmerman assigning you new quarters, or will you remain housed here with the maids?"

"He said for now that things would remain as they are. In time, however, if they are pleased with my work, I will be moved to a private apartment. Either way, I'm sure the change in my position will create more division between the girls and me. At least I have Emma to talk with. I will answer directly to Mr. Zimmerman, so she and I can be friends without fear of favoritism interfering."

"And you'll always have me to talk to," he added.

Melinda's smile faded. "I don't have you very much of the time, Evan. Whenever I want to talk, you're busy."

Her comment was a reminder of his forthcoming trip. "I know I'm not around much, but I think that will begin to change once the racetrack is operating and the golf course has been completed." He inhaled a deep breath. "When you saw me speaking with Mr. Hubbard this morning, he was giving me instructions about the golf course. I must leave for Savannah in the morning to meet with a new golf course specialist hired by the investors."

"So I heard."

His eyes widened. "How could you?"

She touched a finger to one ear. "Surely you know that most of the staff members listen in on conversations whenever possible. Daisy overheard part of your conversation with Mr. Hubbard and repeated it to Emma, who told me."

"I hope no one made any alterations to the conversation before you heard it, because I want you to know that I did my best to avoid the trip to Savannah, but Mr. Hubbard wouldn't hear of it." Evan shrugged a shoulder. "He says the project will run more smoothly if I meet with the specialist in person so there are no mistakes once we begin. There's a special event planned for March, and he's insistent the course be completed." He rubbed his forehead. "I'll need to be gone several days, and with Harland ill, it means the other work will fall behind. Still, I don't think I have any choice."

"If I said I didn't mind, it wouldn't be the truth. I wish you didn't have to go, yet I do understand." She placed her hand on his arm. "And what's this event you mentioned? Perhaps I can develop some ideas for the ladies if there is to be something special planned for the men at the golf course."

"I didn't receive any details—only that a special event is occurring and there can be no delays with the course." He hoped she wouldn't quiz him further, for he couldn't give her any additional information.

"Well, once you know more, perhaps we can coordinate events. And let's hope that when the golf course is well underway, you'll have more free time."

He was thankful for her understanding. With her new duties, Melinda likely realized the added pressures being placed upon him. If he didn't receive Harland's position, he couldn't continue at Bridal Veil. He knew pride played a part in his thinking, but he couldn't possibly support a wife on his current wages. And he certainly wouldn't be dependent upon his wife to support him.

"Once you begin planning all of your parties and social events, you may be busier than I. Then what will we do?"

"I don't think that will happen. I plan always to make time for you." She pushed a lock of hair back from her forehead as Daisy and a couple of the other maids sauntered past them. Evan nodded in greeting, but they turned and looked away.

"It appears they're not any more pleased with me than with you." He chuckled and waited until they were out of earshot before he scooted a bit closer. The branch wobbled under their weight, and Melinda grasped his arm. "I promise it won't break."

She smiled. "I'm sure you're right, but I really do need to return. I've been gone all day shopping, and I'll need to unpack some of the items I purchased before going to bed. I'm to start my new job in the morning."

He had hoped for a little more time, but he couldn't very well object when he expected her to be understanding of his own duties. "I'll walk you over. There's one other thing I wanted to mention before I leave for Savannah."

Their talk had gone better than he'd expected, and he now wondered if he should broach the subject of Lawrence, though he didn't want an unpleasant exchange prior to his departure. Thus far, his uneasiness about Lawrence was unfounded, yet he worried that with Harland's recent illness and Garrison having to take charge of so much, Lawrence might find some way to take advantage of the situation.

"What is it? Something about my new position?"

He shook his head. "Actually it's about your brother."

"Lawrence? What's he done?"

"Nothing that I know of, yet he's made some comments that make me uneasy. I hope it's merely foolishness on my part, but on several occasions he's mentioned gambling. With guests beginning to arrive for the season, I'm concerned he may attempt to elicit an invitation to join some of the gentlemen in their card games." They stopped at the bottom of the steps leading into the clubhouse. "I'm told some of those games are played for high stakes. Of course, it's up to the guests if they wish to participate, but I don't want Lawrence to think he has the same privilege." He watched her expression for any sign of anger, but she appeared more concerned than annoyed.

She glanced toward the darkening sky. "I worry a great deal about Lawrence's love of gaming. He told me he wanted to create a new life here, and I hope he is sincere in that regard. If it will make you feel better, I'll speak to him tomorrow." She smiled up at him. "I won't mention your name. I wouldn't want to create a rift between the two men I love."

He looked over his shoulder before stepping forward and wrapping her in a warm embrace. "I don't deserve such a wonderful woman, but I am very thankful you will soon be my wife." When she rested her palms on his chest and looked into his eyes, he could no longer resist. Lowering his head, he captured her lips in a lingering kiss that would carry him to Savannah and home again.

CHAPTER 21

Before Evan left the following morning for Savannah, he stopped outside Harland's bedroom. He placed his suitcase near the door and forced a smile before he entered.

"The sun is out and it looks like it's going to be a beautiful day, Harland." Evan grabbed the spindles of a straight-backed chair and placed it beside the older man's bed. "How are you feeling this morning?"

Since Harland had taken to his bed, Delilah had claimed a small space near his legs. After standing to see who'd intruded upon her sleep, she stretched her furry body, gave a feeble purr, and plopped back into her space on the bed. Harland's thinning white hair fanned across the pillow like a halo of dandelion dust. "I'm doing just fine. Don't you spend your time fretting about me. You've got lots to accomplish in the next few days, and worrying about an old man isn't one of them. I've been praying everything will go real smooth so you can return and get started on that golf course." His voice was weaker than usual. "No telling what the doctor's going to decide about me. He's talking about a doctor in Savannah, so Delilah and I may not be here when you return." As if she'd understood, the cat purred and moved closer to his leg.

Harland's words hit like a crushing blow. For a moment Evan couldn't gain enough breath to speak. He shook his head. "Please, Harland. I don't think I can do this without you."

"Now, don't you be saying what we both know isn't true. I've trained you well. You're equipped for the job, and you've got the Lord to lead you through the rest of your journey. He's a better guide than I am. You just need to remember to keep your eyes fixed on Him rather than on everyone else. Keep Him first in your life, do your work as if you're doing it for Him, and make decisions you know will please Him."

He lifted his hand and placed it on Evan's arm. "That will be the most difficult part of your job. In a place like this, you're dealing with men who have both power and wealth. Some of them may expect you to do things that are wrong." Harland squeezed his arm. "Be willing to take a stand when you must, Evan. Honor God by making decisions that glorify Him."

A lump formed in Evan's throat. The thought of being on Bridal Veil without Harland's wisdom and guidance pained him. Not since his mother's death had he experienced such a sense of loss. "I will, Harland. I promise. But it's my prayer that you'll be here when I return."

"And if I'm not, you can come and visit me when you have a few days off. Bring Melinda with you. She'd like my brother's wife. I'll expect an invitation to the wedding, too." He grinned and released Evan's arm. "Now you best get moving or Captain Fleming and the *Bessie II* will leave for Biscayne without you. Have a safe trip to Savannah."

"I'll do my best. Thank you for everything, Harland, but like I said—I'm praying to see you right here when I return."

The older man waved toward the door. "Go on, before I have to get out of bed and shoo you out of here like a pesky fly."

In spite of his sadness, Evan chuckled. He leaned over the bed and gave Harland a fleeting hug. "You are the earthly father I always wanted."

"And you are the son I never fathered." A tear slipped down Harland's cheek, and he turned his head toward the wall. "Go on now."

Evan hurried from the room, grabbed his suitcase, and rushed down the steps and out the front door, nearly colliding with Emma.

"Ya almost knocked me flat as a pancake, Evan. Best watch where yar going."

He apologized as he came to an abrupt halt. "Are you going upstairs to sit with Harland?"

"I'm gonna check on him, but then I got to get over to the clubhouse. Guests are arrivin' and there's work to be done. I've got one of the new lasses who hasn't yet been trained for her cleaning duties to come over and sit with him. She's a sweet girl and she knows to send for the doctor if there's a problem." She nodded toward the upper portion of the house. "Did Harland tell ya he may be leaving for his brother's before ya return?"

"Uh-huh." Not much happened on Bridal Veil that escaped Emma's watchful eye and keen ears. "I'm praying he'll still be here when I return, but I bid him good-bye just in case."

"Aye, that was smart of ya. And did our Melinda tell ya of her new position over at the clubhouse?" Emma didn't wait for Evan to answer. "I'm guessin' you're mighty proud of her. Mr. Zimmerman places a lot of confidence in her." She nudged Evan. "And to think you won her heart."

He smiled and agreed. "It is a surprise, isn't it?" A horn blasted from the *Bessie II*, and Evan waved and took off at a gallop. Captain Fleming knew of Evan's plans to ride over to Biscayne this morning, but he wouldn't wait on him. The man prided himself on timely arrivals and departures, and he deemed leaving tardy folks behind a good lesson in punctuality.

❦

Melinda's schedule hadn't permitted time to seek out Lawrence, and he hadn't been around the clubhouse since Evan's departure three days previously—at least not that she'd noticed. Although Mr. Zimmerman had predicted later arrivals this year, five families had come to the island on Thursday and Friday, and seven families had already opened their cottages for the season. Yesterday, the supervisor had been flustered by several letters from guests who had asked to move their arrival dates to next week.

Today, Mr. Zimmerman appeared every bit as disturbed as he had yesterday. He flapped several envelopes back and forth as he approached the door of Melinda's small office. "More guests requesting early arrival dates. I do not understand people who change their plans at the last minute. I doubt these women operate their households in such a lax manner, yet they expect me to be prepared no matter when they step onto the dock." He massaged his forehead. "And you can imagine how the chef is reacting to the influx of guests. He's even more upset than I am."

Melinda bit back a smile. She couldn't imagine any of the staff being more distressed than Mr. Zimmerman. Bridal Veil's supervisor was the epitome of organization, and he operated the clubhouse on a rigid schedule. However, the guests sometimes made it difficult for him to maintain his routine. They expected their desires to be met by a pleasant staff and without question. Watching Mr. Zimmerman attempt to remain calm and organized during these ever-changing circumstances, Melinda caught a glimpse of what might lie in store for her as the season continued. After working for Mrs. Mifflin for the past four years, she understood how quickly boredom could set in among the wealthy crowd.

"How have your plans progressed?" He peered over her shoulder at the ledger book in which she'd been writing. He tapped on one of the lines. "This looks good. I like the idea of rotating teas so the ladies become acquainted with one another. I am sure you have checked with the chef and serving staff to make certain this will not prove overtaxing for them?" His mustache twitched as he stared down at her.

"Yes. Chef Durand has appointed his assistant, Chef Bickerstaff, to oversee all of my activities while Chef Durand will continue with the full meals served in the main dining rooms. Chef Durand agreed we may use the sunroom for many of the activities I have planned."

Mr. Zimmerman gave his mustache a slight tweak. "Good. I'm glad to hear you are keeping well organized. I think you should place a bulletin at the front that will list the activities for each day and another one that will show upcoming activities. That way the guests can register in advance."

Melinda pointed to the wall on the other side of her desk. "We think alike, Mr. Zimmerman. I have already printed the first bulletin and will be posting it later in the day."

"Excellent." He gave a firm nod. "I knew you would be the perfect choice for this position, Miss Colson." He glanced toward the main parlor. "As time permits, you should circulate among the guests. It will give you an opportunity to encourage participation."

"Indeed, I will do exactly that, Mr. Zimmerman. I appreciate your support and your ideas. I'm sure it's going to be an exceptional season."

"Let us hope so, Miss Colson. And let us hope the remainder of the guests register at their appointed times rather than send me more of these letters." He tucked the envelopes into his jacket pocket. "I do believe there are already enough ladies present that you could host the first tea tomorrow afternoon."

Melinda inwardly cringed. She had hoped to wait until Monday. That was what she and Chef Bickerstaff had already planned. "My first tea is scheduled for Monday, but I am going to see if some of the guests would enjoy a game of charades out on the lawn tomorrow, weather permitting."

"Excellent! Just keep them content." He turned and marched away, his shoulders at a rigid posture that would have pleased a military officer.

After another full hour of scheduling events and checking supplies, Melinda took Mr. Zimmerman's suggestion to heart. Closing her ledgers and tucking them into the desk, she strolled into the main parlor, surprised at the number of guests mingling in the room. A small group of women gathered at one end of the room were visiting while their children played on the lawn outdoors under the careful supervision of nurses or nannies. Several young people had joined together, and from Melinda's quick observation, it appeared the girls were vying for the attention of the young men in the circle.

Perhaps she should suggest a game of croquet. As she started toward the group, she felt a hand on her shoulder. Startled, she whirled around. "Lawrence! I couldn't imagine who—" She fell silent when she noticed her brother's companion, unable to do any more than nod in recognition.

"It is a genuine pleasure to see you, Miss Colson. Your brother has been entertaining me this afternoon. He promised I would have the opportunity to see you today. I'm pleased to see he is a man who keeps his word."

Melinda cleared her throat. "Mr. Powers. I didn't realize you were going to be at Bridal Veil." Her thoughts raced back to her initial meeting with Preston Powers at the milliner's shop in Savannah. He had given her a bit of information about the hurricane damage at Bridal Veil and mentioned relatives who owned a cottage on the island. She glanced toward the group of women. "Have you arrived at Bridal Veil with your relatives?"

His eyes sparkled with delight. "You have an excellent memory, Melinda. Yes, I'm with the Radcliffes—my Chicago family members who are wintering at their cottage here on the island."

He was obviously enjoying the opportunity to surprise her. She didn't know what bothered her more: the fact that Preston Powers had decided to visit Bridal Veil or the fact that he was in the company of her brother. He'd been clear that he had never before visited the island, so why had he decided to visit this season? She looked at her brother. Had Lawrence encouraged him to come? He had enjoyed far too many late evenings sitting at the gaming tables during the delay in Savannah.

"I believe you told me you'd never before visited Bridal Veil, Mr. Powers. Why the sudden interest? You don't seem the type who would give in to the cajoling of relatives."

He tilted his head back and laughed. "You are right on that account. However, both Rupert and Vonita are delighted I joined them." He stepped closer and leaned toward her ear. "I decided this was the perfect time for a visit for several reasons. One, of course, was because I knew I'd have the pleasure of seeing you again. The other is because I'm extremely interested in the new racetrack. I've brought two of my horses to the island and hope that I'll make a great deal of money while I'm here."

"I'm pleased to hear that you've come for some reason other than to see me, for the staff members of Bridal Veil are not permitted to socialize with the guests. Isn't that right, Lawrence?"

Her brother shrugged. "I believe the staff members have been told to respect the wishes of the guests. So when Preston requested my company here at the clubhouse, I felt obligated to honor his request."

She narrowed her eyes and glared at Lawrence. Evan had been

correct—her brother needed immediate correction or he was going to slip back into his old habits. She could feel the heat rise in her cheeks. From all appearances, Lawrence somehow planned to use these wealthy guests to his advantage, and such foolishness could damage his future—and her own.

CHAPTER 22

By the second week of January, activity had increased, and many of the Bridal Veil cottages and clubhouse suites had been filled. Each day brought new challenges and a variety of events, most of them planned or coordinated by Melinda. Mr. Zimmerman hadn't failed to point out that Melinda's position had been his idea. And when the guests continued to lavish their praise upon him for the new and resourceful activities, he accepted each compliment as if he'd personally planned every event.

At first, Mr. Zimmerman's behavior surprised Melinda, but she soon learned that the guests preferred speaking to a supervisor rather than to those individuals actually performing the tasks. She decided it mattered little, for if Mr. Zimmerman remained pleased, then her position would be secure for the rest of the season. He'd already increased her salary and had promised more in the coming weeks as well as a new apartment. To her, the additional pay was of greater importance than flattering words.

The influx of guests during the last two weeks had afforded her little time with Evan. However, she hoped to see him that afternoon. Other than when he'd returned from Savannah, Melinda had seen him only one brief time. During Evan's trip to meet with the golf course specialist, Harland had moved to his brother's home outside Savannah. Not only had the older man's return to the mainland placed more responsibility on Evan's shoulders, but the loss also left a huge void in his life. During their last visit together, Evan had spoken of nothing but Harland's departure and how much he missed the older man's guidance. She hoped that today they would have time to discuss some of their own plans for the future.

Although the investors had placed full responsibility on Evan's shoulders, they hadn't yet given him the title of supervisor—or the pay increase. At least not so far as she knew. The board members had met at the clubhouse at the end of last week, and she hoped Evan's promotion had been a part of their agenda. Surely they could see that Evan had the ability and determination to succeed. She held out hope that they had deemed him worthy of both the title and the pay. The very thought sent unexpected shivers of excitement racing up and down her arms. She glanced at the clock above her desk. Only two more hours and she'd be on her way.

She turned at the sound of footfalls outside her door. Preston Powers stood framed in the doorway of her office. "Ah, here's the lovely lady I've been hoping to see." He grinned down at her and then turned enough for her to capture a glimpse of Lawrence. He'd obviously accompanied Mr. Powers into the clubhouse again.

Nowadays, she saw more of her brother than she did Evan. Lawrence managed to slip away from his duties quite easily, and although she'd spoken to him at length regarding visits to the clubhouse, her warnings had gone unheeded. Time and again, Lawrence appeared in the clubhouse with Preston. And she'd heard from some of the other workers that her brother frequented many of the other facilities that were considered off limits to the staff. Of course, Lawrence made certain Mr. Powers remained nearby to defend his presence. On one occasion, Mr. Zimmerman had stopped Lawrence and questioned his right to enter one of the clubrooms where the men gathered for cigars and after-dinner drinks, but after Mr. Powers had spoken briefly with the supervisor, Lawrence had been permitted entry. Since then, she'd not seen Mr. Zimmerman question her brother's presence.

Lawrence's attitude worried her. After years of separation, she had hoped that her brother had matured and accepted the fact that they no longer possessed elite stature. Instead, Melinda feared he'd become intent upon gaining entrance to the inner social circle in any way possible. She feared his cavalier behavior would lead him down a path to destruction. And why was Mr. Powers so eager for her brother's companionship? She'd questioned her brother at length, but his lips were sealed as tight as a jar of Emma's peach preserves.

Melinda peeked around Mr. Powers. "Good afternoon, Lawrence. I thought you would be working at the racetrack today."

"I've already been there. Everything is under control." He gave her an exaggerated wink. "The sign of a good boss is being able to teach others and then let them do their work."

Melinda couldn't believe his cocky response. She dug the tips of her fingers into her palms and tried to remain calm. "I didn't realize you were in charge of the racetrack. I thought Evan was supervising that project. The last I'd heard, you work for him." She arched her brows. "Or have you received a promotion?"

Lawrence chuckled. "Evan is busy with the golf course, and I believe he knows I'm capable of handling any details at the racetrack."

When Mr. Powers cleared his throat, Melinda looked in his direction. "I'm sorry, Mr. Powers. Is there something with which you need assistance?" She picked up her pen. "Do you wish to register for one of our activities?"

"I was hoping that you could give me a private tour of the

island this afternoon. My relatives tell me some of the scenery on the other side of the island is quite beautiful." He leaned forward and glanced at her ledger. "Why don't you put my name beside the empty space at three o'clock, and I'll return."

Melinda tapped her pen on the ledger. They didn't give private tours of the island. All tours were for groups of eight to ten people, and there were no tours scheduled for that day.

"I'm sorry, but we don't offer private tours. There is a group tour scheduled for tomorrow morning if you'd like to register." She did her best to maintain a friendly tone. Mr. Powers remained as determined as she'd observed in Savannah, but since arriving at Bridal Veil, he'd developed an increasingly arrogant manner. A characteristic she disliked. "Shall I write your name down?"

He bent down a bit closer. "No. I'm not interested in sharing you with a group of other guests. How much does a private tour cost?"

She glanced at Lawrence. Why didn't he help her? "Be assured that *if* we offered private tours, I would place your name on my ledger, Mr. Powers."

He stood and straightened his shoulders. "Since you have nothing listed at three o'clock, perhaps I should ask your supervisor about the possibility of such an arrangement."

She wanted to kick Preston in the shin, but she forced a smile. "I won't be here at three o'clock, Mr. Powers. That is why there isn't anything posted. It is my afternoon off work."

Melinda jumped when he clapped his hands together with a loud crack. "Perfect! We can make this tour our own little social outing. I'll call for you at three."

The man knew no limits! "I'm sorry, but I have a prior engagement. You may recall that when we met in Savannah, I was returning to Bridal Veil to make certain the man I love hadn't been injured in the hurricane."

"Yes, I do recall." He nodded his head. "Evan is the fellow that acts as Lawrence's supervisor. However, your brother told me you haven't wed, and I don't see an engagement ring on your finger. Any man who is willing to keep you waiting is a fool." He shrugged and gave a dismissive wave. "I realize what a prize you are, but it seems Evan isn't worried about losing you." He chuckled and beamed a roguish smile. "Evan must not be a very smart fellow. If I were your beau, I'd be very worried about another man stealing your heart."

She could feel the heat rise beneath her collar and climb to her cheeks. She didn't know whether to be flattered, embarrassed, or offended by his bold remarks. Given her position, it mattered little how she felt—she had to be kind to the guests. "I will pass along your words of caution, Mr. Powers."

She turned a hard gaze on her brother. "However, I've discovered that there are some men who don't heed warnings—regardless of how frequently they're given."

Lawrence didn't acknowledge her remark, and Mr. Powers continued to rest against the doorjamb with a smug look on his face. "You may as well know that I don't give up easily, Miss Colson. Eventually I'll convince you to grant me the honor of your company."

Melinda pushed up from her desk. Obviously Mr. Powers considered her response a challenge rather than a refusal. "If you will excuse me, Mr. Powers, I need to go over some ideas with members of the staff before I depart." She waited until Mr. Powers stepped from the doorway before she exited her office. Stepping close to her brother's side, she nudged his arm. "I hope that you're not shirking your duties, Lawrence. You could carve out a good future here if you'd try."

"That is exactly what I'm doing, Melinda. My approach may be different from yours, but I have the same goal as Evan and

247

you—to succeed." Lawrence stepped around her and walked into the parlor with Mr. Powers.

She wasn't certain what her brother meant about his approach, but the comment nagged at her long after their conversation ended.

As she returned to her room, Melinda's heartbeat increased with every step. She could hardly contain herself. Once she changed her dress and arranged her hair, she would be off to spend the remainder of the afternoon and early evening with Evan. Although she'd offered to make plans for their time together, Evan had insisted upon making the arrangements. "You spend all of your time planning activities for others; let me arrange for our outing," he'd said. His offer had touched her. Over the past years, she'd become unaccustomed to others caring for her. She smiled, enjoying the luxury of going off to enjoy her own special event with Evan.

A buggy was waiting outdoors, and the young driver saluted her with great decorum. "Mr. Evan said I was to deliver you to the hunting lodge, Miss Melinda."

Her thoughts whirled as the young fellow helped her into the buggy. She had guessed they would go to Biscayne, but if Evan was meeting her at the lodge, perhaps he'd thought of another plan. Then again, maybe he was having her come to the lodge to keep her in suspense. If so, his idea was working quite well. Maybe if she engaged the young driver in conversation, she'd learn something about their final destination.

"We're having lovely weather, don't you think?"

The boy's forehead scrunched as though he needed to give the question deep thought before responding. "Yes, ma'am, it has been nice." His lips tightened into a thin line, and he kept his gaze fixed on the path.

So much for conversation! Might as well come straight to the point. "Is Evan waiting for me at the lodge?"

The boy shrugged his shoulders. "I wouldn't know. He gave me my instructions yesterday morning, and I haven't seen him since. Fact is, I had to go and help with yard work at the cottages this morning. I took the buggy with me so I wouldn't be late to pick you up at your quarters."

"I see. Well, I appreciate your promptness, and I'll be certain to tell Evan you arrived on time and that you've been most courteous."

The boy grinned. "Thank you, ma'am." They made the remainder of their short journey in silence. Once they arrived at the lodge, the young man jumped down, circled the buggy, and assisted Melinda down. "I guess you can go inside. Unless you want to wait on the porch."

Melinda slipped the boy a coin and smiled at his delighted chortle. To offer him a little of the joy she'd been experiencing all day pleased her. The sounds of chatter and laughter drifted from inside the lodge, a reminder that one of the families staying in the clubhouse had scheduled riding lessons for that afternoon. She narrowed her eyes, trying to recall the family's name. Polter—yes, that was it, the Polter family. This was their first time at Bridal Veil, and Mr. Polter was a business associate and close friend of Victor Morley. The Polters had mentioned they'd named their daughter Victoria in honor of their deep friendship with Victor Morley. Melinda wondered if the racetrack had been the primary reason Mr. Polter decided to bring his family to the island this year, for he'd asked several questions about race schedules.

Before they'd even checked into their rooms, the Polters' son and daughter had expressed interest in riding lessons. Melinda had expected Mrs. Polter to discourage her daughter, a striking young woman who appeared to be eighteen or nineteen years of age. Instead, both parents had been quite supportive, and Melinda had registered them and made the arrangements. As with all guests who signed up for riding lessons, the Polters had been advised their lesson would begin at the hunting lodge. Last season Garrison had decided he preferred to limit the number of people entering the barn. Nowadays the instructor greeted guests at the lodge and escorted them to the barn, where horses would be waiting for them in the small corral near the barn.

Melinda's eyes widened and she came to an abrupt halt just inside the door. Evan glanced over his shoulder. When he caught sight of her, his laughter ceased. "Melinda!" He scooted between Victoria Polter and her father and then hurried to Melinda's side. "Didn't you receive my note this morning?"

Her gaze traveled from the tip of his riding boots to the knot in the bright kerchief tied around his neck. He certainly wasn't dressed for dinner in Biscayne, and she wasn't dressed for riding. Melinda shook her head. "The only message I received was from the young man who said you'd sent him to transport me here." A small lump formed in her throat.

Evan glanced toward the Polter family. "Would you excuse me? This won't take long, and then we can begin your lessons."

The lump in Melinda's throat increased to boulder-sized proportions as Evan grasped her elbow and led her to the front porch. Once outdoors, she turned to face him. "Exactly what is going on?" She forced her words around the mountainous bulge in her throat. Tears threatened when she looked into his eyes.

"I promise I'll make it up to you, Melinda. I wrote a message and asked Garrison to see that it was delivered. I completely forgot that I'd told Paul to take the buggy and bring you over here."

"That much appears obvious, but I don't understand." Her voice trembled and she bit her quivering lip.

"Mr. Morley insisted that I personally take Victoria and John for their riding lessons. I tried to change his mind. I even gave him suggestions, but he said Mr. Polter insisted I be the one to take his children."

"That makes no sense. How would he know anything about you?" She brushed her clammy hands down the front of her skirt. "You've been busy over at the golf course."

Evan looked toward the main room of the lodge and then directed her down the porch steps. "I'd rather the Polters didn't overhear our conversation." When they were a short distance from the porch, he took her hand. "Mr. Morley brought the entire family over to see where we're laying out the golf course. During the conversation, Victoria mentioned she had signed up for riding lessons."

Melinda arched her brows. *"Victoria?"*

"Miss Polter." He shrugged. "She insisted I call her Victoria. She says *Miss Polter* is too formal."

"Really? She didn't seem to mind when *I* addressed her as Miss Polter. So while she was at the golf course, she asked that you take her riding?"

"Sort of. Well, not exactly." Evan sighed. "Mr. Morley was telling them about my different tasks. He mentioned that the investors depended on me for everything from keeping the game well stocked to giving riding lessons to overseeing construction of the racetrack—something like that. I don't recall his exact words." Seeming to sense her displeasure, he squeezed her hand. "Anyway, as the conversation continued, Miss Polter said she'd like me to give her and her brother their riding lessons." He inhaled a deep breath. "I agreed without asking when the lesson had been scheduled."

Melinda's heart squeezed. She wanted to be understanding; she knew their jobs must come first. But try as she may, she couldn't set aside her disappointment. "Why didn't you explain that it was your afternoon off and you had plans that couldn't be changed?"

"I did, and I thought the matter had been settled. But later in the day, Mr. Morley came to see me. It seems Miss Polter insisted that I be the one to take her riding. Mr. Morley wants to make them happy. He's hoping Mr. Polter will invest in the island, and they are longtime friends. How could I refuse?"

A tear rolled down her cheek. The guests came first—all of the staff learned that lesson the minute they secured employment on Bridal Veil. Still, it didn't seem fair. With all the extra hours Evan had worked during the past months, Mr. Morley shouldn't have asked for even more.

She removed a handkerchief from her pocket and wiped her cheek. "I suppose you'd better go back and take care of the guests. I'll see if Paul is still at the barn and ask him to drive me back to the clubhouse."

"I'm truly sorry." Evan leaned down and brushed a kiss on her cheek. "Thank you for being understanding, Melinda. Mr. Morley promised me an extra afternoon off next week."

"We had best wait and see if he keeps his promise before we make any plans." Head bowed, she turned and trudged toward the barn, her joy and excitement nothing more than a memory now.

Minutes later, she spotted Paul in the corral. At least she could be thankful he hadn't yet departed. Hastening her step, she waved and called his name. He exited the corral and trotted toward her. "Something wrong, ma'am?"

"My plans have changed, and I need a ride back to the clubhouse. Have you unhitched the buggy?"

"No." He pointed to the barn. "It's around the side over there. If I get you settled in the buggy, would you mind waiting until I finish putting out feed for a couple of the animals in the barn?"

She shook her head. "That would be fine, but you go ahead

with your chores. I don't need help getting into the buggy." In truth, it didn't matter how long it took for the young man to complete his chores. She could wait until morning, if necessary, since she no longer had anything to do. As if to protest such a thought, her stomach rumbled a reminder that she hadn't eaten since that morning. She'd worked through her lunch so that she could have the extra time with Evan. That had proven to be a mistake.

Then again, if she'd arrived an hour later, he'd be gone for Victoria's riding lesson, and Melinda would have had no idea what happened. Why hadn't Garrison given the note to his wife? Emma could have delivered it to her. She would ask Emma when she returned.

Melinda was still deep in thought when Paul returned to the buggy. He tipped his hat and gave her a sheepish grin. "Sorry to keep you waiting. Took longer than I thought."

"That's quite all right, Paul. I'm in no great hurry."

He flicked the reins and the horse stepped forward. Moments later, Paul pulled on the left rein and the horse began to round the edge of the barn. At the sound of Evan's boisterous laughter, Melinda glanced toward the barn. Inside the doorway, Victoria stood gazing at Evan, her blond curls coiffed to perfection beneath her veiled riding hat. She clung to his arm and leaned even closer when she caught sight of Melinda in the buggy. Victoria appeared to be delighted with her catch. And by the smile on Evan's face, he looked as if he enjoyed being caught!

Melinda clenched her jaw as she struggled to maintain her composure. How could he?

CHAPTER 23

While Evan rode toward the golf course, he attempted to focus upon the work that needed to be completed that day. But instead of creating a mental picture of where to assign his workers, he recalled all that had gone wrong with Melinda during the past week. He'd done his best to convince her that Victoria Polter's riding lessons were no more than a job—the same as his work at the golf course or tracking different species of game available for the hunters. Unfortunately, he'd failed to sway her. After Victoria had personally visited Melinda's office to schedule more riding lessons, Evan's explanations had fallen upon deaf ears, even though he'd told her Mr. Morley had given him no choice. The investor's instructions had been clear: Accommodate Victoria's requests for riding lessons. And Victoria's requests had been abundant.

With each new appointment, Evan received a crisp note from Melinda that said nothing more than the date and the time, along with the words *Riding lesson for Victoria*—never Miss Polter—always Victoria. The pointed use of Miss Polter's first name hadn't escaped him. And though he would never tell Melinda, Miss Polter presented a number of challenges. After their first lesson, her young brother had been scheduled for a different time and with a different instructor—all at Victoria's request. Another fact that wouldn't have escaped Melinda's notice, for Melinda scheduled the lessons.

Evan guided the horse onward, his attention drawn to a patch of wild flowers in hues of scarlet and purple. For a moment he considered stopping to pick some for Melinda but soon changed his mind. By day's end they would be wilted. Besides, he had no idea when he'd see her. How he wished he could schedule time with Melinda rather than Victoria.

With each lesson Victoria acted more familiar, and he became more uncomfortable. So much so that Evan asked some of the younger lads to remain close by when Victoria was present in the barn or corral. Of course, once the two of them were out on a trail or riding along the beach, he had little choice if she asked to stop and rest. During those times, he did his best to keep his horse between them, though he'd not always been successful.

To make matters worse, Mr. Morley had never allotted Evan additional time off. His promotion had not been forthcoming, yet his duties and work hours continued to multiply—and so did his frustration. Still, he had no recourse. If he was going to wed Melinda, he needed that promotion, and he couldn't refuse assigned duties or offer objections. Though he had hoped Melinda would understand, their brief encounters over the past week or two revealed she'd lost patience. He understood her frustration, for he experienced the same disappointment. Yet his concern had heightened when he'd seen Preston Powers standing close to Melinda while she directed a group of children in a croquet game on the lawn of the clubhouse.

Evan's time with her had been relegated to Sunday morning church services and a brief visit afterward. Although Sunday was a day of rest for most, it was not so for the workers of Bridal Veil—at least not during the season. Meals and planned activities were still expected to commence on Sunday afternoons and evenings. For Evan, it meant work at the golf greens. The special event planned for mid-March required completion of the course. Although Mr. Morley had finally secured a monthly bonus for Evan, if he didn't succeed, the possibility of securing Harland's old position and a permanent increase in wages would diminish. Mr. Morley hadn't specifically said those words, but the investor was keeping a close eye on the project—and on Evan.

After issuing instructions to the workers, Evan mounted his horse and rode back toward the lodge for yet another riding lesson with Victoria. How he wished these interruptions could be avoided.

His thoughts scattered in a thousand directions. There was so much that must be completed over the next several weeks and he prayed the weather would remain favorable. Otherwise, they didn't stand a chance of completing the course. He reined in the horse as he entered the corral and dismounted.

Paul came to the door of the barn. "Miss Polter is waiting inside. She wasn't happy that you weren't already here. I went ahead and saddled her usual horse."

"Thank you, Paul. Everything else going well today?"

The boy shoved his hand into his pants pocket and withdrew a shiny coin. He grinned and held it aloft. "Couldn't be better, Mr. Evan. Look what I got from one of the gentlemen."

Evan congratulated the boy. "Looks like you're pleasing the guests. When they give you a tip, it means you gave them exceptional service, Paul." He patted him on the shoulder.

"I didn't do much of anything for him, but he was happy with what I told him."

Confused, Evan stopped and looked at the boy. "What is it that you told him?"

Paul hiked a shoulder. "He said he saw a man out riding a beautiful horse. He described Mr. Lawrence's horse and said he came over to the barn to see it." Paul took hold of the horse's reins and walked him toward Evan. "I told him we didn't keep that horse at our barn."

"What else did he ask?" The fact that someone had come to the barn asking about Lawrence's horse heightened Evan's attentiveness. He hadn't truly understood Lawrence's reasoning for stabling the horse away from the barn.

"Wanted to know the horse's name and where we keep him stabled."

Evan's heart thumped like a beating drum, yet he couldn't understand his strange reaction. Lawrence had papers on the horse and said everything was in order. There was no reason for concern. Still, he'd said he didn't want anyone around the horse.

"What did you tell him, Paul?"

"The truth. I don't know where Mr. Lawrence keeps the horse. I said the horse's name was Priceless Journey. When I told him the horse's name, he looked kind of disappointed and left. Did I do wrong, Mr. Evan? Should I give him his money back?"

"No, Paul. You keep the money—you did fine."

Evan strode toward the lodge. He'd take Victoria for her riding lesson, but he doubted his thoughts would be on anything other than Lawrence and Priceless Journey. Victoria hurried over to him the moment he stepped into the lodge.

"There you are, you naughty boy." She tightened her lips into a moue and tapped his chest with her index finger. "I don't like it when I'm kept waiting. Especially by you." She stepped closer, leaving a mere inch between them. When Evan took a backward step, she moved forward. "I've missed you, Evan, and when you're late for our time together, it causes me to believe you don't care about me." She formed her lips into another pout. "I'm sure you wouldn't want me to speak with Mr. Morley, would you?"

Evan stared down at the young woman. How he wished to tell her he detested being controlled by the whims of a spoiled young woman—but he knew such a comment would result in unwanted repercussions. "I do have other duties that need my attention, Miss Polter."

She leaned in and rested her palms against his chest. *"Victoria,"* she whispered. Before he could move, she raised up on her toes and kissed him full on the mouth. "Perhaps that will help you remember my name."

She nearly fell when Evan abruptly backed away from her. Evan glanced toward the door, feeling the heat rise in his cheeks. What if Melinda had been nearby and observed the scene? She would never forgive him. "I am your riding instructor. Nothing more and nothing less. Please don't do that again."

Victoria giggled. "Your lips say no, but I believe your heart will soon say yes, Evan."

❖❖

"Melinda!"

At the sound of the familiar voice, Melinda spun on her heel and came face-to-face with Mrs. Mifflin. She clasped a hand to her bodice. "Mrs. Mifflin. H-h-how good to see you." She did her best to sound pleased but feared her voice had betrayed her.

Mrs. Mifflin gave her a feeble smile. "You need not fib to me, Melinda. I imagine you feel quite the opposite." Her former mistress stared at her open hand, still resting on the bodice of her shirtwaist. "I don't see a ring on your finger. I do hope your fellow—Evan wasn't it? I do hope he wasn't injured in the hurricane."

She tried to reply, but her lips wouldn't move.

"I don't blame you for being angry with me. I was unduly harsh when you departed. I owe you an apology." She cleared her throat. "Cyrus will be the first to tell you that I don't apologize often, but when I do, it comes from the heart."

The room momentarily swirled and she wondered if she might faint. Today's schedule had been hectic. She'd arranged and overseen a surprise birthday party for a set of ten-year-old twins that had included lunch, outdoor games, and birthday cake. Following that exhausting event, she'd hurried indoors to make certain supplies and easels had been set up for the ladies enrolled in painting classes. Each class was followed by a sumptuous tea, which also required Melinda's oversight. She couldn't be sure if the ladies enjoyed the painting classes, but all of them delighted in the extravagant array of tea and pastries offered after the sessions. In all of the rush, she'd failed to eat lunch. And then she'd been surprised by Mrs. Mifflin and her uncharacteristic apology. No wonder she felt light-headed.

Melinda snatched one of the activity sheets from a nearby table and fanned herself. "I'm sorry. I'm feeling a little faint. I failed to take time for lunch today." She couldn't decide if Mrs. Mifflin's wrinkled forehead was due to concern or irritation.

The older woman grasped Melinda's elbow and propelled her toward a couch in the small parlor. "Do sit down before you fall down." The moment she was seated, Mrs. Mifflin motioned to a maid passing through the outer foyer. "Bring me a glass of water and a sandwich." Before the girl could respond, Mrs. Mifflin waved her off. "And be quick about it." Removing her gloves, she settled on the divan beside Melinda. "Now tell me about Evan and your marriage—or lack thereof."

"I'm not married, but Evan is fine. He wasn't injured in the hurricane."

Mrs. Mifflin dropped her gloves onto her lap. "Then why aren't you married? I thought that was the plan when you made your hasty departure."

"Evan thinks it's better if we wait until—"

"When Cyrus received word that you were being considered for this position, I was certain that the young man had backed out on his proposal. I don't want to say I told you so, but I did tell you that young men who work in these places are not the marrying kind. They'll tell a girl most anything in order to—"

"Mrs. Mifflin! Evan is not like that at all." The moment she'd uttered the words of defense, a picture of Victoria and Evan came to mind and taunted her.

The older woman's lips drooped into a frown. "Then explain why there isn't a wedding ring on your finger."

With thoughts of Victoria dancing in her head, Melinda's explanation sounded hollow, and Mrs. Mifflin didn't fail to read between the lines.

"Forgive me, Melinda, but you don't look or sound like a young woman planning for marriage in a month or two."

"That's because Evan hasn't received his promotion, and we have no idea when or if that will happen. The circumstances are difficult. He's dependent upon the investors to make the decision." The thought of Victoria clutching Evan's arm flashed to mind, and Melinda leaned against the back of the couch.

Mrs. Mifflin picked up her gloves and flapped them in front of Melinda's face like two limp fans. "You've become pale again. Please don't faint. You know I'm not good at dealing with illness." She glanced over her shoulder. "Where is that maid with the water and sandwich?" As if on cue, the girl rounded the corner carrying a tray. Mrs. Mifflin heaved a sigh. "Good heavens, it's about time you got here. A person could die of thirst."

The girl gave a tiny curtsy as she placed the tray on the nearby table. Her eyes shone with fear when she glanced at Melinda. "Thank you, Molly." The maid leaned down to pour water into the glass. "We can take care of the water." Melinda smiled, hoping to set the girl at ease. Melinda turned to Mrs. Mifflin as Molly scurried off. "It's her first week. She's trying very hard."

"Well, if anyone understands the difficulty of locating good help, it's me." The older woman poured water into one of the stemmed water goblets and handed it to Melinda. "Do take a drink and then eat." With a stern look, she motioned toward the sandwich. "I insist."

Melinda let the cool water slide down her throat. She should be reviewing tomorrow's events with Chef Bickerstaff, but Mrs. Mifflin would cause a scene if she attempted to excuse herself. Besides, she didn't think her legs would hold her if she attempted to stand up.

She lifted the silver dome from atop the sandwich. "I'm going to feel rude eating in front of you."

Mrs. Mifflin picked up the linen napkin, snapped it open, and settled it across Melinda's lap. "I hope you don't expect me to feed you." She picked up the plate and placed it on the napkin. "I'll talk while you eat."

Melinda wasn't certain she liked that idea. No telling what Mrs. Mifflin had on her mind. She'd best deflect her. Otherwise, the older woman would use the time to further berate Evan and her. She picked up a piece of the sandwich and held it between her fingers. "How is Sally? I've had only one letter from her since I left, although I've written her several times."

Mrs. Mifflin straightened as though she'd been poked with a hatpin. "Sally?" The question had obviously disturbed her train of thought. "Oh, she's doing fine. She's far too busy reading everyone else's mail to take time to write her own letters. And of course she's still busy passing gossip from one servant to the next. I never could trust Sally to keep a confidence. Unfortunately, I still can't." She frowned as she uttered the comment. She pointed at the sandwich. "Keep eating."

Melinda dutifully took a bite of the sandwich. She hoped Mr. Zimmerman didn't choose to walk through the front portion of the clubhouse any time soon. The sight of his leisure activities manager sitting in the parlor nibbling a sandwich and sipping water wouldn't set well with the supervisor.

"While you're eating, I want to make you a proposition. Please don't answer right away. I want you to take time and think before you respond. Will you do that?"

Melinda bobbed her head and pointed to her mouth. Why did the woman instruct her to eat and then ask questions?

"Ever since you left Cleveland, I have been struggling with one lady's maid after another. Heaven knows I've done everything possible to be kind and to give them opportunity to learn, but it has proved impossible." She pointed to her head. "If you could see my hair beneath this hat, you would be appalled by the mess. I can't find one maid who can fashion my hair. I end up with some hideous style, or the minute I walk out of the room, the pins are falling and so is my coiffure."

She closed her eyes and shook her head. "I need you to return, Melinda. I will double your wages. You would be paid more than any other lady's maid in all of Cleveland. And I promise that in addition to Sundays off, I'd permit you two, no three, additional days a month off work." She bowed her head and stared at her hands. "And I promise I'll do my best to treat you with much greater kindness. I truly want you to return, and I hope that you'll consider my offer."

Melinda gulped hard to force down the piece of sandwich now lodged in her throat. Had it not been for the pain in her throat, she would have believed she was in the midst of a strange dream. She picked up the plate and moved it back onto the tray before wiping the corners of her mouth with the napkin. "Thank you very much for your kind offer, Mrs. Mifflin, but—"

She held up her hand. "You promised you wouldn't give an immediate answer. I want you to take several days to think about my proposal." She patted Melinda's hand. "You should thoroughly consider not only what I've offered but your future here at Bridal Veil. I don't want to be negative, but it does seem that your young suitor isn't as intent upon marriage as you are."

The words scorched her heart like a hot branding iron. Thankfully, Mrs. Mifflin didn't want to hear any further defense of Evan's position, for Melinda had already begun to wonder about Evan's commitment to her. Did his delay hinge upon the offer of Harland's old position or upon his hope for time to win Victoria?

CHAPTER 24

February 1899

Evan strode toward the barn, surprised to see several of the guests gathered nearby. All of them were men who'd become regulars at the racetrack—either because their horses were competing in the races or because they enjoyed gambling. They were circled together and appeared to be deep in discussion, though the fact that they'd chosen to talk near the corral rather than go into the lodge surprised Evan. But long ago he'd learned not to intrude on private conversations, so he bowed his head, skirted the edge of the path, and continued toward the barn.

"Evan! Come over here!"

He turned to see Mr. Jacoby, one of the guests and an owner of a racehorse, waving him toward the group. As Evan took long determined steps in their direction, the short rotund man with a ruddy complexion continued to motion him forward with frantic gestures.

"How can I help, Mr. Jacoby?"

The man shifted from foot to foot, his protruding belly swaying with each movement. "We have some questions about the horse stabled in that structure over near the chicken coops. Mr. Zimmerman tells me the horse belongs to Lawrence Colson. He also tells me that Lawrence works for you."

Evan frowned. "I think Mr. Zimmerman may have been confused. Garrison O'Sullivan is Lawrence's supervisor. I was in charge of some of the work at the racetrack when it was being constructed, and Lawrence helped a great deal with that project. However, Mr. O'Sullivan is actually his supervisor." Thoughts of his earlier conversation with the young stableboy came to mind. Evan had intended to meet with Lawrence, but he hadn't had time to seek him out, and their paths hadn't crossed. "Is there some sort of problem regarding the horse?"

Mr. Jacoby rested his arm on the wood fencing. "I took a ride over there earlier today, and that horse looks a lot like Fulton Overbrook's horse, Midnight Flight."

The man looked at Evan as though his comment should evoke some response, but Evan didn't know Mr. Overbrook or his horse. "I suppose you could speak to Lawrence. I don't have any information about the previous owner." Evan didn't want to mention that Lawrence had won the animal in a game of cards.

"Mr. Overbrook lives in Cleveland." Mr. Jacoby inhaled as though he couldn't get enough air. "I live in Cleveland, as well."

This entire conversation was making no sense. Evan couldn't be rude, yet he didn't have sufficient time for idle chatter. "I'm certain Cleveland is a fine city." As he uttered the response, realization struck. "Lawrence Colson has lived in Cleveland, so you two should have a little in common. I understand he's sometimes in the clubhouse with Preston Powers. You might be able to find him there of an evening."

The men nodded and someone muttered, "I'm not sure they

spend as much time in the clubhouse as they do *entertaining* in the Radcliffes' guesthouse."

Several of the men snickered, and another said, "They host private card games, and I understand the stakes get quite high."

Mr. Jacoby arched his bushy brows and waved the men to silence. "Here's the thing, Evan. The racehorse, Midnight Flight, was stolen from Mr. Overbrook back in October. I don't want to make false accusations, but the horse that Lawrence supposedly owns bears a strong resemblance to the stolen horse." He cleared his throat. "And the fact that Mr. Colson lived in Cleveland raises my suspicion. When did you say he came to Bridal Veil?"

Evan clenched his hands. He was being baited, and he didn't like it. If these men truly believed what they said, they should confront Lawrence, not him. In spite of the afternoon warmth, the idea that the horse might be stolen caused a chilling effect to sweep over Evan. Melinda would be devastated if the accusations proved to be true. Although she acknowledged her brother to be a bit of a rogue, Lawrence was her only living relative, and she loved him. "I didn't say when he arrived, Mr. Jacoby. However, it sounds as though you have a good idea where to find Lawrence. I suggest you speak to him if you have concerns."

Mr. Jacoby's complexion deepened to the shade of a beet. "One of the maids who cleans our rooms tells me that Miss Colson, the activities manager, is related to Lawrence. A sister, I believe she said." He reached into his pocket and withdrew a pipe. "The maid also mentioned that you and Miss Colson have plans to marry." He tamped tobacco into the bowl of the pipe, and then looked at Evan. "That being the case, I'm thinking you might be willing to protect Mr. Colson."

Every muscle in Evan's body tightened. A flash of pain shot from his clenched jaw to the top of his head. This man was accusing him of being involved in a crime. And not just any crime, but horse thievery. He knew the rules of courtesy required he remain civil, yet everything within him wanted to punch Mr. Jacoby's bulbous nose.

He inhaled a calming breath and forced himself to speak in a normal tone. "I believe there are any number of people who can assure you that I am not a horse thief, and I would not knowingly protect anyone who had stolen a horse. However, let me again suggest that if you have questions, you direct them to Mr. Colson. My information on the subject is truly limited."

"I have every intention of doing so, Evan. And I do hope he has some answers that will prove me wrong." Mr. Jacoby lit a match, held it to the pipe tobacco, and puffed. "Otherwise, I may have to come back and visit further with you."

Evan's anger mounted as the other men nodded and murmured their agreement. He had known some of these men since he'd first arrived at Bridal Veil. How could they possibly believe he would be involved in stealing a horse? Blood pumped through his veins like a raging river.

Evan shook his head in disgust. "If there are no further accusations you wish to make, I have work that needs my attention, gentlemen." No doubt one of the men would report his cutting remark to Mr. Zimmerman, but at the moment he didn't care.

A few of the men appeared shocked, but Evan didn't apologize. Instead, he strode toward the hunting lodge. Once he completed Victoria's lesson, he would make time to seek out Lawrence. He only hoped he could speak to him before Mr. Jacoby and his group returned to the clubhouse and began to hurl accusations.

After closing the distance between the barn and lodge at a breakneck pace, Evan took the porch steps two at a time, flung open the door, and let it slam behind him. He did his best to fight against an inward groan when he caught sight of Victoria. His riding student sat perched on the edge of the sofa and jumped to her feet as soon as he crossed the threshold.

She hurried toward him, her lips in a pout. "You're late again, Evan." She shook her finger like an annoyed mother reprimanding a young child.

After the heated exchange with the men over at the barn, Victoria's behavior set his teeth on edge. Rather than performing his primary duties, it seemed his every action had to delight the Bridal Veil visitors. How could he oversee daily operations at the racetrack, continue progress on the golf course, and make certain enough game was available for the hunters, plus complete all of his previous duties? The thought made his head hurt, and Victoria's reprimand caused his pain to reach new heights.

She grasped his arm and gazed at him. "You're a very bad boy, Evan. I've been waiting for nearly half an hour. I thought we'd come to an understanding the last time you were late." She lifted her free hand and traced her finger across his lips. Evan tipped his head away from her touch. "You're going to make me think that I'm not important to you." Pushing her lips into another exaggerated pout, she leaned against him. "I truly don't want to tell Mr. Morley you're not giving me the attention I deserve." Still clutching his arm, she leaned close.

Evan couldn't possibly say what he was thinking. He'd be fired if he told Victoria what she truly deserved. He nodded toward the barn. "I was delayed by other guests at the barn. If they're still out there, I suggest you voice your disapproval to them." He forced a weak smile. "Whether I have an appointment with you or not, I can't ignore other guests when they approach me. If it makes you feel any better, I would have been a few minutes early had I not been detained at the barn."

Her pout diminished and she gave a slight nod. "It does make me feel better. I'm pleased to know you were eager to spend time with me."

He attempted to pull loose from her grip. How had she come to that conclusion from what he'd said? Victoria could twist a string of words into a knot faster than anyone he'd ever met.

He looked down at her hands on his sleeve. "If you don't release my arm, I'm not going to be able to change clothes and take you for your riding lesson."

"You don't need to change clothes. I won't mind getting a little dirt on my dress—as long as it comes from you."

He took a sidestep and put a little distance between them. He should have stayed outside with the men; it would have been safer. He glanced at his arm and then at her. "Either way, you're going to have to let go of me."

She grinned and nodded as she loosened her hold, but the moment he turned toward the door, she tucked her hand into the crook of his arm and held on with a death grip.

So much for his momentary freedom.

Instead of taking one of the longer trails, Evan suggested they have a brief lesson and then ride over to the clubhouse. "I have some business to see to over there, and I can return your horse when I ride back to the lodge."

Victoria responded with a shriek of delight that caused him to think he'd made a horrible mistake. "Oh, that will be great fun! I do hope there will be lots of people out on the lawn to see me riding with you."

Her words singed him like a hot flame. He longed to abandon the suggestion, but Victoria would obviously object. What had he been thinking? He prayed that if Melinda was present, she'd give him an opportunity to explain.

During Victoria's lesson and afterwards as they rode toward the clubhouse, he silently condemned his foolishness. Granted, he needed to speak with Lawrence, but riding to the clubhouse with Victoria was pure folly. The moment they were in sight of guests playing bocce on the front lawn, she began to wave her riding crop overhead.

Evan gritted his teeth while wishing he could vanish into thin air. "Hold the reins properly, Victoria. You don't have correct form when you're waving your arm. And the horse doesn't understand why you're bouncing about, either."

Any number of guests ceased their activities and turned to stare at them. Although Victoria's horse appeared unperturbed by her frantic movements, Evan was greatly troubled. No doubt Melinda would receive a full report of this event. He cringed at the thought and knew he must find her and explain before he returned to the lodge.

They dismounted at the side of the clubhouse and Evan tied the horses. Rather than go inside immediately, Victoria waited for him and clung to his arm as they walked inside, he in his dirty work clothes, she in her perfect riding skirt and matching jacket.

"Please excuse me, Victoria, but I have business that requires my attention. I'll see you for your next lesson." He had to yank in order to free himself from her clutches.

Once again, her lip protruded into a larger-than-life pout. "I wish you would play a game of croquet with me."

"I am not one of the guests, Victoria. I think there are any number of young men who would enjoy your company out on the lawn." He backed away. "Now, if you'll excuse me."

Not wanting Victoria to follow, Evan continued to walk backward toward Melinda's office. Victoria motioned, but he ignored her and backed into Mr. Zimmerman with a thud.

Victoria giggled as she lifted a hand to her lips. "I tried to warn you."

Mr. Zimmerman brushed his suit with the palm of his hand. "Do watch where you're going, Evan. What if you'd backed into one of the maids carrying a tea tray? Think what a mess we would have had in the middle of the foyer."

"I'm terribly sorry, Mr. Zimmerman. It won't happen again."

Evan glanced toward Melinda's office, and the supervisor shook his head. "This is her afternoon off work, and she's gone out with Mr. Powers, I believe." He tugged on his thin mustache. "I don't approve of the staff mingling with guests, but Mr. Powers can be quite insistent. The man positively badgered me until I agreed. . . . After all, we must keep the guests happy."

So Melinda was keeping company with Preston Powers, and the talk among the maids was correct. Evan felt as though he'd received a fist to his midsection. The silence stretched between the two men until Mr. Zimmerman finally arched his brows. "Was there some other matter you wished to discuss?"

"Lawrence—Melinda's brother," he stammered. "Do you know where I might find him?"

Mr. Zimmerman tipped his head. "Lawrence works for Garrison O'Sullivan, doesn't he? Why would I know his whereabouts?"

"I'm told he spends a great deal of time around the clubhouse, and I thought he might be here."

"If you haven't been to the racetrack, you might see if he's there. I heard several gentlemen say they were going over there to speak with him."

Evan sighed. "Was one of those men Mr. Jacoby?"

Mr. Zimmerman nodded. "Yes, and he didn't appear any too happy." One of the guests approached to speak with Mr. Zimmerman. Bidding the supervisor good-bye, Evan hurried out the side door. He spotted Paul across the way and motioned to him.

The boy came trotting toward him with a smile on his face. "Afternoon, Mr. Evan."

"Good afternoon, Paul." He glanced around. "Why are you over here at the clubhouse?"

"Mr. Zimmerman sent word to bring one of the guest's horses over here." He shifted his weight to his other foot. "I'm heading back to the barn right now. I just stopped to say hello to my cousin, Marie. She works cleaning in the clubhouse." He curled his bottom lip inward and bowed his head. "I know I should have gone straight back. I hope I'm not in trouble."

Evan chuckled and ruffled the boy's hair. "You're not in trouble. In fact, I have an extra horse over here. I'd like you to ride him back."

"That'll let me make up for any lost time." He pointed to his shoes. "And save me some shoe leather, too."

With a grin, Evan directed the boy to the horse Victoria had ridden to the clubhouse and then mounted his own. He reined the horse to the road leading to the racetrack, but when he'd gone about halfway, he met Mr. Jacoby and his friends on their return.

Mr. Jacoby stopped in the road and nodded toward the racing complex. "I went looking for Colson, but he's nowhere to be seen. If you see him, tell him I'd like to have a word with him."

"I'll do that." Evan continued onward, hoping Jacoby would think he had other business at the track. In truth, things had run smoothly after the first few races and, except for any repair problems with the structures, little had been required of Evan. Once the construction had been completed, the operations had fallen under Garrison's supervision, and it seemed that the older man had hired dependable help.

Soon he'd traveled far enough that it would be closer to circle around the racing facility and take one of the bridle paths back to the hunting lodge. He tightened his knees and the horse broke into a gallop. Once they neared the track, Evan pulled back on the reins and the mare slowed to a trot. The late afternoon sun danced across the grandstands, the rays casting long shadows onto the track. A lone rider was circling the track. Evan shaded his eyes, but he was already certain of both the rider and the horse.

He approached the edge of the track, removed his hat, and waved it overhead. Lawrence raced the horse to the final turn and then reined him to a halt. "Evan! Didn't expect to see you out here."

"I came looking for you. We need to talk."

Lawrence leaned forward and patted his horse's neck. "I wanted to exercise my horse. Can it wait?"

"Afraid not." Evan didn't miss the look of aggravation that pinched Lawrence's features. "Did you happen to see Mr. Jacoby and a group of other men out here a short time ago?" When Lawrence shook his head, Evan continued. "That's strange because I passed them on the road between here and the clubhouse only a short time ago. They'd been here and said they couldn't find you."

Lawrence shrugged. "Maybe they didn't look in the right place. I hadn't even made a lap around the course when you stopped me. What's the problem?"

"The problem is your horse." Evan explained what Mr. Jacoby reported. "He wants a closer look at Priceless Journey. If you can't prove ownership, I'd say there will be more questions than you may be able to answer." Only the nickering of Evan's horse broke the silence between the two men. "Is there anything you'd like to tell me?"

Lawrence leaned back in his saddle and met Evan's gaze. "Let me introduce you to Midnight Flight."

CHAPTER 25

If she'd had roller skates attached to her feet, Melinda could not have turned any more quickly. "Did I hear you correctly?" The blood pounded hot in her veins, and she wondered if one of her blood vessels might explode and kill her in the middle of her tiny office.

Lawrence assumed a casual pose in her doorway and radiated a genial smile. "No need to work yourself into a frenzy, sister. I wouldn't have told you, but when I talked to Evan yesterday, he insisted I do so." He stepped forward and pulled out her chair. "Maybe you should sit down before you faint."

His relaxed countenance sent her anger soaring to new heights. "I do not feel faint, Lawrence!"

His mouth gaped open and he feigned a pained expression. "You don't need to raise your voice. Surely you believe me."

When he'd first arrived at her office, Melinda had listened quietly as her brother explained that several guests had been questioning his ownership of the horse he'd brought from Cleveland. But as his story continued and he revealed he'd changed the horse's name, she became wary. Melinda didn't want to believe her brother had stolen another man's horse, but the story took a deeper twist when he finally admitted the ownership papers were missing.

"It matters little whether I believe you or not. If you don't find those papers, you'll be arrested for horse stealing. And I'll likely be charged as an accomplice." Merely saying the words caused her stomach to lurch.

Lawrence chuckled. "You're being a bit dramatic, Melinda. They aren't going to haul you off to jail."

"How can you laugh? We left Cleveland together. After the fuss I made to the ticket agent about paying the transport fees for that horse, I'm sure he'll remember me. And he'll be happy to tell those wealthy guests when they question him."

"I don't recall your being so melodramatic in your younger years." He raked his fingers through his hair and dropped into the chair opposite her desk. "You're making me sorry I told you."

She walked around the desk and sat down. "When and where did you last see the ownership papers you were given on Priceless Journey—I mean Midnight Flight?"

"They were in my valise when I boarded the train. I had no reason to look for them before now. I didn't steal that horse, Melinda. I can explain the entire mishap. I think."

"You think?" She lunged forward and leaned across her desk.

He leaned back in his chair and motioned for her to do the same. "There's a little portion that has left me confused. Otherwise, I can explain."

She sat back. "Then please do. You have my undivided attention."

"I won the horse fair and square, and Fulton Overbrook signed the papers over to me. Problem is, he didn't want his wife to know he'd lost the horse in a game of cards. I gave my word I wouldn't race the horse, and I'd do my best to keep it out of sight until he could figure out how to explain to her."

Her brother stared at her as if she should be satisfied. Melinda gestured for him to continue. "And?"

"And that's it. I don't know how things got in the newspaper about the horse being stolen. I've never heard from Fulton since he gave me the horse."

Melinda pointed a finger at her brother. "You need to go back to your quarters and look until you find those papers, Lawrence. Otherwise, you and I are both going to be in more trouble than I want to think about." Her head pounded as though she'd been hit with a sledgehammer. "How long did Mr. Jacoby give you to produce the papers?"

Lawrence shrugged. "Look at your book and see when he's leaving. I figure I have at least until his departure date."

She couldn't believe his nonchalant attitude. "What makes you think you have until they depart? What if they decide to ride the launch over to Biscayne and wire the authorities in Cleveland? Have you thought of that possibility?"

"I suppose I'll have to think of some way to stall them. I'm usually good at that sort of thing, so you need not worry." He pushed up from his chair. "I shouldn't have told you any of this. If I hadn't been concerned one of the men or their wives would mention the whole affair, I wouldn't have said a word."

"Perhaps you should write a letter to Mr. Overbrook and explain the situation. He could send you a new bill of sale for the horse, couldn't he?"

Her brother nodded. "I could, but I don't know Mr. Overbrook very well. If he discovers I've lost the bill of sale, he may use that information against me. He's a gambler and he may see this as a chance to regain the horse." He frowned. "Do you understand?"

"Yes, Lawrence, I'm afraid I do. Please, just go find those papers." She closed her eyes and listened to his departing footsteps.

How could Lawrence and Evan, the two men she loved, create such uncertainty in her life?

❖

Lawrence had departed a half hour earlier, yet Melinda's head continued to throb. She closed her eyes and massaged her temples but startled at the sound of a knock.

"There you are!" Her former employer stood outside Melinda's office doorway, peering into the room.

Melinda glanced up and forced a smile. "This is where I am every day, Mrs. Mifflin. Have you had difficulty finding me?"

"Indeed, I have. When I stop by, they tell me you're off organizing parties or managing receptions."

"I'm sorry to have missed you. How can I help?" From the glint in the older woman's eyes, Melinda had a good idea Mrs. Mifflin had come to discuss her employment offer.

The older woman pulled the straight-backed chair from the wall, sat down, and scooted forward until she blocked any possible route of escape. "I thought it was time we had another little chat." A hairpin dropped from Mrs. Mifflin's coiffure and landed on her lap. She picked it up and held it between her thumb and forefinger. "As you can see, I am in desperate need of your help. I do hope you've given my offer further consideration and are prepared to tell me you'll return to Cleveland." Melinda opened her mouth to reply, but was stopped short when Mrs. Mifflin handed her the hairpin. "Would you?"

Melinda stood and tucked a curl into place before securing it with the pin. The entire coiffure needed to be refashioned, but Melinda didn't mention that. Her own head ached and she longed for a few minutes of rest, but Mrs. Mifflin had settled in and wasn't going to permit Melinda any such luxury.

"Thank you, my dear. My curls feel much more secure."

She patted the side of her head and smiled. "I do miss our time together, Melinda. I could always trust you to keep my confidences. I no longer have anyone I can trust." She clasped Melinda's hand. "You probably read in the papers that Ida McKinley's brother was murdered shortly after you left Cleveland."

Melinda gasped at the shocking news. "Murdered? No, I'd not heard. I'm sorry to hear such sad and dreadful news. I'm sure it has been a very difficult time for Mrs. McKinley."

"And for me!" Mrs. Mifflin dropped Melinda's hand and reached for a handkerchief.

"You knew Mrs. McKinley's brother?"

"Yes, I know the entire family. I know I told you that before she visited last year."

Melinda didn't recall hearing any such thing, but to say so would serve no purpose.

"The death was a horrible tragedy. Murder!" Mrs. Mifflin shook her head. "Of course, the scandal that followed was horrid. And there I was without help—you'd deserted me only a short time before, and I had to travel to the funeral." She clasped a hand to her chest. "I shudder to think how I suffered. I had to deal with that simpleton maid who couldn't pick out a proper gown or lace my corset correctly." She leaned closer. "To make matters worse, the minute we returned home, she repeated every word she'd heard about George being murdered by one of his former . . . lady friends."

The conversation was becoming more and more confusing. "Lady friends?"

"Yes. George Saxton, Ida's brother, was single and lived in Canton with his sister Mary Barber and her family. He had been keeping company with a widow, Eva Althouse, and was on his way home when his former lady friend, Anna George, shot him." Mrs. Mifflin *tsk-tsk*ed and shook her head. "I cannot believe you

279

didn't read any of this in the paper. Don't people down here keep abreast of what is going on in the country?"

Melinda flinched as though she'd been slapped. "You may recall that there was a flood and much devastation here in the South during that time, Mrs. Mifflin. We didn't have time to worry about anything other than cleaning up after the destruction."

Melinda's response had been somewhat sharper than she'd intended. Mrs. Mifflin leaned back in her chair and crimped her features into a look of disapproval. "Well, yes, I suppose you did have your problems down here, as well. However, the whole affair was staggering for both Ida and me."

Melinda wasn't surprised that Mrs. Mifflin had immediately returned to the topic of her own suffering. In her time away from Mrs. Mifflin, Melinda hadn't forgotten the matron's selfish attitude. "I'm sorry you were forced to endure such difficulty. I do hope Mrs. McKinley's health hasn't deteriorated any further."

Mrs. Mifflin's features relaxed. She glanced over her shoulder and folded her hands in a tight knot. "I don't know if you've heard, but the president and Mrs. McKinley will be visiting Bridal Veil next month."

The shocking revelation left Melinda speechless. When she finally gathered her wits, she looked at her calendar and then back at Mrs. Mifflin. "Ex-ex-exactly when is this supposed to occur?"

"This is not a supposition, Melinda; it is a fact. Both the president and Ida are going to visit Jekyl Island on the twenty-second of March, and then they'll come to Bridal Veil for a visit. Ida said she couldn't bear to be so close and not see me."

"You're absolutely positive? I haven't been told anything about a presidential visit, Mrs. Mifflin." Her stomach lurched at the thought. She'd be expected to host a gala that would surpass anything on Jekyl Island. The throbbing in her head now heightened to a stabbing pain.

Mrs. Mifflin glared. "Didn't I just say it was a fact? You need not ask the same question over and over, Melinda." She sighed. "Now then, we need to discuss matters of importance."

Had the woman lost her mind? What could be more important than a presidential visit in six weeks' time? "Does Mr. Zimmerman know about the presidential visit?"

Mrs. Mifflin's forehead wrinkled into a frown. "Well, of course. Victor Morley knows, so I'm certain he would tell Mr. Zimmerman so that all will be in readiness." She snapped open her fan and waved it back and forth. "Now, what have you decided about your return to Cleveland? Do give me an affirmative answer. Otherwise, I don't want to hear a word."

Melinda remained silent and Mrs. Mifflin stood. "I'm going to convince you before the season ends."

A single hairpin dropped from Mrs. Mifflin's coiffure and pinged on the hardwood floor as she turned and marched across the foyer.

❖

Melinda waved at Mr. Zimmerman as he entered the clubhouse late in the afternoon. She'd been trying to locate him ever since Mrs. Mifflin's departure. When he didn't approach, Melinda jumped up from her chair and hurried toward him.

The moment she reached his side, she grasped his arm. "We need to talk. It's very important."

"During the season, everything is important, Miss Colson. I trust you have the arrangements completed for the banquet being hosted by the Bridal Veil Rowing Club? You remember it's to be held after the competition next Sunday." He tugged on the end of his mustache. "Jekyl has always had the privilege of hosting the event, and we want to outshine them."

"Of course, I remember." She wanted to tell him she'd made

the arrangements long ago. Surely he realized food, décor, plaques, and trophies needed to be ordered far in advance of the event. "It is another event we need to discuss." She leaned close. "The president's visit to Bridal Veil in March."

He arched his back and pinned her with a dark gaze. "How did you hear that information?"

"From a guest. One who trusted me to keep her confidence. I am speaking to you because she said you'd already been informed of the anticipated visit."

Mr. Zimmerman grasped Melinda's elbow and propelled her toward his office. He pushed the door closed behind them, apparently concerned about privacy rather than propriety during this conversation.

"The information you received is correct. Sometime in March, the newspapers will be notified that the president intends to visit Biscayne. I don't know what other information will be given to the public regarding the president's schedule, but it will not come from employees of this resort." A ray of sunlight glistened on Mr. Zimmerman's black hair as he stepped across the room and settled at his desk. "We can't control what guests tell one another, or even what they tell the resort employees. However, any employee repeating this information will be discharged. We have promised secrecy. It is up to the president or his advisors to determine whether they will publicize the visit. Is that clear, Miss Colson?"

"Yes. I had no intention of repeating—"

"I'm sure you didn't, but I like everything clarified."

Never before had Mr. Zimmerman acted in such an abrupt manner. He obviously feared losing his own position if anything went amiss. "How am I to prepare for such esteemed guests if you don't give me proper notice of their visit?"

Mr. Zimmerman folded his hands atop his desk. "You aren't,

Miss Colson. I will oversee this visit. If and when I need your assistance, I'll let you know."

Melinda bowed her head and backed toward the door as warmth spread up her neck and across her cheeks. If Mr. Zimmerman had intended to embarrass her, he'd succeeded. She walked back to her office, uncertain if she should feel offended or relieved that Mr. Zimmerman would oversee the presidential events. However, one thing remained unchanged: the pounding in her head.

She tried to push aside a feeling of defeat as she stepped inside her office. How silly to feel slighted. The last thing she needed was additional work. Rubbing her temples, her gaze fell upon an envelope bearing only her first name. Her heart fluttered at the sight of Evan's handwriting. She needed something to cheer her today. Somehow he had known. She sat down, slid her letter opener beneath the seal, and withdrew the single sheet of paper.

Dear Melinda,

I'm sorry, but I must cancel our plans for tomorrow due to my workload at the golf course. Please forgive me. Perhaps next Friday?

Love,

Evan

The paper fluttered from her hand and dropped to the desk. How could one day provide so many disastrous events? She sank back in the chair and covered her eyes. She would *not* cry. It would only make her head hurt all the more.

As if to taunt her, a vision of Victoria Polter came to mind. The girl made it a practice to stop at Melinda's office each time she returned from her riding lessons with Evan. She reveled in recounting her time with him. Melinda was certain Victoria exaggerated a bit, but today the memory of a remark by Victoria's lady's maid haunted Melinda. She'd overheard the maid comment to one of the other Polter servants that Evan and Victoria appeared quite enamored with each other.

Her confidence faltered as she stared at Evan's note and considered the servant's gossip. In the past she'd been successful in pushing the thoughts from her mind. After all, such stirrings were prompted by nothing more than childish jealousy—and she didn't want to be considered either childish or jealous. But today her feelings seemed neither childish nor jealous. They seemed far too real and very frightening.

CHAPTER 26

Melinda had had little contact with Evan during the past few weeks other than their time at church on Sunday mornings, and the chasm between them was broadening. She'd held out hope he might remain for a time after services this morning, but before they'd walked out of the church, he began to offer an apology.

"I'm sorry, but—"

Melinda held up her hand. "But you have to return to work. Will that golf course never be completed, Evan?"

His mouth dropped open. "Are you forgetting the blizzard that covered the entire southern coast with snow two weeks ago?"

How could he ask such a question? The unexpected storm had created countless problems for all of them, including a postponement of her taking the new apartment. Because of the snow, Melinda had been required to rearrange dates for previously scheduled events while keeping the Bridal Veil visitors happy. The children had enjoyed the astonishing weather changes, but critical comments from the adult guests abounded until the weather finally turned warm.

"I remember quite well. My work more than doubled," she said.

"And mine came to a halt. With six inches of snow on the ground and cold temperatures, I've only been able to resume work the past two days. And even now, the ground is so wet, it's nearly impossible to accomplish much. How can I make progress when we have one disaster after another on this island? The golf course is important, Melinda. I must have it completed by March twenty-fourth. An important guest is visiting, and if it's not complete . . ." His forehead creased and he lifted his open palms toward heaven. "What am I to do?"

She bit back her comment. Did Evan know the identity of the important guest? A month ago she would have asked him. But with their relationship on unsteady ground, she decided to follow Mr. Zimmerman's warning.

"Do whatever you must, Evan. I've told you that the promotion isn't important to our future. It's the two of us working together that will make us stronger, but you don't agree." He opened his mouth to object, but she shook her head. "I know you promised yourself you would never marry until you could support a wife and children. There's no need to tell me again. Perhaps it's best if we reconsider our future. Although you still manage to have time for *Miss Polter*, you aren't able to fit me into your busy schedule."

"That's unfair, Melinda. You know my time with Victoria is a necessity—one over which I hold no control."

She arched her brows. "Really? I didn't realize that sharing affectionate embraces or kissing was considered a requirement of riding lessons."

His features contorted into a strange mixture of surprise and irritation. "I don't know how you got information about embraces or kisses, but I have no interest in Victoria Polter. She has been very forward and controlling, even threatening to carry tales to Mr. Morley if I don't comply with her every request."

Her frustration mounted at his excuses. "You're a grown man, Evan. I find it difficult to believe you couldn't stop her advances if you truly wanted to. I think we should both take time to evaluate what we want for our future. You need not worry about finding time for me in your busy schedule."

She turned and walked away before he could see the tears forming in her eyes. Keeping to the circular path leading from the church, she raised her parasol and walked toward the clubhouse. Her stomach clenched in a tight knot as she attempted to gain control over her roiling emotions. The impact of her final words to Evan replayed like a haunting melody. Why had she said he need not worry about finding time for her when she wanted nothing more than to spend her time with him? Why had she said they should evaluate their future together when she already knew she wanted to share her future with him?

She kept her gaze fixed on the path. "What does *he* want? That's the real question," she muttered. He hadn't followed after her—he hadn't even called her name. Did he believe his position at Bridal Veil more important than marriage to her? A lump formed in her throat, and she swallowed hard to keep her tears at bay. The clubhouse lawn had filled with guests, and she didn't want anyone reporting her emotional state to Mr. Zimmerman.

In the distance she spotted Lawrence riding off with one of the guests. Two days ago, her brother still hadn't located the bill of sale for Midnight Flight. When Melinda questioned him, he'd adopted a cavalier attitude that had annoyed her. In turn, she'd become snappish, and they'd parted with no resolution.

In her brother's mind, there was no problem. He always adopted the position that by ignoring a problem, it would some-how disappear. Melinda embraced the belief that procrastination intensified difficult dilemmas. Her brother's delay tactics had become increasingly worrisome, and Melinda wanted him to take the matter seriously before the police became involved. But right now her worries over Evan were of greater concern than Lawrence and his irresponsible behavior.

"Here's the lovely lady I was hoping to see." Still lost in thought, Melinda startled and turned to see Preston Powers striding toward her. He chuckled. "I didn't mean to frighten you. I thought you heard me approaching."

"No. My thoughts were elsewhere." From his attire, she guessed he'd spent the morning riding rather than attending church.

"I'd like to believe your thoughts were on me. Is that possible?" His lips curved in a flirting grin.

She frowned and took a backward step. Over the past weeks, Preston had become increasingly familiar with her. At times she enjoyed his company, but his personal comments caused a sense of discomfort and uneasiness. "My thoughts are personal, Mr. Powers, but they were not of you."

He clasped a hand to his chest and pretended he might fall to the ground. "You've wounded me, dear Melinda. How could I have become enamored with a woman who treats me so heartlessly?"

She inwardly cringed at his remark. What if someone heard him? They were drawing near the clubhouse, and visitors were scattered across the area playing croquet, bocce ball, and horseshoes. She considered taking him to task for his bold remarks but knew it would likely encourage him to continue his foolish banter. And one of the guests would certainly overhear.

"I take it you've been riding or on a hunt this morning."

He glanced down at his riding boots. "A hunt, but I went along only for the ride. I don't enjoy shooting at birds or animals, though I might consider taking aim at a few of my enemies."

She stopped midstep and stared at him.

He grasped her elbow and urged her forward. "Don't look so alarmed. I was only joking."

She didn't consider his remark amusing but let it pass. "Did the other men meet with success on the hunt?"

"I believe the animals would count it successful—they managed to remain well hidden." He laughed and followed her into the clubhouse.

Melinda removed the key to her office door and turned toward Preston. He had moved much too close, and she backed against the door. "I have a couple of matters that I must attend to." She hoped he would consider her comment the end of their exchange.

"By all means." He gestured toward the office door. "I'm going back to the cottage and change clothes. I doubt they'd permit me entry to the dining room in my riding clothes. I do hope you'll be here when I return."

She smiled and gave a tiny shrug. "I find it impossible to know where I will be from one minute to the next."

"Then I shall have to come in search of you." He winked before he turned and strode toward the door.

The man was impertinent, but at least he found her interesting enough to seek out. Her heart tugged and the familiar loneliness grabbed hold again. If only Evan would pursue her with half as much fervor.

She withdrew her appointment book from the shelf and ran her finger along the page. Next week was booked for several events, but there were several days that weren't particularly busy. She sighed, grateful for the break in her schedule, for there were always guests who wanted Melinda to arrange a last-minute card party or tea.

"Ah, Miss Colson! I didn't expect you to be in your office, but it pleases me to see your dedication." Mr. Zimmerman stepped into Melinda's office and sat down in the chair opposite her desk. "I have changed my mind."

A lump as hard as last week's bread formed in her stomach. "Changed your mind about what?" The supervisor seldom changed his mind about anything, and when he did, it usually wreaked havoc on the staff.

"About the visit from our special guest." He glanced at the door. "You understand whom we are discussing?"

"Yes." An involuntary tremble assailed her. Had Mr. Zimmerman now decided to drop all of the planning in her lap?

He leaned forward and peered into her eyes. "I have decided that we should hold the costume ball while our special guests are here." His thin mustache quivered as his lips curled into a broad smile. "Isn't that an excellent idea?" His eyes glistened with anticipation as he leaned back and awaited her response.

"No!" The answer burst from her lips with unexpected vehemence. Mr. Zimmerman flinched, and Melinda apologized for her forceful response. "The costume ball is scheduled in April. The guests are aware of the April date. I've already arranged for the musicians. I don't think I'll have enough time to prepare."

Mr. Zimmerman shrugged. "Contact the musicians and change the date or find new ones if they don't wish to accommodate your request. The ball will be held on March twenty-fifth. I'm confident you'll complete the necessary preparations. You have a month. That should be more than sufficient."

"But the other guests—"

"If they create a fuss, tell them we are having two balls, one in March and one in April. You can make the first a costume ball and the second a masquerade. The ladies will be pleased to have an additional party. The gentlemen perhaps not so much, but they won't offer too many objections. They want to keep their wives happy." He swiped his hands together. "That was easily solved."

She folded her hands and squeezed until her fingers turned

numb from the pressure. Mr. Zimmerman would accept no argument. "I'll begin seeing to the arrangements right away."

❦

Melinda hadn't fully recovered from Mr. Zimmerman's unexpected decision when Preston returned. He stood in the doorway and extended his hand toward her. "I've arrived to take you to lunch, Miss Colson." Before she could protest, he stepped closer. "No need to worry. I've already received Mr. Zimmerman's permission to have you join me in the dining room."

How dare he do such a thing? She swallowed the objection lodged in her throat. Her thoughts were drawn to Evan and Victoria, and she wondered if she'd been hasty to judge his behavior. Still, she'd held Mr. Powers at bay, and she certainly hadn't permitted him to embrace or kiss her! Employees were expected to accept any *proper* request from a visitor, but they weren't obliged to tolerate unseemly behavior. Personally, she didn't deem an invitation to lunch with a guest an appropriate duty for an employee, but Mr. Zimmerman had given Preston his consent without gaining her approval. Therefore, she had no choice in the matter.

The guests were accustomed to seeing Melinda mingle at their various events, so none of them appeared surprised to see her walk into the dining room and sit down with Preston. Perhaps it wouldn't be such an uncomfortable situation. Besides, she was hungry and Chef Durand was known for his sumptuous cuisine. While she was reviewing the menu, a shadow fell across the table, and she glanced up.

"My, my. Aren't you two a lovely couple. Enjoying your Sunday afternoon, Miss Colson?" Victoria stood beside the table with her younger brother in tow, while her parents were seated at a nearby table.

Melinda looked up with a steady gaze. "I'm preparing to enjoy my noonday meal, Miss Polter. I hope you will enjoy yours, as well."

"Oh, I've already finished. We're on our way to meet Evan. He was delighted to accept my invitation to go horseback riding this afternoon. I'll be sure to tell him that you and Mr. Powers are enjoying the afternoon together." She lifted her chin and flashed a triumphant smile before she turned and sashayed out of the room.

Melinda clutched her napkin. Her heart plummeted. No matter how Victoria spun her tale, Melinda knew Evan would presume Preston Powers had played some part in her decision to reevaluate their future.

❖❖

Evan sighed as he caught sight of Victoria arriving from afar. He'd done his best to keep the young woman at a distance, but Mr. Morley was intent upon pleasing Mr. Polter. And pleasing Mr. Polter meant keeping Victoria happy, even at the expense of his relationship with Melinda. There seemed no way to maintain any balance in his life, but one thing was certain: This year he would be pleased to see the end of the season arrive. And at the very least, he would have some extra money saved for the future, and with Victoria and the other guests gone, he'd have time to focus all of his attention on Melinda.

"Evan! Over here!" Victoria waved her handkerchief overhead. Several of the workmen turned to look at the young woman and then at Evan.

He wasn't surprised to hear their murmured complaints—and he didn't blame them. They wanted time to enjoy their afternoon, but they had to continue working. "I'll be back as soon as I can," he told one of the men before striding off to meet Victoria.

She rushed toward him and clutched his arm. "I'm so glad you agreed to take me riding. I knew you'd change your mind once you had time to give it a little more thought."

"I can be gone for only an hour." Over and over he'd emphasized the amount of work he needed to complete, but she ignored his comments.

She clung to his arm like a small child. "You know how I told you that I see Preston Powers and Melinda together all the time?"

The hairs on the back of Evan's neck prickled, and his muscles tensed. On several occasions Victoria had mentioned that she'd seen Melinda and Preston keeping company. Initially he'd been jealous and even a little angry, but he knew Melinda was required to spend time with the guests. After all, he had to do the same thing. Still, hearing they were together so soon after Melinda had placed their future in a state of uncertainty gave him pause.

In the past he'd done his best to tamp down his jealous feelings, but when he'd seen Preston with Melinda out on the lawn last week, he'd spoken to Emma. She'd confirmed what Victoria had told him. Mr. Powers appeared to be quite smitten with Melinda. However, Emma had quickly come to Melinda's defense and assured him he need not worry. Now he couldn't help but wonder if Emma had been wrong. Perhaps it wasn't Victoria's attentions toward him, but an attraction to Preston Powers that had caused Melinda's change of heart.

Victoria poked his arm. "Are you listening to me? I just said that Melinda and Preston Powers were having lunch together in the hotel dining room. Isn't that a bit uncommon for a guest and employee to dine together—in the formal dining room, no less?" With a syrup-sweet smile on her lips, she waited for his reply.

But Evan had none.

❦

MARCH 1899

During the following week, Evan did his best to find time to speak privately with Melinda, but to no avail. He had hoped to settle their differences before Preston gained any further advantage. On Thursday he'd gone to the clubhouse while the workmen ate their lunch, but Melinda hadn't been in her office. He'd looked around the grounds but hadn't met with any success. That evening at supper Emma told him Melinda had gone into Biscayne.

"I thought Mr. Zimmerman had taken responsibility for the trips to Biscayne," Evan said as he helped himself to a couple of warm biscuits.

"That he had, but Mr. Zimmerman is changing plans for the ball, and Melinda needed to check on her orders and see if they'd be arrivin' on time." Emma spooned fried potatoes into a bowl and placed it on the table. "Did the two of you have some sort of spat?"

Evan jerked around to look at her. "Why do you say that?"

The older woman shrugged. She pushed the bowl of potatoes toward him. "Mr. Powers went with her to Biscayne, and she seemed pleased to have the company." The older woman nudged his arm. "Melinda's lonely, and Mr. Powers has lots of time. Am I makin' myself clear?"

All thoughts of supper disappeared and so did Evan's appetite. He pushed the food around his plate and attempted to force aside thoughts of Melinda and Preston. How could he compete with a man like Preston Powers when he couldn't even manage an afternoon away from work? Emma's words troubled him like a festering splinter.

"I'm sorry Emma, but I'm just not hungry." Evan shoved his chair away from the table and stood.

The older woman chuckled. "Love will do that to a fella."

Evan didn't acknowledge the remark. Love might do it, but so did anger and frustration. One way or the other, he was going to get off work and talk to Melinda.

In spite of his best efforts, it was Sunday before Evan managed time to be alone with Melinda. As they departed the Sunday morning service, she turned to leave, and Evan reached for her arm. "Where are you going?"

"Back to the clubhouse to go over my schedule. There's a tea this afternoon, and I need to make certain everything is in order." She arched her brows. "Why do you ask?"

"I have a few hours and thought we could spend them together. We need to talk."

She hesitated. "You could walk me over to the clubhouse, and after I go over the arrangements, I could go for a short stroll along the river." She hesitated for a moment. "But this doesn't mean that I've changed my thoughts about evaluating our future."

He did his best to smile. "We can't very well determine our future if we don't spend time together."

She tipped her head to one side. "That's what I've been saying for months, but you haven't seemed to hear me."

He reached for her hand. "Now that we have a little time, let's not argue." He glanced over his shoulder and then leaned a bit closer as they continued to walk. "Did you hear about our visitor?"

She looked up at him. "You know who it is?"

"It was in the newspaper on Friday. Mr. Morley said the president's office released his schedule to the newspapers, and Bridal Veil is listed as one of his stops. That's why the golf course must be completed." Evan shook his head. "If I hadn't heard it from Mr. Morley, I never would have believed it was true. Did you know?"

She gave a slight nod. "Yes, but I wasn't permitted to say anything. Do you think you'll have the golf course ready by the time they arrive?"

"We'll do our best to get nine holes completed, but I'm still not sure it's going to be possible." He fixed his gaze on the walkway. "I don't know what will happen if I fail. The promotion . . ." The words caught in his throat, and he couldn't continue.

"They know how hard you've worked on the golf course, Evan. I don't think they'll withhold your promotion. If they do, then I think God must have something else in store for you."

"I pray that you'll be included in those plans." He stopped and turned to her. "I understand Preston Powers has been enjoying your company while I've been working. You've had lunch and he even escorted you to Biscayne."

She met his gaze. "And I understand that you continue to enjoy Victoria Polter's company during both your working hours and free time."

"That's not the same."

"I believe it is exactly the same." Melinda folded her arms across her waist and jutted her chin. "As I told you the other day, I think we need to take time and evaluate our future. Clearly we see things differently."

CHAPTER 27

The days flew by far too quickly to suit Melinda. The president would be arriving in exactly one week, and the costume ball would take place the following evening. That thought alone caused Melinda to review her checklists for the third time since entering her office this morning.

"Melinda, Melinda!" Emma clutched a bundle of mail against her chest and panted for air. "I need to talk to you." She leaned against the doorframe leading into Melinda's office. "Can I close the door?" Without waiting for a reply, she stepped inside and gave the door a hefty push. The ring of keys attached to her waist jangled against her well-padded hip as she fell into the chair opposite Melinda's desk.

Melinda stared at the head housekeeper. "Whatever is wrong, Emma?" Ever since news of the president's visit had been released two weeks ago, Emma had been fluttering about like an excited schoolgirl. Today, however, she was as white as a ghost, and her pale blue eyes shone with fear.

"You're not gonna believe what I've been hearin' upstairs." A strand of hair fell across her forehead, and she brushed it away. "I was delivering the mail like usual, and when I went in room 220, I heard men arguing next door." She inhaled a deep breath.

"You know I'm not one for listenin' in on the guests, but when I heard them talkin' about the president and his visit, my ears perked up." She leaned forward. "It sounds like there's a plan to kill the president."

"What?" Melinda scooted to the edge of her chair, certain she must have misunderstood. "Tell me exactly what you heard, Emma."

"I didn't hear all of it. They said something like the easiest way would be a huntin' accident or poison. And then one of them said that having the president on the island was a perfect opportunity." Her eyes widened. "You believe me, don't ya? I'm not making this up."

Melinda didn't know what she believed, but she didn't want to discourage Emma. Was it possible someone was planning to assassinate the president? "Tell me what else they said."

Emma's brow furrowed. "Somethin' about the president being imperial and tryin' to take over the world, but that didn't make much sense to me."

"Imperialist? Is that what they said—that the president is an Imperialist?"

She shrugged. "Might be. I was so scared, I was shakin' in me shoes. And they said there's some of us that's willin' to help."

"Employees of Bridal Veil?" Melinda's thoughts raced as she asked the question. The employees had been excited to learn of the president's visit. Why would any of them want the president dead? She'd never heard political talk of any sort among the staff members.

Emma bobbed her head. "I didn't hear no names, but they got some sort of plan. I'm sure of it. They said something about some foreign places I never heard of and how President McKinley wants to take over the world." She frowned. "What do you think we should do?"

Perspiration dampened Melinda's palms. "I want you to keep this to yourself, Emma. We don't know who can be trusted, so don't mention one word of this to another soul. Is that clear?"

"But what—"

Melinda tapped the desk with her index finger. "Don't say anything. I promise that I'll take care of this. In the meantime, go and deliver the rest of the mail. And keep your eyes and ears open. If you see or hear anything else, let me know."

Emma stared at the packet of mail. "You want me to go back up there?"

"If the mail isn't delivered at the usual time, guests will wonder and ask questions. Just act normal." Melinda pushed up from her chair. "Come on, I'll walk to the foot of the stairs with you."

"I'll be doing me best to act normal, but I don't know that I'm much good at hidin' me fears."

"You'll do just fine." Melinda gave her a reassuring smile. Men's voices drifted from the second floor, followed by the dull thud of closing doors. Moments later, Preston Powers strode down the stairs and out the front door. Melinda watched him depart. Was he one of the men involved in those talks? She shivered at the thought. How silly! Preston was a gambler and man-about-town, not a devotee of politics.

Once Emma made her way to the second floor, Melinda returned to her office. As she was placing a sign on the door, she caught sight of another man near the stairway. Was that Mr. Mifflin? She strained sideways but could capture only a glimpse. It looked like him, but he would have no reason to be upstairs. A fleeting thought of the clandestine meeting crossed her mind, but she shook her head. Mr. and Mrs. Mifflin were dear friends of the McKinleys. She must have been mistaken.

Melinda's heart pounded as she weighed what could be done. She needed help, but who could she trust? Certainly not Preston

Powers, and though she disliked the thought, she couldn't completely trust her own brother with such frightening information. Her thoughts whirled. Evan! He was the only one she could trust to keep her confidence and lend the help she would need.

She hurried out the side entrance, praying she could find Evan and explain. Once outside, Melinda spotted Paul standing alongside a brougham. Raising her arm, she waved her handkerchief overhead and ran toward him.

If any of the guests saw her, they'd surely think she'd gone mad. "Is Evan at the golf course?" She gasped for air and clasped a hand to her chest.

"Last I knew. Is something wrong, Miss Melinda?" The young man drew closer.

Melinda motioned toward the carriage. "Could you take me there, or have you come to pick up one of the guests?"

"I just delivered a group over here to the clubhouse and was fixing to return to the barn, but I can take you to the golf course." He smiled and opened the carriage door. "Evan sure is proud that he got nine holes of the course ready in time." Paul extended his hand to help her into the carriage. "Just wait till you see how good it looks. Mr. Morley was mighty happy when he saw it, too. Sounds like he's hoping to impress the president."

Melinda was pleased to hear Mr. Morley had been impressed. Perhaps now he'd push the directors to give Evan his promotion. The buggy rolled past clumps of purple hyacinths and occasional groupings of bright yellow daffodils peeking through the tall grasses. The flowers exhibited their beauty and resilience now that the snow had disappeared and warmer temperatures had taken hold. If the landscape wasn't in peak condition by the time the president arrived, it wouldn't be from lack of effort. The employees had all been working long hours preparing for the visit.

Melinda rested her head against the black leather seat and

closed her eyes. Silently she prayed that nothing would happen to the president during his visit to the island.

When they arrived at the golf course a short time later, Paul brought the carriage to a halt and called to Evan. "Got someone in the carriage who wants to speak to you!"

Paul jumped down and opened the door. "Maybe once he sees who I've brought, he'll get over here." The young man cupped his hands around his mouth. "Look who's here, Evan!" He pointed toward Melinda and grinned. "If you don't need me anymore, I'll get the carriage back to the barn. I reckon Garrison's wondering where I am."

"You go ahead, Paul. Thank you very much," Melinda said.

She didn't miss the look of disbelief in Evan's eyes as he trotted toward her. She knew her arrival at the golf course would take him by surprise. "It looks wonderful, Evan."

He turned his gaze to the rolling green sod that had been shipped to the island and laid a week ago. "Thank you." His eyes sparkled with pleasure.

She gestured at the expanse. "I'm amazed at all you've accomplished. You have every right to be very proud."

"I can't take all the credit. The men worked long hours to get everything ready." He grinned like a young boy showing off a prized possession before he turned more serious. "I didn't expect to see you out here. Is there a problem?"

She gave a slight nod. "I know I've told you we need to evaluate our relationship, but there is something amiss at the clubhouse, and you're the only one I believe I can trust to help me."

The hint of a smile tugged the corners of his mouth. "It pleases me to know that I've maintained your trust, even if you're still holding onto your heart."

Pushing aside all restraint, she reached for his hand. "Walk with me and I'll tell you what I've heard." While they strolled along the perimeter of the golf course, Melinda recounted Emma's tale and even included the fact that she'd seen Preston coming downstairs afterward. "I doubt he's any part of this, but it sounds like there are men who consider the president an imperialist and plan to assassinate him because of his policies."

She squeezed his hand. "What are we going to do, Evan? I'm afraid to speak to any of the other employees or managers. I can't begin to imagine who might be involved." Her eyes opened wide and she gasped. "What if they decide to try and kill the president during a hunt? You could be hurt." The thought caused her heart to constrict.

He stopped and turned to face her. "First of all, we shouldn't jump to conclusions. These stories circulate occasionally when the president is traveling. The newspapers report stories about possible attempts from time to time, but they've come to nothing. And the president generally has security guards who travel with him. I don't want you to worry."

"I think this is more than idle talk. I'm worried, Evan. What if we do nothing and the president is killed? I couldn't live with myself. And I doubt Mrs. McKinley would ever recover from such a shock."

Evan nodded. "You're right. Let me see what I can find out. In the meantime, if you or Emma should hear anything else, send word." Using his finger, he tipped Melinda's chin and looked into her eyes. "And promise me you'll stay away from Preston."

❖❖

Thanks to Preston Powers, Lawrence's time on Bridal Veil hadn't been as difficult as he'd expected. Preston had introduced him to many of the gentlemen visitors and included him in some of the card games, where Lawrence had met with some success. Unfortunately, once he won at cards, he used his winnings to bet on the horses. His luck on those wagers hadn't been as triumphant, but because of the many contacts he'd made, Lawrence counted his time on Bridal Veil a success. He'd been careful not to make enemies by winning extreme amounts from any of the men. Maintaining influential contacts was the primary asset of a gambler, a lesson Lawrence had learned long ago. "Win but don't be greedy"—that was his motto, and it had served him well.

Once the racetrack was completed, Garrison's expectations hadn't been overtiring. As long as everything operated smoothly at the racetrack, Lawrence could come and go without a problem. And giving the young lads who worked with him a little of his winnings from time to time gained him loyalty among them. Their loyalty permitted him even more time away from the horses and racetrack, and it didn't cost him much.

He lifted his booted foot into the stirrup of a chestnut mare and waved to the young man mucking a stall. "I'm going over to look after my horse. If anyone comes looking for me, tell him I'll return after lunch." The boy waved in return and continued with his work as Lawrence tugged the left rein and guided the horse toward the path. More than once, Lawrence had considered assigning one of the stable boys the care of Midnight Flight, but in the end, he decided it best to care for the horse himself.

Though he still hadn't located the bill of sale, Lawrence no longer feared the arrival of authorities. Mr. Jacoby had been the instigator, and he and his wife had departed for a tour of Europe a few weeks ago. Once Lawrence learned of Jacoby's departure, he erased the matter from his thoughts. He only wished Melinda would do the same. Each time he saw her, she nagged him about the bill of sale, and he'd begun to wonder if she, too, believed he'd stolen the horse.

He dismounted the chestnut mare and tied her outside the stone building. "There you are, my beauty," he said as he quietly approached the horse. No one could deny the magnificence and speed of Midnight Flight, but he was a well-bred, high-strung racehorse that required a steady hand. "You're happier away from those other horses, aren't you?" The horse nickered as if to agree.

Lawrence lifted the leather reins and bridle from a hook and patted the horse's smooth coat as he moved forward. He continued talking to the horse as he removed the halter and dropped the reins around the animal's neck. After wrapping his arm under Midnight Flight's head, Lawrence stroked the horse's nose. Using his free hand, he lifted the bridle into place. "Good boy."

The horse shifted as Lawrence backed from the stall and stepped to the doorway. Certain he'd heard the sound of an approaching horse, Lawrence squinted against the sun and trained his focus on the path. A moment later he caught sight of a large bay rounding the bend in the road, and his shoulders tensed. He sighed and relaxed once he recognized the rider as Preston Powers. He waved in return and stepped back into the enclosure.

He'd finished cinching Midnight Flight's saddle when Preston strode inside. "One of the boys over at the stables told me I'd find you here."

Preston didn't particularly enjoy riding horses, so either he had something important to tell Lawrence or he'd been unable to find anything better to occupy his time this morning.

"I need to take Midnight Flight for his exercise. Care to join me?"

Preston shook his head. "No, but we do need to have a little chat." He grinned and leaned against the stone wall. "I have an offer you can't refuse. One that involves a bit of mayhem and murder."

Lawrence chuckled. "Must be one fine card game that you've arranged. Just tell me when and where."

"No card game this time." Preston's eyes turned dark, and he pushed away from the wall and drew near. "I'm talking about an actual murder, and I'm enlisting your capable assistance."

The hairs on Lawrence's neck prickled, and he shook his head. "This is some sort of joke, isn't it? You're not a murderer, Preston. What game are you playing?"

Preston grabbed his arm in a tight hold. "Listen to me! This isn't a joke, and it isn't a game. Some of us who are members of the American Anti-Imperialist League are acutely aware that the president must be stopped before he continues to annex more countries. His visit to Bridal Veil has presented us with the perfect opportunity to stop him—permanently."

Lawrence gaped at Preston. He knew him to be a man who enjoyed good liquor, gambling, and women—not a man who would have an interest in killing the president. The man had never uttered one word about President McKinley or annexation. "If you're serious, and it appears that you are, please know that I'll be no part of your plan. I have no grudge against the president. Even if I did, I would never consider murder." His brows drew together into a deep frown. "I can't believe you would consider it, either, Preston. I hope you'll give this idea more consideration." He now was watching Preston's hands, fearful the man might have a gun or knife concealed beneath his riding jacket.

Preston's lips curved in a cunning smile. "Oh, but you'll do whatever I tell you, my *friend*. Who do you think has the bill of sale for that horse?"

"I do. Fulton Overbrook signed the horse over to me. I had the bill of sale in—"

"In your traveling valise?" Preston licked his lips. "I know, because that's exactly where I found it."

Lawrence's thoughts raced back in time as he attempted to piece together what was happening. "But how? When?"

"You're really not very bright, Lawrence. All I needed to do was gain your entry to a few card games, and you thought we were best friends. Your trust was so easily acquired." He snickered. "Once I learned how you'd won Midnight Flight, it was easy enough to locate the bill of sale lodged beneath the leather lining of your traveling bag. You and the horse fit into our plans quite well."

"But I won't—"

"Of course you will. Fulton Overbrook is politically aligned with us. He's already been contacted. He'll do whatever we ask of him. And if going to jail for horse stealing isn't enough to convince you, there's always your sister. I'm sure you wouldn't want any harm coming to her, now would you?"

At the mention of Melinda, Lawrence's fear was replaced by a burst of anger. He grabbed the front of Preston's jacket and pulled him close. "Don't even think about hurting my sister. You're not fit to say her name." With a shove, he released his hold on Preston.

"My, my, you do have a nasty temper, Lawrence. You need to learn to control your emotions." Preston shrugged his jacket back into place. "What happens to you *and* your sister is entirely up to you."

Defeat settled across his shoulders like a heavy weight. "I won't kill anyone."

Preston's lips curved in a victorious smile as he explained Lawrence's part in the plan. When he finished, Lawrence nodded. He wouldn't be required to commit the murder. At least that's what Preston promised.

CHAPTER 28

Evan gave himself two full days to consider what Melinda had told him. He'd prayed and asked God for guidance but hadn't received any clear answer. He could wait a little longer and pray a little more, but he didn't want to wait too long. Melinda would think he didn't believe her—or that she couldn't trust him to help with her problems. He didn't want that to happen. A wife needed to be able to trust her husband—and he prayed that when this was all over, she'd agree to become his wife.

He slipped his arms into his lightweight jacket, walked to the barn, and saddled one of the riding horses.

"Where ya headed off to this bright and shiny mornin'?" Garrison asked as he tromped into the barn with his usual early morning frown.

"Over to the clubhouse for a talk with Mr. Zimmerman."

Garrison tucked a piece of straw in the corner of his mouth. "I'm thinkin' you should be stopping for a talk with Mr. Morley. Now that ya finished the golf course, he needs to push them directors to give you that promotion. And a big raise, ta boot."

Evan nodded. "We'll see. I didn't get the full eighteen holes done, but Mr. Morley said the directors were pleased and planned to take a vote at their meeting. They realize it was the blizzard and not me that caused the delay."

"Them men and their meetin's. Just another way to make a man wait, if ya ask me." Garrison looked around the barn. "Where's them lads that's supposed to be mucking out the stalls? Can't depend on anyone but meself."

Evan pulled out his pocket watch and chuckled. "They're not due down here for another fifteen minutes."

"Oh, go on with ya. Always checking the time for everything. I look at the sun, and the sun tells me it's time they should be here."

Evan mounted his horse. "I'll see you later this morning, Garrison. And don't give those lads a hard time. I'm telling you they're not late."

Garrison mumbled and plodded off toward one of the stalls as Evan rode off. He hadn't made an appointment with Mr. Zimmerman, but he hoped that by going to the clubhouse first thing in the morning, he could speak to him before he began his regular routine. Mr. Zimmerman could be as cantankerous as Garrison when it came to interruptions in his schedule.

"I hope I'm doing the right thing, Lord. If Harland was around, I'd get his advice, but I don't feel like there's anyone else I can look to. I'm not complaining, but I'm not feeling any yes or no from you about whether to talk to Mr. Zimmerman." Evan had come to rely on these talks with the Lord after Harland left Bridal Veil. In the past, he'd been accustomed to Harland steering him in the right direction, but there wasn't time to write a letter and wait for the older man's advice. Besides, Harland would probably think he'd lost his mind if he wrote a letter about folks planning to assassinate the president.

A refreshing breeze drifted from the river as he approached the clubhouse. If Melinda was in her office, he'd stop and talk to her before going to see Mr. Zimmerman. He hadn't heard anything more from her, but it would be best to make certain before he spoke to the manager. And he wanted to assure himself she'd been staying away from Preston.

He tied his horse and ran up the steps of the side entrance. Everywhere he looked, servants were busy dusting and polishing. No doubt, Mr. Zimmerman and his staff hoped to impress President and Mrs. McKinley. Evan wondered how many more times they would dust and polish those same spots before the president finally arrived.

He nodded to several maids as he passed through the foyer and looked into Melinda's office. "She's gone to meet with the gardener over at the greenhouse." Evan turned to see Emma walking toward him. "What with so many of the flowers ruined during the blizzard, we're dependin' on what's in the greenhouse for the arrangements during the president's visit. Melinda has lots of ideas to make everything perfect."

"You're right about Melinda. She does have a way of making life wonderful." And now that the season was drawing to an end, he planned to prove to her that marrying him would make both of their lives wonderful. Hope welled in Evan's chest as he motioned toward Mr. Zimmerman's door. "Is he in his office?"

Emma bobbed her head. "Last I knew he was in there." She wrinkled her nose. "I'll give ya fair warning. He's been in a bad mood these past weeks. Not that he's ever what I'd call a happy man, but he's been like a bear with a sore nose since we begun gettin' things ready for the president."

Evan raked his fingers through his hair and laughed. "That's a bear with a sore tail, Emma."

She shrugged. "Nose. Tail. Don't matter much. He's been like a bear—and I'm knowin' that for sure." She chuckled and nudged Evan with her elbow. "And don't you be tellin' him what I said."

"No need to worry about that, Emma." He patted her shoulder. "I better get in there before the bear comes out of his cave."

Emma giggled and waved her feather duster toward Mr. Zimmerman's office. "Go on with ya, now. If Melinda returns, I'll tell her you're in visitin' with the bear."

As he strode toward the office door, Evan silently prayed for God's guidance. He didn't want to add to Mr. Zimmerman's demanding duties, but the president would be attending several functions in the hotel where the hustle and bustle of the crowd would provide a good diversion for anyone seeking to harm him. Evan hesitated for a moment before he knocked. Should he speak to Mr. Mifflin? After all, President and Mrs. McKinley would be staying with them. Would a possible assassin prefer a crowd or a more peaceful setting such as a private cottage? He'd contemplated the idea but still didn't have any answer.

"Ya goin' to knock on that door or just stand there all day?" Emma tapped him with the end of her feather duster as she walked by.

Evan rapped on the door and waited for what seemed an eternity. He'd raised his hand to knock a second time when Mr. Zimmerman yanked open the door. His brows dipped low and he sighed. "What is it, Evan?"

"If you could spare a few minutes, I need to speak with you about something important." Mr. Zimmerman continued to block the doorway while his dark eyes bored into Evan like an auger digging into a solid piece of wood. Evan moved closer and lowered his voice. "It is a private matter—one of great consequence."

"I suppose if you must, but I am very busy." His dark mustache twitched above his thin lips. "You're sure this can't wait until after the presidential visit?"

"Absolutely certain." Evan inched forward, thankful when

Mr. Zimmerman stepped aside to permit him entry. Without asking permission, he sat down in one of the chairs opposite Mr. Zimmerman's desk.

The supervisor waved to the pile of paper work on his desk. "Do be brief."

The only way he was going to gain the man's full attention was to begin with a frank statement. Evan inhaled a deep breath. "There are men planning to assassinate the president during his visit to Bridal Veil."

Mr. Zimmerman's eyes opened wide, and he dropped into his chair. "What? How do you know this? Tell me everything."

There was a demanding tone to the manager's voice that surprised Evan. "I can't tell you how I've come by the information, but the person is most reliable. I've come to you because I know the president will spend a great deal of time in the clubhouse."

Mr. Zimmerman waved his hand in a circular motion. "Yes, yes, go on. Tell me all of the particulars." He scooted forward and leaned across the desk. "I want to hear every detail—from beginning to end. Take your time. Leave nothing out."

The manager certainly had a quick change of heart regarding his busy schedule. He listened carefully while Evan recounted what Melinda had told him. When Evan finished, Mr. Zimmerman leaned back in his chair.

"Is that everything? You have no names or particulars about when this is to occur?" The manager's steely gaze settled on Evan. "You've left out nothing?"

Evan hesitated. He hadn't mentioned Preston Powers. As much as he disliked the man, he'd decided it was unfair to implicate him simply because he'd walked downstairs after a meeting. Still, he'd do what he could to keep a sharp eye on Preston. With the golf course completed, Evan had much more time and freedom to come and go—and he planned to use the time to his advantage.

"I believe that's everything of consequence, but if I should hear anything further, I'll let you know."

"Please do." Mr. Zimmerman gave him a feeble smile. "I think it would be best if you gave me the name of the person who supplied the information. He or she appears to be quite skilled and could possibly gather additional details for us."

Evan shook his head. "I gave my word that I wouldn't divulge the name. If the person supplies anything more, I'll let you know immediately." Evan stood and reached across the desk to shake Mr. Zimmerman's hand. "I hope that you will do the same. We want to be certain everyone remains safe during the president's visit." Although Evan doubted Mr. Zimmerman would appreciate the advice, he couldn't leave without some mention of the Mifflins. "Since President and Mrs. McKinley will be staying at Summerset Cottage with Mr. and Mrs. Mifflin, do you think it would be wise to alert Mr. Mifflin?"

"Perhaps. Then again, the fewer who know, the better, and word does spread quickly. I'll give it some thought." Mr. Zimmerman extended his hand.

"Thank you, Mr. Zimmerman." Evan shook the supervisor's hand. "I do worry there is truth to this rumor."

"I would remind you there are frequent rumors regarding attacks on this president because he has pursued expansion by annexation of territories, such as the Philippines. He seems to believe it is a proper method to stimulate the country's economy, but many disagree with his beliefs." The supervisor straightened his shoulders and cleared his throat. "While I will do everything in my power to safeguard the president, I'm sure he will have security. We don't want to let a rumor overshadow the grandeur of this event."

Evan frowned. On the one hand, Mr. Zimmerman wanted details, yet on the other, he was referring to the news as nothing more than a rumor. "But you do believe there is a plot of some sort and that safety precautions must be taken."

"Of course, of course." He stepped around the desk and patted Evan's shoulder. "I will take care of everything. You need not worry. I want to make certain nothing unexpected occurs."

Evan strode toward the door but turned when Mr. Zimmerman called his name. "Please keep this matter to yourself. I will speak to the authorities and to the president's security guard. We wouldn't want word of this leaking to the guests or the newspapers. It would be tragic for Bridal Veil."

Evan nodded. "I agree. Thank you, Mr. Zimmerman." He closed the door behind him and walked around the corner to Melinda's office, but she'd not yet returned to her desk.

Over the next few days, Lawrence weighed his options. How had he gotten himself into such a mess? If it weren't for Melinda, he would have escaped the island the day Preston issued his ultimatum. Strange how he'd trusted Preston. Generally he could spot men willing to cut corners and take advantage of every situation. He prided himself on his ability to separate the wheat from the chaff, but Preston had fooled him. If something didn't change soon, he would pay dearly for that mistake. He was willing to suffer the consequences of his actions, but he wouldn't let harm come to Melinda. Not if he could help it. He must keep her safe, and for that, he would need help.

Last night he'd decided to speak with Evan. Telling anyone of Preston's plan would be dangerous, but he knew Evan loved Melinda. Evan was the one person who wouldn't betray him.

Lawrence mounted one of the stable horses and rode to the hunting lodge. Evan had a hunt scheduled for that morning, and Lawrence wanted to arrive before the guests did. As he rode, his thoughts were on two things: how he could protect Melinda and how much he should tell Evan.

The ride didn't take long, and he was pleased when he didn't detect any activity at the lodge. He dismounted, tied his horse, and trotted up the steps. Before he reached the door, Evan opened it. "Lawrence. I wasn't expecting to see you. I was just heading over to the barn. I have a hunt due to start in about forty-five minutes and need to go and select the horses we'll be using."

"If you could hold off for a few minutes, I need to talk to you someplace where no one will overhear our conversation."

Evan's eyes clouded with concern before he waved Lawrence inside. "I have time, and there's no one in the lodge." Taking the lead, Evan stepped toward one of the leather chairs. He motioned Lawrence to the one beside him. "Sit down and tell me what's bothering you."

After dropping to the chair, Lawrence leaned forward and rested his arms across his thighs. "This is going to sound crazy, but hear me out." He kept his gaze fastened upon Evan while he told him there was a plot to assassinate the president and that Preston Powers was involved.

Evan didn't appear as surprised as he'd expected, but Evan was levelheaded—a man prone to evaluate and deal with facts rather than offer a quick emotional response. That was one of the many things Lawrence admired about him.

"Do you know how or when?" Evan rubbed his forehead.

"They are planning to assassinate the president sometime during the costume ball on Saturday night. I wasn't given all of the details. Believe me, I would tell you if I knew more." Lawrence clenched his hands together. "Preston threatened to harm Melinda if I didn't do as he's instructed."

Evan straightened in his chair. "What do you mean he threatened Melinda?"

"He won't hesitate to do whatever he must to carry out this plan. I'm supposed to be at the side entrance with Midnight Flight. The assassin will use the horse to make a quick escape to the dock, where I'm sure they'll have a boat waiting."

Jumping to his feet, Evan paced the length of the room. "We need some sort of plan to keep Melinda safe and away from Preston during the ball."

Lawrence nodded. "Exactly. Can you think of a way that you can be present to help protect Melinda?"

Evan glanced heavenward. "It is a costume ball. I'll need some sort of outfit, and I can have Melinda give me one of the invitations that will permit me entry." He looked straight at Lawrence. "Believe me, Lawrence, I'll do all within my power to keep her safe."

CHAPTER 29

The dock, draped with red, white, and blue bunting that had arrived only two days ago, provided an atmosphere of gaiety and celebration. Until the specially ordered decorations were delivered, Mr. Zimmerman held Melinda responsible, but once they had arrived, he took credit for the display. She truly didn't care so long as all went well during the president's visit. The Bridal Veil board of directors and visiting guests, along with select members of the staff, greeted President and Mrs. McKinley as they stepped off the boat. Mr. and Mrs. Mifflin were the first to offer a welcome.

Melinda's cheeks warmed with embarrassment when Mrs. McKinley beckoned her forward. She touched the president's arm. "This is the sweet young lady who was so kind to me when I was visiting at Cyrus and Dorothea's home in Cleveland." She hesitated a moment and then smiled. "Melinda Colson. Did I get your name correct?"

Melinda bobbed her head. "Yes, that's right." She didn't know if she should bow, curtsy, or extend her hand, but before she could do any of those things, the president grasped her hand and held it between both of his own. "Anyone who has helped my Ida has helped me. I am in your debt, Miss Colson."

"Oh no, sir. It was my pleasure." Melinda glanced back and forth between the president and his wife while she backed away from the couple. She prayed no one would do harm to the president. "It is an honor to have both of you visit Bridal Veil Island."

Following several other introductions, the president made a few brief comments to the crowd. Melinda hoped he wouldn't speak very long, for he was an easy target for any marksman. After a round of applause, President and Mrs. McKinley stepped into the decorated carriage that stood waiting to deliver them to the clubhouse. Even the horses' manes and tails had been embellished with red, white, and blue ribbons. They pranced with heads held high—as if they understood the significance of the event. A procession of horses and buggies carrying guests followed the president's carriage, while staff members followed on foot.

Emma leaned close to Melinda. "You think the president is gonna be safe?"

Melinda nodded, but she wondered the same thing. As they walked behind the carriages, she continued to keep a sharp eye. "I'm praying he will. I know Evan is doing everything he can to make certain nothing happens."

Emma brushed dust from the skirt of her black uniform. "I'm pleased I was chosen to be one of the first to greet the president, but walkin' behind all these buggies was a foolish idea."

"Not so loud, Emma." Melinda glanced toward the hotel supervisor. "This was Mr. Zimmerman's idea."

Stepping closer to Melinda's side, Emma tipped her head near Melinda's ear. "Well, if he can't use his noggin any better than this, we can be glad he isn't in charge of any other events."

After checking to see that Mr. Zimmerman had moved beyond earshot, Melinda said, "Well, there is that skit he promised. He hired an outside troupe for the entertainment, but he had one of the seamstresses create a couple of the pirate costumes."

"Is he having a boat full of sailors brought in for his pirates to capture, or are they only takin' some of the ladies as hostages?" Emma covered her mouth and laughed.

"Goodness, I hope not. I don't think any of the ladies would be amused."

Emma's comment was enough for Melinda to decide it would be wise to know a little more about Mr. Zimmerman's skit. A formal dinner was scheduled for tomorrow, with the ball to follow afterward. Melinda had no idea when or where Mr. Zimmerman planned to present the skit. Personally, she thought the entire idea peculiar.

Once they returned to the clubhouse, she stepped around several servants and hurried to his side. "Do you have a few moments, Mr. Zimmerman?"

He pressed his lips together. "Is it absolutely necessary, Miss Colson?" Irritation dripped from each word.

She straightened her shoulders. "I believe it is. We need to detail a few of the arrangements for tomorrow night."

Waving her into his office, he followed and closed the door. "I can't imagine that there is anything left that must be clarified. We've been over the lists several times now."

"We haven't discussed the skit. I'm confused as to how and where it will take place."

He rounded his desk and dropped into the chair. "I told you I would take care of the arrangements, and I have. The skit will take place after dinner in the annex dining room."

"But there won't be—"

He held up his hand. "Let me finish, Miss Colson." The supervisor leaned forward. "The skit will take place in the annex dining room near the side entrance. I've arranged for a small stage to be placed along the east wall near the doors."

Melinda frowned. "It would make more sense to have the stage on the north wall away from the doors. Think of the congestion."

"I want the stage on the east wall." He cleared his throat and assumed a less strident tone. "The performers can move in and out of the room with less distraction if the stage is along the east wall."

"It sounds as though this is going to be a longer production than I'd anticipated. I told the musicians the ball would begin following dinner."

Mr. Zimmerman twisted one end of his mustache. "Why this sudden interest in the skit, Miss Colson?"

"Because it seems like too much activity for one evening, Mr. Zimmerman. I was thinking that it might be better if we had a thespian night on Sunday evening. We could ask the guests if they'd like to perform, and then you could present your skit." She folded her hands in her lap and forced a smile. "Don't you think that would be better?"

"No, I do not think that would be better. Everything from the actors to the staging is arranged for tomorrow night." He pushed up from his desk. "There will be no changes. The skit will take place following dinner." The supervisor circled his desk and strode to the door. "If there's nothing else, I have other matters that require my attention." He opened the door and waited for her departure.

There would be no further discussion.

With guests using the dining room for their meals, it was impossible to begin decorating until after lunch the following day. Although the centerpieces had been created, there wouldn't be much time to finish the remaining décor. Melinda enlisted the help of as many staff members as possible. The decorations would continue the patriotic theme established at the dock yesterday.

Huge floral arrangements of red, white, and blue flowers contained ivy streamers that Melinda intertwined with colorful ribbons. The ivy and ribbons flowed from the centerpieces down the length of each table. She placed large candles atop pillared stands and surrounded each one with fluffy white netting. Palms in sturdy jardinières were placed throughout the room, each one adorned with silver stars that would twinkle in the candlelight.

"Understated yet beautiful—just like you."

Melinda swirled around and found herself toe-to-toe with Preston. Taking a quick backward step, she lost her footing and Preston leaned forward to catch her. Melinda glanced at the entrance to the dining room and gasped. Evan stood in the doorway staring at them.

"Let go of me!" she hissed at Preston, who had lifted her to an upright position and was now holding her close to his chest.

He followed her gaze to the doorway and smirked at Evan. "Just helping a lady in distress."

Evan strode toward them, his fists balled in tight knots and his eyes flashing. "If you have a moment, there's a matter related to work that we need to discuss." He turned his angry eyes on Preston. "In private."

"Why, of course." After an exaggerated bow from the waist, Preston winked at Melinda. "I hope to see you later, Miss Colson." With a jaunty wave, Preston strode from the dining room.

The muscles along Evan's jaw twitched. "I thought you promised to stay away from him."

Melinda stiffened at the accusation. "I have stayed away from him, but he walked up behind me. I startled and tripped." She narrowed her eyes. "If he hadn't caught me, I would have fallen. I hope you don't consider tumbling to the floor a more suitable outcome."

His features softened. "No, of course not, but if you'd come upon me holding Victoria Polter in my arms, how would you react?"

Her anger faded. "You're right." She smiled and reached for his hand. "I likely would have assumed the worst."

He squeezed her hand. "I'm sorry for jumping to conclusions. Forgive me?"

"Yes, and I'm sorry for my angry response. I know you're worried about my safety."

"You're right—I am concerned. About your safety and about our future together. I love you, Melinda, and want you always near my side. Even though others may try to come between us, I pray that God will keep us faithful to each other. I don't need time to evaluate my feelings, and I pray you have come to the conclusion that it's time we commit to our love."

She gazed into his eyes. "I had committed, Evan, but when Victoria began to monopolize your time and you wouldn't set a wedding date—"

"Would a date help you to realize my seriousness in marrying you? Is that what this is all about? Is that why you've chosen to believe Victoria Polter rather than me . . . rather than your own heart?"

Guilt plagued Melinda. She'd placed more faith and trust in the words of Victoria Polter than in Evan or, for that matter, God. Instead of seeking God's will for her life, Melinda had been listening to the murmurings of a foolish schoolgirl. In truth, Melinda liked to believe she had placed her trust in God, but she'd taken back control when she departed Cleveland many months ago without seeking His guidance. And though she'd made intermittent attempts to wait upon the Lord for guidance, she continued to snatch back the reins and take control. Only now did she realize her mistake. Now she realized how foolish she'd been with her attempts to make Evan jealous. Now she realized God was giving her another chance. Only time would reveal whether she would fully and completely place her trust in Him for the rest of her life.

"I'm sorry, Evan." She positioned her hand against his heart. "I don't need a date to know that you will honor your marriage proposal."

He touched her cheek and smiled. "Is all forgiven between us?"

She nodded. "To be sure."

Evan grinned. "Then the moment the presidential visit is completed, we'll set a date."

Not caring if the servants saw her, she tipped back her head, raised up on her toes, and kissed Evan full on the mouth. Heat stole across her cheeks as she gestured around the room. "What do you think?"

"I think I'd like another kiss."

She giggled and shook her head. "Perhaps later."

"The room is quite lovely, but it is no match for your beauty." He grinned down at her. "I'm sure everyone will be amazed at what you've accomplished." Still holding her hand, he led her away from the maids who were busy arranging the place settings. "Have you heard anything more about this evening?"

Keeping her voice low, she glanced toward workmen carrying a makeshift stage toward the annex. "Emma says there's been nothing more happening upstairs—at least nothing she's detected." She hesitated a moment. "I wish I could convince Mr. Zimmerman to cancel his skit. It's going to delay the ball, but he insists."

"It's probably best to accept that he's going to go forward with it. He probably wants one event for which he can take full credit. He likes to impress people, and with all of the investors as well as the president in attendance, he probably considers this a one-time opportunity."

She shrugged. "You're probably right, but it makes my job all the more difficult."

"And Preston Powers makes everything more difficult. I want

you to keep him at a distance. I don't trust him." He cupped her cheek in his hand. "Are you certain I couldn't steal a final kiss?"

Melinda glanced toward the workmen and shook her head. "Don't forget that you need to return later this afternoon. Emma will have your costume. It's almost finished." She grinned. "You'll have to wear a wig, but I thought it would better conceal your identity."

He chuckled. "And who am I to be?"

"George Washington. I think you'll look quite handsome in breeches, a cape, and a tricorn hat. Emma will have an invitation for you to use if it you need it. The cape can also be used to conceal your face, if you find it necessary."

He nodded. "You've thought of everything. What about your costume?"

Heat flooded her cheeks. "Martha Washington. I hope you don't object that I'll be dressed as your wife."

"From the pictures I've seen of Martha Washington, you're far too beautiful to portray her. Still, I'm delighted you chose to attend as my wife."

"To be your wife has been my choice for a very long time, Evan."

Using short flicking motions, Lawrence brushed loosened dirt from Midnight Flight's coat. "You're looking quite sleek, you beauty." He continued along the side of the horse, but stilled his movement at the sound of galloping horse's hooves in the distance. One look down the path and he groaned. *Preston.* The last person he wished to see. Had there been sufficient time, he would have saddled Midnight Flight and ridden in the opposite direction.

Hoping to make this a brief encounter, he stood in the doorway and waited. As Preston drew nearer, he slowed his horse to a trot. When he was beside the doorway, he pulled back on the reins. Looking down from atop the horse, he nodded. "Glad to find you here. I wanted to be sure you completely understood what's expected tonight."

Lawrence leaned against the rough timber of the doorframe. "Quite clear." He made no effort to hide his contempt. "I'm to be at the side entrance of the clubhouse with Midnight Flight at eight o'clock."

"And if anyone asks why you're waiting there with the horse, tell them you're helping one of the guests in a portrayal of Paul Revere and his midnight ride." He chuckled. "Uncanny that the horse is named Midnight Flight, don't you think?"

"I think you're making a grave mistake, but I don't expect you to listen to anything I have to say."

"This is no mistake. We're saving the nation from an imperialist." Preston pointed his riding crop at Lawrence. "Keep in mind that the weapons used by the pirates in their skit won't all be fake. If anything goes wrong, your sister is the first one I'll look for." Preston tightened his legs against the side of the horse and nudged it into a trot. "Until tonight."

Lawrence bowed his head. His stomach twisted. What if Evan failed in keeping Melinda safe? If anything happened to her, how could he ever forgive himself? This was one gamble he wasn't willing to lose.

CHAPTER 30

Dressed as Martha Washington in rich green brocade, Melinda acted as hostess for the party, greeting the guests as they arrived for dinner and directing them to their assigned tables. It had already been decided that the president and his wife would not be in costume, and because of this, Mr. and Mrs. Mifflin had chosen to do likewise. Melinda had arranged for Mr. and Mrs. Mifflin to flank the president and his wife, with the security guards standing close behind. The ladies looked beautiful in their evening finery and the men quite dashing in their tailed tuxedos. It rather reminded Melinda of royalty keeping watch over their court.

The other guests at their table had been selected in a drawing held the previous week. The possibility of being selected to sit with the president had elicited a great deal of excitement, and Melinda had encouraged Mr. Zimmerman to employ the same method for seating at the skit. But after a stern comment that the seating had already been assigned and everything was in order for the skit, he had shooed her from his office. The man's attitude baffled her.

Other than what was likely the lumber for a makeshift stage, Melinda had seen little evidence of anything being completed in the annex. Each time she'd attempted to peek inside, the doors had been locked. After weeks of planning each detail for this evening's event, she hoped the skit would add to the perfection but feared it would not be so.

Melinda approached the front door of the dining hall and smiled at the approaching guests. "Welcome, Mr. Morley—or should I say Uncle Sam?" She accepted his invitation and nodded toward his wife, who was wearing a costume of Betsy Ross and carried both a small flag and a sewing basket. "You and your patriotic bride are assigned to table one with President and Mrs. McKinley."

With each arriving guest, the variety of costumes amazed Melinda. She had feared that with so little time to arrange for their outfits, the guests would not have much choice in their attire. She was delighted to see otherwise and supposed that with enough money all things were possible.

The attendees appeared costumed as Robin Hood, Cleopatra, and Julius Caesar, as well as Abraham and Mary Todd Lincoln, among others. When Victoria Polter entered the foyer dressed as an Indian maiden, Melinda worried she might spot Evan, but she had walked by him without notice. Apparently the white wig served well to disguise him from the overly amorous young woman. Melinda sighed. The last thing she needed right now was to worry about Victoria's trying to engage all of Evan's time at the ball.

An Egyptian pharaoh presented his invitation only minutes before Preston Powers entered. He looked a bit outlandish in a Viking costume, complete with fur-lined vest, horned helmet, and sheathed dagger.

"My, my," he said, giving her a quick once-over, "don't you look charming. I'm particularly fond of that shade of green on you. It brings out your lovely eyes."

Melinda forced a smile. "Thank you. For a Viking . . . you are quite civilized."

He laughed. "It's merely a costume, my dear."

What did he mean by that? But she had no time to further consider the statement because a group of pilgrims arrived carrying a turkey they'd borrowed from the island taxidermist. Melinda laughed aloud. "You do know that you're going to have a bit of trouble if you try to cook that bird. I think it will be a little dry."

The pilgrims chuckled and moved deeper into the room to admit several of the other guests. Cowboys, Indians, a sheik, and a crowned king and queen followed behind the pilgrims and quickly located their seats.

There were even two guests in pirate costumes. Melinda wondered if Mr. Zimmerman worried that those men would detract from the actors in his pirate skit—or if he'd even considered the possibility that some of the guests might choose pirate costumes. If it bothered him, Mr. Zimmerman said nothing. He merely stood to one side, dressed in his boring black suit and white shirt. For whatever reason, he'd chosen not to embrace the party spirit.

Once the guests were seated, Mr. Morley walked to the front of the room. "Mr. President and Mrs. McKinley"—he smiled and nodded toward the couple—"it is my great honor to welcome you to Bridal Veil Island. The board of directors and our guests count it a tribute that you have taken time from your busy schedule to visit us." He gestured toward Mr. and Mrs. Mifflin. "Cyrus and Dorothea, we thank you for convincing them that a visit to the South would not be complete without a stop at Bridal Veil." A round of applause followed his brief remarks, and soon the waiters appeared.

Course after course, the dinner proceeded without incident. The guests expressed pleasure in every dish, from clams and oysters to quail and petit fours. Though she didn't have the privilege of eating the meal, Melinda sighed with pleasure when the guests had completed the final course. Perhaps any plot to assassinate the president had somehow been thwarted. By evening's end, she prayed they could count the event a complete success.

When Mr. Zimmerman entered the dining room moments later and made his way to the presidential table, Melinda's stomach lurched. They hadn't planned for him to make any announcements. The program that had been placed at each table setting clearly instructed the guests to exit the dining room following dinner and be seated in the annex to view the skit. Mr. Zimmerman was to remain in the annex with the performers and direct the guests to their seats.

Glancing toward the hallway, she spotted Evan stationed in the foyer near the door leading to the annex. She tapped her folded silk fan against her chin, their agreed-upon signal that something might be amiss.

Mr. Zimmerman approached Mr. Mifflin, whispered in his ear, and then backed away and strode toward her. A look of satisfaction glimmered in his eyes. "President and Mrs. McKinley will lead the guests into the annex. Mr. and Mrs. Mifflin will follow them."

Melinda frowned. That hadn't been the way she'd arranged the procession to the annex. Why did Mr. Zimmerman insist on making simple things difficult? Did he always have to look like the one in charge?

She had planned to excuse the guests table by table, beginning with those seated near the exit to the foyer leading into the annex dining room. "That will create greater confusion. I prefer to do it table by table beginning back here."

"You will do as you are instructed, Miss Colson." His mustache quivered, a sure sign she'd agitated him. "This is for the president's safety." Whether she liked it or not, Mr. Zimmerman had taken charge. Moments later, he signaled to Mr. Mifflin. The two couples rose to begin the procession, while the remainder of the confused guests whispered and looked at their programs.

"They don't know what to do," Melinda hissed to Mr. Zimmerman.

He stepped forward to address the crowd. "Please remain seated. Once I have the president and his party seen to, I will arrange for everyone else. When I point to your table, please proceed through the foyer and into the annex." Turning to Melinda, he nodded toward the door. "Go and accompany the president and his wife to the annex."

Melinda was as confused as the guests. Why did he want her to take them to the annex? This performance was his portion of the entertainment, not hers. She had no idea what he'd planned or where he wanted the McKinleys to sit. And she could only hope that the doors were unlocked. Hurrying ahead of the two couples and a security guard, she turned the door handle, pulled open the doors, and backed away to permit President and Mrs. McKinley to enter.

She remained by the door and looked over to the makeshift stage. With nothing more than a sheet hanging over some sort of pole, clearly no scenery had been created. There weren't even places to sit, with the exception of one ladder-back chair that sat on the stage. What had Mr. Zimmerman been thinking? This wasn't fit for the president. Something was very wrong.

A lump formed in her throat and her mouth went dry. She looked toward Evan, who had moved closer to the president, and tapped the fan to her chin.

Before she could make sense of the situation, a man in a pirate costume stepped from behind the sheet.

"Death to imperialists!" He raised a gun and took aim at the president. Evan lunged forward and pushed the president aside as a shot rang out. Both men fell to the floor, and Mrs. McKinley crumpled in a faint atop them.

The assassin rushed from the end of the stage, and Melinda stuck out her foot, tripping him. The man scuttled to his feet, but the president's security guard threw him back to the floor. A feeling of elation filled Melinda's chest as the guard wrestled the would-be assassin into a stronghold.

The black patch that had covered one eye now swung from the captured man's neck. "Wait! Wait! I wasn't working alone."

The security officer propelled him away. "Don't worry, mister. All your friends will be walking the plank before this is done."

Mr. and Mrs. Mifflin both hurried to Mrs. McKinley's aid and, along with another security guard, gently rolled her from atop Evan and the president. Someone else took off his suit coat and folded it into a pillow. Mrs. Mifflin began to fan her with a vengeance.

"Ida, all is well. All is well," she told her friend over and over.

"Young man, I do believe you saved my life. I owe you a debt of gratitude." President McKinley dusted off his pinstriped pants. He cast a glance at his awakening wife. Ida McKinley strained to catch sight of her husband. "I am quite all right, my dear. Thanks to this fast-thinking young man."

Melinda beamed at Evan, but the muffled uproar of the guests filtered through the closed doors leading into the main dining room and kept her from telling him how proud she was of his bravery. When had those doors closed?

Mr. Zimmerman must have shut them, and now he was shouting at the crowd. "Keep your seats! It's part of the entertainment. In a few minutes, you'll all see what is happening."

Part of the entertainment? What was he talking about? Melinda started toward the doors, but an arm surrounded her upper body, and she felt the sting of cold, sharp metal against her throat.

"Zimmerman is doing just fine without your help, dear Melinda. If you don't want this knife to ruin your beautiful neck, I suggest you do as you're told." Preston's menacing voice hissed in her ear.

Melinda's hands trembled and her heart pounded a frenzied beat. She spotted Evan inching toward them and swallowed hard. *Please, Lord, don't let him do anything rash.*

Preston tightened his hold. "If you don't want me to hurt her, stay where you are, Evan."

When Evan took another step, Melinda thought she might faint. "Please, Evan. Don't do anything foolish. He'll kill both of us."

"You'd do well to listen to her, Evan. She's a smart girl. And she's quite beautiful—at the moment. If you want her to remain that way, you'll all do as I say." He waved the dagger toward the side doors before returning it to Melinda's neck. "Now, I'm going to go out that door, down those steps, and mount a waiting horse. If you want this young lady to remain unscathed, you'll do nothing to stop me. Is that understood?"

Melinda looked at Evan. Anger and determination shone in his eyes. When no one answered Preston, he tightened his hold until she yelped in pain. "Please answer him," she begged.

They nodded and murmured their agreement.

"That's better." He pressed his lips close to Melinda's ear. "Now begin moving with me toward the door, where your brother is waiting for me with his horse."

"My brother? I don't believe you." Her mind whirled. Preston and Lawrence had become gambling friends. Had Preston truly convinced her brother to become involved in this attempt to kill the president? Her body went limp as sadness mingled with escalating fear.

"Stand up straight and turn to the right. I'm not going to drag you!" Once again Preston tightened his hold. Melinda forced herself to remain upright and keep pace with Preston's movements.

They had just turned toward the door when Melinda heard a noise behind them. Preston turned to look over his shoulder just before Melinda heard a loud thwack and white fabric descended over both of them. Preston fell to the floor, and she heard the clunk of the dagger. When the sheet was pulled away, Evan was holding Preston on the floor and Mrs. Mifflin was standing over Melinda with a wooden pole in her hand.

The older woman's eyes were as large as saucers. "I do hope you aren't injured, but I had to do something to stop him, and that pole was the only thing nearby."

"I'm fine. Thank you for taking action. I don't know what I would . . ." Her voice trailed off as she caught sight of a security guard entering the side door and holding Lawrence at gunpoint.

The guard shoved Lawrence forward. "I got this one before he took off on his horse."

"No! He's on our side!" Evan shouted to the guard. "Come and secure this man's arms." Evan lifted Preston to his feet and pushed him against the wall. "He's one of the ringleaders."

With his powdered white wig askew, Evan rushed to Melinda's side as she attempted to stand. "Are you all right?"

She nodded, not trusting her voice.

Tipping her chin, he eyed the welt on her neck and winced. Lawrence joined them and laid a hand on Melinda's shoulder.

Evan pulled Melinda close. "Tell the president's guards I'll be with them in a minute."

"You take care of Melinda, and I'll help the guards take Preston and his henchmen to the jail in Biscayne." Lawrence trotted off in the direction of the security officers.

Melinda shook her head. "I don't understand all of this, Evan. Preston said Lawrence was helping him with the assassination attempt. Is that true?"

"No. Your brother came and told me Preston was forcing

him to bring his horse to be used in their escape. Preston stole the papers for Midnight Flight and threatened to have Lawrence thrown in jail for stealing the horse, but when Lawrence still refused to help, Preston threatened your life."

"My life?"

"Lawrence had to go along with the scheme until he knew you were safe, but it was his information that helped us foil the assassination plot."

Melinda exhaled a sigh of relief and a sense of pride washed over her. Both her brother and Evan had helped save the president. "I'm so proud of you, Evan." She leaned forward and brushed his lips with a fleeting kiss, then scanned the room for Lawrence. She wanted to thank him, but he'd disappeared.

The doors to the dining room opened, and a security guard, along with Mr. Morley and two other investors, escorted Mr. Zimmerman and the two men dressed in pirate costumes into the foyer and out the side door.

Melinda shook her head. "I can't believe Mr. Zimmerman was involved in this. How did you know?"

"At first I didn't. I unsuspectingly made things worse because I went to him after you told me what Emma heard."

Melinda gasped and covered her mouth. "Oh no!"

"Fortunately, it all worked out, with Lawrence's help. Had I known Zimmerman was involved, I would have spoken directly to the security guards when the president first arrived. Instead, I only asked if he'd notified them."

"And when he told you he had, naturally you believed him."

Evan nodded. "I knew only you and Mr. Zimmerman were aware of my involvement. It wasn't until I heard Mr. Zimmerman shout to the other guests that the gunshot was part of the skit that I realized he was involved. But thankfully, nobody was injured." He touched his finger to the welt on her neck. "At least not too badly."

Melinda gave him a reassuring smile and leaned closer. "Where is Lawrence? He was here only moments ago, and now he's nowhere in sight." She'd barely uttered the question when her brother bounded into the room waving several papers overhead.

He stopped in front of her, his smile as bright as a summer day. "Look what I found in Preston's room." Lawrence pointed to the bill of sale. Melinda began to unfold the papers. "These are the papers that prove I own Midnight Flight. Preston stole them from my valise so that I couldn't prove ownership of the horse. He also threatened to harm you if I didn't aid him in his plot against the president."

Melinda wrapped her arms around him and held him tight. "Evan told me you came to him. I'm so proud of you, Lawrence. And I'm delighted you've located the bill of sale for the horse." She stepped back and grinned. "I suppose this means I no longer have reason to nag you."

Lawrence chuckled. "I'm sure you'll find something else that needs improvement, dear sister."

"Well, there is the gambling . . ."

He turned his attention to Evan. "You see? There's no pleasing this woman."

"Perhaps. But I'd like to spend the rest of my life trying." She grasped Evan's hand. "Nothing would make me happier."

Once the guards removed all of the perpetrators from the room, Melinda looked toward the president. He was standing beside his wife, who still appeared pale. She tipped her head in their direction and Evan understood. Together they crossed the room. Melinda took a deep breath. "I am so sorry, President and Mrs. McKinley. I'm very grateful no one was hurt, but I doubt you'll ever want to return to Bridal Veil again."

The president tugged on his jacket. "Nonsense, my dear girl.

There's no denying that the ordeal gave both my wife and me a fright, but there's been no harm done." He patted Melinda's shoulder. "Now that the officials have removed the perpetrators and order has been restored, the orchestra members need to gather their instruments and offer us some music. We came here for a ball, and we're not going to let those criminals spoil our good time."

He leaned closer and lowered his voice—his bravado fading. "I can't deny the attempt on my life has given me a good scare—and I must keep a close eye on my wife. However, we don't want the crowd to become even more alarmed. To continue with the festivities will send a message that all is well."

"You're absolutely certain you want to proceed?"

He glanced at his wife, who had regained a bit of color in her cheeks, and then gave a firm nod. "The best way to dispel the significance of what they've attempted is to carry on as planned."

Melinda looked at Mrs. McKinley. "Do you think you're up to any more excitement this evening?"

She smiled at Melinda. "I may not dance more than once, and I may depart earlier than some of the other guests, but I agree with my husband. The best way to set minds at ease is to carry on as planned."

Evan wrapped a protective arm around Melinda's waist. "Are you certain you can do this? You've had a terrible fright, and I think everyone will understand if you decide to leave." He smiled down at her. "I care more about you than anything else."

"If President and Mrs. McKinley can stay, I believe I can, too." Melinda looked into Evan's dark eyes that shone with love. "So long as you promise to remain by my side for the rest of the evening."

He leaned close. "I promise to always remain by your side, my love."

A short time later the president quietly explained the foiled assassination attempt to the guests. He then signaled the musicians. "Now, I ask that you please join my wife and me in the first dance." The president escorted Mrs. McKinley onto the dance floor, and the remaining costumed guests took to the floor, also.

Evan took Melinda's hand. "Shall we?"

She bobbed her head. "Please."

Evan gathered her into his arms, and as they swirled around the room, the palms adorned with silver stars twinkled in the candlelight—just like the stars in Melinda's eyes.

"I've been thinking." He pulled her a little closer. "June the third is a Saturday."

Melinda's eyebrows crimped in puzzlement. "If you say so. Is that day of some importance?"

"If you don't need additional time to evaluate your feelings about marriage, I think it would make a wonderful wedding day . . . don't you?"

She looked at him with wide innocent eyes. "Our wedding?"

"Who else's?" He chuckled. "I certainly have no interest in any but ours."

She smiled and leaned in. "Why, President Washington, I believe that would be quite acceptable to me. Provided, of course, that the country can get by without you at the helm for a time."

He laughed and whirled her in a wide circle. "I'm the president. Who would dare to interfere with my wedding day?"

CHAPTER 31

JUNE 3, 1899

Melinda stood as impatient as a child on Christmas morning while Emma secured sprigs of waxed jasmine petals to her wedding veil.

"Yar for sure the most beautiful bride in all the world," Emma declared, taking a step back. "It was most generous of Mrs. Mifflin to pay for the gown. A pretty penny that must have cost her."

It had been a surprise that the Mifflins had not only insisted on being invited to the wedding but had taken up the position of parents of the bride. Aided by the McKinleys, they had insisted that Evan and Melinda marry in a beautiful clubhouse wedding. And because this request had come from investors and the President of the United States himself, Victor Morley and the other investors had readily agreed. They asked only that the couple wait until after the official island season had concluded.

"I still can't believe Mrs. Mifflin did this," Melinda said, touching her hand to her neck and the turquoise and silver pin Evan had given her last Christmas. The high-necked bodice made the perfect place to display the family keepsake.

"Well, ya look grand." Emma wiped a tear from her eye.

"As do you," Melinda said, motioning to the woman's new gown. "I think you should always wear that shade of blue."

"Mrs. Mifflin called it niagara." Emma turned to show off the dress, which was a hue somewhere between turquoise and peacock blue. "And your brother said it shimmers like the falls themselves."

"That it does. You look like quite the grand lady."

A knock sounded on the door, and Emma hurried to answer. "Why Harland, and don't ya look like the grand master himself in that new suit."

Melinda smiled as Harland stepped into the room. "I'm nothing compared to the two of you."

Taking hold of his hand, Melinda hugged him close. "How is Evan holding up?"

"He's mighty impatient. I'm here to tell you that it's time to get on with this affair. Pastor Webley had to fight to keep him from coming here himself."

Emma laughed. "Well, we'd best get this affair underway then. Tell Lawrence that we have a bride in need of an escort down the aisle and request the music to begin."

Harland nodded. "I'll do just that." He leaned over and gave Melinda a quick peck on the cheek. "I wanted to be the first to do that. Blessings on this marriage and your life here on Bridal Veil."

Melinda fought back tears. "Thank you, Harland. I'm so glad you were well enough to come and stand with Evan. You mean the world to him. You are practically the only family he has."

"Then you must do your duty and remedy that matter quickly." He turned to walk to the door. "I'm thinking Evan would like a dozen or so children now that he's been promoted."

Melinda felt her cheeks grow hot, but she said nothing. Instead, as Harland left she took up her bouquet of flowers and drew a deep breath. "I'm ready," she said in a barely audible voice. "I feel as though I've waited forever for this day, and now that it's here . . . well . . . it all seems to be happening so fast."

"The best days pass quickly. That's why God gives us memories." Emma gave Melinda's arm a gentle squeeze.

Just then the door opened a fraction of an inch, and Garrison O'Sullivan called out. "Are you ladies ready to put an end to our misery?"

Emma laughed and pulled open the door. "And fer sure ya'll be a sight more miserable if ya don't mind yar wild manners."

He gave her a wink. "I'll be teachin' ya all about me wild manners after we get these two hitched."

Lawrence entered the room behind him, and Melinda's breath caught in her throat. "You look like Papa."

He came alongside Melinda and took hold of her arm in a most gentle fashion. "And you look like a princess."

"Thank you for being here to give me away." Melinda gazed into her brother's eyes. "And thank you for agreeing to mend your ways. It's the best possible wedding gift to hear that you will put aside gambling."

"Well, what with a full-time job offer from the investors, I could hardly refuse." Lawrence leaned down and kissed her cheek. "Besides, we all have to grow up at some point."

"Papa and Mama would be proud."

He nodded and smiled. "Indeed they would—especially of you." He reached up to pull her veil into place. "Come along, princess. Your prince awaits."

❦

Evan watched as Emma made her way down the aisle of the little church. He'd never seen her so grandly attired, but the older woman looked quite regal and very happy. She threw him a wink before stepping to the side opposite of where he and Harland stood.

The congregation stood just then, and the piano boomed out in a wonderful wedding melody. Evan wiped his moist hands against his suit coat and gave a small tug at the mail-coach cravat Mr. Mifflin had helped to secure at his neck.

And then the moment he'd waited for came, and Melinda, gowned in white satin, appeared in the doorway on the arm of her brother. Evan swallowed hard, unable to push down the knot that had formed in his throat. She was beautiful—angelic, like something from a dream. Her veil hid some of the details of her face, but Evan knew without a doubt that she was smiling.

Pastor Webley stepped forward as Lawrence came to a stop with Melinda on his arm. "Dearly beloved, we are gathered together here in the sight of God, and in the face of this congregation, to join together this man and this woman . . . in holy matrimony. Who giveth the bride?"

Lawrence grinned at Evan. "I do . . . her brother." He extended Melinda's hand to Evan and pressed his hand atop Evan's as he took hold of her. "Treat her right or you'll answer to me."

Evan nodded. "I promise you, I will."

Lawrence then stepped back and took his seat as the pastor continued. Evan hoped Melinda didn't feel the trembling in his hand as he tucked her arm against his. He thanked God for bringing the two of them to this point. His only regret was that his mother hadn't lived to know Melinda. He was sure they would have been the closest of friends.

The vows were given and repeated and the rings exchanged. Before Evan knew it, Pastor Webley was instructing him to kiss his bride. His heart swelled with joy as he lifted his wife's veil and could see her face in full.

She smiled and whispered, "My husband."

"Beloved," he murmured and settled his lips on hers for a most passionate kiss.

❦

"Where are you taking me?" Melinda asked as Evan drove the buggy farther from the clubhouse and past the hunting lodge. She looked at him in confusion.

"It's a surprise." Evan snapped the reins to hurry the horse a bit.

Making their way along a lovely little lane, Melinda was surprised when a small cottage came into sight. She'd never seen the little house before, but it was quite fetching. Someone had gone to a great deal of trouble to pattern it after some of the grander dwellings but on a much smaller scale.

Evan pulled the horses to a stop in front of the house and set the brake. "Well, what do you think?"

Melinda looked at him in confusion. "About what?"

He laughed and jumped down from the carriage. "Our new home—Mr. Morley's gift to us for as long as I'm overseeing Bridal Veil Island."

Her eyes grew wide and her heart leapt. "Ours? Truly?"

Evan helped her down from the buggy. "Ours indeed. I think you'll be quite pleased. Mr. Morley spared no expense. He said he was under the direction of the investors and the president himself to make us a suitable place to start our new life."

Melinda shook her head. "I can scarcely believe it. It's beautiful."

"As are you." Evan lifted her into his arms.

Melinda giggled and wrapped her arms around his neck.

"I know you didn't like the wait, but I promise you now that we're married . . . you'll realize just how worthwhile the delay was. I want to give you the best life." He leaned down to kiss her forehead as he carried her toward the house. "I never want you to be afraid of going hungry or of having a roof over your head."

Melinda sighed and buried her face against his neck. A hint of bayberry and spice tickled her nose. The heat of the day bore down on them, but she didn't mind at all. To be in his arms was all that she had ever wanted.

"God purposed our lives together." Evan stepped up to the porch and shifted her enough to open the screen door. "And I intend to honor that purpose by making you a promise here and now. The same promise I gave in our ceremony. I will love and cherish you, Melinda Colson Tarlow. Every day, every moment."

She tightened her hold on him as he carried her over the threshold. Her heart nearly burst with joy. The long wait was over, and God had blessed them on their journey. The love He had given them was richer than she could have ever imagined.

Looking up, Melinda met his intense gaze. "And I will love and cherish you, my most precious Evan . . . with all of my heart . . . always and forever."

AUTHOR'S NOTE

Dear Reader,

The idea for this independent series was born when a reader attended one of our book signings for the Broadmoor series set in the Thousand Islands. She'd stated that now that we had written about the Thousand Islands, we should consider a series set on one of the islands along the southeastern coast of the United States. She mentioned both St. Simons Island and Jekyll Island as possibilities. We tucked away the idea, and when the time came to develop another series, we decided the rich history along the southeastern coastline would provide another unique setting for us.

As in most of our books, there are fictional characters and settings, as well as authentic people and places. While Jekyll Island is an amazing resort in the southeast, we decided we would enjoy creating our own island, just as we had in the Broadmoor series.

Bridal Veil Island is fictional, as are Bridal Fair and the Argosy River. However, we do make many references to Jekyll Island, so we wanted to point out that because our books are set prior to 1929, you'll notice that the spelling appears as "Jekyl" Island rather than "Jekyll" Island. It wasn't until the summer of 1929, at the instigation of club members, that the Georgia legislature passed a resolution to correct the spelling of Jekyl by adding a second "l." The resolution noted that the island had been named by General Oglethorpe in honor of his friend, Sir Joseph Jekyll, and the correct spelling had been corrupted by omitting the last letter. Thereafter, Jekyll became the proper spelling for the island.

The city of Biscayne is also fictional, although loosely based upon Brunswick, Georgia. However, never doubt that the live oaks are very real and exceedingly breathtaking trees.

In the second book of the series, *To Love and Cherish*, you'll discover President McKinley makes a visit to both Jekyl Island and to Bridal Veil. The president did visit Jekyl Island, and it was, of course, the highlight of the season for those wintering on the island. Names of some well-known wealthy industrialists and entrepreneurs of the time period are sprinkled throughout the series, but the characters we hope you will come to know and love are the fictional ones that we have developed in our imaginations.

In the final book of the series, *To Honor and Trust*, we introduce you to some new characters who have unique positions on the island. You'll also experience some of the difficulties extreme weather caused prior to the 1913 winter season at Bridal Veil and in the City of Indianapolis, the home of our protagonist.

If you'd like to learn more about Jekyll Island, please visit their Web site http://www.jekyllislandhistory.com/ and consider a visit in the future. You'll fall in love with yet another part of our beautiful country.

We hope you'll enjoy this series.

~Tracie and Judy

ACKNOWLEDGMENTS

No book is written without the help and support of many people. The entire Bethany House staff constantly amazes me with their creative talents and ability to make each book shine. Special thanks to editors Sharon Asmus and Charlene Patterson for their encouragement and assistance. It is a genuine privilege to work with such talented editors as well as every member of the Bethany House family.

Thanks to Mary Greb-Hall, Lorna Seilstad, and Mary Kay Woodford for their prayers, critiques, expertise, and friendship.

Thanks to Gretchen Greminger, curator of the Jekyll Island Museum, for her speedy replies and helpful responses to my questions.

And special thanks to you, dear readers, for your e-mails and letters of encouragement, your expressions of kindness and love, your prayers, and your eagerness to read each book.

Above all, thanks and praise to our Lord Jesus Christ for the opportunity to live my dream and share the wonder of His love through story.

~Judy

Judith Miller is an award-winning author whose avid research and love for history are reflected in her bestselling novels. Judy makes her home in Topeka, Kansas.

Tracie Peterson is the bestselling, award-winning author of more than eighty novels. Tracie also teaches writing workshops at a variety of conferences on subjects such as inspirational romance and historical research. She and her family live in Belgrade, Montana.

For more information on Tracie and Judith's books, including behind-the-scenes details and photos from the BRIDAL VEIL ISLAND series, check out the Writes of Passage blog at *writespassage.blogspot.com*.

Don't Miss the First Journey to Bridal Veil!

For more information on Tracie, Judith and their books visit traciepeterson.com and judithmccoymiller.com.

When greedy investors set their sights on Audrey Cunningham's ancestral home on Bridal Veil Island, Marshall Graham is charged with protecting the fiery young woman who seems to disdain him. But her refusal to sell could cost more than they know.

To Have and to Hold by Tracie Peterson and Judith Miller
BRIDAL VEIL ISLAND

More History and Romance From Authors Tracie Peterson and Judith Miller

When three cousins are suddenly thrust into a world where money equals power, each is forced to decide what she's willing to sacrifice for wealth, family, and love.

THE BROADMOOR LEGACY by Tracie Peterson and Judith Miller
A Daughter's Inheritance, An Unexpected Love, A Surrendered Heart

Discover a Piece of Amana's History

In the picturesque Amana Colonies, family secrets, hidden passions, and the bonds of friendship run deeper than outsiders know. As three young women come of age, must they choose between love and their beloved community?

DAUGHTERS OF AMANA by Judith Miller
Somewhere to Belong, More Than Words, A Bond Never Broken

♦ BETHANYHOUSE

Stay up-to-date on your favorite books and authors with our *free* e-newsletters. Sign up today at bethanyhouse.com.

Find us on Facebook.

Free, exclusive resources for your book group! bethanyhouse.com/AnOpenBook

an open book

3 1901 05216 5695